BOILING POINT

HE'S HER PROFESSOR.
SHE'S THE ONE VARIABLE HE CAN'T CONTROL

BOILING POINT

NADINE THEISS

Paperback ISBN: 979-8-9907745-6-8
eBook ISBN: 979-8-9907745-7-5

Edited by HEA Author Services
Formatting and interior design by Joanne Martin
Cover design by GetCovers

This is a work of fiction. Names, characters, places, and incidents are either the product of the author's imagination or are used fictitiously. Any resemblance to actual persons, living or dead, events, institutions, or locales is entirely coincidental.

Published by Saffron Ink, LLC
Summerville, South Carolina

Library of Congress Control Number: 2025921075

For anyone who's ever fallen for someone they shouldn't—and loved every dangerous second of it.
The forbidden fruit is so much sweeter.

PLAYLIST

"Angels" — Robbie Williams
"Beautiful Things" — Benson Boone
"You Are The Reason" — Callum Scott & Leona Lewis
"Can't Help Falling In Love" — Kina Grannis
"Hanging By A Moment" — Lifehouse
"Falling Like The Stars" — James Arthur
"Lose Control" — Teddy Swims
"This I Promise You" — Ronan Keating
"Don't Look Back In Anger" — Oasis
"Shattered (Turn The Car Around)" — O.A.R.
"It Will Rain" — Bruno Mars
"Wake Me Up When September Ends" — Green Day
"Maybe It's Time" — Sixx:A.M.
"Wherever You Will Go" — The Calling
"She's The One" — Robbie Williams

Author's Note

Boiling Point is a contemporary academic romance intended for **mature readers**. It contains explicit sexual content, parental loss (off the page), and themes of secrecy and power imbalance within a forbidden relationship. While these elements are integral to the story and are handled with respect, they are presented unapologetically. Some content may be triggering. I encourage you to proceed with caution and take care of your well-being as you read.

This story grew from my fascination with the razor's edge where passion and consequence meet. I wanted to explore what happens when two people—both intelligent, both deeply aware of the risks—choose each other anyway. It's not a fairy tale, and it's not without fallout. But for Gabrielle and Cal, love is worth burning for, even when the world says it's reckless.

Though Page College—where much of this story unfolds —is fictional, it was inspired by my own alma mater, with just enough twists to make it its own world. If you know me (or the campus behind it), you'll probably spot a few familiar landmarks. Just don't try to use this book as a campus tour—you'll end up hopelessly lost. I've moved buildings, invented spaces, and twisted geography to suit the story. Along the way, I've included a few respectful nods to people and places that shaped me, but those are homage, not biography. If you think you recognize yourself, you don't.

This applies to other settings in this book as well. I write immersively, and I write what I know, so many of the locations are drawn from real places. But every one of them has been nudged, borrowed, or outright stolen and re-stitched to fit the story. So if you go looking, don't expect Google Maps to help. This is fiction's turf, and the signposts point wherever I say. Which means the only map you'll need is the story itself.

So brew the tea, get comfy, and fall headlong for a professor who has no business making physics this interesting. Step into a story about defying the lines we're told not to cross, about burning for someone you can't have, and choosing them anyway. If you've ever touched the forbidden and come away changed—*welcome*.

Enjoy the fire,
  Nadine

P.S. To my UK readers: Yes, Cal is English, and yes, his voice is English too. But at the relentless insistence of my (American) editors, I've kept the spelling, grammar, and punctuation firmly in US territory. As someone raised in British schools, it was a small act of violence to drop my Us, swap my Ss for Zs, and generally Americanize (there, I've done it again) Cal's perfectly good Queen's English.

If you find yourself mourning the missing letters, here—have a few cheeky ones on me: sssssssss uuuuuuuuu. Cheers.

PROLOGUE

CALLUM

S mall towns are supposed to be safe. Nothing of consequence happens in a forgotten speck on the map. My sins shouldn't be able to haunt me here.

But they can.

And they are.

The reaper has come for my soul.

And her name is Gabrielle.

CHAPTER 1

CALLUM

Another semester.

Another herd of barely conscious undergrads clinging to caffeine, shivering in hoodies, readjusting to early mornings after winter break.

January in North Texas reliably meant a biting, dry cold and an utter inability to dress for it. Hoodies counted as coats. Scarves were decorative. Gloves, apparently, were a foreign concept.

Eight o'clock on a Monday. Welcome back to Page College.

"Good morning," I said, straightening my tie and adjusting my cufflinks—a small ritual that helped me stay composed. A few students looked up, but most remained hunched over glowing screens, already disengaged. "I am Dr. Hawthorne, and this is Physics 112. If you're in the wrong room, I suggest you leave now."

A ripple of laughter passed through the hall, tepid and obligatory. I scanned the rows, cataloging the usual types—the eager ones in the front row, already armed with laptops, highlighters, and pristine notebooks; the indifferent middle-section slouchers; and, of course, the back-row escape artists who thought I couldn't see them texting under their desks. My eyes snagged briefly on a young woman sitting in the third row closest to the window. She wasn't slouching or scrolling like the others. She sat upright, pen in hand, focused entirely on me. She didn't even have an open laptop—just a simple notebook and printed copies of my syllabus and lecture slides.

I avoided eye contact and started the lecture. "Physics isn't a subject for the weak. It demands discipline, accuracy, and—most importantly—a willingness to fail spectacularly before you succeed." The words came out sharper than I'd intended, but I didn't soften them. They weren't here for coddling. "Since you're in second-semester physics, I'll assume you're still committed. But the second course is much more challenging than the first, so…buckle up."

I clicked through the first few slides, outlining the course structure, key dates, and my expectations. "You will, of course, have already had Physics 111 with Dr. Watkins. This course will be structured similarly. Instead of the traditional lecture-lab setup, this course is integrated. We meet Mondays, Wednesdays, and Fridays from eight until ten, and the lab component is incorporated. Physics—applied physics, anyway—is very hands-on, and studies show that a more kinesthetic approach to the material produces superior retention." I caught a few blank stares. My words may have coasted over their heads. I made a mental note to remember these were first-year students, and the wheat had not yet been sufficiently separated from the chaff.

Page had high standards, but it was still a liberal arts school. Bright students, yes—but not all of them were built for science. Especially not in a place this small, where the top physics minds shared a residence hall with theatre majors and poets.

"Attendance is crucial," I continued, "though not sufficient for success. Engagement is what will see you through. And yes, that means putting away your phones." A collective groan rose from the classroom. I allowed myself a thin smile. Several students begrudgingly stowed their devices, though a few in the back held out with a defiant nonchalance.

My gaze drifted to the young woman in the third row. Unlike the others, she hadn't needed to put anything away. Her focus remained unbroken, her eyes like two deep wells of intent. I wondered, briefly, what her story was—and why she seemed so different from the rest.

"Discipline is the cornerstone of this course," I continued. "You'll find that physics has little tolerance for approximation or halfhearted effort. The same can be said for me." I paused, letting the weight of my words settle over them like an iron cloak. "If you're here to coast, you might as well drop now and save yourself the trouble."

I flipped to the next slide, which displayed a list of bullet points in stark white text against a navy blue background.

"Let's talk about expectations," I said. "First, late work will not be tolerated. The universe may be flexible, but deadlines are not. I won't take attendance because I'm not your father. However, don't expect any grace from me if you fail to show up and then struggle with the material."

I advanced the slide to my office hours and contact information. "These are my office hours," I said, pointing to the screen. "I strongly encourage you to make use of them. If you find yourself struggling with the concepts, don't wait until the last minute to seek help. I am more than happy to assist those who show initiative and are willing to put in the effort."

She was staring at me. Unflinching. A spark of something— determination, perhaps—flickered in her eyes.

"And before you ask," I continued, breaking away from her gaze with a reluctance I didn't quite understand, "yes, I'm English; no, I don't know the king; and yes, I drink tea."

Another ripple of laughter, this one slightly warmer. I'd used that line for years.

"Are there any questions?" I asked, knowing full well that there wouldn't be—not yet. The first lecture was always a monologue. Questions came later, once they started struggling.

"Then let's begin with a brief overview of what this course will cover." I clicked to the next slide, which displayed a series of diagrams and equations. "In your first semester, you focused on kinetics—things you can see and measure directly, like velocity and acceleration. This term's curriculum is far more abstract. We'll explore circuits, magnetism, and waves—the concepts that govern the unseen forces of our universe."

I noted the shifting postures, the subtle twinge of anxiety on faces. The abstract had a way of intimidating even the most confident students. "Don't be discouraged," I said, almost gently. "While these topics are less tangible, they are no less real. Understanding them will give you a deeper appreciation for the world around you—and perhaps even change the way you see it."

The next slide showed a simple electric circuit diagram. "We'll start with circuits. Electricity is a fundamental force, one that powers nearly every aspect of modern life. Yet how many of you actually understand what happens when you flip a switch?" A few students put their hands half in the air, then thought better of it and pulled them back down. "Don't worry —by the end of this unit, you will."

The remainder of the lecture passed in a blur of diagrams and definitions, my voice on autopilot as my mind wandered dangerously.

Who was she?

"That will be all for today," I said, closing my laptop. "Make sure to read the first chapter and complete the introductory problem set before our next class."

The lecture hall erupted into a flurry of movement and noise as students hastily packed their bags and made for the exits. I methodically slid my laptop and papers into my soft-sided leather briefcase and cast a final glance at the student in the third row.

Unlike the rest, she moved with an unhurried grace, neatly capping her pen and closing her notebook with a soft pat. She stood, hesitated for a moment, then walked toward me, weaving through the departing mass like a salmon swimming upstream.

"Dr. Hawthorne," she said as she reached the lectern. Her voice was soft but clear, cutting through the residual din of the classroom. "I just wanted to thank you for the lecture."

I hesitated, searching her face for disingenuousness. I found none. "You're welcome," I said, perhaps more curtly than I'd intended. Compliments from students were rare and usually laden with ulterior motives.

Her eyes didn't waver. "I appreciate the structure. It's… refreshing."

I nodded, unsure how to respond. Most students balked at my rigid expectations. Her gratitude was disarming. "What's your name?"

"Gabrielle." She shifted her weight and fidgeted with the strap of her backpack. "Gabrielle Clark."

I filed the name away, knowing somehow that it would be useful. "It's always nice to put a name to a face," I said politely. Her face would be impossible to forget—beautiful in its simplicity, not masked by excessive makeup. She had delicate features, sharp green eyes, and natural blonde hair pulled back in a loose plait.

She lingered a moment longer, and I braced for the real reason she'd stayed behind. Perhaps an appeal for special consideration, or an excuse proffered in advance. Instead, she simply said, "See you next class," and walked away.

I watched her until she disappeared into the corridor, then shook my head as if to clear it. Students like Gabrielle were rare but not unheard of—bright sparks in a sea of mediocrity. Yet something about her felt different, more compelling.

Or perhaps I was mistaken, and she'd be no different from the rest.

Chapter 2

Gabrielle

"How was the first day of classes?" Aunt Suzy's sugary, sing-song voice carried through the phone's speaker.

"It was good," I answered, balancing my phone and travel coffee cup in one hand as I unlocked my apartment door with the other.

"Remind me what you're taking this semester."

I kicked the door shut behind me. "Today I had physics, calculus, and psych." I flipped on the light and dropped my backpack and purse on the couch. "Tomorrow I've got French."

"Sounds heavy."

I tugged off my hat and jacket and draped them over a nearby chair, then walked into the kitchen, where I set my now-cold coffee in the microwave to reheat. "It's not so bad," I said, switching the phone to my left ear as I rummaged through the fridge for nothing in particular. "I'm used to heavy. Though I think my physics professor is going to be a hard-ass."

"After putting up with my brother at the end of his life, that's nothing you can't handle, sweetheart." She paused, and

I could almost hear her biting her lip. "You know, Gabrielle, it's okay if you want to take things a little slower."

I sighed. This was a conversation we'd had many times, ever since Dad died. "I know, but I want to get my degree and be done with it. Slowing down would just—"

"Would just give you more time to breathe," she interrupted, her usual cheer dampened but not extinguished. "To enjoy college. To figure out what you really want."

The microwave dinged. I took my coffee out and gave it a swirl, watching the steam rise and bead along the rim. "I'm twenty-five—not eighteen like everyone else here. I don't need to soul-search and find myself. I've actually lived a bit of life. And I know what I want."

There was another pause, longer and heavier. "Okay," she said finally, though she didn't sound convinced. "Just remember I'm here for you, no matter what."

"I know. Thanks, Aunt Suzy."

"So…any cute guys?"

I rolled my eyes but smiled. "In this tiny town? That's rich."

My brain, of course, chose that moment to conjure up Dr. Hawthorne. Not that he was cute—he was way too intense for that. But there was something about him. Maybe it was the sharp angles of his face, those calculating gray eyes that cut straight through you, or the near-perfect sweep of his short dark hair. He was tall with a swimmer's build, and his suit clearly wasn't off the rack. He wore it like it was cut just for him. It probably was. And then there was his accent. *Swoon.* Like every other girl, I was weak for a British accent. He made physics sound like Shakespeare.

I shook my head, pushing the thoughts away. He was my professor, and that was reason enough to keep my head down. I had more than enough to focus on without adding an unethical crush into the mix.

"So?" Aunt Suzy persisted, her expectation practically humming through the phone.

"So I'm not looking for a guy right now."

"Doesn't mean you can't window shop."

"I'll keep that in mind." I knew she was just trying to lighten the mood. "Look, I've got to do some reading and a problem set before today's physics lecture escapes my head. Thanks for checking on me."

"Anytime, sweetie. Love you."

"Love you too." I ended the call and set the phone on the counter, staring at it for a moment like it might chide me further.

I took a sip of coffee—hot enough to burn my tongue— and settled onto the couch with my physics textbook and Dr. Hawthorne's lecture notes. AP Physics was eight years in the rearview, and I'd slept, lived, and cried a proverbial river since then. I had a lot of rust to knock off, and I wasn't about to take any chances. If Wednesday's class was anything like today's, I'd need every advantage to keep up.

I skimmed the pages, but the diagrams and equations wouldn't stick. My mind kept slipping back to the lecture hall, to Dr. Hawthorne's precise, measured voice. He spoke with absolute confidence, and he commanded the classroom without even trying. When I'd thanked him after class, his eyes on mine—reserved, cautious, but not unkind—had unsettled me more than I'd care to admit.

He didn't look or move like the other professors at Page, with their sweater vests and easy familiarity. He was sharper, formal, almost refined—as if he belonged somewhere else entirely. Younger too—definitely not fresh out of grad school, but not gray and grizzled at the edges like most of the faculty. Late thirties, maybe?

Stop it, Gabrielle. You're acting like a schoolgirl with a crush.

I groaned and rubbed my temples. This was the last thing I needed. He was my professor. Any interest beyond that was a distraction—and worse, a liability. I had goals. Real ones. There was no room for silly infatuations.

Not to mention, I was an engineering major. I still had three and a half more years of classes, most of them connected to the physics department—*his* department.

I glanced at the textbook again and read the same paragraph three times. I still couldn't tell you what it said. Circuits were supposed to be easy—the teething ring of second-semester physics. My dad and I had built plenty of circuited projects in the garage over the years. But tonight, none of it made sense. My brain was a tangled mess of resistors and capacitors, overloading and short-circuiting.

Enough. I shut the book harder than necessary and dropped it onto the coffee table. A hot shower—that would help clear my head. And maybe even knock some sense back into me.

CHAPTER 3

CALLUM

A soft tap at my door pulled me out of a mind-numbing email from the dean of students.

"It's open."

The door inched forward, revealing a young woman with hesitant eyes and a loose plait spilling over her shoulder. I recognized her immediately as the third-row student who'd spoken to me after our first class.

"Gabrielle Clark," I said, my surprise bleeding through more than I'd intended. Students rarely appeared at my Thursday afternoon office hours until desperation drove them here, usually closer to the first exam—or afterward, to plead for their grade.

Her eyes widened. "You remember me." She tentatively stepped inside, notebook clutched to her chest.

"It's rare to be thanked for a lecture."

Her cheeks flushed, a delicate shade of pink against the muted gray afternoon light filtering through the window. Rain was coming. She brought an odd warmth to the drab little box that passed for my office—cinderblock walls, shelves of textbooks lined like sentries, and institutional beige metal furniture. The only hint of life was a failing fern slumped on the windowsill. She wore an oversized forest-green cable-knit jumper over dark indigo jeans—well put together in a classic sort of way.

"Am I interrupting?" she asked, glancing at the papers scattered across my desk—the detritus of administrative tedium.

"Not at all. It's refreshing to see someone here so early in the term." I gestured toward the chair opposite me. "Please, have a seat."

She moved with an unpretentious grace, settling into the chair and placing her notebook on her lap. I caught myself watching her slender, elegant fingers as she traced the cover.

"I was reviewing your notes from the first two classes," she began, her voice steady but soft. "I'm having trouble with capacitors, I think? Unless it's something more basic that I've missed."

Her directness caught me off guard—so unlike the artifice or evasion I'd grown accustomed to hearing from students who darkened my door. I leaned back slightly in my chair and considered my response.

"Capacitors are tricky devils, but not nearly as devilish as they seem at first glance." My tone softened, knowing she was likely out of practice but certainly not out of her depth. "Let's take it from the top."

She nodded, her expression one of complete focus. There was something surprisingly gratifying about having an audience of one.

"Think of a capacitor as a container—like a balloon—that stores electrical energy. It fills up when connected to a power source and then releases that energy when needed."

The tension in her shoulders eased ever so slightly, though I knew she wasn't entirely convinced.

"This 'balloon' effect allows capacitors to control the flow of electricity," I continued. "They can release their charge all at once or gradually. This is especially useful for things like camera flashes, where you need a sudden burst of energy."

"That makes sense," she said slowly, as if testing the words before committing to them. "So in a circuit…?"

"They function as gatekeepers," I replied. "Balancing the current or providing bursts when needed."

"I was making it too complicated," she admitted, tucking a loose strand of hair behind her ear. A simple gesture, and yet, I noticed.

"You wouldn't be the first. It's easy to get bogged down by the maths, but it makes sense when you understand the meaning behind the numbers."

Another knock at my door. Surely not another student.

Bill Watkins, my colleague and resident of the adjacent office—tenured long before I'd arrived—stuck his head through the doorframe. "Hey, Cal, did you— Oh, sorry! I didn't mean to interrupt."

Gabrielle turned to face him, and her eyes lit with recognition. "Hello, Dr. Watkins." Her voice was sweet but not vapid or disingenuous.

"Gabrielle!" Bill exclaimed with a grin, eyes crinkled at the corners. "Camping out in office hours already?"

Her laughter was a quiet ripple, and it struck me as unexpectedly musical.

He leaned against the doorframe, arms casually crossed over his plaid jumper. "Gabrielle here was in Physics 111 with me last fall." He turned his attention back to her. "Has Dr. Hawthorne learned yet that you'll be a permanent fixture in his office until you're satisfied you've conquered every concept?"

"Consider me warned," I said, drawing Bill's attention back to me. I couldn't be sure, but Gabrielle looked relieved to have the focus removed from her. "How can I help, Dr. Watkins?"

"Oh, it's nothing important." He scratched at his beard,

more gray than red these days. "I just wanted to know if you could make heads or tails of that cryptic email from the dean. We can chat later."

"Of course. I'll pop by your office when I'm done here."

"Great!" He turned back to my student. "Nice to see you again, Gabrielle. Good luck with classes this semester."

"Thank you, Dr. Watkins," she replied with a slight dip of her head.

Bill turned to leave, then paused. "You're in good hands with Dr. Hawthorne. He's the brightest of us all."

"Don't lie to the lady," I teased, shooing Bill out of my office. I dropped my voice to a whisper. "Sorry about that."

She blushed ever so slightly, her cheeks again flushing a lovely pale rose.

"Now, what else can I help you with?"

By the time I left the science building, it was pitch dark outside. The faculty lot lay under those ghastly sodium streetlights that washed everything in amber and gray. Every time I stayed late on campus, I felt like I was walking through a noir film—flat light, no color, no warmth.

I approached my car, the mid-January chill biting through my overcoat. The air carried a damp tension that always preceded rain—a North Texas specialty, where winter meant a dreary damp and bone-deep cold rather than snow. As I reached for my keys, a fine drizzle began to fall. That's when I saw her—a figure standing under the sepia glare in the adjacent student lot. She was beside her car, its bonnet propped open like a defeated banner. Even from this distance, I recognized Gabrielle.

As the drizzle thickened into proper droplets, I pulled my umbrella from my satchel and unfurled it. Rain tapped against the fabric. I broke into a jog, footsteps sharp against wet asphalt, and came up beside her.

"Miss Clark," I called, just loud enough to rise above the rain.

She startled slightly, straightening and brushing damp hair from her face. I lifted the umbrella over her head. The proximity to her—innocent enough—still kicked up my pulse.

"Oh! Dr. Hawthorne," she said, voice laced with both surprise and relief. "What are you doing here so late?"

"I might ask you the same," I replied with a trace of humor. "Trouble with your car?"

"It won't start," she grumbled, glancing down at the engine with a mix of frustration and resignation. "I think it's the battery."

I couldn't help but smirk at the irony. "Battery troubles? Rather fitting, considering what we've been covering in class."

Her lips curled faintly, a flicker of amusement in her eyes despite the situation. "You don't happen to have jumper cables, do you?"

"Regrettably not. And even if I did"—I gestured back toward my car—"I drive a hybrid. It doesn't play nicely when it comes to jumping other batteries."

She let out a breath. "Just my luck."

"I'd be happy to give you a ride," I offered, careful to keep my tone professional. Still, something tightened in my chest at the prospect.

"Really? That would be amazing." She shut the bonnet and brushed rain from her hands.

"Come on then, let's get out of the weather."

The umbrella strained against the wind as I walked her to my car. The scent of rain on wet pavement and pine hung in the air. Her shoulder nearly brushed mine. Her damp hair glistened, and her cheeks were flushed from the cold.

Once inside the dry haven of my car—a sleek silver sedan

—we shook off the rain. Gabrielle rubbed her hands together to chase away the cold while I adjusted the climate controls.

"Shall I switch on your seat heater?"

She grinned. "Fancy. Yes, please."

"Which residence hall do you stay in?" I asked, hoping to dispel any awkwardness that accompanied having a student in one's passenger seat. I pulled out of the monochromatic car park and onto the rain-slicked street, the windscreen wipers swishing in a steady cadence.

"I actually live off-campus," she said with a hint of pride.

I raised an eyebrow. "You've managed to circumvent the university's strict on-campus residency policy? Impressive." I glanced at her, intrigued. "Local, then? Living with your parents?"

She flinched slightly at the word "parents," and I immediately regretted my curiosity, cursing my breach of discretion.

"No, I have an apartment. Nothing fancy, but it's all mine," she said quietly, gaze fixed on the rain-streaked window. "I'm twenty-five. The residency requirement only applies through twenty-four."

I nodded, absorbing that. She was older than most students. Perhaps that explained her focus and determination. It also meant she had more life experience than I'd assumed, something that drew me to her in a way I couldn't quite articulate—a way that left me unsettled.

"I'll take you home then, if you'll permit me."

"Thank you, that would be great." She chewed on her bottom lip and fiddled with the hem of her jumper. "If it's not too much trouble."

"Not at all. Where to?"

CHAPTER 4

GABRIELLE

The streetlights blurred into streaks as we drove through the rain-soaked roads. The town was ghostly in the downpour, a watercolor of muted hues and shifting shapes. Dr. Hawthorne's car was a warm cocoon as water streamed in steady sheets down the windows. I stole glances at him—his focus on the road, his profile sharp against the dim light—and I felt a curious blend of comfort and uncertainty.

He pulled into my apartment complex, an array of modest buildings with khaki-colored siding nestled behind a grove of trees, their outlines softened by the deluge.

"I'm in building five, just over there," I said, gesturing toward my place on the ground floor.

He nodded silently and steered the car into a parking spot as close to the front as he could get. "Here we are," he said, shifting into park.

"Thank you so much," I replied, clutching my backpack close to my chest. I couldn't quite mask my reluctance to leave. The thought of braving the rain again felt daunting, but I reached for the door handle anyway.

Dr. Hawthorne's voice stopped me. "You'll be drenched

before you get inside." He retrieved his umbrella from the back seat. "Let me walk you to your door."

I hesitated, sensing this wasn't an offer he made lightly. But I didn't have a better option. "You're sure you don't mind?"

"I insist."

He was out of the car before I could say anything else. He jogged around to my side and opened my door, and I dashed alongside him through the parking lot, water sloshing up around us with each hurried step. By the time we reached my apartment, my shoes were soaked through, and the cuffs of my jeans dripped steadily.

"Thank you," I said breathlessly, fumbling in my purse for my keys.

He stood beside me, droplets trailing down his cheekbones, dark hair clinging in errant strands across his brow. "It's really coming down," he remarked, shaking some of the water from his sleeves.

I paused before unlocking my door, feeling an unexpected reluctance to let this strange evening end. "You should come inside," I suggested, trying to sound nonchalant, though there was a tremor of hopefulness in my voice. "At least until it calms down. You could barely see the road on the way out here."

His hesitation was palpable, an internal debate flickering across his features. "I wouldn't want to impose," he said softly.

"Nonsense," I insisted. "If it weren't for you, I'd still be stranded on campus. At least let me return the favor by offering somewhere dry to wait out the weather."

He seemed about to protest, but then he glanced up at the deluge pouring from the slate-gray night sky. "Very well," he said with a resigned nod.

I led him inside, the rain muffled by the door's solid thud as I closed it behind us. The space was small and unassuming, but it was mine—framed vintage aviation prints and Dad's old nineties-era furniture claiming every corner. The air was warm and dry, laced with the faint scent of lemon and lavender from a half-burned candle on the coffee table.

"Make yourself at home," I offered, hoping he couldn't hear my heart racing. He stood awkwardly near the door, gaze sweeping over the place before settling back on me.

"It's charming." His expression was unreadable.

"Can I get you anything?" I brushed damp strands of hair off my forehead. "A cup of tea, maybe?" I winced internally, afraid I'd sounded trite—offering tea to a Brit—but he did mention he liked tea during our first class.

He raised an eyebrow, a glint of humor lighting his eyes. "You can certainly try."

Relief washed over me. "Challenge accepted. I make tea all the time." I rummaged in the cabinet and pulled a box of assorted tea. "I've got Earl Grey, spiced orange, lemon, peppermint, and English breakfast."

He chuckled as he shed his coat and draped it over the back of a dinette chair. "Of those options, English breakfast would be best."

I pulled out a packet of English breakfast for him and spiced orange for me, taking a moment to enjoy the delicious aroma of the orange tea before grabbing two navy blue ceramic mugs and filling them with tap water.

I turned to find Dr. Hawthorne standing at the entrance of my tiny kitchen, his eyes following my every move with glib curiosity. I could practically feel the disapproval rolling off him as I dunked the tea bags into cold water, their strings draping over the rims of the mugs like tiny life rafts.

"It appears," he said, a playful lilt in his voice, "that I have more to teach you than just physics."

"What?" I asked, tugging the microwave door open.

He stepped closer, crossing the worn linoleum with an air of gentle authority. "Tea tends to perform better in hot water."

"Oh!" I laughed and quickly pulled the tea bags from

their chilly bath. The color had barely begun to leech, leaving behind only pale, earthy wisps. "Heat the water first. Got it."

When I moved to put the mugs in the microwave, he shook his head. "Not quite," he chided softly, the corners of his mouth lifting in an almost smile. "Since we haven't covered magnetism and waves in class yet, I'll let that slide. But microwaving water is generally not a brilliant idea."

I set the cups down on the counter and muffled a self-conscious sigh.

"Do you have a kettle?" he asked, still teasing but not unkind.

"No kettle," I admitted. "I guess I'm hopeless. How about a small saucepan?"

"That'll do."

I pulled a tiny pot from the depths of a cabinet and handed it to him. Our fingers brushed for the briefest moment. He took the pot, filled it with water, and set it on the stove. There was something strangely captivating about the way he moved—deliberate and precise, like brewing tea was an art I'd hopelessly butchered.

The burner hissed to life, electric coils glowing orange. He leaned back against the counter, arms crossed, glancing around my apartment.

"Interested in aviation?" he asked, gesturing with his chin to one of the framed prints on the wall.

"Oh yes, as long as I can remember. If it has wings, I'm in love."

He nodded, an almost boyish spark in his eye. "Jets too, I take it?"

"Especially jets." I moved to join him, savoring the shift from awkward hostess to something more familiar. "I grew up with them."

"Air Force?" His voice was curious, nothing like the clipped tone he used in class.

"Nope. My dad." The words floated between us, carrying more weight than I'd intended.

He seemed to consider this, then diverted his attention to the pot on the stove. "The water is nearly ready." Steam curled from its surface. He grabbed two clean mugs from the cabinet and dropped in fresh English breakfast tea bags from the box I'd left on the counter. He pulled the pot from the stove just as it started to boil, waited a few seconds for the turbulence to calm, and then carefully poured steaming hot water into each cup.

The ritual of it felt new and exciting, as if I were sharing some small intimacy with him—beyond the tea. We lingered in the kitchen while the tea steeped. He watched me closely, as though searching for something beyond books and lectures.

Finally, he angled his head. "And you? Do you fly?"

I smiled. "I had my pilot's license before I could even drive a car," I replied proudly.

Dr. Hawthorne raised his eyebrows, clearly impressed. "You're full of surprises, Miss Clark."

Hearing him say my name again was a surprise, too—formal, but tender and more intimate than I'd expected. And in that accent…

He glanced at his watch—gold with a black leather band. The kind with hands and numbers instead of pixels and notifications. It suited him. "Time's up. The tea should be ready now."

"You really take your tea seriously."

"Guilty," he replied. "Please tell me you have milk."

Silently, I pulled a carton from the fridge and set it on the counter.

He took it from me, poured a splash into each mug, and gave them both a careful stir. "There we are," he said, handing one to me with a nod of approval. "A proper cup of tea."

The ceramic was warm beneath my fingers, and the steam

carried a stout, earthy aroma. We stood there, close enough that I could see rainwater still glistening in his hair like tiny beads of glass. I sipped delicately, watching his reaction over the rim of my mug. He tasted his tea with all the scrutiny of grading an exam, then cracked a smile that reached his eyes.

"Sorry about my paltry tea service," I offered with a shrug.

He shook his head, the smile lingering. "No need to apologize. We redeemed it." The warmth of his gaze took the sting out of my self-deprecation.

I laughed and gestured toward the living room. We settled on the couch, and somehow, Dr. Hawthorne's presence in my modest apartment felt entirely natural as he glanced around at my eclectic mix of belongings, sipping from his mug.

"I'm guessing your place has a few more textbooks and a bit less nineties plaid?" I mused, leaning back into the cushions.

He let out a dry chuckle. "And perhaps a kettle or two. Though I admit, my place leans heavily toward function over form. Just me, so I've only myself to please."

The words slipped into the quiet like a dropped pin.

Just him.

I nodded slowly, lifting my mug to hide the smile tugging at my lips.

His eyes found mine again—bright and engaged. "I suppose I'm curious about how you started flying. Not the most common hobby."

I leaned forward, setting my tea on a crocheted coaster on the coffee table. "It was my dad's hobby first. He had a knack for getting me obsessed with his favorite things. We started with models—half our garage was full of them." I laughed, the energy of nostalgia flowing through me as memories flooded back, vivid as daybreak. "Then we moved up to the real deal—Cessnas, mostly. I got to sit up front while he flew. We'd spend hours at the airport just watching jets land and take off."

The words brought a sudden wistfulness, and he must have noticed a change in my expression.

"I sense this is a sore subject," he said gently, setting his cup down with care. "Forgive me for prying."

I shook my head, surprised at how easily I'd let those pieces of myself slip out. "No, it's fine. He died just over a year ago."

His eyes darkened with empathy. "I'm so sorry. That's dreadful to go through at any age—but especially when you're so young."

"He had ALS—diagnosed just before I graduated from high school." Talking to Dr. Hawthorne, even about this, was surprisingly easy. My words flowed like a current. "So that put the brakes on college. He felt guilty that I stayed back to take care of him, but who else was going to do it?"

"That's an enormous sacrifice to make so early in life."

"It didn't feel like a sacrifice. It felt…" I searched for the right words. "It felt like a gift—time with him that I wouldn't have had otherwise."

"When are you going to stop that?"

I shot up straight, back rigid. "Stop what?"

"Stop surprising me."

The rain continued to beat against the windows. For a moment, I couldn't think of a thing to say.

"I'm not trying to surprise you," I finally offered, my voice subdued.

Dr. Hawthorne's expression shifted, something unguarded flickering across his face. "Most people your age would resent having their lives interrupted. They'd view it as a burden, not a gift."

I grabbed my mug from the coffee table and traced the rim with my finger. "Maybe. But most people my age haven't lost someone they love inch by inch, watching them fade away physically but still mentally all there." It was all still so clear— Dad's frustration as his body betrayed him, his determination to maintain dignity, his insistence that I pursue my dreams. "When someone you love is dying, you realize how precious every moment is."

The intense way he stared at me made my skin tingle. "That's a wisdom most don't acquire until much later in life. If at all."

"I'm not sure it's wisdom," I admitted. "Just reality."

Our eyes met and held, and something tightened in my chest—a peculiar ache, both pleasant and painful. The burgundy-and-green plaid couch seemed to shrink beneath us, the space between our bodies suddenly charged with an electricity that had nothing to do with the capacitors we'd discussed earlier. His fingers rested mere inches from mine on the worn cushion, and I found myself acutely aware of that proximity—of how easy it would be to bridge the tiny gap…

He glanced at his watch, breaking the spell. "I'm afraid it's getting late," he said, voice low, reluctant. He crossed to the window and parted the blinds, peering outside where the rain had softened to a steady patter. "It looks calm enough to drive."

He carried our empty mugs to the kitchen sink, rinsed them, and tucked them into the dishwasher. The image of refined, precise Dr. Hawthorne doing dishes in my tiny apartment felt surreal.

"Can I offer you a ride to campus in the morning?" he asked, drying his hands on a blue towel. "I can pick you up on my way."

I hesitated, not wanting to impose more than I already had. "It's okay, I'll order a rideshare."

He chuckled, a low, rich sound that flooded the room. "Good luck finding one around here."

He pulled on his coat, fastening each button with an unhurried precision that felt strangely intimate.

When I didn't reply, he said, "I'll be by at seven." His eyes met mine.

My heart skittered. "All right. Seven."

He paused at the door, his hand resting on the knob. The air between us almost tingled. "Good night, Miss Clark," he said softly. My name hung like an echo in the room.

"Good night," I replied, surprised at how much weight those two words carried.

He lingered at the door a moment longer before stepping out into the chilly night. Rain-scented air swept in to fill the space where he'd stood—sharp and clean, mingling with traces of tea and warmth.

CHAPTER 5

CALLUM

Gabrielle opened her front door and immediately thrust a green travel cup into my hands.

"Good morning," I said, mildly startled. I glanced down at the mug, its warmth seeping through the hard plastic into my gloved fingers. "What's this?"

"Tea. And before you protest, I made it the right way." She beamed like a five-year-old unveiling a finger-painted masterpiece.

I smiled. "That's kind, thank you." A spiced aroma rose as I lifted the mug. "What blend is it?" I asked, though the peppery notes were a dead giveaway.

She fiddled with the hair tie at the end of her single blonde plait. "Earl Grey. We finished off my English breakfast last night."

"I see." I took a tentative sip. The bergamot hit sharp and fast. Not my preference, yet I wouldn't dream of telling her so.

Gabrielle stood in the doorway, bundled in her coat, backpack slung over one shoulder.

"Shall we?" I gestured toward the car park, where daybreak cast a pale glow, glistening off the wet pavement like scattered diamonds.

As we walked to my car, a comfortable quiet settled between us—charged with everything I wished I could say. There was a pull toward her that both intrigued and disturbed me. It would be far too easy to cross lines better left intact.

The morning was crisp, the cold air scrubbed clean by rain—damp earth and dormant grass stirred awake by last night's storm. As we reached my vehicle, I unlocked it and opened the door for her. She looked up at me with an almost sweet eagerness, then slid into the charcoal leather seat.

I started the car. The hybrid engine whispered into the hush of wet roads and early morning stillness. We drove past the grove of trees that bordered her building, their dark trunks glistening with moisture. I was acutely aware of Gabrielle beside me as I took a polite sip from the travel cup. I didn't care for the taste—too piquant—but I couldn't bear to let her gesture go to waste.

Silence stretched—not uncomfortable, but substantial enough to demand filling. I considered switching on the radio —an easy, impersonal soundtrack. But something stopped me. Perhaps it was the unfamiliar weight of my hesitation—the awareness of how easily she disarmed me.

"What classes do you have today?" I asked, choosing conversation over music.

She turned toward me, her eyes finding mine in a way that made concentration on the road seem secondary. "Well, I have your class at eight," she began with a teasing lilt. "But you already knew that."

A faint smile pulled at my lips. "Yes, I believe I did."

"Then calculus at ten and psychology at one."

"That's a full day," I said, merging onto the main road toward campus.

"Luckily, I only have French on Tuesdays and Thursdays, so it balances out."

"French?" I chuckled, more to myself than to her. "That takes me back."

"To what?"

"To a drafty classroom just outside London, where I learned that French is most definitely not my forte."

"When did you come here? To Texas, I mean." Her gaze was steady, as if searching for more than just a timeline.

"About five years ago," I answered, aware of how simplistic that sounded. How much it omitted. "After a bit of time on the East Coast."

"What was on the East Coast?"

"I did my postdoctoral studies at Princeton."

"And before that?"

"Before that, I was at Oxford."

Her eyebrows shot up. Not an uncommon reaction, but admittedly a tiresome one. "So how did you end up a physics professor in a tiny town in North Texas?" She tilted her head slightly. "Don't get me wrong—Page College is a great school. But you could have gone anywhere."

"I needed a change," I replied, keeping my response as tidy as possible.

She didn't press, and for that, I was grateful.

We crested a curved bridge over the railroad junction— the closest thing this town had to a flyover. Silly, perhaps, but it was my favorite part of the drive to work each morning.

"Do you have a plan for your vehicle?" I asked as I turned right onto one of the college's perimeter streets.

"I looked up a couple of repair shops last night. I'll call between classes and see what I can find."

"I know a mobile mechanic," I offered as I turned into the faculty lot. Campus was still sleepy—Friday eight o'clocks were never popular.

"Oh, if you wouldn't mind giving me his number, that'd be great."

I parked and turned to Gabrielle. "Why don't you give me your keys, and I'll take care of it?"

"Seriously?" Her tone caught me—surprise, maybe. Or reproach.

"Of course," I said. "It's no trouble."

She hesitated, gripping the strap of her backpack. "I really don't want to impose."

"You're not imposing." I leaned back in my seat, the leather creaking softly. "You have a full day of classes. I only have ours at eight."

She studied me, uncertainty flickering behind those bright green eyes. Then she exhaled, a soft sigh of grateful resignation. "All right." She handed me her keys. They felt oddly significant in my palm. "Thank you," she added, absolute sincerity in her voice.

We sat a moment longer than necessary, silence suspended like blown glass. I knew what needed saying before we stepped out of the car and into roles far better defined.

"Miss Clark—"

"You can call me Gabrielle, you know."

I smiled. "That brings me to my point, actually."

Her face dropped. "Oh gosh, I crossed a line." She shook her head violently. "I didn't—"

"No, not at all." A beat. "Not at all, Gabrielle."

Her eyes shone when I said her name.

"Once we step out, I'll have to go back to acting like a stuffy professor. I may come off as cold or distant." The words landed more clumsily than I'd intended. "I don't want you to take it personally," I added quickly.

Her brow furrowed before understanding smoothed it over. "I get it, Dr. Hawthorne." She tried to mask her disappointment with a small smile. "Thanks for the heads-up."

I nodded. "Drop by my office when you're finished with classes this afternoon, and we'll see how much progress I've made with your car."

A moment passed, one that felt both fragile and precious.

"See you in class. And thanks again." She opened the door and got out, her backpack swinging lightly as she walked toward the science building.

I lingered in the car for another breath, unmoored by how easily she accepted what I couldn't bring myself to say aloud—this was only temporary.

Chapter 6

Gabrielle

I wasn't the first student in class, but the room was still sparsely populated. I counted four others—earbuds in, laptop screens glowing. My third-row seat by the window was vacant and waiting for me. Overhead lighting bounced off the white tile floor, casting a sterile glow that made me long for glowing lamplight and worn book pages. I could already imagine myself curled up on the couch with a soft blanket and the new Savannah Evans novel I'd saved for the weekend—my reward for surviving the first week of the spring semester. That and—weather permitting—a few glorious hours in the cockpit of a Cessna Aerobat.

I flipped open my notebook to Wednesday's lecture: diagrams, equations, and my meticulous color-coded notes on electric current, circuit configurations, and capacitors. I heard each word in Dr. Hawthorne's voice—smooth and rich, accented just enough to make every technical term sound like poetry. I imagined him on my sofa again, explaining the difference between series and parallel circuits.

I snapped back to my notes: *Current always flows through the path of least resistance. A short circuit can cause a discrepancy between intended and actual voltage levels.* My mind wandered again to this morning in his car—how he hesitated before starting the conversation, his wry sense of humor when he relented that French was not his forte. The way he said my name.

Stop it, I chided myself. *Focus.*

The room began to fill, most of my classmates looking as bleary-eyed as I felt after my restless night. A half-asleep student tripped over his laces, muttering more with irritation than pain as he slumped into a chair. Yawns rippled through the hall. The Friday morning exhaustion was contagious.

I took a deep breath and refocused on my notebook. *Current,* I read to myself. *The rate at which charge flows through a surface…*

Dr. Hawthorne entered precisely at eight, his stride buoyant enough to rouse the half-asleep class from its stupor. "Good morning," he said, his voice rich and resonant as it filled the room.

A few mumbles greeted him in response.

"Tough crowd," he mused as he placed his laptop onto the lectern and connected it to the dock. He scanned the still-sparse classroom with cool gray eyes. "I see more empty seats than I'd have liked this morning."

A few students chuckled awkwardly. I watched him with thinly veiled admiration. Without the winter coat he'd worn earlier, his appearance was even sharper: crisp black button-down shirt, cobalt-blue tie, stone slacks with surgical creases, and polished black leather shoes that reflected the fluorescent lights. His style was formal but uncomplicated—commanding attention without demanding it. How had I missed that earlier?

"Before we get started," he said, sliding effortlessly into professorial mode, "are there any questions?"

A student near the front shot his hand up. "Can you explain when it's better to use a series circuit instead of a parallel one?"

Dr. Hawthorne nodded. "Excellent question. Let's review

the difference. In a series circuit, the same current flows through all components. That even distribution is the primary benefit, and you can control the current with a simple switch. The drawback is the lack of redundancy. If there is a break anywhere in the circuit, the current stops. You're all probably too young to remember, but Christmas lights used to be wired in series. It was a simple, effective setup—every bulb received the same current, so the lighting was consistent. But"—he paused for effect—"if one bulb burned out, the rest of the string went dark."

"So," the student interjected, "in that situation, would a parallel circuit be better?"

"Yes," Dr. Hawthorne replied. "Which is why modern Christmas lights are wired in parallel." He pushed off the lectern and walked toward the front row of desks. "But that's not quite what you asked. You asked when a series circuit would be superior to a parallel circuit. And that would be something like a flashlight. Two 1.5-volt batteries wired end-to-end give you a cumulative three volts of reliable, non-fluctuating power to the bulb, with a simple on-off switch to control the circuit. If it were wired in parallel, you'd potentially get uneven depletion of the batteries. And since you don't need redundancy in a flashlight—it's either on or off—you don't need a parallel circuit." Dr. Hawthorne stopped in front of the student's desk. "Does that answer your question?"

The student nodded quickly, his unruly mop of dingy brown hair bobbing with his head. I took quick notes while Dr. Hawthorne spoke, but my attention was split between his words and the fluidity with which he delivered them. His voice wrapped around each concept with an easy command that left me half mesmerized.

"Any other questions?" he prompted, scanning the room.

No hands.

He gave a single nod. "In that case, let's see what stuck

during your first week." He picked up a stack of papers from the demo table at the front of the room. "You'll have ten minutes."

There was a collective groan as he began to distribute what was clearly a pop quiz.

"Think of it as an opportunity to assess retention," Dr. Hawthorne continued, tone even. "And too bad for your colleagues who chose not to come to class on Friday morning."

The quiz reached my desk faster than I expected—three questions printed neatly down the page. The first asked us to compare series and parallel circuits—convenient following this morning's review. The second was a question about calculating the net current of a circuit based on a diagram. I stifled a grin at the third question: Briefly explain the function of a capacitor in a circuit.

I glanced up, catching Dr. Hawthorne's eye across the room. There was a flicker of recognition in his gaze—a flash of acknowledgment—before he dipped his head and returned to the lectern.

"Your time starts now. Bring your paper to the front when you're finished."

The afternoon crawled.

1:25.

Dr. Monroe prattled on—I couldn't have told you the topic if you'd paid me.

From the second-floor classroom window, I looked out over the barren trees and brown grass that spanned the winter campus. My gaze hung on the science building across the quad.

I imagined Dr. Hawthorne in his office. Did he review our quizzes right away, or save them for later? Perhaps he had a meeting with Dr. Watkins, their contrasting styles an entertaining prospect to envision. Maybe he was meeting with earnest graduate students and research assistants. Maybe he was thinking of circuits and capacitors and—maybe—me.

A brief wisp of sun broke through the overcast sky, casting bold shadows that hinted at the clear weather promised for tomorrow—a perfect flying day if it held.

"And remember," Dr. Monroe said, snapping me out of my reverie, "your first analysis paper is due next Friday. So you might want to pay attention to this section." Her gaze landed on me, and I rushed to jot something down—anything that looked like I'd been paying attention.

Seemingly satisfied, she turned back to the projector screen and continued lecturing about research ethics in psychology and the horrific incidents that brought them about. She was tall with silky chocolate hair styled in a neat chignon. She wore a cornflower-blue collared blouse tucked loosely into a pair of bootcut jeans, her overall look effortlessly elegant.

Finally, the clock hit 1:50. "Have a good weekend," Dr. Monroe announced as she dismissed the class. I gathered my belongings and rushed out of the room as quickly as I could without drawing attention.

The hallways were full of students streaming toward dorms and an early weekend, but I pushed my way through, bursting into the chilled afternoon. I hurried past the imposing administration center and over the mud-striped paths leading to the science building. My breath rose in brisk white puffs, dissipating into the steely sky above.

I darted up the building's stone steps and slipped inside, slowing down just enough to seem composed as I made my way up to Dr. Hawthorne's office on the third floor.

His door was cracked open when I arrived, and I lingered outside for a moment, catching my breath. He was at his desk, absorbed in a stack of papers that looked like our morning quizzes. There was something almost intimate about watching him unnoticed—the subtle concentration etched across his features, the methodical way he set each paper aside before reaching for the next.

I knocked softly.

He looked up, eyes brightening with immediate recognition. "Miss Clark," he said, standing as he gestured me in. He consulted his watch. "Right on time."

I entered, drawn toward him despite the little voice in my head frantically waving red flags.

"Did you hear from your mechanic?" I asked, my voice too hopeful to hide.

Dr. Hawthorne nodded, a slight, knowing smile curving his lips. He opened the top drawer of his desk and lifted out my car keys, presenting them with a quiet flourish. "I did. And it's all fixed. Good as new."

"Wait—what do you mean it's fixed?" I blurted, too stunned to play it cool.

He raised an eyebrow, the playfulness in his expression almost teasing. "I'm not sure how I could be clearer."

My thoughts scrambled to catch up. "What about the bill? I can't let you pay for—"

"It's taken care of." He set the keys on the desk, as if that settled everything.

"I really can't accept that," I tried again, but he was already shaking his head with calm resolve.

"Think of it as a thank you for your hospitality."

"But—"

He held my gaze, steady and insistent. "It was no trouble at all."

Silence stretched, and the room somehow felt smaller— dense with a tension I felt in my chest more than I understood.

At last, I reached for the keys—slowly, deliberately, half afraid they might disappear if I moved too fast. I closed my fingers around the familiar metal, and with it came a rush of relief tangled with another, more complicated emotion I couldn't yet name.

"That's…really generous," I said, my voice catching. "Thank you."

He dipped his head. "My pleasure." He gestured to the chair in front of his desk. "Please have a seat. How were your other classes?"

"Calculus was pretty straightforward," I said, letting my backpack slip from my shoulder and drop to the floor. "And psychology was on the dry side today—all research methods and ethics. It should get more exciting next week."

"Remind me, what's your major?"

"Engineering," I answered, easing into the seat across from him.

Dr. Hawthorne leaned back in his chair and smiled. "I should have guessed."

"Specifically aerospace engineering," I added, the pride in my voice just barely outrunning the insecurity. "Assuming I can survive enough physics to get there."

His smile widened. "I think you'll do just fine. Most students don't have your drive and tenacity. It will serve you well."

The compliment wrapped around me like a warm blanket, and some of the tension left my body.

"Most of these kids—I hesitate to call them kids—but in many ways, they still are." He leaned forward, resting his elbows on the desk. "They don't know a thing about life. You, on the other hand, for better or worse, have already seen your fair share of it. It gives you focus."

His assessment clung to the air, as if daring me to correct him. Instead, I took a leap.

"I've got some flight time booked at the airfield tomorrow afternoon," I said, trying to sound more casual than I felt. "If you'd like to come."

There was a pause, just long enough to make me wish I'd phrased it differently—or not at all.

"Is that an invitation?" His tone was light, but his gaze was searching.

"Yes." Heat spread across my cheeks. "It is." My words tangled on my tongue. "Just…as a thank you. For the car. And…everything."

He studied me, and I wished I could shrink into the chair. But then he leaned closer and in a hushed voice replied, "I'd be delighted."

CHAPTER 7

CALLUM

I sang along to the chorus of "Don't Look Back in Anger" by Oasis—a favorite band from my adolescence—as I sat in my car outside the Grayson County Municipal Airport. The dashboard clock read 1:47 p.m.—a full thirteen minutes before Gabrielle had asked me to meet her here. A handful of pickup trucks sat in the car park, their bumpers crowded with aviation decals. A gust of wind rattled the bare branches of a nearby tree, and I adjusted the heat and turned up the music.

In our youth, my sister Isabel and I had frequently argued over which band was superior, Oasis or Blur. She was two years my senior, so I lost by default. Or rather, conceding was strategic—better for my peace. And there were more important things in life.

I was early, and there was time to reconsider, though I knew I wouldn't. The music crooned on—one of Oasis's smoother tracks—but it failed to settle my nerves. I tapped restless fingers against the steering wheel as I glanced around the car park, half expecting someone to spot me and wonder why I was here, waiting alone like an indecisive teenager. Guilt gnawed at the edges, and I told myself again and again that this was harmless. A friendly gesture. A simple kindness repaid. As if repetition would make it true.

My pulse kicked up as reality struck. Here I was, a tenure-track professor with a hard-fought career, edging closer to lines I'd sworn never to cross, trying to justify it all with clever semantics.

A sharp rap at my window yanked me from my thoughts. I turned to see Gabrielle smiling through the glass, her breath misting against the cold air.

"You're early," she said as I opened the door and stepped out into the chill, fumbling to recover my composure.

"Punctuality is a virtue." I closed my car door. "Or so I was taught."

She was, in a word, stunning. Gabrielle wore a brown leather bomber jacket with a fur collar, complemented by a cozy cream jumper underneath. Her fitted tactical trousers struck a perfect balance between flattering and functional. Sturdy ankle boots gripped the pavement, and vintage-inspired aviator sunglasses perched on her head. She embodied the striking spirit of an adventurous aviatrix.

Words eluded me. Here was a woman who could remake the world in her image, sweeping away the gray with every self-assured stride. I stood in awe, the chill of the afternoon forgotten as my heart drummed a desperate improvisation.

"Are you ready to go?" Her eyes sparkled like spring's first green, her voice as crisp and clear as the air.

"Yes." My voice had bolted ahead without consulting me. "Where should I watch from?"

She dipped her head back and laughed—a sound so light it rose above us, carried by the wind. "Watch? No, silly. You're coming up with me."

I must have gone pale because she offered a quick smile—the kind meant to reassure, though it only compounded my panic.

"I thought..." My words faltered as I imagined the

dizzying height, the earth shrinking beneath us, and my stomach turned traitor, somersaulting wildly.

"You're not afraid of flying, are you?" she asked, a hint of disbelief mingling with concern.

"No," I lied. A fierce wind whipped across the lot, rifling through my hair and sending a shiver up my spine. My mind reeled—of course she meant for me to join her. How had I not realized? The prospect of being airborne filled my mouth with the tang of metal and nerves.

Gabrielle watched me, expectant and eager.

I took a cleansing breath. "Lead the way."

She turned toward the tarmac, her stride confident and sure. I followed, legs stiff with dread and exhilaration—a peculiar cocktail that blurred sense and certainty.

The smell of aviation fuel hit me first, sharp and strangely sweet. A compact plane sat waiting for us, its propeller still and wings gleaming in the pale sunlight. White with sleek blue stripes along its fuselage and a red-and-blue checkered tail, it looked almost playful—deceptively harmless.

I swallowed hard, feeling absurdly large for something so compact.

"Is this it?" My voice cracked as I took in the plane's intimate dimensions.

"This is it." She ran her hand affectionately along the fuselage. "A Cessna 150 Aerobat." She pulled open the door, revealing a cabin just wide enough for two snug seats. She gestured to the right-hand side. "Hop in."

I hesitated at the word "hop"—as if ease and agility were required qualifications—and considered my long legs and lack of coordination. My brain scrambled for plausible excuses—any reason to remain earthbound—but none came except cowardice. I forced a smile, even as my stomach executed another nauseating tumble.

She gestured toward the right-hand seat again. The tangle of brown canvas restraint straps made my heart lurch.

"Are you sure I'm meant to sit up front?"

Gabrielle chuckled softly, reading my expression with unnerving accuracy.

"Ah," I ventured, trying for nonchalance. "It's just…I assumed there'd be a back seat."

She smirked. "It's a basic two-seater. Up front is all there is."

I took a step, then stopped. "Am I dressed appropriately?"

She glanced at my gray trousers and black jumper, clearly fighting back laughter. "You're fine," she said gently, sensing my last-ditch attempt at delay.

With no further excuses, I climbed in, maneuvering with all the grace of a giraffe folding itself into a shoebox. I wedged myself into the seat, wondering how I was meant to get back out again. Before I could fumble with the harness, Gabrielle leaned in to assist. Her closeness sent a jolt through me— equal parts thrill and panic. I focused on breathing as she threaded the straps into place.

She cinched the four-point harness, gave it two sharp tugs, then flashed a devilish grin. "You're gonna want that nice and tight."

My breath caught, and my pulse thrummed erratically.

Gabrielle climbed into her seat and shut the door with a solid clunk. The sudden enclosure magnified everything—the close air, the scrape of fabric, the creak of sunbaked metal as the cabin settled around us. Heat radiated from the panels, pressing in until it felt as though the machine had swallowed me whole. She reached for the ignition key, fingers moving in confident rhythm across the switches. Then she paused and turned to me, her tone suddenly serious.

"Last chance to escape."

I stiffened.

She smirked. "Do you trust me?"

I let out a nervous laugh that felt more like a hiccup. "I'm here, aren't I?"

"Good enough." She reached forward, her voice light again. "*Clear prop!*" she called out the window.

Before I could ask what it meant, she twisted the key.

The engine roared to life, an explosion of sound slamming into me. The entire plane vibrated through my seat, up my spine, and into my teeth. I clutched the harness instinctively, my mind screaming, *What have I done?*

Gabrielle adjusted the throttle, and the deafening rumble settled to a steady, throbbing drone—but still loud enough to rattle my skull. She grabbed a pair of bulky aviation headsets from beside her seat and handed one to me.

Her voice barely cut through the din—something like, "*Put these on!*"

"*What?*" I shouted back, though I could scarcely hear myself.

"*Headset!*" she repeated, tapping the ear cups and miming putting hers on.

I fumbled with mine, nearly dropping it as I fit the clunky earpieces over my head. The moment the headset sealed over my ears, the world changed.

The engine noise collapsed into a muffled hum, like being dropped beneath deep water. Everything felt insulated, distant —as if reality had slipped a layer away from me. My breath, now loud and rhythmic inside the headset, sounded like rolling waves in an empty ocean. For a moment, the contrast was disorienting—as though I had been yanked from one world and deposited in another, where the rules of sound had shifted.

Gabrielle's voice crackled through the headset—clear, close, and strangely intimate. "Better?"

I let out a shaky breath and nodded.

She grinned. "It's too loud without these. This is the only way we'll hear each other."

I adjusted the clumsy, alien-feeling headset, still not used to the insulated silence. "Seems our roles are reversed today," I managed, clutching my harness. "You, the instructor. Me, the pupil."

She smiled, the expression genuine and disarming—and for an instant, I thought she might have blushed before she turned away and slid her hands over the throttle, her voice crackling back into my ears.

"We'll keep it simple," she said. "A quick hop over Lake Texoma and back. You ready?"

I nodded, though I had no idea if I was or not.

Gabrielle flipped the radio switch, her tone shifting to calm and practiced—professional but effortless.

"Grayson traffic, Cessna 150 Aerobat taxiing to runway two-niner."

No response—just the steady crackle of an open frequency. A beat passed before Gabrielle released the brake, and the plane rolled forward. No permission granted. No unseen authority approving our fate.

"Isn't someone supposed to answer?"

"Nope," she said easily. "Not unless there's a problem. This is Class G airspace."

"What does that mean?"

"There's no control tower. We announce our moves on an open frequency. If no one objects, we're good to go."

My stomach twisted as she maneuvered onto the taxiway, feet on the rudder pedals, hands light on the yoke. The aircraft bumped and rattled over the pavement, the vibrations crawling up my spine.

Yellow taxi lines stretched ahead, curving past painted numbers and runway markers that meant nothing to me but seemed to anchor her. Gabrielle moved with certainty, following rules I couldn't decipher, her gaze flicking between the tarmac and the horizon.

Painted on the asphalt in stark white: 29. Bold and final. The end of solid ground. We paused at a white line just short of the runway—the place where everything stopped. She scanned the sky, eyes sharp and assessing, and keyed the mic again.

"Grayson traffic, Cessna 150 Aerobat departing runway two-niner, northbound."

She tilted her head, listening. Nothing but silence.

She looked at me, her expression edged with amusement. "Last chance to back out."

I swallowed hard, gripping the seams of my trousers. "Just get us in the air before I come to my senses."

Her smirk widened. "Copy that."

She pushed the throttle forward, and the engine roared, surging us down the runway—slow at first, then faster. My spine pressed into the seat as we gathered speed, the centerline blurring beneath us. The plane's nose lifted.

A sudden lightness stole my stomach as we left the ground, the wheels parting from the earth in a moment so unnatural, I forgot to breathe.

Wind nudged the aircraft, and it responded with a subtle, fluid tilt—nothing violent, but enough to remind me just how small we were up here.

Beside me, Gabrielle was composed—a study in serene focus—as she coaxed the plane into a smooth upward path, her hands light on the controls. Her calm accentuated my disarray.

My breaths came shallow and quick inside the headset's cocoon, each one deafening in its isolation.

Her voice filled my brain. "How are you doing over there?"

I hesitated on honesty and settled on something close enough. "Holding together."

"You're shaking like a leaf, Dr. Hawthorne."

"Cal."

She glanced over, puzzled. "What?"

"My name is Cal," I clarified. "You hold my life in your

hands right now. I think you've earned the right to use my first name."

A smile spread across her face. "All right, then. You're shaking like a leaf, *Cal*."

The sweetness in her voice twisted something in my chest, and for a moment, I forgot the thousand tiny deaths waiting beyond these thin walls. I managed a laugh—tinny and nervous inside the headset.

"I'm better now," I lied, watching in a terrified awe as the world fell away beneath us. Fields and roads shrank into a patchwork quilt, each line and square growing smaller, more abstract. The whole of it seemed impossibly fragile, like a child's model left carelessly out in the garden.

Gabrielle leveled the plane, and, at last, my stomach caught up—a welcome relief after the gut-twisting terror of ascent. The engine's roar eased into a steady hum, like the breath of a sleeping beast.

"See? Not so bad," she said, her voice laced with teasing confidence.

I forced my fingers—stiff, foreign things that barely seemed mine—to unclench. "Not so bad," I agreed, though I was still acutely aware of every shiver and sway.

"Weather's perfect today," Gabrielle went on. "Smooth air up here."

The sky stretched, flawless and blue in every direction. Wisps of clouds lingered far below—delicate streaks painted on a vast canvas.

I risked another glance at the ground. What I assumed to be Lake Texoma emerged like a splash of spilled ink against paper, its shimmering surface reflecting fragments of sky.

"This your first time in a small plane?"

I nodded, trying to outrun the churn of disbelief and adrenaline. "And possibly my last."

"Don't worry," she teased, voice warm. "I haven't crashed a plane yet, and I don't want a black mark on my record."

My laugh sputtered, too thin to cover the chaos of fear and exhilaration exploding in my chest.

Gabrielle banked right, and I felt the shift before I saw it. The sky stretched vast and endless, an indifferent expanse that cared nothing for the fact that I was entirely out of my element. Far below, Lake Texoma shimmered like a forgotten world—distant and unreachable, the last solid thing before gravity ceased to matter.

Gabrielle leveled us off, and her voice crackled through my headset. "So," she said casually, as if we were merely out for a Sunday drive, "are you ready to have some fun?"

"Gabrielle," I said slowly, "I struggle to define what we're currently doing as 'fun.'"

She laughed, easy and warm. "Come on, Dr. Hawthorne—sorry, Cal. You're a physicist. You understand the principles of flight better than most."

"Yes, and I also understand the physics of crashing, which terrifies me infinitely more."

"You should be fascinated, scientifically speaking."

"Oh, I'm utterly fascinated," I assured her. "That humans, in all their wisdom, looked at the ground—a perfectly good, solid place to exist—and thought, 'No, let's strap ourselves into a tin can and see what happens if we defy nature.'"

She smirked. "You're going to love this next part, then."

Dread coiled in my already twisted stomach.

She keyed the mic again. "Grayson Traffic, Cessna 150 Aerobat maneuvering over Lake Texoma, aerobatics in progress, four thousand five hundred."

I inhaled sharply. "Did you just warn the public? Should I be concerned?"

Gabrielle's grin was entirely too satisfied. "Just good etiquette. Let's start with something easy."

Easy, she said.

The plane tilted sharply, banking into a tight, steep turn. The horizon slanted at an unnatural angle, and the G-force pressed me into my seat. My pulse tripped over itself as I watched the world spin sideways, the lake rising unnervingly toward the cockpit window.

"Nice, right?" Gabrielle asked, holding the bank effortlessly.

I managed a breath. "That was very…turn-like."

She rolled us back level, the horizon righting itself as if nothing had happened. My vital organs, however, remained unconvinced.

She shot me a look. "Not bad, actually. You didn't scream."

"I'm British," I muttered. "We internalize our suffering."

She chuckled, then reached for the throttle. "Okay, you ready for a roll?"

"A what?"

The plane pitched up, and before I could object, she turned the yoke smoothly to the left.

The world tilted—no, flipped—entirely over.

For an impossible moment, we were upside down, sky where earth should be, ground where sky had been.

The harness bit into my shoulders as gravity upended every expectation I had of it, pressing me down in ways that felt fundamentally wrong.

And then, just as suddenly, we were upright again.

At some point, my hand had found Gabrielle's arm, fingers clutching the cool, supple leather of her jacket. She glanced at it, amused.

I let go immediately. "Right. Well. That was…" I swallowed. "An entirely unnecessary perspective shift."

Gabrielle grinned, her eyes glinting with mischief. "You survived."

I forced my shoulders to relax. "So I did."

"Which means you're ready for a loop."

"If this is payback for yesterday's quiz, I stand by it."

Her laughter was instant and bright. "Oh, you are absolutely paying for that."

I barely had time to process my impending doom before she pulled the nose up. The engine strained as we climbed—too steep, too fast. My stomach dropped as we arched backward into a full vertical loop. G-force pinned me into my seat, the pressure so intense I experienced my own weight in a way I never had before.

Until the top of the loop, where we hung weightless.

For a breathless second, I was floating, suspended, the world still.

And then—

The nose pitched down, the shift from weightless to crushing snapping through me as the lake rushed back into view.

Gabrielle leveled us out smoothly, her hands steady, her breathing infuriatingly normal.

I, meanwhile, was gripping the harness as though it were my only tether to the living.

She let the silence stretch, then finally asked, "So? Worth it?"

I blinked at her, forcing my fingers to uncurl. "Gabrielle," I said, voice hoarse, "I believe I saw my soul leave my body somewhere over the lake."

She laughed. "And did it look impressed?"

"I think it was questioning my life choices."

She grinned, easing back into straight and level flight. The engine settled into its steady hum, the world mercifully calm again.

For a long moment, neither of us spoke. My heart slowed. I loosened my grip. My body accepted its survival.

And then Gabrielle turned to me, a quiet warmth in her expression. "You did good," she said, softer this time.

I exhaled, glancing at her—the golden sunlight catching the curve of her smile, the easy confidence in her surroundings, the way she still looked at home here in a way I never would.

Something twisted in my chest, something that had nothing to do with physics or aerodynamics.

I looked away, out at the vast, endless sky, and found myself smiling.

"Maybe," I admitted. "But I'd still prefer the ground."

Chapter 8

Gabrielle

Cal wobbled slightly as we crossed the tarmac toward the diner. But there was a shift in his posture, as if surviving the flight let him stand taller.

The airfield diner—really just a glorified snack bar with delusions of grandeur—buzzed with laid-back chatter and the clink of glasses. The air smelled of fried food and aviation fuel, a peculiar perfume I'd always found oddly comforting.

Cal stood close at the high-top counter, tugging at his sleeve, hair a little mussed. He looked like a man grateful to have both feet back on solid ground.

"I owe you a drink," he said, running a hand through his hair as he eyed the menu board.

"This is my turf. Let me buy." I smirked. "Besides, you'll need your money for therapy after that flight."

He shook his head, suppressing a smile. "You returned me to earth in one piece. It's the least I can do."

I shrugged and leaned against the counter as he ordered beers and a basket of fries. The cashier handed over two frosty mugs, amber liquid sloshing against the sides, condensation already fogging the glass.

We claimed a small table by the window where sunlight

poured over the worn vinyl checkered tablecloth. I slid the basket of fries closer, the scent of salt and grease rising up. Cal settled across from me, taking a tentative sip of his beer.

"That's actually not bad," he conceded, surprise flickering over his face.

"See?" I teased. "You're discovering all kinds of new things today."

His laugh was low and genuine. "I suppose it's good to challenge one's comfort zone every decade or so."

He relaxed with each sip, the tension from our flight slowly unspooling from his shoulders.

"So, you do this sort of thing often?" His tone was teasing, but I caught the thread of genuine curiosity beneath it.

I nodded, dipping a fry in ketchup. "Every chance I get. Though fuel prices have skyrocketed, so I have to watch my budget. But yes. Call it my version of therapy." I took a sip of my beer, hoping to nudge the conversation somewhere lighter. "You were a very good sport."

"Good sport," he mused, leaning back in his chair and taking another drink. "Does that include the part where I nearly lost consciousness?"

I laughed, the sound mingling with the clatter of plates and the low rumble of a plane taking off outside. Voices rose and fell in an easy cadence around us, but our little table felt like its own quiet world.

Cal followed my gaze out the window to the runway beyond. "I can see why you love it," he said, quieter now. "There's a freedom to it."

"It's like nothing else."

I watched him over the rim of my glass, and the sunlight caught in his hair—glints of gold and chestnut woven through the deep brown. There was something fragile about this— sitting here together, letting go of everything but the present— and I wondered how long it could last before reality intervened.

"Do you have plans for the rest of the weekend?" Cal asked with an intentional offhandedness that made me smile.

"Studying, mostly," I replied, trying not to sound sheepish. "Some homework for your class. And a psych paper due Friday."

He raised an eyebrow. "Homework for my class? I intentionally don't assign weekend work."

I shrugged, looking down at my beer to hide the warmth creeping into my cheeks. Sunlight spilled through my mug, rippling gold across the tablecloth. "The assignment due Wednesday."

He narrowed his eyes. "Which is based on Monday's material."

"Yes…" I hesitated, considering. "I struggle with the hybrid experiential setup of the course. I'm more of a top-down learner rather than bottom-up, so I compensate by working backward. I look at the homework, which assesses the overarching concept, get a feel for it, and then the integrated lecture and lab activities make more sense to me."

He blinked, jaw slightly slack. "You are," he said, voice dipped in admiration, "terribly overachieving. And remarkably well-versed in pedagogy."

"Oh, that's my Aunt Suzy. She's a professor of education at the University of Houston. When I struggled in Dr. Watkins's class last fall, that was her assessment. It took us halfway through the semester to figure out that I needed to work backward, but it solved my problem."

A plane roared to life outside, the vibration thrumming through the window and into my bones. His eyes were on me, intent and searching, and that familiar twist tightened in my chest—a blend of thrill and fear, but not from the flight.

"I'm nothing short of impressed, Gabrielle."

I took a long gulp of beer, trying to cool the heat in my cheeks. "Anyway," I said, hoping to deflect his gaze with a quip. "What about you? Grading papers all weekend?"

Cal tipped his head back. Light skimmed across his hair again, accentuating an errant lock that never stayed put. He looked like every serious thought he'd ever had was a little further away today, just out of reach.

"I'm afraid so," he said, looking faintly amused. "And reviewing a few research proposals that have been glaring at me all week." He paused, the hesitation just enough to give away whatever pretense he intended. "But my plan is to finish tonight and free up the day tomorrow."

I tilted my head. "What's happening tomorrow?"

He glanced around the diner, then leaned across the table under the guise of reaching for a fry. His voice was low and inviting. "I'd like to claim your day tomorrow, if you're open to it."

Surprise fluttered through me, leaving me momentarily without words. He was close enough for me to notice the fine stubble along his jaw, feel his presence humming in the air like static.

"Oh," I managed, smiling despite myself. "Well, when you put it so sweetly…"

A hint of mischief flickered in his eyes before he settled back in his chair, looking entirely too pleased with himself.

"Are you sure you can handle two days in a row?" I teased, feeling suddenly bold.

"I'm willing to risk it. But…"

"There's a catch?"

He grinned. "I get to choose the activity."

My imagination sprinted straight for the gutter before I could stop it. I ducked my head, willing my face not to give me away. But when I risked a glance up, Cal's eyes shot wide, and he shifted awkwardly in his seat.

"I didn't mean…" He fumbled, retreating into his beer. "I was referring to…" He covered himself with a guilty cough.

A laugh bubbled up, but I swallowed it down. "No harm done. What's the plan?" I asked, leaning in, suddenly daring.

He set down his mug with deliberate care, a faint flush creeping up his neck as he reclaimed a measure of composure. "That," he said, affecting a mysterious air, "is for me to know."

I raised my eyebrows.

"I'll pick you up at ten," he added, dodging my gaze by staring out the window.

"Don't I get a hint?"

His eyes flicked back to mine, gray and earnest. "Dress warmly."

"Warmly?"

"Similar to how you're dressed now." A beat. "Which is quite becoming, by the way. Though I probably shouldn't say that."

The warmth in my chest had nothing to do with embarrassment and everything to do with the way he looked at me. Like we were alone in this crowded room. Like nothing existed but this crazy stolen moment.

CHAPTER 9

CALLUM

For the third time in less than a week, I stood at Gabrielle's door. This time, however, I hadn't arrived empty-handed.

She opened the door, eyes wide at the sight of the blue gift bag in my hands. Her flaxen hair was tied back in its usual intricate plait, and her emerald eyes sparkled in the morning sunlight. She wore jeans, a high-necked red jumper, and the brown leather bomber jacket that still carried a trace of yesterday's adventure.

"Hi," she said at last, her voice bright with a mix of delight and uncertainty.

"Good morning," I replied, unable to keep the smile from my own voice.

We stood there for a moment, the air between us charged. Curiosity flickered as she looked at the bag, then back at me.

"This is for you," I said, handing it to her.

Gabrielle accepted it with a hesitant grace, her fingers brushing mine for a moment too brief. "You didn't have to get me anything," she said, though the delight in her voice betrayed her.

I smiled, enjoying her reaction more than I ought to. "Happy to. Though I'll confess, the gift is rather self-serving."

She tilted her head, interest piqued. "Now I'm worried," she teased, stepping aside to let me in.

I laughed as I crossed the threshold. "Go on, open it," I urged, shrugging out of my black leather jacket.

Her gaze swept over me, an involuntary flicker that caught on my fitted black shirt and dark denim jeans—a marked departure from my usual university attire. She looked away, but not before I caught the faint flush coloring her cheeks.

We settled in the living room, where she placed the bag on the coffee table before peeking inside. Her face lit up as she pulled out an electric kettle and a box of Yorkshire Gold.

Her laugh was bright and unguarded. "Clearly for your benefit."

"And yours. If I fail at everything else, I'll at least have you making tea properly."

Her flat was warm and intimate, scented faintly of cinnamon and coffee. Morning sun poured through the sliding glass doors, scattering pools of light across the sand-colored carpet.

She set the kettle aside and met my gaze with a mix of shyness and boldness that left me breathless. "Can I make you a cup now?" she asked. "Show off my new skills?"

"Perhaps when we get back," I replied.

"Where are we going?"

I couldn't help but savor her curiosity as it flared again. I rose, watching her follow suit. "Come with me and find out," I said, pulling on my jacket. At the door, I turned to Gabrielle, holding her gaze. "One more thing. No handbag today."

Her brow knitted in confusion, curiosity mounting. "Really?"

"Everything you need should fit in your pockets," I insisted, relishing her hesitation before she nodded.

I watched, amused, as she locked the door and tucked her phone, wallet, and keys into her jacket. The sun shone brightly, casting long shadows across the block of flats as we made our way outside.

We approached the car park, and there it was—sleek, black on black, every inch built for speed and temptation. A machine designed to purr beneath you on the open road, all clean lines and quiet power, poised like a predator waiting to charge its prey.

I glanced sideways at Gabrielle. She froze, eyes wide, mouth half-open.

"Cal…" Her voice was a mix of awe and incredulity. "Are you serious?"

A grin stretched across my face. "Entirely."

"I've never been on a motorcycle in my life," she confessed, glancing from me to the bike and back. "Death machines, my dad used to call them."

"That's rich," I replied with a chuckle. "Seeing as you put me in a flying tin can yesterday."

I unlatched the pannier, pulled out the spare helmet, and handed it to her, watching trepidation play across her face.

"It's your turn to be brave and trust me."

Gabrielle hesitated for a heartbeat, then slid the helmet on. I couldn't see her expression, but apprehension clung to her movements as she fumbled with the strap. I stepped closer and gently adjusted it, her warm breath skimming against my fingers. She stilled as I fastened it beneath her chin, my touch lingering a moment too long.

I unclipped my helmet from the handlebars and settled it on my head, watching her closely. The look in her eyes was priceless—a cocktail of thrill and dread that echoed how I'd felt in the air with her yesterday. The slight tremble in her hands as she touched the helmet's visor didn't escape me.

"Where are we going?" she asked, her muffled voice threaded with curiosity.

"It'll take just over an hour to get there," I replied cryptically, fastening my chin strap. "You'll like it."

She tilted her head skeptically, but I could tell she was intrigued. I swung a leg over the bike and patted the seat behind me in invitation.

Gabrielle approached with careful, deliberate steps, uncertainty stitched through every moment. She climbed on with more grace than I expected, yet perched stiffly on the seat.

"What do I do?" she asked, her voice small and uncertain.

"Start by lowering your visor."

She obeyed with almost comical caution, her movements stiff and mechanical.

"And relax," I said with a soft laugh. "Lean with me when we turn."

"What about my hands?"

"Those," I said with a grin, "go here." I guided her hands to my waist. "Just hold on to me."

She hesitated, her palms hovering before they settled against my sides. Her grip was tight, every muscle coiled as if bracing for calamity. The contact was electrifying.

I started the engine, and it vibrated to life beneath us, its growl shattering the quiet morning air.

"Last chance to back out," I said over the din, echoing our exchange from the day before.

Her laughter was nervous but defiant. "Do your worst."

"I'll get you back home in one piece," I promised as I flipped down my visor, protectiveness surging through me. Her weight against me was heady and intoxicating.

I eased the bike out of the car park, and Gabrielle's hold tightened as we picked up speed. The world blurred past us in a kaleidoscope of color and sound—along with my carefully kept boundaries.

We wove through the surface streets, wind whipping around us in exhilarating gusts. Each turn moved like a dance,

Gabrielle's body following mine with growing comfort, her earlier apprehension giving way to trust. The stiffness in her grip gave way to a more relaxed hold as her confidence grew with each passing block.

We approached a red light, and I slowed the bike to a stop and glanced over my shoulder. "How are you holding up?" I asked over the engine's rumble.

Her laughter was muffled but unmistakably gleeful. "I'm still alive!" she called back, her voice threaded with exhilaration.

"Try to relax a bit more," I advised, feeling the tension in her grip. "And keep your eyes open. It's better if you can see the turns coming."

She nodded, eager but unsure. "I'll give it a shot," she said, voice wavering between determination and doubt.

The light changed, and I accelerated smoothly, savoring the way her grip tightened reflexively before loosening again. A surge of something dangerously close to affection caught me as we merged onto the highway, leaving the city behind.

The miles blurred beneath us—asphalt, adrenaline, and the steady thrum of the engine. We crossed the Red River into Oklahoma as clouds dragged lazy shadows over stretches of pastureland and empty sky.

The scenery unfurled like a moving canvas. I merged onto US 377, and the landscape shifted—the prairie stretched beneath a winter-bleached sky, the horizon sharp and unbroken.

The wind knifed through my gear in wild, liberating torrents. Gabrielle's arms tightened around me—not from fear, I suspected, but from the chill seeping past leather and fleece. She pressed closer, seeking warmth, and I couldn't deny the satisfaction curling in my chest.

We veered onto OK 7, where the land softened into rolling foothills, dotted with cedar clusters, the bare-limbed oaks and sycamores etched stark against the sky. Gabrielle shifted behind me, her excitement clear in the way she moved, her body instinctively mirroring mine as we descended into the hills surrounding the Chickasaw National Recreation Area.

The air turned crisp with the scent of damp limestone, dormant grass, and the faint trace of evergreen as we slowed to cruise alongside Travertine Creek. The water ran glassy and smooth, reflecting the pale sky, winding through the hush of the winter-stripped woods. I eased off the throttle, coasting toward an overlook where a small waterfall spilled down limestone ledges into a crystal-clear pool below.

Gabrielle lifted her visor, cheeks flushed from wind and cold, eyes wide as she took in the view.

"Wow." Her voice was breathless. "I had no idea this was so close."

"It's one of my favorite places to escape," I said, removing my helmet, watching her drink in the moment.

"Incredible," she murmured, fixated on the cascade of water as it tumbled into the pool, the surface smooth except where ripples fanned outward. The landscape, stripped of autumn's warmth, held a raw beauty—silvered bark, frost-kissed grass, and the dark, unyielding green of the cedars.

She turned to me, her breath clouding faintly. "That drive was…"

I raised an eyebrow, waiting.

"Exhilarating," she confessed, laughing—a sound that wrapped around me like warmth in the cold. "And kind of peaceful, once I started breathing again."

"Shall we walk a bit?" I asked, savoring her delight as she nodded. "Stretch our legs?"

We left our helmets on the bike and set off along a narrow trail through the quiet woods. The path, dusted with frost in shaded patches, crunched beneath our boots. Winter had stripped the landscape bare, but in that bareness was something unguarded, exposed—like the silence between words unsaid.

Gabrielle walked beside me, closer than usual, the space between us thinning with every step.

"You seem different out here," she said, dipping her head. "In a good way. More relaxed. Free." She met my gaze again.

"And which version do you prefer?"

She smiled. "Don't get me wrong. I like you as you are. But it's nice seeing this side of you. Feels like a peek behind the curtain."

"And what do you see behind the curtain?" I asked, catching the glint of mischief in her eyes.

She stopped walking and turned to face me, the corners of her mouth tilting upward. "I think there's more to you than meets the eye," she said, playful but earnest. "You hide it well."

"So you're saying I'm dull?" I countered, feigning offense —or trying to. Her laughter undid me.

"Not at all. Just…reserved." She hesitated, then added, softer, "I like knowing there's more to you."

"I could say the same about you."

The space between us thrummed with tension. I had to keep moving, or else I'd succumb to the temptation to close it entirely.

We continued down the path, our strides slower, as if we had all the time in the world. Of course, we didn't—just a few stolen hours.

The path drew us deeper beneath a lattice of pale limbs and evergreen. The air was crisp and clean, a sanctuary broken only by the soft rush of the creek and our footfalls on the dormant ground. Gabrielle hiked beside me, her cheeks still flushed, her breath misting in delicate curls.

The trail curved toward a secluded spot where the creek widened into a crystalline pool, fed by a small waterfall spilling over limestone terraces. The turquoise water, impossibly clear, was cradled by smooth outcroppings that rose like petrified waves. I guided Gabrielle to a weathered wooden bench overlooking the view. We sat in silence, absorbing the wild serenity of the place.

"This is incredible," Gabrielle said softly, her eyes alight as she took in the view. In the hush, the waterfall's rhythm was almost musical. She absorbed the landscape, or perhaps it absorbed her, the way it mirrored her clarity and depth. "You look like you have something on your mind," she mused, turning toward me with an inquisitive smile. "What could possibly pull you away from this?"

For a moment, I considered deflecting with humor. But the raw openness of this place demanded honesty. I kept my gaze on the tumbling water. "A thousand thoughts I shouldn't be having," I confessed, my voice nearly lost in the rush of the falls. "Things I've no right to think."

She didn't answer right away, instead shifting beside me. "That makes two of us," she said at last, her words threading into the crisp air with quiet intimacy.

I turned to face her. The tension between us hung sharp in the cold, biting air, thrilling and terrifying in equal measure. If I were a better man, I'd have ended this now—a clean severing before the attachment dug any deeper.

But she was here, and the moment was here.

And I wasn't a better man.

I leaned toward her, drawn by a force as certain as gravity. She didn't flinch or look away, and for a breathless moment, I imagined closing the distance, feeling the warmth of her mouth against mine, letting this reckless impulse take hold. But I hesitated, the weight of it crashing into me all at once. I pulled back, my pulse roaring like the waterfall.

"This place," I said at last, grappling for composure. "It's where I can escape everything—real life, responsibility…the bloody employee handbook." Her eyes widened slightly at that last confession. "I thought you might need an escape too."

Her expression softened, her gaze tender, making my restraint feel both noble and absurd. "I knew you were a rebel," she teased, though a quiet seriousness lingered beneath it.

I exhaled, my breath dissolving into the cold. "Out here, I can be free in ways I can never be on campus." I looked at her directly, letting every conflicting emotion hang like unfinished notes.

"I want to be free too," she said softly, sliding her hand along the bench until her fingers brushed mine. The touch landed like a spark.

The sun slipped behind a cloud, muting the light, but the colors around us—pewter sky, white limestone, green cedars—were still vivid and arresting.

I turned fully toward her, the ache of wanting so fierce it drowned out every protest and consequence. She shivered slightly, the cold pressing in as the sun slipped away, and without thinking—without rationalizing—I caught her hand and pulled her toward me. She came willingly, eyes bright with wonder and resolve, her breath uneven as our faces drew close.

For an agonizing heartbeat, I expected her to recoil, to remind me of all we stood to lose with a single word or movement. Her silence was deafening, and my own fear roared over it, threatening to consume everything.

But she did neither.

I kissed her, reckless and terrified, still half convinced she'd wrench away in horror or disbelief. Instead, she wound her arms around my neck and pressed into me with a fervor that made my head spin. It was all the invitation I needed. The flimsy lines I'd drawn between us dissolved entirely.

She leaned into the kiss, her lips soft and eager beneath mine. The certainty of her response obliterated every hesitation. The world around us—icy air, muted light, rushing water—collapsed inward until there was nothing but this impossible moment.

She traced the rough edge of my jaw, as if memorizing this fragile transgression. My restraint shattered. I pulled her closer still, deepening the kiss with an urgency born of uncertainty and longing.

It was madness. It was chaos. It was perfect.

CHAPTER 10

GABRIELLE

"So what made you turn vegetarian?" Cal asked as he perused his scratched-up laminated menu.

"A streak of rebellion when I was eleven," I answered. The meat-free options at Tia Maria's Mexican Cantina were sparse, but I settled on a veggie quesadilla.

Cal glanced up at me over the top of his menu. "You can't just leave it there. Tell the story."

"It's not much of a story," I said, watching his lips curve into a knowing smile—the same one that had undone me so thoroughly by the creek. "There was some epic battle between Dad and me. I can't remember what it was about now, but it seemed important at the time."

The restaurant was worn but welcoming—a hole-in-the-wall joint with cracked vinyl booths and strings of chili pepper lights dangling haphazardly from the ceiling. The air was thick with the scent of cumin and sizzling meat, while laughter and the clatter of plates bounced off the brightly painted walls.

"Dad had grilled steaks for dinner, but I was mad and declared I was a vegetarian." A flood of memories rushed in as I spoke.

The menu slipped from his fingers as his laughter filled the small cantina—rich and unguarded, an echo of the forest moment we were both reluctant to leave behind. "How did he take that?"

I could still picture the look on Dad's face, half-amused and half-exasperated. "He didn't miss a beat. He just said, 'Suit yourself, eat your broccoli.' He thought it would blow over in a week."

Cal's eyes crinkled with amusement. "But you were too stubborn to let that happen."

"Exactly," I said, smiling at the memory of my dad's resigned patience. "I'm still a vegetarian to this day."

"A vegetarian rebel," Cal mused as he set his menu to one side. "How very…fitting." His voice was light, but an edge of genuine admiration lay beneath it. "And here I was expecting a plea for the plight of livestock."

"It's not an ethics thing," I clarified. "Though I am in favor of humane treatment of animals." I took a sip of my iced tea. "Somewhere along the way, I lost my taste for meat entirely." I shook my head. "Actually, that's not quite accurate. For me, it's a texture thing. I don't mind the flavor, like if something is cooked with meat. I just can't eat it."

"I'll remember that when I cook you dinner."

Warmth bloomed inside me at the thought of a next time beyond this stolen weekend. "You cook too?" I asked, aiming for casual when it was anything but. "I'm impressed."

Our server returned to the table, notepad in hand, an amused tilt to her lips. Her look made me wonder just how obvious Cal and I were.

"Ready to order?" she asked, pen poised in her French-tipped fingers.

"Ladies first," Cal said, nodding to me.

"I'll have the veggie quesadilla," I told her, handing over the weathered menu. "With an extra side of sour cream, please."

"And I'll have the tacos al carbon."

"I'll have that right out." She clicked her pen closed and glanced at my nearly empty glass. "Need a refill? Sweet or unsweet?"

"Sweet," I answered. "Thanks."

She left the table, and I caught Cal trying—and failing—not to laugh.

"What?"

"You keep finding new ways to assault tea."

"You're in the South," I shot back, sipping the remnants through the striped plastic straw. "Sweet tea is a staple here. I'll accept your way of making hot tea, but leave my iced tea alone."

"Fair enough." He reached across the table and brushed his fingertips along the back of my hand. My skin tingled.

"Your turn," I said, eager to shift the focus before my emotions unraveled. "What got you into physics?"

Cal patted my hand lightly before leaning back in the booth. "Rebellion against my own father, I suppose. Though far less noble than yours."

"Rebellion against what?" I asked, dragging my straw through the ice in my glass.

A shadow flickered across his face—fleeting, but unmistakable. I wondered if he'd retreat into himself, but he didn't. "Against a future that had already been decided for me."

"That sounds ominous." I tilted my head, intrigued by this glimpse behind his composed exterior. "What kind of future?"

"The kind with a seat at the head of a boardroom table," he said, lifting his glass. "Private banking, investment, development, that sort of thing. Back in the day, it was railroads and sea lanes. Now it's mostly banks, real estate, and an exhausting amount of polished small talk." He took a sip, then added dryly, "My father was thoroughly unimpressed when I chose quantum mechanics over capital markets."

"Family business?"

He nodded. "Going back generations."

The image of Cal in some glossy London office—bespoke suit, dead eyes, too-tight tie—was so wrong it made me smile. "So you went from rebel son to—"

"Rebel professor," he finished, the smile returning. "Or as my father calls it, 'an expensive disappointment with—'"

"Tenure?" I guessed.

"Almost." His chuckle was soft, almost a sigh. "Which somehow makes it worse."

"Almost?"

"I'm up for review next year." His words were so casual, but I could hear the gravity beneath them.

"For tenure?"

He nodded.

"You'll have to explain tenure and the whole university rank structure to me sometime. My aunt has tried, but it never sticks."

"It's not complicated." He gestured layers with a flat hand. "Adjunct, assistant, associate, professor with tenure."

"And you are?"

"Associate."

The waitress returned with our food just as a knot of guilt tightened in my stomach. She set the steaming plates before us, but the rich, savory aroma did nothing to quell my sudden unease. I poked at the melted cheese spilling from beneath the crisp tortilla, my appetite evaporating as quickly as it had arrived.

"You've gone quiet." Cal's voice was gentle, probing. I felt his gaze on me—steady, unflinching—unraveling every thought I tried to keep hidden. "What is it?"

I hesitated, searching for words that wouldn't ruin everything. "It's just…" I toyed with the frayed edge of my napkin as his expression shifted from curiosity to concern.

"What if this"—I gestured between us—"jeopardizes your career? Your shot at tenure?"

He reached across the table again, capturing my restless hands in his. "Of all the things I might have expected you to say," he murmured, "that was not one of them."

"I'd hate to get in the way of something so important." The words tumbled out. "I can't stand the thought of being responsible if—"

"Gabrielle." He squeezed my hand, silencing my anxious spiral. "If anyone should be worrying about impropriety and consequences, it's me." The intensity in his eyes softened, and I saw something else—a vulnerability I hadn't expected. "I just hope you don't think..." He trailed off, searching for the right words. "The last thing I want is for you to see me as some sort of...creep."

I blinked, startled by the confession. "There's no way I'd ever think that."

"Because I know how it looks—a lecherous professor chasing after a beautiful, young"—he kissed the back of my hand—"irresistible student."

Heat rose in my cheeks, mortifying and reassuring all at once. "Believe me," I said, ducking my head and catching his gaze through lowered lashes. "You're nothing like that. I've had my share of sleazy advances." A leering football coach in high school, a too-friendly manager with wandering hands... I shuddered. "You've been nothing but a gentleman."

Cal relaxed his brow, relief softening his features. But behind those gray eyes, a shadow lingered—old scars not yet faded. He squeezed my hand again, as if to reassure us both. "I'm glad to hear it," he said quietly. "And I hope you don't think I see you as some devious, self-serving student trying to—"

"Secure an A in your class?" I finished, smiling despite myself.

He nodded, a hint of wry humor tugging at his lips. "I know the type."

"And I'm not it?" I teased.

"You"—he leaned in, dropping his voice to a conspiratorial whisper—"are definitely not that." A grin broke free. "Those girls don't filter into my office until end of term."

Chapter 11

Callum

Gabrielle stepped outside, bathed in golden light, and lifted her face to the sun, eyes closed.

"It's warmed up a little," she said as she zipped up her brown leather jacket.

Her blonde hair lifted in the breeze, sunlight catching the soft waves and igniting them like a halo. I couldn't look away, struck again by how effortlessly beautiful she was—lovely in her simplicity, enchanting for it. She opened her eyes and caught me staring.

"You're right," I said as I shrugged on my jacket. "Feels almost like spring."

"We have different definitions of spring," she jabbed with a teasing smile as she pushed her hands into her pockets.

We had barely taken a step toward the car park when Gabrielle's phone buzzed. She fished it out, glanced at the screen, and hesitated before sending it to voicemail.

I arched an eyebrow. "Need to take that?"

"No," she replied with a breathy laugh. "That was my aunt. She's a talker, so I try to preplan our conversations."

"Not one for quick chats?"

"There's no such thing as a quick chat with Aunt Suzy."

She thumbed out a text. "I'll just tell her I'm out with a friend and will call her later." She smiled up at me, tucking the phone away again. "There, off the hook."

I rocked back on my heels. "A 'friend?'" I teased. "Is that what I am?"

"As far as she's concerned? Yes."

I stepped close enough to feel her warmth. "And as far as you're concerned?"

She met my gaze, and the world around us paused, the lazy hum of Sunday afternoon small-town traffic fading to a whisper. For a moment, I thought she might evade the question—until she spoke, her voice low and sincere. "What do you want to be?"

I drew Gabrielle off the pavement toward a shuttered storefront, its windows dark behind a rusted gate. I pressed her gently against the faded brick wall, slipping my hands from her arms to her waist, anchoring her there. Her breath caught as I dipped my head and grazed my lips along the delicate line of her jaw.

"So many things," I whispered as she trembled beneath me. "Some I dare not mention."

The words were an exhale against her skin, and I felt rather than heard the soft moan that escaped her lips. She leaned into me, pliant and warm, and all my fears unspooled, melting away like ice in the spring thaw. Her fingers curled into my shirt, holding me as if afraid I might disappear, and the tender desperation of it made my pulse kick up.

"Cal," she breathed, threading one hand into my hair, pulling me closer still. The sound of my name was a revelation —intimate, electric, charged with all the possibilities she'd offered but left me to define.

I kissed her slowly, a claiming, and something in me shifted irrevocably. Her lips moved beneath mine with exquisite urgency, and the universe narrowed to the cadence of our breath and the delicate press of her fingers on my skin. The world dimmed to nothing, the silent street vanishing behind the symphony of sensation she stirred in me. I tasted the hesitant tang of her longing, felt her heartbeat racing against mine.

As we broke apart, a shiver passed between us—a thin seam of air, fragile and fleeting. I cupped her face, unwilling to release her from this moment. Her cheeks were flushed, her green eyes luminous.

"Wow." The single word was an admission and a benediction. She blinked slowly, as if waking from a dream.

"Wow indeed."

I heard a throat clear behind me and whipped around. An older woman—short, stout, and impeccably dressed in Sunday finery—stood there clutching a colossal handbag.

"Be sure to leave some room for Jesus now, you hear?" she said, her accent thick, twangy, and unmistakably Southern. I stiffened, and Gabrielle bit back a laugh.

The woman surveyed us with genteel disapproval, her painted lips pursed beneath a feathery church hat. "It's Sunday," she declared, clutching her handbag tighter. "And y'all ain't in California."

Heat crept up my neck. I stepped back from Gabrielle, my hand trailing down her arm until only our fingertips touched. Despite my irritation, I couldn't suppress a smile at the absurdity of it all—caught like teenagers by the town busybody.

"Some advice, young man?" she added with a smile that was anything but warm. "Save some of that energy for your wedding night."

Gabrielle stifled a giggle behind her hand, and my irritation dissolved into an awkward chuckle.

I nodded, hoping I appeared respectful. "I'll keep that in mind."

She gave us one last curt nod before continuing down the

street with a self-satisfied air of triumph, her heels clacking an indignant rhythm on the pavement.

As soon as the woman rounded the corner, Gabrielle doubled over in laughter.

I tried to look stern but failed miserably. "We've been shamed in the name of Jesus," I said, pulling Gabrielle back into my arms. "By a woman with a handbag larger than her head."

"Small towns." She sighed, nestling against me as if she belonged nowhere else.

Her warmth seeped into me, dissolving whatever discomfort lingered from our ambush. We stood there for a moment longer before I kissed the top of her head and pulled away. "We should probably head back before it gets too late," I murmured, though every part of me rebelled at the thought.

Gabrielle tilted her face up, eyes searching mine. "I suppose."

Her reluctance echoed my own—a shared hesitancy to leave behind the anonymity and abandon we'd found, tucked over an hour away from everyone and everything. Here, in this small, sleepy town, time bent just for us. But as we walked hand in hand through the empty streets, that fragile spell had already begun to unravel.

We reached my motorcycle, parked solitary and defiant at the edge of an empty lot. I paused, fished the keys from my pocket, and turned to Gabrielle with a grin.

"Want to try driving?"

Her eyes widened in a perfect blend of horror and incredulity. She took a step back, shaking her head emphatically. "Absolutely not."

"Why not?"

"Because I'm fond of living," she said, hands on her hips, trying to look stern but adorably missing the mark.

I spread my arms wide, my grin lingering. "I'll teach you."

Gabrielle crossed her arms, a playful defiance in her bright eyes. "Not a chance."

With a laugh, I relented, holding up my hands in mock surrender. "Fine. Another time."

She arched a brow—half skeptical, half daring—and I reached into the pannier to pull out her helmet. I tossed it lightly and caught the small breath she released as she caught it—satisfaction in winning this tiny standoff.

We geared up in familiar silence. Every movement—sliding gloves on, tightening helmet straps—was methodical, but beneath it, a charged awareness buzzed, one neither of us dared acknowledge. We were leaving the cocoon, reentering the world. I mounted the bike and waited.

Gabrielle slid in behind me, and the second her body pressed against mine, the spell broke and reformed into something sharper—less magical, more magnetic. Her warmth seeped through both our jackets, and her hands settled around my waist, slow and possessive.

I braced myself, my thumb hovering over the starter, when she leaned forward, her breath tickling the skin just behind my ear.

"Can I ask you something?"

"Of course." I turned, catching her eyes beneath the visor.

"Why are you okay riding this thing when you're terrified of flying?"

I tensed, caught, then forced a short laugh. "I'm not terrified of flying."

She didn't answer—just rested her chin on my shoulder, her silence more persuasive than any argument.

I exhaled. "All right. Not fond of it."

"Yet you'll take corners on this beast at eighty miles an hour with me clinging to your back?"

"At least if I wipe out, I've got a fighting chance." I kept my tone light, but it didn't mask the truth.

Her arms shifted slightly, sharing warmth in the way she was holding me.

"I think I'll take the long way back," I said, adjusting my grip on the handlebars. "Back roads. Fewer cars. More curves."

She went still for half a beat—then pressed in.

"Should be a fun ride," I murmured.

Her fingers flexed against my jacket, body stiff.

"You flipped a plane upside down yesterday," I said, glancing back at her. "Surely you can handle a few tight turns."

Her laugh gusted warm against my neck, but it quickly melted into something else—something quieter and more focused.

I swallowed, suddenly aware of every point where she touched me. "Do you trust me?" I asked.

"I'm here, aren't I?"

The echo hit—my own words turned back on me—and it landed deeper than I was prepared for. I slid my hand along her forearm, found one of her gloved hands, and lifted it to press a kiss to her knuckles.

Then, deliberately, I guided her arms tighter around my waist. "Much better."

Her laughter was warm, breathy, and far too distracting.

"The ride might get a little wild," I said, adjusting my grip again. "Best hold on—nice and tight."

CHAPTER 12

GABRIELLE

"Okay, so how do I work this thing?" I fumbled with the electric kettle Cal had given me.

"First, you add water," Cal said with a trace of amusement. "Then you plug it in, switch it on, and wait. It's not rocket science." He leaned against the kitchen counter, arms crossed, his face full of mischief.

I rolled my eyes, filling the kettle with exaggerated care.

"If you have trouble boiling a kettle, I'm genuinely concerned about letting you near the lab kit tomorrow," he continued, his accent slipping into something painfully posh for effect. "We'll be adding resistors and capacitors to circuits."

I tossed a dish towel at him. He caught it easily.

"Very funny." I set the kettle on its base with a decisive click, refusing to look at him until I could smother my grin.

He tugged me toward him, the towel forgotten on the floor.

Cal kissed along my neck, each touch like a spark. I stood still, caught in the delicious thrill of it, breath going shallow. His lips lingered just below my ear.

"The kettle won't work if you don't plug it in," he

whispered, his voice a teasing rumble. "And switch it on." He pulled back, eyes alight with playful reproach. "Haven't I taught you anything?"

I laughed, the sound embarrassingly shaky as I plugged in the kettle. The switch, however, eluded me, and I fumbled to find it, growing increasingly frustrated. Before I knew it, Cal was behind me, pressing the flat button at the base of the handle with infuriating ease.

"It was hiding," I defended weakly.

"I'm sure."

I turned toward him, surrendering to his proximity and the blaze of attention that pinned me there. "How long will it take?"

"A minute or two." His lips brushed the side of my jaw between syllables.

"I suppose I could've calculated it," I said, a nervous tilt to my voice.

"You could have." Another kiss, more insistent than the last. "Or you could just trust me."

Cal spun me across the kitchen with a sudden, playful fierceness. I let out a small yelp before he caught me at the waist and lifted me onto the counter in one swift motion. I gasped, but it quickly became a soft exhale as he stepped between my thighs and kissed me—deeply, fiercely—with a hunger that turned my bones to sand.

I moaned against his lips, instinctively wrapping my legs around him, pulling him closer. He tangled his fingers in my hair, and I threaded mine through the dark strands that fell over his forehead. Everything—the heat of him, the solid press of his body—flooded my senses. My pulse surged with each insistent kiss. His name escaped my lips in a breathless pant.

He pulled back just enough to meet my eyes, and the raw intensity there left me unmoored. He rested his forehead against mine, chest heaving like he'd just run a race.

"Christ," he murmured into the space between us. "If you keep making sounds like that, I don't think I'll ever be able to let you go."

His heart beat frantically against my own.

He brushed his lips against mine again, lingering with a tenderness that carried just as much urgency as before. I clung to him.

The kettle clicked off, but neither of us moved.

"You'll want to get that," Cal finally said, the words low and ragged.

"Already?" I was breathless, still clinging to him. "Was that even a minute?"

He drew away just enough to catch his breath, reluctance in every motion, and went to the cupboard. The absence of his touch left me cold and aching. He placed Yorkshire Gold tea bags into each mug and poured the steaming water over them. The faint, earthy aroma of tea curled through the air.

He returned to me with renewed urgency, words punctuated by demanding, insistent kisses. "We have another" —his lips sealed over mine, insistent and consuming—"three minutes now."

I laughed against his mouth, but the sound turned needy, dissolving into a moan as he skimmed his hands up my back, pulling me closer. He captured my gasp with another kiss— deep, devouring—as though making up for every moment he'd resisted.

I arched into him. The bottom edge of the cabinet bit into my neck, but it didn't matter. Nothing mattered except the wild pulse beneath my fingertips as I traced over his chest.

He slipped his fingers beneath the hem of my sweater, the heat of his touch scalding against the sensitive skin along my spine.

"Your skin is like silk."

Cal traced his lips down my neck, his breath a fevered rush against my skin. He caught the neckline of my sweater between his fingers, tugging it down to press slow, deliberate kisses along my collarbone.

"Can't get enough," he murmured, voice thick with need.

Desire coiled tight within me, an electric pulse that spread to every nerve. I dug my fingers into his shoulders as I arched into him. His mouth was relentless, leaving a trail of sensation that made it impossible to think beyond this moment, this need.

He paused, searching my eyes with an intensity that both thrilled and unsettled me. The weight of what we were doing hung between us—unspoken but undeniable. Still, he didn't stop.

I slipped my fingers under his collar, savoring the heat of his skin beneath the fine wool of his sweater. It should have been enough—but wasn't.

I took hold of his belt and gently tugged.

"Gabrielle," he breathed into my ear, raw and almost pleading.

The sound of my name, so far removed from his usual polished reserve, was unbearably thrilling.

"Gabrielle," he said again as I tugged more insistently at his belt, the word almost a groan. He drew a shuddering breath. "You're an exquisite tease." He moved to my neck, lips grazing, each touch electric. He nibbled my ear, and I trembled.

"You're one to talk." I pulled the belt free from the buckle only for him to put his hand over mine, halting me with gentle restraint. I pulled back, self-conscious.

"Gabrielle," he said softly, urgency and affection warring in his voice as he kissed me again and again, each one reaffirming. "Do you know what it's like?" His words were fire against my skin. "To want you this badly?"

He traced his mouth along my jaw, and I sighed.

"I'd love nothing more than to toss you on your bed right

now," he murmured between ragged breaths, "and ravish you completely."

The image seared through me, sharp and delicious, leaving me aching. A delicious flutter unfurled in my stomach.

"This afternoon…" He paused, drawing my earlobe into his mouth with exquisite tenderness before he found his voice again, words rasping. "When you were riding with me…your body pressed into mine with every turn." He gripped my hips, hard and sudden, and traced my collarbone with his tongue, and I shivered. "I thought of pulling off the road and bending you over my bike."

The image made me go liquid in his arms. He caught and steadied me against him, laughing softly at my reaction.

"God, Gabrielle. I longed to know what it would feel like, having those stunning thighs wrapped around me." The words were a groan against my skin.

I could barely breathe, dizzy with wanting him so much. He slid his hands to the hem of my sweater again but paused there, leaving me burning at his hesitation.

"But—" His voice was raw, stopping me as well. He pulled back enough for me to see the war in his eyes. "If we don't stop now, I won't be able to hold back."

He kissed me then, fiercely tender and achingly sweet, like he had just laid something bare between us he couldn't take back. I exhaled in a rush, almost a sob, feeling both relieved and wrecked as he gathered me close again, his cheek pressed against my hair.

"And unless we want builder's tea, I suggest we pull those bags out."

I tilted my head. "What's builder's tea?"

He stepped away with a laugh. "Sorry—I forget myself sometimes. It's easy to do with you."

At the counter, he plucked the bags from the mugs and tossed them into the trash. "Builder's tea is what you get when you steep it until it's strong enough to fight back. The kind of thing you serve blokes in high-vis jackets before sending them off to pour concrete. Black, bitter, and drowned in milk and sugar to make it drinkable." He flashed a grin. "Not exactly what I had in mind for us."

Cal grabbed the milk from the fridge and poured a splash into each cup. He turned, a flash of self-reproach in his eyes. "Do you take sugar? I didn't think to ask before."

I took the mug with a smile. "This is perfect. I'm trying new things."

He followed me to the table, one eyebrow raised in curiosity.

"I usually drink my tea sweet, no milk," I admitted, watching his expression shift. "And flavored."

He crinkled his nose.

"What?"

"To each their own," he said diplomatically.

"No, tell me," I pressed, eyes narrowed in mock challenge.

"Flavored tea..." He gave an exaggerated shudder. "It's like potpourri in a cup."

I laughed, the sound rising between us. The tea was warm in my hands, but the company was warmer still. I watched him over the rim of my mug, savoring both.

"What does your day look like tomorrow?" I asked, careful to sound casual, even though I already didn't want him to leave.

He furrowed his brow for a moment, then a small smile tugged at his mouth. "Our class at eight," he said, ticking it off on his fingers. "Another lecture at ten. Then a string of meetings with my research students in the afternoon."

I nodded, absorbing his schedule like it mattered more than it probably should. "What else are you teaching this semester?"

"In addition to our course? Electromagnetism and quantum mechanics."

He said it without fanfare, but I caught the faint shift in his voice—a quiet pride behind the words.

"That sounds…intense," I said, setting my mug down. "I'm impressed."

He shrugged, his expression flickering between modesty and amusement. "It keeps me busy. Out of trouble."

I smiled. "What's your specialty?"

He studied me for a beat, like he was deciding how much to say. "Theoretical physics. Quantum field theory, mostly."

I didn't know the full meaning of that, but the way he said it—like it mattered, like it was the part of him that ran deepest—made me want to learn.

He took another sip of tea, cradling the mug loosely in one hand. A crease carved between his brows as he stared into the middle distance—not distracted, just thoughtful—like he was building equations behind his eyes.

"What about your research?" I asked. "What are you working on?"

He looked back at me with the faintest flicker of amusement. "You really want to talk about that?"

"Why not?"

"Because I'd rather not bore you out of the room," he said, though his smile undercut the warning.

I leaned forward, resting my chin in my hand. "I can keep up."

He gave a short laugh. "I don't doubt that." He reached for his mug again. "But let's get you through second-term physics before we tackle quantum field theory."

I narrowed my eyes. "That sounds suspiciously like a challenge."

"It's a public service. I'm preserving your sanity."

"You're just stalling."

He tilted his head, conceding the point. "Fine. One of my students is modeling quantum entanglement in a chain of spin particles. Very simplified stuff, but elegant when it works.

Another's playing with broken symmetry in particle systems—trying to force equations to misbehave so he can study the fallout."

I blinked. "You're letting undergrads break physics?"

"I supervise closely," he said with mock solemnity. "No damage to the fabric of space-time. Yet." He set his mug down on the bright blue-and-yellow checkered tablecloth beside a cobalt vase of silk sunflowers. "And I'm impressed that you followed all that."

I dipped my head. "Not really. Just the last bit. The rest went clean over my head."

Cal took my hand and pressed a kiss to the inside of my wrist. "Still impressed."

My tea was finally cool enough to take a long drink. I'd definitely add sugar next time, but, no lie, the way Cal made it was the best I'd ever had. Maybe it was the right way, as he'd insisted. Or maybe it was because *he'd* made it. Either way.

I toyed with my mug, turning it slowly between my fingers. "Do you think there's ever a chance I could do research with you?"

Cal froze, conflict clear on his face—the tug between desire and decorum, between what he wanted and what was wise. He caught himself quickly, but not quickly enough.

"As an engineering major?" he said at last, carefully neutral. "No, probably not." He shifted in his seat, drumming his fingers lightly on the table. "That would fall more under my colleagues in applied physics. Dr. Watkins, perhaps, or Dr. Lee."

I felt an unexpected pang of disappointment. Cal must have seen it because he reached across the table, capturing my hand in his.

"I think," he began softly, brushing his thumb along my knuckles, "we need to talk about what things might look like when we're in class tomorrow."

My pulse kicked up, and I swallowed past the dry lump in

my throat. I nodded, my heart already squeezing tight at the edges. "Because of the professional implications."

He held my gaze, serious and steady. "We need to be absolutely discreet. Not because I'm ashamed—"

"Because you might lose your job," I finished. The words were like stones in my mouth.

He didn't look away. "Precisely. A relationship with a student—regardless of the circumstances—is the fastest, most assured way to find oneself unemployed."

A shiver ran through me despite the warmth of his hand, and I pulled back, wrapping my arms around myself. Guilt coiled in my chest, sharp and insistent. "I feel bad," I whispered. "Putting your career on the line like this."

He tilted his head, studying me with a tender smolder. "I know what I'm doing," he said quietly. He held his hand out again, palm up, waiting. I placed my fingers in his, tentative but wanting. "Your company is well worth the risk."

I wanted to believe him—needed to—but couldn't help the doubt that whispered cold in my ear.

"But I do plan to wine and dine you in splendor," he said, brushing his lips across my knuckles. "And I need to keep my job in order to do that."

I looked down. "What if I dropped your class?"

His expression darkened, like the idea genuinely pained him. "I can't have your academic course disrupted because of me."

"But—"

"Engineering at Page College is housed firmly within the physics department, Gabrielle. There's no way you could major in engineering and steer clear of my courses." His voice was firm, but I sensed a pleading note beneath it.

"I could change my major," I insisted, though even to me, it sounded ridiculous.

He shook his head, a soft impatience edging into his tone. "It's a moot point. University policy prohibits relationships with students—full stop. Whether they are in one's course or not. You could major in comparative unicorn studies, and it wouldn't make the slightest difference." Cal caught my gaze, his intensity almost fierce. "I don't believe there are formal consequences against students for...inappropriate relationships. The responsibility falls solely on the instructor, as it should." He curled his fingers around mine, grip tight, eyes searching and tumultuous. "But if there were informal consequences for you? If your academic path is disrupted because of me? I wouldn't forgive myself."

"You think I'd forgive myself if you lost your job because of me?"

Our words collided in the air, clashing and falling between us like stones on the carpet. A pause stretched, taut and uncertain, until he let out a slow, resigned breath.

"Absolute discretion then," he said quietly.

I nodded, bunching the hem of my sweater in my fist. "Yes. Absolute."

Cal rose from the table, finishing his tea in a single swallow. He carried his mug to the sink and rinsed it, his movements unhurried and deliberate. He checked his watch, then said reluctantly, "I should head home. I've got a few things to finish up for tomorrow."

Disappointment bloomed sharp beneath my ribs, but I tried to hide it behind a smile as I stood. He held out his hand for my empty mug, and I gave it to him.

"Thanks."

He nodded and rinsed my cup too, placing both neatly in the dishwasher.

"When will I see you again?" My voice was quiet, almost tentative.

He turned back, amusement flickering in his gray eyes. "In class at eight?" he ventured.

I shook my head, determined now beneath the hesitation. "No." I stepped closer, searching his face with all its careful restraint. "I'll see Dr. Hawthorne tomorrow at eight," I corrected gently. "When will I see *you*?"

Cal's expression softened. He cupped my face and traced his thumb gently along my cheek. "When do you want to see me again?" he asked with a playful lilt. "I don't want to monopolize your time."

"If I had my way, you wouldn't be leaving now," I confessed, heat rising beneath the soft stroke of his finger. "But I can't be selfish."

A smile tugged at the corners of his mouth, slow and warm, curling around my heart. "Then let's compromise," he suggested, his voice low and persuasive. "We'll play the week by ear." He paused, holding my gaze with a tender gravity. "Especially these first few weeks. I tend to front-load the term —lecture prep, research design, the usual."

Disappointment pinched at my chest before I could stop it, and my face must have betrayed me.

Cal tilted my chin up, coaxing my eyes back to his. "As I said," he repeated, smiling again, soft and reassuring, "we'll take the week as it comes. But—I did promise you a home-cooked meal."

I blinked as the realization sank in.

He added, "Friday night seems perfect. If you're free, of course."

The days between now and then felt endless, but I nodded. "You'd better not cancel on me," I warned lightly.

He leaned in, resting his forehead gently against mine for a moment that stretched, sweet and suspended. "I wouldn't dare." He reached into his back pocket and pulled out his phone. "Might I have your number?"

I dipped my head to hide my smile. His formality was endearing.

I took his phone, entered my number, and promptly texted myself to ensure I had his as well. A moment later, my pocket buzzed.

"Efficient," he remarked with an approving nod. He moved into the living room, grabbed the black leather jacket he'd draped over the couch, and shrugged it on, the motion fluid and easy. The worn leather sculpted itself to his frame, and something in me fluttered at the sight.

I crossed over to him, trailing my fingers in an appreciative path up his chest. "You look good in black," I said, unable to keep the note of admiration from my voice. "Makes your eyes look even more…" I searched for the right word, settling on a breathy laugh. "Striking."

He caught my hand and pulled me closer, kissing me with a lingering sweetness that sent warmth spilling through me. "I'll keep that in mind," he murmured against my lips.

I exhaled softly as he pulled away, the absence of his touch leaving a quiet ache behind. He paused at the door, one hand on the knob.

"Don't forget to call your aunt back," he reminded gently.

I rolled my eyes and gave him a light shove. "Go," I said with mock exasperation. "Before I change my mind."

CHAPTER 13

CALLUM

The morning sun strained against the classroom windows, casting oblong patterns across the tiled floor. I stood at the lectern, loading my slides for the morning's lecture, when a voice—shrill and syrupy—pierced my focus.

"Dr. Hawthorne?"

I vaguely recognized her as one of my nameless, middle-row slouchers, but her casual air of entitlement was infuriating—the type with a bountiful trust fund and an unswerving belief in her own exceptionality. Glossy bottle-blonde hair swung like a metronome against her designer peacoat as she shifted her weight from one foot to the other.

"I was absent Friday," she announced, though her inflection made it sound more like a question.

"So I noticed," I replied.

She narrowed her eyes, clearly unaccustomed to indifference, and angled her head. When she spoke again, her words were pitched with a nascent whine. "I heard we had a pop quiz. Since I wasn't here, I'd like to make it up."

Perfectly predictable. I set my pen down and regarded her

with the detached curiosity I might show an unexpected lab result. "I'm afraid not."

Her mouth fell open slightly. "But the quiz wasn't on the syllabus," she protested, composure slipping. "How can you grade us on something we couldn't possibly prepare for?"

My patience thinned, irritation prickling beneath the surface as I folded my arms. "Pop quizzes are, by definition, unexpected."

Gabrielle entered, a soft halo of light catching her hair as she slipped quietly into her seat. My irritation eased, and a frisson of awareness passed between us before I schooled my expression.

"But there's not even a grading line on the syllabus for quizzes," the student pressed, arms crossed, hip cocked. She jutted her chin in defiance, expectantly waiting.

"Read your syllabus again. They're included in your participation grade."

She didn't move.

"Your name?" I asked as I opened my email on my laptop.

"Sloane," she said, adding a haughty pause before delivering the rest like a trump card. "Cartwright."

Of course that was her name.

She studied my face for a reaction, then added impatiently, "Yes, *those* Cartwrights."

I couldn't resist a faint smile at her presumption. "Should that mean something to me?"

"As in Cartwright Tower?" Disbelief sharpened her tone.

"Never heard of it," I lied.

Her expression faltered, and I could almost hear the gears grinding as she recalculated her approach.

The room began to fill, the scraping of chairs and unzipping of backpacks providing a welcome distraction. She opened her mouth to speak again, but I preempted her.

"No communication from you about missing class," I remarked, gesturing to my laptop screen.

Sloane pressed her lips into a flat line.

"One missed quiz won't sink you," I continued evenly. "I recommend attending class on Fridays."

"Fine." She tossed the word like a gauntlet. Her glare tested my patience. "I'll just have my dad—"

"Take your seat, Miss Cartwright." I dismissed her with a flick of my hand. Her shoulders stiffened, and she flounced to the fourth row, a minor rebellion in each footfall. I exhaled, turned back to my laptop, and adjusted my tie—black on black today, especially for Gabrielle. *Makes your eyes look even more striking.*

I allowed myself one fleeting glance. She sat near the window, pretending to leaf through her notebook, smiling at the page. Something in me settled, soothed by her presence.

"Let's get started," I announced, redirecting my attention to the room at large. A few stray murmurs faded, and once I was satisfied with the silence, I continued. "This morning we'll be expanding on last week's work with circuits."

I paused, letting that take hold.

"And speaking of last week, Friday's quiz results are uploaded to the portal. For those of you who missed out on the riveting experience, try attending class."

Several groans issued from the back row. I didn't dignify them with a response.

"We'll begin today with electrical resistance," I said, letting my gaze sweep the hall, marker poised against the whiteboard. "Let's start with Ohm's Law. You've likely seen the simplified version before—V equals IR, where V is voltage, I is current, and R is resistance."

I wrote it out, underlining each variable. A few students scribbled, others typed, and a few simply blinked, debating whether this was worth taking down.

"Think of resistance as how stubborn the material is. Voltage is the push. Current is what actually moves. Increase resistance, current drops. Double the voltage? Double the current. Simple—when mass and complexity aren't in the way."

I advanced to the next slide.

"In calculus terms, current is the rate of change of charge over time—I equals dQ/dt. Don't worry, no integrals today. Just a clean relationship between voltage, current, and resistance."

I let the silence stretch long enough to leave a mark.

"For today's lab, you'll build circuits with both resistors and capacitors. Start simple, then make it messy. Pay attention to how the capacitors affect current and voltage over time— especially as they charge and discharge. We'll get into time constants next lecture."

Chairs scraped as students began gathering materials from backpacks and folders. The usual rustling chaos of lab setup unfolded across the hall.

"Also," I added, loud enough to carry, "when your circuit fails and your LED doesn't light, resist the urge to tell me physics is broken. Start by checking your resistor values. Then your wiring. Then your ego."

A few students laughed. Even Gabrielle looked mildly amused, though she didn't lift her eyes from her notebook.

Which was probably for the best.

The room settled into the drone of lab work, ambition and frustration humming in equal measure. A student twisted to read his neighbor's notes; another tapped a pencil against her teeth. Sloane slouched insolently on her stool, as if passive resistance might bend the laws of physics to her will. I left them briefly to their own devices before making my rounds.

At one end of the room, I leaned over a table where a trio stared, perplexed, at a circuit board. "Your resistors are in parallel," I pointed out, adjusting a connection. "Try series."

A few steps away, a student with bright pink hair and a perpetual scowl mumbled something about blown fuses.

"Current too high?" I asked, examining the tangle of

wires before nodding toward the assortment kit. "Try something less dramatic. Higher resistance."

Across the room, hands raised tentatively like flags on a battlefield, each signaling for attention or aid. I moved among them, untangling misinformation and missteps until I reached Gabrielle's table.

She caught my eye as I approached. Her expression was focused but warm—bright with the challenge of getting this right without my help.

A gleaming perfection lay before her: capacitors and resistors in flawless sequence, LEDs winking at full brightness. She held my gaze with teasing confidence, and I felt a disobedient warmth—pleasure I shouldn't have indulged.

"You've been busy," I remarked, my voice pitched low enough for her alone.

Her smile widened, ever so slightly, and I had to bite back an answering grin, too aware of the risk. She shifted, a subtle movement closing the space between us. Her shoulder brushed my arm as she reached for a small screwdriver—a touch so brief it might not have happened at all. Yet it did, sharp and distinct, like a spark on a frayed wire.

For an eternal second, our eyes met, and I was seized by an almost physical need to suspend this moment in time. To let it unfold beyond the confines of this room, beyond every rule that bound me. Then sense reasserted itself with cold clarity.

"Looks good," I said, stepping back to reclaim professional distance. "Try adding another capacitor. See if it behaves."

She nodded, but her eyes held mine as I retreated.

I returned to the whiteboard with manufactured purpose, feigning interest in equations already etched in my mind. I needed to focus. On circuits. On anything else.

CHAPTER 14

GABRIELLE

Physically, I was sitting in calculus, but my mind was back in my kitchen—pinned between the counter and Cal's body, my sweater tugged halfway down one shoulder, his mouth tracing the curve of my collarbone like he was trying to memorize it.

Dr. Huber was writing something on the board—definite integrals, maybe?

I couldn't focus.

The only function I could remember was the sharp spike of sensation when Cal had whispered, "If you keep making sounds like that, I don't think I'll ever be able to let you go." My pen hovered uselessly over my notebook as heat burned in my ears.

The room was stifling, the radiators hissing like snakes beneath the windows. I pushed my sweater sleeves to my elbows in an attempt to cool down or distract myself, but it did neither. I propped my chin in my hand, feigning interest as Dr. Huber droned on about limits and continuity, but the numbers blurred into a tangled mess of possibilities.

Should I text him?

Would he text me?

What if everything fell apart before it even began?

I shifted my legs restlessly under the desk, crossing one ankle over the other, then uncrossing them again. I glanced at my phone, tucked discreetly between the pages of my notebook. The screen was dark.

Focus, Gabrielle.

The last twenty minutes of class trudged by to a soundtrack of marker squeaking frantically on the whiteboard, but nothing sank in. Thankfully, Dr. Huber lectured to the board—not the class—and spoke with such a thick Cajun twang I would never have understood anyway. Even if I had been listening. Sweat beaded along my hairline as I fidgeted in my seat. Relieved when class was finally over, I gathered my things in a flurry.

Outside, the air was crisp against my flushed skin. It revived me instantly, and I pulled out my phone with renewed hope. Cal should be done teaching now, right? Would he call between classes? I tried not to check for messages too obviously as students streamed past, scattering like particles in random motion.

I'd just reached the sidewalk when the phone buzzed in my hand. My heart leaped, only to plummet when I saw the caller ID: Aunt Suzy.

I let out a long breath and answered as I ducked into the student center and settled onto a sagging leather couch in the foyer. "Hey."

"You never called me back yesterday!" Aunt Suzy's shrill voice pierced through the line. "I was worried."

"Sorry," I said, trying to sound contrite. "I got caught up in something. Everything's fine."

"Oh?" she prompted, suspicion crackling like static. "So, who were you out with yesterday? A guy…?"

I could picture her perfectly—eyebrow arched, painted lips pursed, manicured fingers tapping against her phone.

"Just a friend," I deflected.

"Aha! A friend!" She seized the word like a hawk on prey. "Anyone I should know?"

"No," I stalled. "Just someone from my physics class." The words felt dangerous, teetering too close to forbidden territory.

"Well, I hope that means he's smart."

I laughed nervously, eager to steer the conversation far from anything incriminating. "We just went over circuits for lab. Lunch and study." My cheeks burned with guilt. It wasn't quite a lie...

"A *friend* from physics?"

"Uh-huh."

"And you're sure it's just—"

"Yes," I cut in, sharper than intended. I winced at how transparent I must have sounded. "We have our first lab report due Wednesday," I explained, trying to wrap my words in a veneer of routine and academic obligation. Desperate to redirect, I asked, "How's the start of your semester been?"

"Well," she said with a huff, caught off guard but not entirely displeased by my change of subject. "It's been a nightmare, to be honest. I've had to take on an extra class at the last minute because one of my colleagues is under investigation."

"Investigation?" The word struck me like a cold draft.

"No one's officially saying anything, but we all know." She paused for effect. "Sleeping with a student," she said pointedly, as if the scandal were a personal affront to her.

"Wow," I said, trying to keep my tone carefully empathetic. "That sounds rough."

"It is! Honestly, I don't know how much more of this I can take," she went on. "I should really think about retiring."

My stomach twisted uncomfortably, Aunt Suzy's words hitting far too close to home. It wasn't difficult to imagine Cal in the same situation if anyone found out about us. The thought chilled me more than the cold air blustering against the window.

"Are you…are you going to be okay?" I asked, clumsy in my attempt to sound sympathetic while swallowing down my rising dread.

"Oh, I'll manage." She sighed theatrically. "But it's such an inconvenience!"

"Well, I shouldn't keep you then. I bet you have mountains of work to do."

"Ain't that the truth! Just make sure you keep me in the loop about this 'friend' of yours," she added, her voice coy but edged with genuine affection. "I need my drama fix."

"I will," I promised, smiling despite myself. As overbearing as Aunt Suzy could be, she was the only real family I had left, and I didn't want to lose her too.

"Good! Talk soon, sweetie." She hung up, leaving a faint echo of herself in the silence.

I checked my phone again. No new notifications. I set it down and let out a long, slow breath. The foyer buzzed with the chaos of students passing in and out, each absorbed in their own small universes.

I drummed my fingers restlessly against my thigh and closed my eyes for a moment, willing myself to be calm. We were being careful. No one would find out.

The phone buzzed in my lap like it had read my thoughts. My heart seized and then released when I saw Cal's name on the screen.

> You've been on my mind all morning. Not great for my electromagnetism lecture, but excellent for morale.

I stared at the message, warmth flooding through me in slow, delicious waves. The corners of my mouth lifted before I could stop them. I stared at the message as if it might vanish if I blinked. My pulse quickened, sweeping away the invasive doubts Aunt Suzy had planted.

> Same here. Pretty sure I didn't absorb anything in calculus. I couldn't explain a definite integral if you paid me.

The response came almost immediately.

> I'm flattered. Deeply concerned for your GPA. But flattered.

I laughed out loud—soft and involuntary. A few students glanced over from the vending machines, but I didn't care. The release was like sunlight after a storm. I grinned, the tension in my chest unraveling a little more. My thumbs hovered over the keyboard, then tapped out a reply before I could second-guess myself.

> I have a 4.0. Plenty of wiggle room.

With a spark of satisfaction, I hit send. Let him chew on that.

> We can't go tarnishing a perfect record. I'd be happy to explain definite integrals later. Privately, of course...

> I'd hate to waste our time on calculus.

I held my breath, eyes fixed on the screen, and released it in a rush when his response appeared.

> A tragic misuse of resources, indeed. But I thought, perhaps, it would give me a convenient pretense to see you again.

I could almost feel him there with me—the distant echo of his voice in the words, the relentless pull that made everything else fall away. The room blurred into a backdrop of motion. Students came and went like apparitions, their chaotic energy reduced to a whisper against the steady drumbeat of my pulse.

> Since when do you need a pretense?

> I don't.

My heart tripped over itself. The words were simple but charged, sparking a thrill that coursed through me like electricity. I hesitated, biting my lip. I wanted to ask him when I could see him, but fear of seeming too eager held me back for one agonizing moment before desire broke through.

> When can I expect to see you then?

I exhaled shakily and waited, the seconds stretching unbearably. Finally, the phone buzzed.

> Are you free tomorrow afternoon?

He could have asked *Right now?* and I would've said yes. My pulse rushed in my ears. I tried to stifle it with deep breaths, but giddiness overtook me instead.

> Yes.

I winced at the starkness of the message. It felt naked and exposed and true. Vulnerability wrapped tight around anticipation, and my thoughts spun in dizzy circles as I wondered what tomorrow might hold.

> If memory serves, you don't have afternoon classes tomorrow. I'll plan to pick you up at your apartment at 2 p.m., if that's convenient.

My mind whirled with infinite possibilities, each more intoxicating than the last. I could hardly contain the surge of elation that made my fingers hover impatiently over the screen.

> Car or motorcycle? So I know how to dress.

His reply was swift.

> Car. Weather won't be good for the bike tomorrow. We got lucky this weekend.

I read the message twice, a flush creeping into my cheeks at the unintentional double entendre. My giddiness gave way to shyness, and I paused. I wanted to sound casual, nonchalant—but my excitement seeped into every word.

> By the way…the all-black look today was a choice. A good one. Just saying.

> I'm pleased you noticed. I do listen, occasionally.

My smile widened.

> Is there anything you'd like me to wear?

I stared at the message a second too long before hitting send. Bold. Maybe too bold.

> That's a dangerously loaded question.

> I like living on the edge.

There was a pause, and then—

> The safe answer is that green jumper you wore to office hours last week. Very becoming.

My heart skipped.

I bit my lip, my thoughts spinning faster than I could catch them. The urge to see him—to really see him—was rising fast and bright in my chest. I had to redirect.

The reply came seconds later, like he hadn't even paused to think.

My stomach flipped so hard I nearly dropped the phone. I heard the words in his voice—low, measured, velvet-edged. I curled in on myself, tucking my knees beneath me, grinning like a lunatic into the collar of my sweater.

God help me, I was in so much trouble.

CHAPTER 15

CALLUM

"You brought me to an Air Force museum?"

Gabrielle's voice echoed off the corrugated metal walls, caught between disbelief and delight.

I locked the car. "What were you expecting? A champagne cruise down the Seine?"

She glanced up at the tan aluminum building with royal blue shutters, its sloped roof gleaming in the afternoon sun. The sign read *Perrin Air Force Base Museum*. She looked at me like she was torn between concern and reluctant admiration.

"Unconventional," she said, "but you do know how to make a girl swoon."

"I do my best."

Inside, the cool air carried the scent of aged metal and sun-warmed concrete, layered with the ghost of jet fuel long since dried. Gabrielle had barely made it two steps before she stopped short, her gaze locking on a gleaming blue-and-white jet planted like royalty at the center of the exhibit floor.

"Oh my God," she whispered.

I leaned in. "Careful. I think you're drooling."

She shot me a look over her shoulder—mock-scathing,

entirely fond. "You brought me here just to watch me geek out, didn't you?"

"Guilty," I said, utterly unrepentant.

She took off like a shot, circling the aircraft with wide eyes and a reverence usually reserved for priceless art. I followed at a more leisurely pace, letting her enthusiasm set the course.

The museum's interior was cavernous but crammed, its layout more passion project than polished curation. Artifacts from every era of military aviation filled the space—propellers suspended from the rafters, flight suits sealed behind plexiglass, training manuals stacked beside polished engine components. A mannequin pilot in full gear slouched in a cockpit shell, painted eyes fixed on the middle distance.

Gabrielle barely noticed. She was already halfway around the jet, vibrating with excitement. "Cessna T-37B Tweet," she rattled off, practically bouncing. "Twin-engined trainer jet, used for decades. She's gorgeous."

"She?"

Gabrielle ignored the question, pressing her palms to the stanchion rope like proximity alone might satisfy her hunger. "I've only ever seen one in photos. Look at the cockpit! And they've got the J47 over there too—I can't believe it."

I followed her line of sight to the back corner where a General Electric turbojet engine sat on its stand like a metallic beast, its polished casing flayed open to expose its gleaming heart.

"First jet engine with a thrust-to-weight ratio over one," she said, spinning to face me. "Changed everything."

I smiled at how she came fully alive. This was Gabrielle in her element—sharp, unfiltered, electrified. And no idea how stunning she was. I wondered, fleetingly, if she had the faintest notion what it did to me—watching her like this.

I cleared my throat.

"Why are you looking at me like that?" She fixed me with a penetrating gaze, her head tilted.

I shook my head, a smile still tugging at my lips. "Your enthusiasm is exhilarating. Not that I needed more proof, but seeing you like this tells me you've chosen the right field of study—and eventually, the perfect future."

Her expression softened into something vulnerable and luminous—a look that threatened to unravel the last of my composure if I stared too long.

"Speaking of which, what do you plan to do with your engineering degree?" I asked, steering us back to safer ground. "Graduate school? Engine design? Flying? Military? Perhaps an astronaut?"

She laughed again, full and bright. "Let's start with grad school." Her face dropped for a moment before the light returned. "I'm not qualified for the military, so astronaut is definitely out too."

"Why are you disqualified from service, if you don't mind my asking?"

"Heart condition." She tapped her chest. "Mitral valve prolapse."

"Is everything all right?" I asked, only then catching the edge of worry in my voice.

She waved a hand. "I'm fine. I just have a good relationship with my cardiologist." She paused, gaze drifting to the jet before snapping back to me. "It doesn't affect me in any real way—just made both the Navy and the Air Force turn me down."

I stepped closer, as though proximity might lessen the impact of what she'd said. "The same reason being an astronaut is ruled out?"

She laughed and nodded. "And the fact that I'm perfectly happy on this planet and don't feel the need to leave it." Her expression turned wistful. "My dad had the same heart condition, and it kept him out too."

"Then I admire your tenacity even more." The words escaped before I could temper them, but they rang true.

She glanced away, a light flush coloring her cheeks as we passed a wall of sepia-toned photographs—aviators mid-laugh or mid-stride, their lives frozen and framed. Gabrielle studied them, perhaps finding echoes of herself in their imagined stories.

"How about you? Why physics?"

I considered the question, momentarily distracted by her nearness. "A lifelong fascination," I said. "Not merely how things work, but why. I suppose that sounds terribly dull."

"Not at all," she said, green eyes keen and curious.

I paused before a display case of radio components, weighing the right words to articulate a passion that had always defied explanation. "In a world where everything is gray and in flux, the pursuit of answers—real answers, without spin—feels practically spiritual."

She smiled—undeniably mischievous. "You almost make physics sound sexy."

"Almost?" My pulse quickened as I stepped closer. "You don't think physics is sexy?"

She laughed, light and unrestrained. "I think you're doing your best to convince me."

"Physics is exceedingly sexy," I insisted, feigning indignation. "The sexiest of the sciences."

"Not chemistry?" she teased as we passed another row of exhibits. "Or biology?"

"They're just applied physics," I said. "And they wish they were as sexy." I grabbed her hand and tugged her behind a mannequin in full flight gear. "Allow me to make my case more effectively." She barely had time to gasp before I pulled her close. My mouth was at her ear, my voice low enough to be indecent. "Physics is energy," I murmured, tracing a finger along her jawline. I pulled her flush against me. "Bodies in motion."

"Heat?" she breathed.

"Thermodynamics," I corrected, nipping at her earlobe. Her shiver was immediate and gratifying.

We were scandalously hidden, obscured by aviation memorabilia in a strategic corner of the exhibit. Her back pressed against the cool metal wall as I loomed over her with a barely civilized hunger. She tilted her head back, eyes alight with challenge.

"Wavelength is why your eyes are that stunning shade of green." I kissed her neck. "Why your cheeks flush pink when I kiss you."

"Frequency." She was breathless, her voice soft and teasing. "Is why I can hear your voice."

I groaned, filled with want and urgency. I placed her palm flat on my chest. "That jolt you feel? That's your nervous system—pure electricity." I took her face in my hands and kissed her, slow and heated.

She returned the kiss with a fervor that made my head spin, then pulled back just enough to whisper, "What about acceleration?"

I chuckled as I kissed along her collarbone. "You mean the way we're moving dangerously fast?"

"Mm-hmm." She tangled her fingers in my hair.

"That's velocity," I said, every neuron firing as she pressed closer.

"And gravity?" she asked, wrapping her arms around my neck.

"Undeniable." I lifted her against the wall and claimed her mouth again.

A loud, theatrical throat-clearing broke the moment, followed by the steady shuffle of footsteps. I eased Gabrielle back to the floor, and we stepped apart just as an elderly museum volunteer passed, her hair a cloud-like halo dyed a whimsical shade of violet. She offered no admonishment beyond a knowing smirk and a dramatic wink. She walked on without a word, eyes fixed on the ceiling as if admiring a pipe.

Gabrielle stifled a laugh, mischief dancing in her eyes.

We wound through display cases and tributes to local veterans until Gabrielle paused before an exhibit entirely devoid of modern machinery. It was a modest section on the American Revolution—glass cases of weathered documents and rows of tarnished muskets, their bayonets dulled by time. A cracked drum and rusted tin plates sat beneath faded banners.

"I didn't think they'd have anything this old here," she said, bending to examine a tricorn hat that looked ready to dissolve. Her delight was palpable, tinged with disbelief.

I couldn't help the chuckle that escaped.

She shot me a curious glance. "What's so funny?"

I hesitated, knowing I was caught either way. "I always find it amusing what Americans consider 'old,'" I said, leaning against the case with a smirk.

"And what do you consider old, then?" Her eyes sparked with challenge.

"Let me take you to England sometime, and I'll show you." The words lingered, charged. A future both imagined and terrifyingly real.

Her lips parted in surprise, then softened into a smile— unguarded. It unraveled me in ways I couldn't have anticipated. Heat pooled in my chest.

"Well," she said, teasing yet tender. "I suppose I'd better renew my passport."

CHAPTER 16

GABRIELLE

I carried a mug of herbal tea to bed, the scent of chamomile and orange blossom rising with the steam in delicate curls. The tea was flavored, yes, but brewed with care—the way Cal had taught me. I smiled, remembering his meticulous instructions. He'd be proud.

The cup warmed my fingers as I curled up beneath my purple duvet. I nestled into the pillows, their downy softness pure indulgence. A novel lay open face down on the nightstand. I picked it up and tried to lose myself in the story, but it couldn't hold my attention. The words felt flat and uninspired next to the real fairy tale I was living.

My thoughts drifted back to the museum. The precision of Cal's touch, the electricity in his voice as he turned science into seduction—everything replayed in vivid detail behind my closed eyes. My pulse quickened at the memory of our daring retreat behind the flight suit exhibit, lost in our secret universe of kinetic energy and charged kisses.

I reached for my phone, half expecting a message from Cal. Nothing. I set it aside, only to pick it up moments later. Impatient with myself, I sent one instead.

> I had fun today. The museum was amazing.

I hit send before I could second-guess myself and hugged the phone close, listening for a reply. My apartment was silent except for the hum of the refrigerator and the soft whir of the heater. It felt like eons before the phone vibrated, the screen lighting up with Cal's response.

> Not nearly as amazing as you.

I laughed softly, feeling giddy and unguarded. Like a teenager with her first crush—only more reckless and more real. I typed back quickly.

> Flattery will get you everywhere.

His reply came almost instantly.

> Is that so? I hope you mean it...

A beat later, another message popped up.

> What are you doing this evening?

> I'm in bed, attempting to read a book (but failing), and drinking a cup of herbal tea I made. I used the kettle! See, I can learn!

I could picture him—brows raised, eyes full of mischief—even before he replied.

> It's still potpourri in a cup, but you are indeed learning if I've got you to use a kettle.

My turn to hesitate.

> See you tomorrow?

My heart stuttered as I waited.

Of course, unless you're planning to cut my class.

I grinned at his predictability.

I wouldn't dream of it.

Dream of me instead?

The words left me breathless. I could almost hear the low, coaxing note in his voice. My fingers hovered over the screen before I sent my final reply.

Good night. And yes…see you tomorrow.

Good night, Gabrielle.

The silence that followed was different this time—buzzing with satisfaction and possibility, anticipation like a live wire beneath my skin. I set the phone down and sank into my cocoon of warmth and softness.

I picked up my novel again, determined to make a dent in its pages before sleep claimed me. Still, the words danced before my eyes. I reread them several times, but it was no use. My mind kept drifting to Cal—to his voice, his touch. And to Friday, a lifetime away.

Chapter 17

Callum

"This is a solid proposal." I finished a few notes in the margin. "Flesh out these sections of your lit review"—I gestured to the highlighted passages—"and tighten the design description. Then we can move forward. Let's see…today's Thursday." I paused, considering. "Have the revisions to me by Monday."

"Yes, Dr. Hawthorne," said Jackson, one of my senior research students, as he gathered his papers. "Thanks!" He rushed out of my office. I might have said he moved with urgency, but Jackson was a classic overachieving perfectionist—always moving like he was late for the train. Urgency was his normal speed.

A soft tap sounded at the door.

"Dr. Hawthorne?"

Her voice lit up the room more than any fluorescent bulb could hope to manage. Gabrielle stood there, her presence an unexpected gift. I reined in the impulse to greet her with too much familiarity and instead offered a composed smile and returned formality with formality.

"Come in, Miss Clark."

She held her notebook tight to her chest, fidgeting with the spiral binding. I wondered if the color in her face owed as much to me as to the chill outside.

"How can I help?" I asked, keeping my tone carefully neutral.

She took a seat in front of my desk and flipped open her notebook, eyes bright and intent.

"I have a few questions about complex circuits," she said, then hurried on, as if eager to justify herself. "When it's just a circuit in series or in parallel, I have no problem with the calculations. But when both setups are involved, I'm lost."

I leaned back, allowing myself an indulgent moment to admire the wayward strands of hair curling to frame her face. It was dangerous having her here like this—alone and entirely within reach—but danger had never felt so exhilarating.

"I can build the circuits in the lab, and I get the overarching concepts, but the math is eluding me." She paused, looking up at me. "Can you walk me through it?"

I couldn't resist the opportunity—her words were a bit too tempting. "Perhaps a bit more focus in calculus, Miss Clark?"

She blushed, and I could have sworn the color alone could warm the room. I tapped my pen against the desk, allowing her a moment to recover before shifting seamlessly back into professional mode. "Show me where you're getting stuck."

Her pencil flew across the paper, gestures animated and passionate. Each page was filled with diagrams, numbers, and lines of equations tangled like a maze. I leaned closer as she explained her process, acutely aware of how near we were.

"So here, on this one," she said, "I added the voltage in series…but I'm not sure that's right."

I nodded slowly, feeling that familiar pull—wanting to teach her, and wanting something far less academic. "You're overcomplicating it," I said gently. "You're treating the configuration as a single system, but you need to break it down. Analyze the series elements first, then reduce to solve the parallel components." I picked up a pencil and marked the misstep, correcting the sequence, graphite skating smoothly over the paper.

Understanding dawned in her eyes as I walked her through it, step by careful step. Her focus was absolute—both endearing and maddening in its intensity.

"Does that make sense?" I asked.

She absorbed it like sunlight.

"Yes," she said at last. "As usual, I made things more complicated than they need to be."

I chuckled softly, leaning in and lowering my voice to a near whisper, ensuring our conversation was insulated from any wandering ears in the corridor. "You know you have access to me whenever you want it," I murmured. "No need to wait for office hours if you're having trouble." I hesitated, my words deliberate. "Though I'm always pleased to see you, whatever the reason."

She seemed to weigh my words, her expression thoughtful and teasing all at once. "I'm just trying to maintain separation of church and state."

"Which is which?"

"Well," she started, playing with her hair, "state governs laws and action. Church governs the heart and soul. So I suppose this"—she motioned around the room—"is state."

"And church?"

She glanced up at me through her lashes. "Tomorrow evening?"

I nodded slowly. "I look forward to…worship."

The temptation was maddening—her presence a gravitational force pulling me toward her even as we both strained against propriety and expectation. I leaned back, widening the space between us, though the distance did nothing to diminish the magnetism.

"How are your other courses this term, Miss Clark?" I asked, unnecessarily louder to ensure we were heard.

She smiled. "Going well, thanks. In fact, I have a paper

due for psychology tomorrow. I'd better get going if I don't want to be up all night." She stood, gathering her things with a fluid grace that completely stole my focus.

"Best of luck with that." I straightened a few errant papers on my desk. "For what it's worth," I continued, unable to disguise the warmth in my tone, "I'm very glad you stopped by."

"So am I."

CHAPTER 18

———

GABRIELLE

"What are we drinking to?"

I raised my wineglass, the deep red catching the overhead pendant light above Cal's kitchen island. He stood across from me, sleeves rolled up, a chef's knife in hand, slicing zucchini with maddening precision.

He set the knife aside, looked up, and—of course—smirked. "To…worship." He picked up his glass and touched it lightly to mine.

The first sip warmed me all the way down—dry and velvety smooth. I tried to focus on the wine. The kitchen. Anything but the slow, deliberate way his gaze lingered when he thought I wasn't looking.

"This is really good," I said, eyeing the bottle—a red foiled tree on a slate-gray background.

Cal gave an amused huff. "Well, that's a relief. I only bought it because I liked the label, if I'm honest."

I leaned on the counter as he took up the knife again. The steady slice of metal against wood was strangely hypnotic. "I didn't realize you lived so close to me."

The blade faltered for half a second before finding its

118

rhythm again. "Had to preserve a bit of mystery. Though… the proximity has been tempting."

"Tempting how?" I asked, pulse kicking hard.

He didn't answer. But the glint in his eyes said everything.

Moving to the stove, he tossed the vegetables into a skillet, and reached for a wooden spoon.

I looked down at the food, trying to distract myself. "What's on the menu?"

"Sautéed vegetables over herbed risotto," he said. "With a side of I-remember-you're-a-vegetarian."

My breath caught. "I'm touched you remembered."

He finally turned, leaning one hip against the counter, wineglass in hand. "There's very little about you that's forgettable."

Before long, we'd settled at the table, my nerves easing with the first bite. The risotto was warm and creamy, the wine mellowed to a hum beneath my skin, and the conversation— easy and open—unfolded between bites. Nothing weighty— just music, movies, the merits of fresh herbs versus dried. Cal was a deft host—attentive without hovering, dryly funny in a way that made me lean in to catch his inflections. By the time we'd cleared the dishes, I realized I hadn't checked the time once. I didn't want to.

I lingered at the edge of the dining room, wineglass in hand, watching the track lights paint long shadows across the walls.

"How did you learn to cook like that?" I asked, turning to face him. "That was…legitimately impressive."

Cal shrugged as he wiped the counter, a flicker of mischief in his eyes. "YouTube. And an embarrassing amount of trial and error."

I raised a brow. "Seriously?"

He leaned against the counter, drying his hands with a towel. "We always had cooks growing up. Staff. Meals were prepared and served." His tone was light but somehow brittle underneath. "My parents thought cooking was beneath us. Said it was domestic work—not meant for someone with the Hawthorne name."

I took a slow sip of wine, giving him space. "And you disagreed?"

"I did," he said. "Eventually. Turns out, self-righteous defiance and the fear of starvation are powerful motivators. That, and the grim realization I couldn't survive on takeaway and toast forever."

Before I could reply, he stepped in close, settling his hand at the small of my back—steady, certain, and quietly electric. His touch sent a shiver through me.

"So," he said, voice low, "I believe I promised you a tour."

"Lead on," I managed, more breathless than I meant to be.

He gestured around us. "Well, you've seen the kitchen."

I laughed, the sound light and a little giddy. "Seen it and been thoroughly spoiled by it."

We stepped into the living room, and it was nothing like what I'd imagined. Instead of dark woods, smoky colors, and books stacked to the ceiling, the space was sleek and modern —almost austere. Black leather furniture with sharp lines contrasted against bursts of saturated color—a red throw, a yellow pillow, geometric patterns that danced across the area rug. Bold, abstract art lined the walls.

"This is…wow."

Cal rocked back on his heels. "What were you expecting?"

"Not this hyper-modern," I admitted. I scanned the room again, noting details that didn't quite fit the Cal I thought I knew. A gaming console sat tucked beneath a large flat screen TV. In a corner, two guitars rested on stands—one acoustic, one electric. "And definitely not rockstar gamer."

He stepped closer, gray eyes bright with amusement. "I'm not all work."

"I'm getting that."

"Here," he said, taking my hand and leading me down the hallway. His thumb skimmed across my knuckles—a fleeting caress that left sparks in its wake. "I think this next room will feel more…on brand."

We stopped at a door, and he let go of my hand to open it, revealing a room both familiar and yet wholly unexpected. A large espresso desk dominated the space, covered in neat stacks of notebooks and papers. Bookshelves lined the walls, heavy with physics and mathematics texts, ordered by a system only he could understand. A whiteboard spanned the far wall, dense with quantum field equations and abstract diagrams that seemed to hum with the energy of his mind.

"Should I be impressed or intimidated?"

His laughter was soft, close behind me. "Let's go with impressed."

I moved to the whiteboard, searching for a familiar anchor in a sea of complex math and abstraction. "What are you working on?"

He stepped beside me. "This?" He gestured to the board like a maestro before his orchestra. "This is what happens when you're too stubborn to admit you don't know everything." He moved closer, his presence as consuming as the equations on the wall.

I turned to face him, caught in the gravity of those storm-gray eyes. My pulse fluttered as the world narrowed to this single, charged moment. "Maybe," I said, low and daring, "you're not all work after all."

He closed the distance—a gentle insistence that sent heat rushing through me. His kiss was tender at first—testing—then deepened, like he'd been holding back a tide.

When he finally pulled away, he rested his forehead against mine. "I've been waiting all evening to do that," he murmured, his breath a whisper against my skin.

"What took you so long?"

His low chuckle curled around me like smoke, and I loved

how intimate and wild it felt. Drawing back just enough to catch my hand, his lips found mine again—searing and urgent — breaking only long enough for him to murmur, "There's a more pressing conundrum than what's on the board."

I could barely breathe. "What could possibly be more pressing?"

The corners of his eyes crinkled in that maddeningly charming way. "Trying to work out how a woman so radiant, brilliant, and utterly disarming is here with me."

My heart skipped. My breath hitched. "Oh," I managed, confidence evaporating.

He cupped my face with both hands, voice low and fierce. "I can't figure it out. I keep thinking I'll wake up and find it's not real."

Another kiss—devouring, consuming—cut off my reply, and I didn't care that he couldn't see what was already so achingly clear. His intensity was a drug, and I craved another hit. I kissed him back with a heat that melted time and reason, tangling my hands in his hair as if touch alone could make this real.

"Cal," I breathed as he traced his lips along my jawline.

"Gabrielle," he said—reverent, almost broken.

I pulled back. "You really don't see what I see, do you?"

He smiled, but there was a shadow in it. "I seem to suffer a particular myopia where you're concerned."

I shivered as he skimmed a thumb down my neck.

"Either that," he said, drawing me in with exquisite slowness, "or I'm willfully blind."

I felt the moment he hesitated—the slight shift in his touch as a hint of doubt flickered across his face. He held my gaze, searching for something—reassurance, permission perhaps— anything to steady the uncertainty.

"Well, my eyes are wide open," I said, voice steady despite the wild racing of my heart.

He looked at me like we were poised before some

irrevocable leap, his reluctance to cross our private Rubicon palpable in the charged air between us. The kiss that followed was soft, almost gentle.

"Stay," he whispered against my lips, so quietly it almost wasn't a word at all.

I met his gaze, pulse thudding. "Are you sure?" I held my breath, worried I'd gone too far—or not far enough.

The corner of his mouth lifted into *that* roguish smile that undid me every time. "I've never been more certain of anything in my life."

I curled my fingers into the buttery-soft fabric of his shirt. His eyes searched mine—intense, unreadable—as if measuring just how far this would go.

I tilted my head. "In that case…" I slid my fingers down the line of his buttons. "You'd better finish the tour."

His eyes darkened, lips parting—more reaction than reply. And then, without a word, he took my hand again and led me down the hall.

His bedroom was dark, lit only by the warm spill of light from the hallway. Clean lines. Cool tones. A black headboard framed against a slate-gray wall. Nothing soft. Nothing fussy. Just Cal—sharp, elegant, controlled.

Until now.

He turned to me, and everything shifted.

The change in his eyes was clear before he even touched me—something raw and unguarded breaking loose beneath that careful façade. He reached for me, and I met him halfway.

The kiss was nothing like before.

It was hunger. Fire. A question asked and answered in the same breath.

He slid his hands into my hair, tangling them at the base of my neck as he kissed me deeper, harder—like he needed to make up for every hour we'd spent apart. I melted into him, fingers fisting in his shirt, mouth opening to his like we were made to fit this way.

He walked me back until the bed hit the backs of my knees.

"I can't—" He broke the kiss with a growl, forehead pressed to mine. "If we start, I won't be able to stop."

"Then don't stop," I breathed, dragging his mouth back to mine.

He swore—low, reverent—like I'd just granted him absolution.

Hands on my waist, he pulled me flush against him, the contact igniting something molten. I gasped into the kiss as he slid his fingers under my blouse, sweeping over bare skin. He pulled back just long enough to tug it over my head, his eyes raking over me like I was something precious and half-forbidden.

"You're beautiful," he said, voice rough with want.

"So are you," I whispered, fumbling with the buttons of his shirt. "But wearing too many clothes."

His laugh broke warm against my throat. "Then by all means…"

Clothes vanished between kisses like we'd both been waiting far too long for this. When he eased me onto the cool sheets and came down over me, the last of my doubts dissolved.

This was happening.

And it was everything.

He looked at me like I was sacred.

Not fragile—never that—but important. Desired. Revered.

He was solid and warm, every inch of his body pressed against mine. The weight of him was grounding, his presence a gravity I didn't want to escape. He kissed along my collarbone—soft at first, then hungrier—tasting my skin like it was a language he'd once known and ached to relearn.

"Tell me if I go too fast," he murmured, voice frayed, hands roaming—discovering me inch by inch. "If I do anything you don't want—"

"I want—" I cut him off with a breathless pull of his mouth back to mine. "God, Cal. I want all of it."

That broke him.

He kissed me like he'd been denied for days, like every second we hadn't touched had been torment. I arched into him, hips rising on instinct, and he groaned into the kiss—low, rough, unraveling.

His hands were everywhere, each pass more certain than the last. He traced the curve of my waist, the swell of my hip, the sensitive line where my thigh and torso met. He learned me like he learned everything—thorough, exacting, maddening in his focus. I gasped when he replaced his hands with his mouth—charting lower, kissing across my stomach, teeth grazing just enough to make me tremble.

"I need—" The rest burned away. I couldn't find words. Only fire.

"I know," he said, eyes lifting from between my thighs—dark with something close to worship. "Let me."

And then there were no more words.

Only sensation.

Pressure.

Heat.

Anticipation gave way to devastating relief as his mouth moved against me—slow, sure, relentless.

Each stroke of his tongue was maddeningly precise, coaxing pleasure in rising, measured waves. I arched into him, hungry for more, and he didn't hesitate—hooking my thighs over his shoulders, pressing firm hands to my hips to hold me still as he devoured me like a man starved. For this. For me.

I clutched at the sheets, at his hair, at anything to keep myself from flying apart. I couldn't think. Couldn't breathe. I was reduced to nerve endings and want, unraveling one breathless second at a time. His mouth—God, his mouth—was revelation made flesh. All that intellect, all that control, funneled into the way he moved against me. Methodical. Deliberate. He teased and tormented, then soothed and satisfied, mapping me with a scholar's devotion combined with the hunger of a man who'd waited far too long.

I gave in—utterly, helplessly—hands tangled in his hair, thighs trembling around his shoulders, voice catching on every broken moan until I shattered, a cry tearing free as I came hard against his tongue.

But he didn't stop.

He slowed, softened, licked me through it—through the tremors and the breathless blur and the melt of my bones—until my body begged for mercy.

He finally kissed his way back up, trailing heat along my abdomen, my ribs, my breasts. When his mouth met mine again, I tasted myself on his tongue. It was filthy. Intimate. Honest.

"You all right?" he asked, voice low and barely leashed.

I could only nod. Dazed, I managed, "More than."

He pressed his body over mine again—solid, warm, and impossibly beautiful.

I'd imagined him naked before, but reality was far better. He was all carved lines and shadows—strength wrapped in elegance. The kind of beauty that did things to you if you looked too long. His abdomen flexed under my palms—hard and defined. I traced the sculpted plane of his chest, over his shoulders, down his arms, memorizing him with every pass.

He kissed me again—deeper this time—a groan rumbling against my lips as I slid my hand between us. He hissed when I wrapped my fingers around him—hot, hard, pulsing in my palm. And the sound he made when I stroked was pure poetry—broken, reverent, wrecked. He kissed me harder, like he couldn't help himself, like he might come apart from the sheer intensity of being wanted.

I twisted beneath him, pushing at his chest until he rolled onto his back—his eyes dark, almost disbelieving. I slid lower, kissing down the center of his chest. His muscles tensed as I trailed downward—lips, tongue, teeth—all softness turning to heat.

He trailed his fingers along the curve of my spine, brushing into my hair—his gaze fixed on me like I might vanish if he blinked.

The moment I swept my tongue across his tip, he shuddered—his whole body tensing like holding himself together took everything he had. He dropped his head back against the pillow, a strangled groan breaking loose as I took him deeper. Every inch was velvet and steel, hot against my lips, pulsing with barely contained need. He dug his fingers into my hair, then clenched the sheets—as if caught between anchoring himself to me or holding on to the bed for dear life.

"God," he gasped, hips lifting before he forced them still. "Gabrielle…"

The way he said my name—pleading, awed, and utterly undone—was everything.

I moved over him slowly, deliberately, savoring each twitch of his stomach, each breath that caught in his throat as he struggled against the urge to let go. Each broken sound he made sent a thrill through me, and I reveled in the power of it —this brilliant, carefully controlled man unraveling beneath my touch. He gripped my shoulders, dragging me up his body until we were face to face, both breathing hard.

"Not like that," he managed, kissing me with dizzying desperation. "Not this time."

He rolled us, pinning me beneath him.

"Condom?" I whispered.

"Of course," he said, pulling back just long enough to grab one from his nightstand and tear the foil. He rolled it on, eyes locked on mine, then slid a hand to my thigh, guiding us into place—close, closer—until there was nowhere left to go.

"Are you sure?"

I hesitated—not from doubt, but from awe. From the weight of what this was becoming. "I've never been more sure of anything in my life," I said, echoing his words.

When he finally pushed into me, it was slow. Careful. One sinfully exquisite slide that filled me so completely I forgot how to breathe.

I clutched at him, nails digging into his shoulders, overwhelmed by the feeling of him everywhere. Inside. Outside. Devouring me and holding me together all at once.

"Oh, my God," I breathed—half-groan, half-prayer.

"Not God," he rasped against my mouth, words fraying between kisses. "Just a man. A very, very lucky one."

He stilled—forehead to mine, jaw clenched so tight it trembled, every muscle strained, and the heat in his eyes— God, the heat—made the rest of the world vanish.

"All right?" he asked, voice ragged. Barely holding himself together.

"Oh, yes." I wrapped my legs around his waist, anchoring him to me.

And God, when he moved...

It shattered me.

Each thrust was deliberate—deep, reverent, like he was memorizing the way I wrapped around him. Like worship. Like discovery. I took in every inch—the slow drag out leaving me aching, the sharp rush when he pushed back in stealing what breath I had left. My body opened to him—greedy, grateful, trembling under every relentless stroke.

Pleasure bloomed low and hot, each movement stoking the flame. I arched beneath him, back lifting from the bed, meeting him thrust for thrust as his rhythm deepened—slower now, but somehow more desperate. More certain.

His breath was rough against my skin, hot and ragged in the hollow of my neck. He kissed me between gasps—cheek, collarbone, the swell of my breast—leaving a trail of heat where his mouth lingered. I traced the curve of his back, his shoulders, feeling every flex and shift as he moved over me—inside me.

"You feel—" He broke off with a moan, teeth grazing my shoulder. "You feel like heaven."

I clung tighter, digging my nails deep into his skin. "Don't stop," I whispered, almost pleading.

"I couldn't," he said. "Not even if I tried."

His control slipped further by degrees—each thrust harder, rougher—his rhythm unraveling into something raw and real. His body was fire against mine—sweat-slicked skin, the air between us charged and electric.

I met every thrust, hips rising to take him deeper, chasing that sweet edge with abandon. The pressure surged, cresting higher with every filthy-sweet word whispered against my throat.

"You're perfect," he groaned. "Bloody perfect."

Pleasure coiled in my spine, my thighs. Hot and high. Ready to snap.

"Cal—" I gasped, voice breaking as the orgasm slammed—sharp, overwhelming, stealing the ground from under me. I bowed into him, shuddering, my cry muffled against his mouth as he kissed me through it.

He didn't stop. Neither did I. A few more thrusts, and then he broke—body tense and trembling, face buried in the curve of my neck, spilling into me with a sound that was pure need and surrender.

He slumped against me, panting, every inch of him draped over me like armor. His heart pounded wildly against mine. I held him close, wrapping my arms tight around his shoulders, threading my fingers into his damp hair, not ready to let go.

Not ready to come down.

We sank into each other—a tangle of limbs and ragged breaths—his weight anchoring me in the best possible way.

Minutes passed before either of us stirred.

He braced on one elbow, looking down at me with eyes full of mischief. "Well," he said, voice hoarse, "I think that concludes the tour."

My laughter bubbled up like light. "Best tour I've ever had."

And when he kissed me again—gentler now, slow and soft and aching—it felt like more than passion.

It felt like the start of something that might change everything.

CHAPTER 19

CALLUM

Morning light filtered through the half-closed blinds, casting pale gold across my navy satin sheets and the bare curve of Gabrielle's shoulder. She was still asleep, her hair a soft, tangled halo against my pillow. One arm was tucked beneath her head, the other draped across the sheet she'd dragged to her side during the night.

She looked impossibly peaceful. Like she belonged here.

I should've felt something heavier—regret, at the very least. Shame, maybe. We'd crossed every line, broken every rule. But watching her sleep, all I felt was a dangerous kind of warmth.

And peace.

And if I were honest with myself, an ache that wasn't entirely physical.

I scrubbed a hand over my face and sat up slowly, careful not to wake her. My body protested, sore in all the best ways. She'd left her mark—in the tiny crescents from her nails, the ghost of her mouth along my collarbone. My body was a map of the night before, and I had no desire to forget the terrain.

I stood, padded to the kitchen for a glass of water, then returned to the bedroom doorway. And there she was.

Still asleep, just beginning to stir—brow furrowing, lips parting with a soft sigh.

God help me, she was beautiful.

She blinked once, twice, then looked at me through sleep-heavy lashes. "You're awake."

"I am," I said, voice lower than I'd intended. I stepped closer, leaning against the bureau as she stretched. "Still half convinced I'm dreaming. Thought I'd wake up alone and heartbroken."

She gave me a slow, languid smile. "Are you always such a tragic romantic first thing in the morning?"

"You have no idea." I sat beside her and placed the glass of water on the nightstand. "How are you feeling?"

She rolled onto her back, tugging the sheet to cover herself. "A little sore. But smug."

"Oh?" I leaned down to kiss her bare shoulder. "Why smug?"

She turned to me with a smirk. "Because I'm the one who got the grand tour."

I groaned, half laughing as I buried my face in the crook of her neck. "That line is going to haunt me forever, isn't it?"

"Yes," she said sweetly, brushing her fingers through my hair.

"Mmm." Eyes closed, I leaned into her touch. "I feel like a pampered house cat."

"A house cat?"

"Not even a cool one," I added, looking up at her. "One of the fluffy ones with no survival instincts."

She laughed—head thrown back, hair tumbling over the pillows like sun-drenched silk—and it hit me again, full force: I didn't regret this. Not even a little.

And that should've terrified me.

But all I could think about was how long I could keep her in this bed before life made me let her go. Before the world reminded us why we couldn't stay.

She let out a sigh, soft and reluctant, and rolled to her side, propping herself up on one elbow. "If I don't get up soon, I'll never leave."

"Then don't."

She blinked at me, caught off guard for half a second—then gave a quiet smile. "Tempting. But I need coffee."

I leaned closer, brushing a kiss against her shoulder. "I can do coffee. Somewhere between good and excellent, depending how awake I am when I make it."

She laughed under her breath, then stretched, catlike and unhurried. "Shower first."

"I could be persuaded to join you," I said, brushing my knuckles down the bare line of her spine.

She tilted her head, amused. "You offering help, or just hoping for an encore?"

I didn't miss a beat. "Yes."

"Cute. But that wasn't a yes or no question."

I sat back just enough to meet her eyes. "Yes to both. I'm excellent with soap and shampoo." I slid my hand beneath the sheet, wrapping around to graze the delicate flesh of her inner thigh. "And I remember precisely how you like to be touched…"

Her breath caught. Her resolve wavered, just for a moment, before she laughed and pushed at my chest. "Shameless man. I'll never get out of here, will I?"

"Not if I have any say in the matter." I kissed her shoulder again, then nudged the sheet down to expose a milky, sumptuous breast. "Shall I remind you"—I grazed my teeth across her nipple—"of all the ways you like to be touched?"

The soft sound she made was somewhere between a groan and a sigh as she fell back against the pillows, surrendering. "God, yes."

I smirked. "And we're back to worship."

I pulled the sheet from her body, her bare skin warming

under my gaze. She was breathtaking—every curve and hollow, mine to explore. To memorize.

I slid my fingers along her inner thigh, and she shivered in response. When I grazed over the center of her, she moaned —low and wanton—a sound I could have lived in forever. She was achingly wet. I parted her thighs with reverence, savoring the way she opened to me so easily, so beautifully.

"Perfect," I murmured, voice rough with awe. "Already so wet for me." Tension rippled through her as I slid a finger inside—hot, slick, devastating—finding the spot that made her gasp and pressing into it.

Her hips bucked. "More," she breathed—half-demand, half-plea.

"Greedy girl," I said, pride curling through my voice as I added another finger. Skin flushed, she arched into the sensation—writhing now, chasing more with her hips as I held her open.

"There?" I asked, curling my fingers to stroke her faster.

Her answer was a cry—pure need, exquisite and unrestrained.

I didn't relent. Couldn't have stopped if I'd wanted to. Every fiber of me locked on her—watching her come undone beneath my hands like she had last night.

No, not like last night. Last night had been about breaking through caution, restraint, and convention. Now that those walls had been obliterated, this was about heat, passion, and untethered desire.

Her head tipped back against the pillow, lips parted around ragged breaths. She was endless—a constellation of sensation—and I meant to map every star. She clenched around my fingers, and I answered—faster, deeper—building her higher, pushing her further. She arched nearly off the bed, and then she shattered—coming so hard I thought she might break my hand.

I eased the pressure but didn't stop moving inside her,

riding the waves of her release until they finally subsided. She lay gasping, chest rising like she'd run miles.

She thought I was finished. I saw in the way she started to close her legs and sink back into the pillows.

"Oh no," I said, smirking as I pinned her open. "You're not getting off that easy."

Before she could speak, I lowered myself between her thighs and drew her swollen clit into my mouth—licking and flicking relentlessly. She cried out—surprised, desperate—a sound that sent raw heat surging through me.

"The ability to have multiple orgasms," I said between licks, savoring her tremors, "is a beautiful female gift." I sucked gently until she writhed again. "Which I intend to fully explore." The words were muffled, vibrating against her flesh. "To make sure you get everything you deserve."

She moaned, deep and low, as I teased her with the tip of my tongue. Her body was slick with sweat, flushed and luminous. She was close again—already—but I had no intention of letting up. Not until she came so many times she forgot her own name.

I slid a finger inside, and she clenched around it, desperate. I added another, pumping in rhythm with my mouth. She was liquid heat and velvet, wet and tight, and everything I'd ever wanted.

"You," she gasped, writhing beneath me, "are insatiable."

I smiled against her skin. "As are you, my dear." My voice was a growl, unrestrained from someplace primal. "I want to see how many times I can make you come."

She fisted her hands in my hair, urgent, frantic, pulling me closer as I drove her higher. I felt every tremor—every shuddering wave—as she went taut and called my name like a prayer.

She shattered harder this time—shaking so violently it rocked me. I couldn't have pulled away if I tried, not with her entire body clenched around my fingers and her thighs quivering against my shoulders. I wanted to stay there forever, hear her beg and moan and cry out until she was hoarse, but there were limits to the human body. Even hers. I drew back and let her catch her breath, skimming my mouth along the trembling insides of her legs.

"Numb." She laughed, voice barely coherent. "My fingers…and my toes…everything."

I smirked against her skin, then bit down, gentle but firm. "Shall we try for number three?"

Her groan was pure exasperation. Pure want.

I drank her in—sprawled on the sheets like some fallen goddess, gold hair tangled around flushed cheeks, skin dewy with sweat. She was breathtaking like this—wild and wanton and fully mine.

"Jesus," she breathed—half protest, half invitation. "Give me a minute."

I dragged a hand down her leg, savoring every silky inch. "Is that really what you want?"

She made a sound low in her throat—one that sent another delicious shiver through me.

"That's what I thought."

She squealed as I took her clit into my mouth again. Her hands were everywhere in a frenzy of exquisite need. She thrashed with every stroke of my tongue, one hand twisting the sheets, the other raking fire across my skin. I pinned her hips and sucked. Flicked harder. She clawed at my shoulders as if she could pull me inside her—hold me there forever. Her thighs locked around me, trembling.

"Cal," she panted, voice breaking on my name. "God… Cal!"

I pressed two fingers inside her, knowing right where to touch, and buried them deep. She shattered again, arching in a burst of sound and ecstasy—coming so hard and fast it nearly undid me. The way she tensed and twisted around me was breathtaking. She was incoherent when I finally gave her a reprieve.

I kissed her mouth, silencing the ragged gasp of my name with a deep, claiming possession. Her chest heaved against mine as I held her there, savoring the feel of her body beneath me. I pulled back just enough to catch the dazed look in her eyes.

"Absolutely incredible." There was no other sight like her—not on this earth.

She blinked up at me, lips parting around a breathless laugh. "I think…" She swallowed hard. "I think we've earned that shower now."

"I think we have." I brushed sweat-damp strands of hair from her forehead. "Or anything else you want from me," I added, tracing her cheekbone with my thumb.

"What about you?" she asked, still breathless. "I feel a little selfish this morning."

"Nonsense." I kissed her again, tasting sweat and sweetness and Gabrielle. "Making you come like that gives me more pleasure than you'll ever know."

A real laugh escaped her lips—pure joy. I let it echo in my mind as I reached into the nightstand, holding up a condom for her to see. She groaned in exasperated delight.

"Oh God," she said, laughing again as she batted at my chest. "You really are insatiable."

I stood and helped her off the bed, her warm skin pressing to mine as she linked her arms behind my neck. When I lifted her, she wrapped her legs around my waist, tangling herself against me once more. She was everything—warm, wild, and mine.

We stumbled into the en suite, a tangle of limbs and heat and breathless want, not bothering with the lights. I managed to turn on the water one-handed, still holding her, still kissing her.

She laughed against my lips, that glorious sound echoing

off the tiles. "You're going to have to put me down eventually, you know."

"If you insist," I murmured, kissing her again before setting her down to wait for the water to warm. I nipped at the curve of her neck as it heated up. "But only so I can get you into my shower without falling on my arse."

Her laughter turned to a soft sigh as I trailed kisses along her collarbone. Steam billowed over the glass as I pulled away and took her hand. I led her into the walk-in shower and pulled the glass door closed. The heat cocooned us, wrapping tight around my senses. I set the condom on the tray beside the shampoo and body wash.

She tilted her head into the spray, water sluicing down her luminous skin that caught what little light spilled in from the bedroom. Her hair ran dark down her back like a sheet, and I was breathless—struck by how fucking beautiful she looked.

I lathered shampoo in my hands and worked it into her hair, the silken strands slipping between my fingers.

"Oh," she said, surprised, leaning into my touch. "You weren't kidding."

"Not in the least." I massaged her scalp in slow circles, savoring each sigh.

"That feels…" She paused, voice languid. "Nice. Really nice."

I smiled at the abandon in her voice.

I detached the shower head and rinsed the lather from her hair, careful not to let any get in her eyes. "If you think that's nice," I said, replacing the shower head, "wait until my hands are scrubbing every inch of you clean."

I worked body wash into my palms and slid them over her shoulders, down her arms, then back up. The soap foamed slick between us as I kept my promise, lathering every curve— every supple inch. I lingered on her breasts, watching her expression melt into bliss.

"You spoil me," she breathed, eyes half-lidded, drunk on the sensation.

"That's the idea." My voice rumbled off the tiles.

She took the body wash and returned the favor, sliding suds over my chest and shoulders, down my arms and back in slow, decadent strokes. Her skin against mine was electric—a live current that lit up every nerve. When she trailed her hand down my abdomen, I drew in a sharp breath. The slide of her palm was slow and deliberate, each stroke languid and exquisite as she took hold of me.

"God, Gabrielle," I groaned, letting my head fall back against the tiles. Steam swirled around us as the water rinsed the last traces of soap from our skin. Her touch was sumptuous—silken and sure—sending heat spiraling through every inch of me, scattering thought into light. When I opened my eyes, she was watching me—a wicked smile curling her lips—as she stroked me with the most maddeningly perfect grip. My fingers splayed against the wall, the world narrowing to this moment, this feeling, this woman who unraveled me with nothing but her hand and that look in her eyes.

Water pounded around us, mingling with my ragged breath as I moved into her hand, caught in the delicious cadence of her strokes. She brought me to the edge and held me there—tension coiling tight—until my body thrummed with raw electric need.

Her voice cut through the haze—a hushed whisper, sultry and sure. "I want you inside me."

I grabbed the condom with a groan, tore it open, and rolled it on. "Music to my ears," I said, hiking her leg onto the built-in shower bench and teasing her until she was slick and ready. "Say it again."

"I want you inside me," she repeated, breath catching as I circled her clit.

"Again," I said, watching her shudder from nothing but my hand and will.

She took hold of me, eyes blazing, and guided me exactly where she wanted. "I'll say anything you want if it gets you inside me."

I thrust in, smooth and deep. She squeezed me like a vise —tight, slick, and ready for everything I had. I gripped her hips and drove in harder, faster, losing myself in the rhythm that consumed us. She arched against the tiles, meeting every thrust—a perfect counterpoint to my own urgency.

"Is this what you wanted?" My voice came out rough as she pulled me in deeper.

"More," she moaned, nails biting into my shoulders.

Steam swirled as we moved together, slick and seamless, an impossible cadence of thrusts and replies. I was drowning in the feel of her skin against mine, of her heat enveloping me with every push.

"You feel…" She exhaled sharply. "So damned good."

"Then let me make you feel even better." I pulled out, spun her around, and pressed her down onto the bench. She caught herself with her palms, wet hair a cascade of gold. Hands locked firm at her waist, I thrust in from behind in one swift motion, the angle sharp and exquisite. Her yelp was pure delight, the sound careening off the tiles and straight into my blood. I drove into her with raw power—nothing held back, nothing left to contain me but my own will.

She braced for each thrust as water poured over us in dizzying torrents. "Oh God," she cried, voice breaking with the force of it.

"Like that?" I managed—more of a growl than an actual question.

"Yes," she gasped. "Just—like—that."

I gave her everything—every ounce of want and hunger— until she tightened around me in rippling waves of release. Her body tensed as she came, and she cried out, voice shattering against the tiles. A few more strokes, and heat coiled low inside me. I came hard and heavy—breathless, weightless, untethered.

After a few steadying breaths, I pulled out and drew Gabrielle to me, cradling her against my chest as the water streamed across our skin. Her hair clung to her face in wet tendrils as I kissed her, tasting triumph on her lips.

"God, you're incredible," I murmured, letting each word fall like a benediction.

She nestled closer, a satisfied hum vibrating against my skin. "Says the man who—"

I kissed her before she could finish, stealing her surprise with my mouth.

Her laugh was breathless when I pulled back. "Is that how you plan to win every argument?"

"One tool of many," I said, kissing her again—slow, unhurried. I savored the way her body curved into mine, soft and replete beneath my touch.

"Not fair," she chided, though her eyes said otherwise—wide, warm, unguarded. I kissed her neck, then her shoulder, brushing wet hair from her face. Her skin was smooth and fragile under my touch, like porcelain warmed by fire.

We stayed there an impossibly long time, wrapped in steam and each other, as I murmured praise against her ear and savored every blissful sigh she gave in return.

The sun had climbed higher by the time we stepped out of the shower, towels slung loosely around us. My skin was still damp where Gabrielle's fingers had traced patterns through the steam. She took a light blue button-down from the wardrobe and slipped into it with that easy grace that made it look better on her than it ever had on me.

She caught me watching her. "Going to stand there all morning?"

"Yes," I said, earning another smile.

In the kitchen, I busied myself with the French press while Gabrielle perched on a counter stool. Her wet hair, darkened to honey gold, dripped onto her shoulders, leaving dark splotches on the blue shirt.

"Any plans today?" she asked.

"Have I got your Saturday too?"

"Oh, you can have just about anything you want." She glanced down sheepishly at the countertop, suppressing a smile. "I hope that didn't come across as desperate."

I took the adjacent stool as the coffee darkened in the French press. "On the contrary," I said, brushing a kiss against her temple. "It came across as charming." I pulled back to look at her. "I don't want to monopolize your time." It was meant to sound light, casual. It came out…not quite.

She met my gaze. "Same here." We were quiet for a beat before she continued. "Do you have work you need to do?"

"Just a few updates for Monday's classes. Nothing that'll take more than an hour. What about you?"

"Finishing a calculus problem set," she said, grimacing. "And…homework for your class."

I couldn't help the smirk. I checked my watch and stood, pausing behind her to brush her hair aside and kiss the delicate spot behind her ear.

"Which isn't due until Wednesday," I murmured against her skin.

Her exhale was soft but amused. "Blurring the lines between church and state, Dr. Hawthorne?"

My honorific had never sounded sexy before. I kissed her again, slower this time. "You started it."

I crossed to the opposite counter and poured our coffee.

"How do you take it?" I asked, already assuming the

answer. "Milk and sugar? Cream and three packets of something unholy?"

"Nope," she said, stretching her arms over her head. "Black."

I glanced over my shoulder. "You drink tea—correction, potpourri in a cup—with half a sugar bowl. But coffee, you take black?"

I handed her the mug. She took it with both hands, eyes slipping blissfully closed as she inhaled the steam. And then she glanced at me—eyes coy over the rim of the mug, lips just barely curved into a lazy, wicked smile.

"You're catching on."

Heat stirred low in my spine again. She hadn't even touched me, and already I wanted to drag her back to bed.

CHAPTER 20

GABRIELLE

Cal's shirt smelled like detergent.

Not the cheap kind—warm and crisp, like clean cotton fresh from the dryer. It was soft from years of wear, the kind of shirt that held its shape and still invited touch. I wanted to live in it.

Or maybe I just wanted to live in this.

I was curled into the corner of his sleek black couch, wrapped in a blanket softer than sin, knees tucked under me. The oversized shirt had slipped off one shoulder. I adjusted the collar and, under the pretense, breathed it in—just a second longer than subtle.

"Checking whether I do my own laundry?"

I jolted, heat blooming in my cheeks. Cal stood over me with two mugs in hand and a smirk he wasn't trying to hide. He was barefoot, wearing flannel pajama pants that clung low on his hips and a heather-gray T-shirt that stretched just right across his chest. Comfortable. Lethal. Like some unfair hybrid of homebody and heartthrob. He handed me my second cup of coffee with a perfectly straight face, but his eyes were dancing.

I narrowed mine, pretending to inspect the shirt more

seriously. "Mmm. Scented detergent, very bold. A little floral, a little citrus. I approve."

"Your standards are terrifyingly high."

I shook my head, laughing as he set a plate on the coffee table—croissants, fresh berries, and a sliced apple fanned into a perfect little spiral he'd absolutely done on purpose.

He dropped onto the couch beside me, the heat of him bleeding through the few inches of space between us. He didn't reach for me right away—just let his thigh rest lightly against mine as he nudged the plate closer.

"I can manage a decent cup of coffee, but breakfast is all flaky pastry and dumb luck."

"Could've fooled me."

He draped an arm along the back of the couch, fingers grazing my shoulder. "So, I was thinking…" His tone shifted slightly. "If you're willing to let me keep you captive this weekend—purely consensual captivity, of course—I should probably run you back to your place. Grab a bag. Study materials." He sipped his coffee, then looked up over the rim. "And something criminally flattering for a night out in Dallas."

I raised an eyebrow, croissant halfway to my mouth. "A night out?"

He grinned, slow and sly. "We can't exactly risk dinner in town. Not that there's anywhere properly posh anyway. But Dallas is just far enough to be anonymous."

Dangerous territory. But my pulse fluttered anyway.

I pulled one knee up, turning to face him, enjoying the thrill of the oversized shirt slipping against my bare skin. "Any other weekend demands I should know about?" I asked, trying not to sound too thrilled.

He tilted his head, mock-thoughtful. "You'll be required to indulge in obscenely good coffee. Real tea, of course. Laugh at my bad jokes, even when they don't deserve it."

I snorted. "Sounds like torture."

"And there's one last requirement," he said, turning toward me with a completely straight face, "Looking devastating in my bed, wearing my shirt."

I sipped my coffee to hide the grin. "Tough terms. But I suppose I'll manage."

His eyes dropped to where the blanket had shifted, catching the hem of his shirt high on my thighs—and I felt his gaze like a touch, slow and reverent. The silence stretched—charged, but not awkward.

"I like you like this," he said softly, the flirtation gone.

My throat went dry.

"Like what?" I whispered.

He reached over and tucked a stubborn lock of hair behind my ear, his thumb lingering a second too long. "Comfortable. In my space. Like you belong here."

The air shifted—just slightly. But I felt it. Felt him. Felt the weight of what this weekend might become.

"Careful," I said, trying to keep my voice steady. "You talk like that, I might start leaving things here."

"I'm counting on it," he said, popping a raspberry into his mouth—grinning like he hadn't just rearranged the furniture in my chest.

Headlights painted long golden swipes along the blacktop beneath the inky Texas night sky. The low hum of Cal's car filled the silence like a lullaby. We'd been on the road ten minutes, heading south, small-town lights fading behind us. Somewhere ahead: Dallas. Anonymity. A night out where we didn't have to pretend.

Cal drove with one hand on the wheel, the other tangled with mine, his thumb stroking slow circles over my knuckles. His posture was relaxed, but I could see the set of his jaw, the faint crease between his brows every time headlights passed us.

I watched him from the passenger seat, tucked into the buttery leather.

"We should play a game or something," I said, breaking the silence.

"What did you have in mind?"

"Not a game really. Just questions. I'd like to know more about you."

He flashed a half-smile. "Do your worst."

I paused, chewing on my lip. "What's your favorite color?"

He glanced over. "That's it? You can ask me anything in the world, and you want my favorite color?"

I shrugged. "I'm starting you off easy."

"Forest green," he said. "You?"

"Red."

His grip on the steering wheel was loose and easy as the road curved beneath us. "I had you pegged for blue," he said, glancing over again. "Or purple."

"It's not an entirely reasonable answer. I like them all—color in general. Red's just...bold."

His lips twitched with amusement as the rural terrain shifted into suburban sprawl. The city was still miles away, but the air already felt different—less stifling than the uncertainty we'd left behind.

"How old are you?" My voice came out softer than I'd intended. "Not that it matters," I added quickly. "I'm just curious."

He exhaled through his nose, taking a moment longer than necessary. "Thirty-eight."

I nodded once, squeezing his hand to signal that I was unfazed by the thirteen years between us. More than unfazed—I liked this about him. Older. Steady.

"Why Page College?" he asked. "Out of anywhere you could have gone?"

"I'm a legacy student."

"Which parent?"

"My dad," I answered quickly. "But that's cheating. You asked two in a row."

"I didn't realize the rules were so strict." He lifted my hand and kissed the inside of my wrist. "I'll make it up to you. Ask me three."

"Okay," I said, thinking. "First question: favorite singer or band?"

"Ooh, tough one." He clicked his tongue. "I suppose I've got to fall back on Oasis."

I blinked. "Who?"

His head snapped toward me. "You're joking."

I laughed. "No, seriously—should I know them?" A beat passed. "Wait, is that the band that sings 'Wonderwall'?"

He groaned, tipping his head back against the headrest. "Christ. Yes. That's them."

I grinned. "See? I do know them."

"Barely," he muttered. "That was question two, by the way."

"That wasn't—oh, come on." I laughed. "You can't count a clarification."

He arched a brow. "I can, and I have. You've got one left. Use it wisely."

I hesitated, suddenly unsure. But the words came anyway. "When was the last time you were in love?"

His thumb stilled on mine. He didn't answer right away. "That's a harder one," he said finally. "You sure you don't want to ask what I'd take to a desert island instead?"

I shrugged. "You told me to use my question wisely."

He exhaled, his grip tightening on the steering wheel. "That's the kind of question better answered after a few glasses of wine," he said at last. Not cold. Just carefully folded.

I nodded, sensing the edge I'd touched. "Okay, we'll shelve it."

He glanced at me, then back at the road. "If I answer that

one…" His voice dropped. "Can I ask you something personal in return?"

"Of course." My curiosity spiked, but I didn't press. Not yet.

"I was engaged once. Back in England. It was one of those matches that everyone wanted, but we did actually care for each other. A win-win, I suppose."

His gaze was firmly fixed ahead—not just on the road, but on some glassy memory out there in the dark.

"But Claire died," he said finally. "And that was that." A pause. "I've had a few casual girlfriends since, here and there. But that was the last time I was in love."

His voice was infuriatingly neutral, like a lecture or a lab report. I sat frozen, the warmth of his hand no match for the chill that had crept into the car with us.

My mind snagged on that throwaway line: *a few casual girlfriends here and there.*

Was that all I was? Another casual fling neatly slotted into the margins of his life?

I pulled away before I could stop myself, my fingers slipping from his grip.

"Gabrielle," he said—urgent, panicked. He looked over, eyes wide with the awful clarity of realization. "Oh God, no."

I tried to smile, but it felt borrowed—flimsy and ill-fitting.

"You've got it all wrong." His words tumbled out, tripping over each other to reach me. "You're not—Christ, Gabrielle, you're so much more than that."

The car flew down the dark highway, but my pulse dragged slow and heavy beneath my skin.

"Listen to me," he said, voice low and insistent. "I've never let anyone in like this. Not like you."

A sharp, needy ache bloomed under my ribs. I wanted to believe him.

"I thought that part of my life was over," he went on, voice fraying at the edges. "Romance. Love. A future with someone…" His eyes cut to me then back to the road. "Until you." The words landed softly, but they echoed.

My pulse quickened as his hand found mine again—this time with an intensity that burned through every layer of doubt.

"I should have left that question on the shelf," I mumbled, cheeks burning. "I'm sorry."

He let out a small, incredulous laugh, his grip tightening like he thought I might slip away again. "What could you possibly have to be sorry for?"

"For…" I hesitated, then took a breath. "For making it about me. For being insecure." I looked down at our joined hands, his warmth slowly seeping back into me. "And…I'm sorry she died."

The highway stretched ahead—dark and endless—but tension bled from his shoulders as though my words had lifted some invisible weight. He brought my knuckles to his lips, slow and soft, and warmth bloomed under my skin.

"Thank you," he said softly. The tenderness in his voice made my chest tighten.

The lights of Dallas shimmered on the horizon—a soft band of brightness encroaching on the night.

"Your turn," I said, nudging his arm with my elbow.

"For?"

"You get to ask me something deeply personal."

He chuckled. "I didn't realize we were still playing." He kissed my hand again. "I won't hold you to that."

"No, no. Rules are rules. Go ahead."

He inhaled slowly. "You speak often of your father. It's clear he meant a great deal to you. Still does. But you've never mentioned your mother. Where does she fit in your story?"

Of all the questions he could have asked.

I stayed silent too long, the words stuck on my tongue, unfamiliar. It wasn't something I talked about. Ever.

Cal's voice was gentle, careful. "Did she die as well?"

I scoffed—bitter, even to my ears. "No," I said. The word landed hard. "At least I don't think so. Though that would've been kinder."

He let out a slow breath, saying nothing. He traced soft, deliberate circles over the back of my hand.

"She walked out on us when I was three," I said finally, struggling to keep my voice steady. The Dallas lights blurred like smudged constellations across the windshield. I stared at them, hoping they'd explain what came next. "Said she couldn't take being a wife and mother." My throat cinched tight around that last word. "That she wanted a different life." My voice wavered, paper-thin against the hush inside the car. "Aunt Suzy says she was heavy into alcohol, drugs, men— anything she could get her hands on." I let out a breath. "I have no idea where she is now. And I couldn't care less."

Cal tightened his grip—a small, solid anchor. He didn't speak, didn't press. The quiet thickened—less like silence, more like space he'd cleared for me to breathe.

He inhaled like he was about to say something, then let the breath go. Whatever words he might have offered, he folded them away and held my hand tighter instead.

Eventually, Cal took the exit onto Mockingbird Lane.

"Wait," I said after a minute, eyeing his sport coat and open collar. "You never told me where we're going."

He squeezed my hand, smiling. "A charming little place called Josephine's."

"What kind of place is it?" I asked, curiosity tugging at my voice.

His smile widened, a playful edge to it. "Do you know how hard it is to find a nice restaurant with a dance floor?"

CHAPTER 21

CALLUM

I walked around to Gabrielle's side and opened the car door, holding my breath against the night's chill. She accepted my hand and stepped out gracefully, a vision in plum silk. Her dress hugged her waist, then flared gently, its low neckline a perfect invitation to everything I wasn't supposed to want. She looked stunning—an elegant risk in every way that mattered.

"In that dress," I said, my breath fogging as I pulled her close, "you're going to make me break all kinds of rules tonight."

"Promise?" Her eyes sparked with mischief—and something softer beneath it.

I kissed her forehead, the heat of her pressed against me, then reluctantly let her go. Still, I kept her close as we walked toward the restaurant.

Josephine's stood at the end of the street like a grand old lady, its exterior an artful imitation of a restored Queen Anne. Twinkling lights danced along the porch railings, and its name glowed in boldly lit letters. Gabrielle shivered as we climbed the stairs, and I slipped my arm around her shoulders.

"Cold?"

"Less so now," she said, tilting her face up with a smile that left me recalculating every boundary I'd ever drawn.

Inside, the restaurant was warm and inviting. Red wine, garlic, and spice hung in the air, each note distinct but perfectly blended. I gave the hostess my name, and she led us to a rounded booth with a high red leather back tucked into the corner behind a delicate screen of greenery. It was intimate without being sequestered—exactly the balance I'd hoped for.

A vintage crystal chandelier cast soft light over white linen tables. The low hum of conversation wove through the gentle strains of a jazz trio near the far wall, and smartly dressed couples swayed lazily on the dance floor.

Gabrielle slid in beside me, close enough that our legs brushed under the table. She leaned into me, her warmth settling against my side like it belonged there.

"This is amazing," she said, her voice low with awe.

"Perhaps I should've worn a tie," I said, glancing around. "I didn't realize Dallas had such potential for sophistication."

"You're perfect." She squeezed my hand—and gave me a look that made me briefly regret booking a table instead of a hotel room.

The menus came tucked into leather folders—elegant, minimalist, and clearly curated for people who didn't blink at the price. Gabrielle skimmed over hers, a flicker of uncertainty playing beneath the edges of a smile.

"This feels...elevated," she said, eyes scanning the page. "I'm not used to dating like this."

I smiled over the rim of my glass. "I'm not used to dating, full stop."

She looked up, surprised into a soft laugh. "Seriously?"

"Seriously," I said. "Plenty of dinners. Fewer I'd call dates."

Her eyes sparkled as she looked back down at the drink list. "What's the protocol? Wine? Cocktails?"

"Depends," I said, glancing up at the waiter approaching our table. "But I'd say this calls for champagne."

She quirked a brow. "Champagne before dinner?"

"Bubbles before dinner. Wine with. It's all about rhythm," I said, voice low and teasing. "The French say it opens the appetite."

"For food, or…?"

I smiled. "Yes."

The waiter appeared, and I ordered two glasses of Saint-Chamant Blanc de Blancs. Gabrielle leaned back slightly as they were poured, watching the fine streams of bubbles rise in her glass.

"To being exactly where I want to be," I said, raising my glass. "And in the most splendid company."

Her lips curled as she raised her glass. "I'll drink to that."

I ordered us a few small plates—warm brie with figs and walnuts, wild mushroom flatbread, and a citrusy beet salad I thought she'd like. She looked quietly relieved not to have to navigate the menu alone.

"You do this well," she said, watching me with faint amusement.

"You mean ordering food?"

"I mean…taking the lead. The ease, the confidence—it suits you."

"Don't be fooled," I said, voice dipping low. "Last week I locked myself out of my office and had to call campus security to let me in."

She bit back a laugh.

"In my defense," I added, smoothing the edge of my voice, "I was a bit distracted that morning. Couldn't stop thinking about a certain someone."

Her eyes flicked to mine—sparkling, curious, just a touch shy—and that glance nearly undid me all over again. "Mm-hmm." She took another sip of champagne. "Still a good look."

As the jazz trio transitioned into something soft and swaying, I reached for her hand and stood.

She glanced up, surprised. "Where are we going?"

"This," I said, guiding her toward the dance floor, "is why I booked this place."

"To feed me mushrooms and fancy cheese?"

I leaned in, brushing my lips against her temple. "Any excuse to hold you in my arms."

She slid her hand into mine. "You're making it really hard not to fall for you."

"I sincerely hope so."

The lights were low, the room humming with warmth and quiet elegance. As we stepped onto the small dance floor, I settled my hand at her waist and drew her close. She hesitated just a moment before she placed a hand on my shoulder, the other resting lightly in mine.

"I should warn you," she said as I led her into the first slow step, "I'm not a great dancer."

"Good thing I am," I murmured, smiling down at her. "Years of lessons. Hated every minute."

"Until now?"

"Until now."

She looked up, a hint of wonder softening her expression. "Was that your charming way of admitting you enjoy this?"

I traced my thumb gently along her spine. "With you? Yes."

We swayed, the music wrapping around us like silk. Her body fit perfectly against mine, and everything else—the restaurant, the rules, the world waiting back home—faded to the periphery.

The song tapered into a lingering chord, and I let it carry us through one final step before guiding her back to the table. Gabrielle's hand remained in mine, her fingers warm and certain. She was quiet as we slid into the booth—the soft rustle of silk against leather, the brush of her knee against mine. She reached for her champagne but didn't drink, only turned the glass, watching the bubbles rise.

Her cheeks were flushed, likely not from the alcohol.

"What is it?" I asked, careful not to press.

She gave me a sideways look—half-curious, half-shy. "How do you know how to do all of this?"

"All of what?"

She gestured—somehow both vague and graceful—toward the chandeliers, the band, the wineglasses. "All this sophisticated glamour. The dancing. The ordering. The bubbles before dinner."

I smiled faintly. "Old habits. I grew up with it."

Her brow lifted. "Really?"

I nodded, keeping it light. "Family dinners with too many forks. Weekend luncheons that required blazers. That sort of thing."

She studied me. "What was it like—growing up like that?"

I traced the rim of my glass, stalling. "Rigidly structured," I said. "Quiet. Very...polished."

She didn't interrupt. Just waited.

"Imagine a house with rooms no one uses, clocks that always chime on time, and staff who know where you're meant to be before you do." I glanced at her with the shadow of a smile. "I had everything I needed. Just...not much of it was personal."

Her hand found mine beneath the table, warm and reassuring.

"I wasn't unloved," I said, softer. "Just...managed."

Gabrielle's eyes held mine, clear and steady. And for a moment I wanted to say more—to tell her about long corridors and closed doors, vacant conversation over breakfast, the coldness only marble and pride can maintain. But I didn't.

She squeezed my hand, and I kissed her knuckles, grateful for the distraction.

"Now," I said, lightening my tone, "tell me something about you. Preferably something scandalous, or I'll be forced to guess."

Her smile flickered in the candlelight. She shook her head, the soft waves of her hair spilling over one shoulder. "I'm afraid I'm not half as exciting as you'd hope. My story's painfully boring."

"I find that hard to believe," I said, leaning back, fingers trailing along her arm. "Surely there's something. What's the wildest, most reckless thing you've ever done?"

"Other than this?" she asked, gesturing between us with a playful, pointed smile.

That smile. That voice. They were going to be the end of me. I nodded, grinning. "Naturally."

She tilted her head, thinking. "Honestly? Nothing. I'm a notorious rule-follower."

"Come on," I said, pressing just enough to see if she'd relent. "Not even a little rebellious streak?"

Her lips curled in amusement as she leaned in, conspiratorial. "I tried a cigarette when I was twelve but hated it. Got drunk once at a party in high school. And accidentally walked out of a store without paying."

She paused, sipping her champagne with theatrical gravity.

"See?" she said, deadpan. "Boring."

I laughed, low and easy. "Anything else?"

"I cheated on a math quiz in high school."

"Ooh." I grazed my lips along her ear and pressed a soft kiss to her skin. "I'll have to keep a closer eye on you in class then. Not that I mind."

Gabrielle turned her face toward mine as candlelight and jazz wrapped intimately around us. "Someone's going to notice," she murmured, voice low with amusement.

I brushed my lips against her again, savoring her warmth and scent. "Let them."

The waiter arrived with our small plates, and I gave him a short nod as he set them down. A second server followed with wine—two perfect stems of Grenache, neither too heavy nor too soft, a deep ruby in the candlelight.

I watched Gabrielle take it all in—the colors, the scents, the warm bread and glistening figs—and felt something dangerously close to contentment settle low in my chest.

She sighed as she took her first bite. "This is decadent," she said, echoing my thoughts.

"As are you." I smiled into my wine and took a long sip.

"Careful," she said, voice low as she sliced a fig in half. "Flattery's going to my head."

"That's probably the wine." I let my gaze linger. "And it's not flattery if it's true."

She rolled her eyes, but I caught the faint flush on her cheeks as she reached for her wine. She curled her fingers around the stem, poised and elegant, and I couldn't help but study her a moment longer—how naturally she moved through this night, how completely she held my attention.

"You continue to surprise me," I said quietly.

Her brow furrowed. "How so?"

"Well…" I shifted, resting my elbow along the back of the booth, brushing my fingers over her shoulder. "You said you're not used to dating like this. But you carry yourself like someone who knows exactly what she's doing."

She tilted her head, skeptical. "So I'm not awkward enough for you?"

I smiled. "I mean, you're confident. Self-possessed. Sexy as hell. And I can't fathom how no one's managed to snap you up yet."

She looked down at her glass, thumb tracing the stem. "I dated a lot in high school. Had a long-term boyfriend senior year—we thought it was serious." Her voice softened. "Then life happened. He went off to college. I stayed back to take care of Dad." She shrugged. "We tried the long-distance thing. Didn't last a semester."

"And after that?"

"I dated here and there," she said. "But as Dad's ALS progressed, he needed more and more care. I guess I just…put everything else on hold."

"Understandable," I said gently.

She glanced up again, her eyes clearer now. "It's not like I didn't have…*fun*," she added, the corner of her mouth quirking. "I just wasn't auditioning for anything serious."

I chuckled, low in my throat. "Well, that clears up one mystery."

"Oh?"

"I was starting to worry you were some kind of divine anomaly—brilliant, beautiful, confident…and somehow still unattached." I took a slow sip of wine, savoring the richness before adding, "Though I will say—"

She raised a brow in warning. "Careful."

I leaned closer, dipping my voice just enough to make her shiver. "For someone without much 'long-term dating experience,' you're remarkably good at…everything else."

Her eyes narrowed, amused. "Did you just compliment my—"

"Technical proficiency?" I asked, all mock innocence. "I'd never dare."

She laughed—quiet and wicked—and it sparked behind my ribs. Whatever darkness she'd carried moments ago had lifted, replaced by something warmer. Lighter.

"Just saying," I murmured, lifting her hand to my lips. "If that's your baseline…I'm frankly terrified to find out what you're like when you *are* auditioning for something serious."

She tilted her head, studying me, that smile still teasing her lips. "Who says I'm not?"

CHAPTER 22

GABRIELLE

I don't know how we made it back from Dallas without a speeding ticket.

Or crashing.

Cal's hand stayed planted on my thigh the entire ride—except when it didn't. Except when it wandered higher, his fingers slipping beneath the hem of my dress with that slow, deliberate confidence that made breathing feel optional. And I let him. Every time.

By the time he pulled into the garage, my pulse was a drumbeat, and my patience had melted into the floorboard.

We didn't even make it fully inside before his mouth was on mine.

Clothes fell away like afterthoughts—my heels kicked off at the door, his jacket tossed across a chair, the zipper of my dress halfway down my back as we stumbled blindly toward his bedroom. Hands everywhere. Mouths hungry and wordless.

By the time we hit the bed, I didn't want soft. Or slow. I wanted him frantic. Desperate. I wanted to feel every ounce of what he'd been holding back.

And God, he gave it to me.

He kissed me like he was starving—like he'd waited all night to strip the composure from my body and see what I looked like coming apart.

I gasped as he pinned me to the mattress—one hand braced beside my head, the other sliding sinfully up my thigh. "Now. Please—"

He caught my mouth again, swallowing the plea with a growl so deep it lit a fuse down my spine.

"I won't be gentle this time," he said against my skin, voice thick with hunger. "You still want this?"

I arched into him. "I want you." I raked my nails down his back before I gripped his shoulders. "I need you inside me—right now—before I rip you apart."

Everything after that blurred—heat and motion and pressure, his name on my lips in a thousand broken pieces.

I barely registered the drawer sliding open, his quick, deft movements. And then he was there. The hard, solid weight of him filled me in one fierce thrust that stole my breath and lit every nerve on fire.

He moved like a man possessed, like this was the only thing keeping him sane. He pounded his hips into mine in a relentless rhythm, each thrust stoking the fire inside of me until I was sure I'd combust.

He groaned—low and deep—as my nails dug into his back. "Christ, Gabrielle—"

I pressed my forehead to his shoulder, my world narrowing to the slick heat of our bodies crashing together and the wild pulse pounding loud enough to drown out everything else. The air turned electric, thick with the heady thrill of every restraint falling away.

I bit down on his neck, arching into him as he shifted— God, that angle—and drove even deeper.

He slid a hand to my hip, fingers digging in before he

flipped us—one swift motion that left me gasping on top of him.

"Show me," he said, voice ragged and demanding but threaded with something raw that split my heart wide open. "Show me how reckless you can be with me."

I rose to my knees, watching his eyes darken as he let his head fall back against the pillow. He bucked into me, grip fierce, guiding me deeper, faster. Every inch of him inside me was glorious friction, building a storm in my blood. I gasped, my breath ragged and broken, as the world shattered and reassembled in brilliant, fractured pieces.

I dug my nails into his chest, clawing at him as I rode out wave after wave of dizzying heat. He clamped my hips in his hands, almost bruising, pulling me down harder until there was only this—heat, motion, and the raw, rapturous ache of finally letting go.

He flipped me beneath him again, groaning low and deep as he thrust hard into me—a desperate rhythm that matched the frantic pounding of my heart.

"Cal," I breathed, my voice catching on a broken gasp.

"God, Gabrielle." His thrusts turned sharp and urgent as he drove us toward the edge.

I raked my hands down his back, feeling the flex of muscle under his skin. I was close again—so close—and his name tore from my lips as I shattered around him.

He followed with a final, brutal thrust that sent us both spiraling into white-hot oblivion.

We collapsed together—chests heaving, breath mingling in a hot, humid blur. The air around us was thick and charged, our bodies slick with effort and the heady release of every restraint. My heart pounded, ricocheting against my ribs like it couldn't be contained.

Our limbs were tangled—no idea where he ended and I began. And I never wanted to know. Everything burned—

skin, lungs, every place he'd left me tender and raw. I felt entirely alive. Entirely undone.

He pulled me close, grip fierce like he'd never let me go, eyes shut tight as though stunned by the enormity of what we'd done. What we'd become.

"God," he said hoarsely. "You're magnificent." He kissed me—forehead, cheekbones, lips—each one steeped in hungry gratitude before he buried his face in the curve of my neck.

He softened his grip just enough to shift and find my mouth again. The kiss was gentle this time—slow, lingering— as though he had all the time in the world. As though we did.

"Bloody hell," he murmured between kisses. "You're going to be the end of me."

I laughed—breathy and weak—and slumped against him.

"But what a way to go." He nuzzled into my neck, leaving a trail of kisses that sent ripples through my trembling body.

I threaded my fingers through his hair, words lost to the wild pulse still thrumming in my blood. This was what I'd needed, what I hadn't realized I'd been missing: a perfect storm of abandon and intimacy that left no room for fear or doubt.

I woke to the scent of him on the pillow and sun-warmed sheets tangled around my legs. For a long moment, I didn't move. My body ached in the best way—sated, heavy, humming with quiet aftershocks. The room was soft around the edges, sunlight slipping through the curtains in muted gold ribbons.

But the bed beside me was empty.

My heart kicked once—stupid, startled—before I heard it: the soft strum of an acoustic guitar drifting in from the living room. A voice followed, low and gravel-edged, just cresting over the chords.

I smiled.

I slid out of bed and crossed to where his shirt was draped over a chair. The same light blue button-down from yesterday. I shrugged into it, savoring the familiar weight, the faint scent of him woven through the cotton.

The hallway air was cool against my bare legs, and the music grew clearer with every step.

When I reached the end, I stopped.

Cal sat on the edge of the ottoman, guitar in his lap, head bent low. The morning light caught in the tousled mess of his hair, painting it gold. He wore a simple T-shirt and flannel pajama pants, and the sight of him like that—barefoot, unguarded, lost in song—hit me somewhere deep.

He didn't see me right away.

He was singing something I vaguely recognized, voice pitched just under the melody. I leaned against the doorway, watching him for one long, quiet moment—swept under all over again.

He glanced up, registering me, and his fingers stilled on the strings. "I believe you've caught me." His voice was laced with playful resignation.

"Don't stop on my account," I said, letting my eyes linger on his hands.

"Ah, but then who'll make you coffee?" He set the guitar on its stand with exaggerated care.

"I can make coffee," I said, pushing off the doorframe and walking toward him.

He stood and stretched, eyes glinting with mischief. "Single-serve pods don't count." He pulled me close, pressing a kiss to my forehead and stroking my hair.

We drifted into the kitchen, where morning light spilled like honey over the countertops. His steps were loose and easy, an odd elegance in every movement.

"When did you learn to play the guitar?" I asked as he flipped on the electric kettle and reached for the French press.

He grinned. "Picked it up at Eton. One of the first steps on my road to delinquency."

"Eton?"

"Sorry—boarding school."

"Wait. Like, actually?"

Cal raised an eyebrow as he pulled a tin of coffee from the cabinet.

"I thought that was just a *Harry Potter* thing," I said, deadpan.

He rolled his eyes and laughed—actually laughed—and the sound warmed the room faster than the kettle. "Oh, it's real. Less magic, more Latin. Fewer house-elves, more smug prefects."

"Wow. Next you'll tell me there were house crests and Latin mottos," I added, half-teasing.

He didn't even glance up. "*Floreat Etona.*"

I blinked. "Wait—that's real too?"

He gave me a look that was equal parts smug and amused. "Let Eton flourish," he translated, voice all posh mockery, accent crisp and clipped. "Did I win your heart with Latin?"

I snorted. "I was joking."

He leaned in, voice dropping. "I wasn't."

Warmth spread across my chest. I leaned against the counter. "So what was it like?"

He measured coffee into the French press, thoughtful. "Strict," he said at last. "Regimented. Unforgiving. Bloody starched collars. Every minute scheduled. Every standard enforced."

I watched him, listening for what he wasn't saying.

"But oddly enough," he continued, "it was the first place I ever felt…free."

"Free?" I blinked. "At boarding school?"

He nodded, fitting the lid onto the coffee canister. "I was thirteen, away from home, finally out from under constant watch by staff and family. There were rules—God, so many—

but for once, I got to choose which ones I'd break." He smiled as the kettle clicked off. "I took to it rather quickly."

"That, I believe."

He poured the water over the grounds in one smooth motion and slid the press aside to steep. Then he reached into the cupboard for two mugs, set them on the counter, and finally looked at me again. "It's also where I picked up guitar. And where I learned that physics came easier to me than most things. Except, apparently, diplomacy."

"You? Diplomatic?" I teased.

He winced with mock sincerity. "Shocking, I know."

"And the guitar?" I asked. "That came naturally?"

"Eventually. There was a boy a few years older who played blues riffs in the stairwell between prep and lights-out. I was meant to be revising French verb conjugations, but…" He shrugged. "Hendrix won."

I grinned. "Total rebel."

Cal's gaze flicked toward me, fond and a little faraway. "It was that, or smoke behind the chapel. I chose the option that wouldn't give me cancer."

He pressed the plunger, poured two mugs of dark, fragrant coffee, and passed one to me—black, just how I liked it.

"Thanks."

He leaned back against the counter, mug in hand, posture easy but thoughtful.

"And physics?" I asked. "You said it came easy, but why stick with it?"

He looked down at the swirl of dark coffee, then out the window where sunlight kissed the bare treetops. "I wanted to understand how the universe worked. Still do. Some part of me always believed that if I could just…decode the rules underneath it all, maybe I'd find my place in it."

Something in my chest pulled tight. I hadn't expected that

kind of honesty before breakfast, but I drank it in like warmth. "And did you?"

He looked at me, long and deliberate. "Not until recently."

My breath caught. I had no words for that, so I didn't say anything. Instead, I stepped in close and kissed his cheek. "I'm glad you picked music over cigarettes."

His smile was slow and real and a little bit shy. "So am I."

CHAPTER 23

CALLUM

The steady scratch of her pencil moved across the page, soft and sure.

Gabrielle was curled on the office sofa—legs tucked beneath her, a red spiral-bound notebook balanced on her thigh, pencil gliding in neat, methodical lines. She wore dark jeans and a soft heather jumper, her hair pulled back in a low twist. Casual, but clearly chosen.

I should have been revising my electromagnetism slides.

Instead, I watched her.

I sat at my desk across the room, both Monday lectures open in separate tabs—Physics II and E&M—notes scattered between them, a half-finished slide on Gauss's Law blinking like it knew I was a fraud. I'd tweaked the example problem three times—not because it needed it, but because my concentration had been shot since she'd stepped into my office with her coffee in one hand and her problem set in the other.

She hadn't said much. Just claimed her spot on the sofa like she'd always belonged there.

The quiet between us wasn't silence. It was shared space.

I forced myself to look back at the screen, double-checking a field diagram as I rewrote the explanation. Something about flux through a closed surface. My mind drifted to the curve of her smile over breakfast, the press of her body against mine in the shower, the sound of her voice muffled by steam and laughter.

Another quiet sigh broke the stillness.

I glanced up. Gabrielle chewed her lip, eyes narrowed at the page like it had insulted her.

I ducked my head to keep up the pretense that I wasn't completely focused on her every move. "You look like you're plotting its demise."

She didn't miss a beat. "I am. This question deserves to burn."

I leaned back, letting the moment stretch. "Calculus or physics?" I asked, though I already knew. I just liked prodding her.

"Calculus."

I sighed with exaggerated relief. "Ah. Good. If it were physics, we'd have to take it up with the author of the blasted question."

Her brow lifted. "Would we now?"

"Certainly. He's known to be a bit of a tyrant, but I've heard he can be bribed with coffee and compliments."

She snorted. "Good to know."

I slid my laptop aside, folding my hands over the edge of the desk. "It's not my primary field, but…" I let the pause hang. "I'm not entirely useless."

Her pencil hovered above the page. She hesitated—pride flickering faintly—then looked up at me, soft and a little sheepish. "I hate to ask, but…yeah. If you've got a minute?"

I was already on my feet.

"For you?" I crossed over to the sofa. "I've got more than a minute."

"Thanks," she said, tucking a strand of hair behind her ear as I sat beside her. The word was soft, sincere, and it warmed the air like an unexpected spring.

She passed me the notebook, and I skimmed the page—the neat scrawl of her pencil, the confident sweep of her integral signs. The problem wasn't particularly daunting—finding the area between two curves, a task that required more patience than brilliance at this stage. One glance confirmed what I already suspected: she'd got tangled in her own complexity.

I handed it back. "As usual, you're overthinking it," I said gently, my shoulder brushing hers. "Try slicing it into simpler parts."

Gabrielle made a low, frustrated noise in the back of her throat.

"Here," I murmured, shifting closer. My fingers brushed hers as I picked up the pencil and sketched a quick diagram. Her eyes tracked my movements with fierce focus—a clarity that made my pulse jump in ways it had no business doing over bloody calculus. "It's easier if you look at it this way," I murmured, sketching two quick curves. "This one's the parabola—y equals x squared. And this is the line—y equals x plus two." My pencil skimmed across the page, knuckles grazing hers. "From zero to two, it's just top minus bottom. Area between curves."

Gabrielle groaned. "Why doesn't Dr. Huber explain it like that?"

I leaned in, brushing my lips just beside her ear before grazing it lightly with my teeth. "I hope Dr. Huber doesn't have my charm."

She shivered—just slightly—but enough for me to feel. "Not even close," she whispered.

I kissed the spot just beneath her jaw, then pulled back before temptation steamrolled good sense entirely.

"Now," I said, reclaiming the pencil and tapping it lightly against the page, "let's get you to the right answer before I forget how to be professional."

She grinned, flushed and breathless, then turned back to

the notebook with renewed focus. God help me, it might've been the sexiest thing I'd ever seen.

"Top minus bottom," she murmured, eyes scanning the sketch. "So…integral from zero to two of x plus two minus x squared, with respect to x?"

"Precisely," I said, lips curving. "See? Brilliant. And devastating."

"You're going to distract me straight into a B-minus." She shot me a look, but her smile gave her away.

"Never," I said solemnly.

She laughed, and the sound wrapped itself around my ribs —warm, weightless, and far too dangerous for a Sunday afternoon.

Gabrielle tapped the edge of her eraser against the notebook, a thoughtful crease forming between her brows as she worked through the problem. Her pencil moved again, more confidently this time, her mouth set with determined focus.

Then she exhaled, set the pencil down, and leaned back with a satisfied sigh. "Okay. Calculus is done."

I didn't say *I told you so*. But I thought it. Just a little.

"What else do you need to finish?" I asked, stretching an arm along the back of the sofa. "I'd rather not be responsible for you falling behind, despite having shamelessly stolen your weekend."

Her mouth quirked. "You didn't steal it," she said, voice low. "I handed it over willingly."

I tucked a loose strand of hair behind her ear. "Still."

She hesitated, glancing at her backpack as if it might scold her. "The problem set for your class."

"Ah," I said, pretending to consider. "I could remind you that it's not due until Wednesday, but I know it's a useless point."

"Completely useless," she agreed, then paused. "I'll probably just start it when I get back to my apartment."

I let the silence stretch for half a beat. "Is that code for 'I don't want to do it in front of you?'" I asked, keeping my tone light.

Her cheeks pinked. "It just feels…weird. Like cheating, or something. Even if you don't say a word. Even if you just exist nearby."

I smiled—softly, but not without mischief. "It's not cheating unless I give you the answers. Which I won't."

"You're not helping your case."

"I'm merely existing nearby," I said, lifting both hands in mock surrender. "I'll even sit over there if it helps. I won't so much as glance at your notes."

She narrowed her eyes, suspicious but playful.

I moved back to my desk. "See? Back to my E&M slides."

Gabrielle looked at me for a long moment, amused resignation softening her features. "Fine," she said at last, reaching for her backpack. "But if you accidentally blurt out anything useful—"

"I won't," I promised, already settling back into my chair.

She retrieved her laptop and set it on the coffee table. "Can I at least have your Wi-Fi password?"

"Absolutely not."

She blinked.

"I'm joking," I said, watching her fake a glare. Then I recited the password.

Her fingers flew across the keys, presumably getting online and logging into the student portal. I pretended to focus on my slides, though my eyes kept drifting to her.

There was something dangerously domestic about it—her curled on my sofa, laptop open, talking deadlines and lecture notes like we'd done this a dozen times before. And I wanted that. All of it. More than I had any right to.

Her fingers paused over the keyboard, and she glanced at me. "Magnetism? What happened to circuits?"

I grinned. "I thought you didn't want to mingle church and state."

She gave a small, disbelieving shake of her head. "I don't. I'm just surprised."

I feigned offense. "You don't trust me to have a plan?"

Her eyebrows arched in a way that made my chest do vaguely idiotic things. "Do you?"

"If you're more patient than curious," I said, savoring the way her focus sharpened, "you'll find out in lecture tomorrow."

She gave me a look. "And if I'm not?"

"Then I'm afraid it'll be a very long day for you."

CHAPTER 24

GABRIELLE

The light in the room had changed.

It slanted in through the windows at a new angle—longer, softer, threaded with the copper tones of late afternoon. The golden kind of quiet that only comes when a day is trying to linger.

I didn't mean to check the time. But my eyes flicked toward the clock anyway.

Almost five.

The thought lodged in my chest like a splinter.

My calculus notes were tucked neatly away, my laptop closed. I'd managed to make it halfway through the physics problem set earlier this afternoon—my usual strategy to stay ahead. If I could wrestle with the structure before class, the concepts clicked faster when I heard them out loud. Aunt Suzy had helped me figure that out last semester, back when I was barely keeping my head above water in Dr. Watkins's class.

I hadn't asked Cal for help. And I wouldn't. That wasn't how I learned. I needed to prove—to him and to myself—that I could hold my own in the room, no matter who I was outside of it.

Still, once he sat beside me with that quiet, amused smile and the soft press of his shoulder against mine, the rest of the problem set never stood a chance. It wasn't confusion that stalled me. It was him—the pull of his nearness, the way his voice dipped when he explained things, the glint in his eye when I finally caught on.

It was nearly impossible to focus when all I could think about was how little time we had left before he'd have to take me home.

I heard him before I saw him—the quiet pad of his steps on the hardwood—and then the soft clink of a mug settling on the table in front of me.

Tea.

I looked up. He didn't speak, just eased down beside me again, his expression soft around the edges in a way that made something inside me ache.

"Thanks." I curled my hands around the mug. It was warm, earthy, and grounding. Of course it would be exactly what I didn't know I needed.

We sat like that for a long time, neither of us speaking, the office wrapped in fading sunlight and quiet resignation. My throat was tight, like if I spoke, it would all collapse into the one thing we weren't saying: the weekend was over.

I let my head fall back against the sofa and closed my eyes, feeling him settle closer beside me. "You know what I hate?" I asked softly, eyes still shut.

His shoulder brushed mine. "What?"

"Time."

He went quiet, like he was weighing how much meaning the word could hold. "It's not very kind," he agreed eventually.

I opened my eyes and turned to look at him. His face was close—so close I could see the faint stubble on his jaw, feel the steadiness of his breath.

"You're a world-renowned theoretical physicist," I said,

watching the sunlight gild the edge of his cheekbone. "Can't you do something about it?"

He huffed a quiet laugh. "Only theoretically. Unless you've secretly designed a vessel that can approach the speed of light and dilate time."

"Not yet." I gave him a sidelong look. "I guess I'll have to finish my engineering degree first."

He turned toward me, the corner of his mouth tugging upward. "That means you'll need to pass my course."

"That sounds like extortion."

"That sounds like the curriculum." He lifted his mug, eyes never leaving mine.

I stared at him, pulse fluttering. "You're enjoying this."

"Terribly." He took a slow sip of tea, then set the cup down. "But I'm afraid there's no stopping Monday morning from arriving."

Cal's words hung in the stillness between us: *There's no stopping Monday morning from arriving.*

"I know," I said quietly, fingers tightening around the mug. I set it down with care, then let my hands fall to my lap, suddenly unsure what to do with them.

I wasn't ready to go. Not even close.

"I just…" I hesitated. "I don't want to go back to real life yet. To being just another student in your eight o'clock physics class. To pretending you're not the best thing that's ever happened to me."

He turned fully toward me, one arm sliding along the back of the sofa until his fingertips brushed my shoulder. "Then don't," he said. "Not here. Not with me."

I looked up at him, studying the way he was watching me. It made everything inside me tilt. Warm. Steady. Unshakable. Like he already knew what I meant, even if I hadn't said it yet.

"I know this isn't…simple," I said, my voice thready. "I know what we're risking."

His fingers brushed a slow path along my shoulder. "It was never going to be simple."

"But it's real," I said, my eyes locked on his. "Isn't it?"

His lips parted like he might answer—but no words came. He just took my hand and kissed the inside of my wrist.

Then he nodded. "Yes," he said quietly. "It is."

My breath caught in my throat. The moment expanded around us, stretched thin by everything we wanted and everything we couldn't have. Not here. Not yet.

Cal exhaled slowly, thumb still tracing along my skin. "I should probably take you home at some point."

I didn't move. "Not yet," I said.

He smiled—soft and crooked and so full of ache it knocked the air out of me. "No," he agreed, pulling me into his arms. "Not yet."

My apartment felt smaller than I remembered. I set my bags on the floor and stood in the middle of the living room, listening to the muted hum of traffic through the closed windows. The plaid couch stared back with dull familiarity, and even the bright vintage aviation prints on the wall seemed to accuse me of abandoning ship.

Cal's car had barely left the parking lot before regret followed me inside, coiling tight around my chest and refusing to let go. Not regret for the stolen weekend. Regret that it had to end.

I sank onto the couch, its worn cushions swallowing me whole. The silence, heavy and suffocating, pressed in from all sides. Normally I loved being alone, loved the lack of expectation and noise. But now? Now all I wanted was his voice curling close to my ear, his breath warm against my neck.

A sudden pulse startled me back into the present as my

phone vibrated where it lay forgotten in my purse. I fumbled for it, almost hoping to see his name on the screen.

No such luck.

Aunt Suzy. Eleven missed calls, four voicemails, and a cascade of increasingly frantic texts. A knot formed in my stomach as I scrolled, each message a small explosion of guilt: *Where are you? Why aren't you answering? Did you get my other texts? Call me!*

I took a deep breath, braced myself for impact, and called her back.

She picked up on the first ring. "Gabrielle! Oh, thank God! I was about to call the police!"

I closed my eyes, sinking deeper into the couch. "Hey, Aunt Suzy."

"*Hey?* That's all you have to say for yourself?" Her voice hit like a rapid-fire assault, equal parts panic and exasperation. "I thought maybe you'd fallen into a volcano or joined a cult or something!"

"I'm fine," I said. "Really."

"Where have you been all weekend? Why didn't you text me back?"

I hesitated too long.

There was a pause on the other end of the line—the kind that sounded suspiciously like gears turning. "You were with that 'friend' from physics again, weren't you?"

I walked to my bedroom and flipped on the light. "Yeah." I didn't know what else to say.

Any trace of worry vanished, replaced by gleeful intrigue. "Good for you, Gabrielle! Now, tell me everything. I want all the details."

I took a breath and let it out slowly. "We went to dinner Saturday night," I said, dropping onto the bed. "And... studied." The word felt radioactive on my tongue, like it might give too much away.

Silence stretched for a beat. "You 'studied'?" she repeated, skepticism bleeding through the line like ink.

"Yes."

My clipped tone didn't deter her. "Did you at least have fun?"

I hesitated again, then found myself saying, "I did. We went to this really nice restaurant, and he's..."—my mind scrambled for something safe—"he's smarter than I expected."

"Smarter?" She practically cackled, the sound popping through the quiet like a flashbulb. "That's a first! Just your type, then?"

"It was nice," I said, evading with more skill than I knew I had. "He's nice."

"This sounds serious," she mused, almost singing. "Did you spend the whole weekend with him?"

"Yeah," I admitted, twisting my fingers in the duvet. "And he helped me with some homework. There's a big problem set due this week." That much was true, at least.

"Do I at least get to know his name?" she pressed.

I hesitated. "Cal." His name slipped out too easily, too familiar. I fumbled to recover it, to cover. "Calvin."

She snorted, a sharp burst of disbelief that made me wince. "Calvin? Please tell me his last name isn't Klein."

"It's not," I said weakly, trying not to dwell on the fact that I didn't actually know what Cal was short for.

"So...when do I get to meet this *Calvin*?"

I froze. "Uh," I said, my mind going blank. "I don't think we're anywhere near that stage."

"Gabrielle, really," she said with exasperated fondness. "What's the point of getting to know him if you're not going to bring him home?"

"We're just hanging out," I said quickly. "I don't want to scare the poor guy off."

"How would I scare him?" She laughed as if the prospect

was delightful. "If he can't handle me, he's not worth your time!"

"He's probably not worth my time then," I deflected, but the words felt unsteady and wrong. "Anyway, it's not that serious." Sandpaper on my tongue.

"Not *yet*," she said knowingly, nearly singing again.

I pictured her on the other end of the line—sitting at the kitchen table back in Houston with a mug of coffee, a bright red nail tapping against its rim as she plotted my romantic future to the last detail.

"I'm glad you're finally meeting people," she said after a moment, her voice softening. "I was worried you were getting too buried in your studies, not getting out into the world at all."

There was no censure in it—only relief. But guilt coiled tighter around my chest, pressing against everything I wasn't saying. Everything I couldn't say.

I mumbled something noncommittal and promised to call her later.

After I hung up, the silence returned—heavier now, threaded through with things I didn't have the courage to voice.

Later, in bed, I lay staring at the ceiling, the sheets cool against my skin and far too much space on either side of me.

My phone buzzed—sudden in the stillness.

I miss you already.

That tightness in my chest unfurled just a bit. Sweet. Dangerous. All want. I typed before I could stop myself:

It's too quiet here. Can't sleep.

His reply came almost instantly:

Neither can I. My bed's empty, and I don't like it.

A smile tugged at my lips despite the ache in my chest.

Maybe you should've kept me.

Don't think I wasn't tempted.

I smiled, imagining how he'd say it—half-sarcastic, half-serious.

What stopped you?

Your future. Your physics grade. My job. Take your pick.

Terrible excuses.

Terribly noble, thank you.

I shifted beneath the covers, the phone warm in my hand, heat curling low in my belly.

What would you have done if I'd asked to stay?

There was a pause. A longer one this time.

Locked the door. Hidden your backpack. Called it an act of God.

Might need to test that theory sometime…

Careful, Gabrielle. I'm still very awake. And very imaginative.

My cheeks flushed. My thumb hovered for a second, the playfulness thinning just enough for something more honest to slip through.

I didn't think I'd feel it this much.

Another pause.

I know. I feel it too.

My throat tightened.

What do we do now?

His reply came slower, but steady.

We survive Monday. Then Tuesday. Then whatever comes next.

I stared at the screen, the ache in my chest sharper but somehow sweeter.

I wish you were here.

So do I, love. More than you know.

CHAPTER 25

CALLUM

I joined the video call at 5:59 a.m.

The house was still, wrapped in the kind of deep winter darkness that resisted morning. Outside, the sky was a solid slate—no hint of light yet on the horizon. My office windows arched high overhead, cold glass reflecting the soft glow of the two lamps I'd switched on. The blinds were half-drawn, shielding the room from the void beyond. Everything was where it should be—books aligned, papers neatly stacked—control in physical form.

I didn't usually notice the silence in here. More accurately, I usually treasured it. But not today. Today, the room felt off-balance, like something was missing.

Or someone.

I straightened my tie—navy with a pale blue diagonal stripe—and adjusted the starched collar of my shirt. Lecture wasn't until eight, but I needed the structure this morning. The discipline. Something to counteract the ache I hadn't quite shaken from the night before.

The laptop fan hummed.

The clock ticked over, and the screen flickered, then filled with Isabel's face.

Auburn hair swept back. Pearl studs. A red silk blouse that probably cost more than my motorcycle. She was sitting in one of her drawing rooms by the look of it—tasteful, muted, curated to the inch.

She didn't smile.

"Well," she said, lifting her teacup in a lazy sort of salute. "It's a bit bloody early, isn't it?"

"Lovely to see you too, sister dear."

Her mouth curled into a wry half-smile. "I'm always glad to hear from my darling baby brother." Her tone turned pouty. "Sometimes I feel you've forgotten I exist."

"Never," I said, stretching back in my chair.

She arched one perfectly plucked eyebrow and set down her teacup with a soft clink. "To what do I owe the pleasure of this 'urgent' call? What time is it there, anyway?"

"Six."

"Ugh," she groaned. "I've barely gone to bed by then."

"Some of us have responsibilities." I glanced at the clock, willing time to move faster and slower all at once.

"Some of us know how to live," she quipped, a sly smile playing on her lips. "And here I thought you'd become a proper American hedonist by now."

"You know me better than that."

"Yes," she said, eyes bright with amusement.

The old game of verbal chess—Isabel's favorite. She played it with surgical precision and a hint of mischief, never revealing how many moves ahead she was.

"How's the wedding planning?" I asked, the weight of what I needed to say pressing at the edge of my words. "Still on for May?"

"Of course." She rolled her eyes. "Mother's being impossible, as usual. It's a second wedding, so you'd think it wouldn't be such a production. But she's got to have it her own way."

"And you're letting her?"

She dabbed at her lipstick with a finger, unbothered. "She'll wear herself out eventually."

"And the groom?"

"Not getting cold feet," Isabel said dryly. "If that's what you're asking."

I gave her a look of mock innocence.

She sipped her tea, watching me with sharp blue eyes over the rim. "You *are* coming, aren't you?"

"Wouldn't miss it," I said, the resolve in my voice apparently surprising us both. "Which brings me to my point." I hesitated. The pause dragged until Isabel's eyebrow crept higher, expectant. "Would it be possible...for me to bring a guest?"

Her jaw practically hit the floor. There was the barest hitch in her response, like a needle skipping on a record. Then she laughed—a short, bright sound that crackled through the quiet. "Of course! You don't even have to ask. But you can't just leave it there. Tell me everything."

I shifted in my chair, painfully aware of how uncharacteristic this was—how reckless, how bold, how necessary. "It's...complicated." The inadequacy of the word hung between us.

Isabel leaned toward the camera, curiosity sharpening every pixelated line of her face. "Since when is anything *un*complicated with you?"

"Since never." I rubbed my temple with one hand. "But this is more than usual."

"You've piqued my interest," she said, settling back into her chair with feline satisfaction. The game had taken an unexpected turn. "Is she brilliant? Beautiful? Actually interesting enough to distract you from your work and your self-imposed exile?"

"Yes," I said quietly.

She tilted her head. "You're serious about this one. I

thought you'd go stag forever. I never imagined you'd bring someone home again."

Her words lanced through me. I winced but kept steady, the old wound throbbing beneath its polished bandage. Isabel's gaze softened as she watched me walk the tightrope of silence.

"You know that's not what I meant," she said gently, reaching for her tea.

I cleared my throat, fumbling for a safer path. "It's still early days."

"But you're ringing at six in the morning about it."

My breath turned heavy, snagging in my chest. "It's… someone I met through the university."

She pounced on the hesitation like a cat with a cornered mouse. "Not saying much, are we?"

"There's not much to say." I paused, reconsidering my approach.

"I know you better than that, baby brother. What's the real story, then?"

I hesitated. "She's one of my students," I said finally, the words unsteady but irreversible.

Isabel blinked—once, twice—then let out the most unladylike snort. She bit it back quickly, coughing into her hand to cover the sound. "Oh, Cal! You've truly outdone yourself!"

The familiar heat of disapproval flared in my chest. "It isn't—"

"I knew your standards were impossibly high," Isabel cut in with a grin sharp enough to draw blood. "But cradle robbing? Really?"

"It's not like that," I said slowly, deliberately. "She's mature. Brilliant. And it's—"

"It's an ethical minefield, darling."

I wrestled for the right words—something to capture the chaos and clarity of it all—but came up short. "It's real."

She leaned back, eyes narrowing. "You're serious then," Isabel repeated, softer now. "More than I realized, clearly. Or you wouldn't have brought it to me."

"Yes." My voice came low but steady. "I've never been more sure of anything in my life."

Her expression eased, a thread of warmth slipping through the curiosity. "What's her name?"

"Gabrielle."

"Pretty," she said with approval. "American, I assume? Is she terribly young?"

"She's twenty-five."

Isabel nodded with a thoughtful tilt of her head. "Not quite an ingénue, then. That's something." She studied me a moment longer, gaze sharp and considering. "Family?"

"Respectable, but not much left. Her father's deceased, and her mother's been absent since the start."

"Well, at least you don't have to worry about meeting her parents."

"No…but she'll have to meet ours at some point."

Isabel's gaze cut straight through me. "That's what's keeping you up, isn't it?"

"It is," I said, rubbing the back of my neck. "I'm worried about dragging her into the family circus. But I don't see any way around it. I can't keep her hidden forever."

"Nonsense." She flicked a dismissive hand, long fingers slicing through the air. "You've weathered far worse."

I leaned forward, imploring in a way that felt painfully foreign. "I can take whatever they throw at me."

"But you're worried they'll rip her to shreds," she finished for me.

"Precisely."

Isabel tilted her head, eyes narrowing. "Since when have you cared what Mother and Father think?"

"I don't," I said, my voice colder than I meant it. "They'll think what they like. They always do."

"Then why the nerves?"

I leaned back, jaw tight. "Because she doesn't know them. She hasn't learned to decode every insult wrapped in charm and etiquette. And I've no intention of watching her be dissected by people who dress up cruelty as civility."

Isabel stilled, amusement draining from her face. She paused, quietly, carefully, before saying, "That's…surprisingly gallant."

A beat passed. I wasn't sure if it was approval. But it wasn't disapproval.

Her gaze didn't waver. "Do you want my advice? Or are you just looking for moral support?"

"Advice," I said without hesitation.

"Bring her anyway." Isabel set her teacup down and leaned in, all trace of sarcasm gone. "You can't make them see her as you do. They won't. But you can frame her first, before they decide who she is. Give her armor, Cal."

I swallowed. "Will you…help me?" It came out low. Fragile in a way I loathed.

She blinked, then nodded. "Of course I will." A pause. Then, quieter, "But do it before Mother starts in on bloodlines over the starter course."

I let out a breath that might have been a laugh. "I'll try."

"So when do I get to meet her?"

"She doesn't know about any of this yet." The admission felt raw, unguarded. "I wanted to see if it was even possible first."

"It is. And it's high time, Cal." She checked her watch. "Right, off with you. I've got a bridal tasting at two and a florist who thinks I've gone completely mad."

I rolled my eyes. "I'm hanging up now."

"Ta-ta."

My video window went dark.

The silence returned, but the ache had eased. Just enough to breathe.

CHAPTER 26

GABRIELLE

I arrived to Cal's class—that is, *Dr. Hawthorne's* class—early, the door creaking shut behind me as I slipped into the empty lecture hall. Fluorescent lights bathed everything in clinical white, harsh against the too-early sky outside. I slid into my usual seat by the window, cracked open my notebook, and tried to corral my thoughts.

Formulas and diagrams blurred in my mind like abstract art. I rubbed my eyes, willing myself to focus. The problem set loomed, but my concentration was a fragile thread, easily snapped by the memory of Cal's voice, lingering in my ear long after he'd had to go.

Three girls burst through the door, their chatter ricocheting off the walls. Sloane Cartwright and her usual crowd—with freshly minted pink sorority jerseys and full-volume energy—claimed seats a few rows behind me.

"I swear, this man is literally the only reason I'll take an eight a.m. class," one girl groaned. "He's stupid hot. Like, criminal levels of hot."

Heat surged up my neck. My pen slipped, leaving a jagged mark in the margin.

"Nope," Sloane replied, her tone flat. "Total hard-ass."

Another girl cackled. "That's the whole appeal. Tell me he doesn't give serious 'ruin your GPA *and* your life' energy."

"I'm sorry," the first one chimed in. "That voice? That accent? He could read the syllabus, and I'd still need a minute."

I didn't turn around, but every syllable crawled down my spine.

"I'm still fucking pissed he didn't let me make up that quiz," Sloane muttered.

"It's one quiz," the other said. "If it tanks your grade, just have your dad call. Isn't he, like, on the Board of Trustees or something?"

"Yeah, but it's the principle."

More students filtered in, jostling the silence with the dull thud of backpacks and the rustle of notebooks. The girls behind me kept up their chatter, but I tuned them out as best I could, every nerve strung tight as I waited for Cal to arrive. He'd probably slip in right at eight and step up to the lectern like nothing had changed. Maybe for him, it hadn't. Maybe he could compartmentalize better than I could.

The door swung open, and there he was.

Everything inside me tipped sideways as he crossed the room. His gaze fell briefly on me, then moved away so quickly I wondered if I'd imagined it. His face gave away nothing.

He set his bag down, connected his laptop, pulled up his slides, and checked his watch.

Eight o'clock.

"Good morning," he said, scanning the rows with that practiced gaze, never lingering long enough on me for anyone to notice. "If you've looked ahead," he said in that steady, deliberate way I loved, "you'll notice we're taking a brief detour from circuits to cover basic magnetism. Any idea why?"

Silence. He paused, scanning for volunteers.

"Perhaps I should let you wake up a bit." He clicked forward a slide. "Up to this point, we've looked at direct current. But to understand alternating current—the electricity you get when you plug something into the wall—you need to understand magnetic fields."

He moved through the next few slides, stopping occasionally to elaborate. I followed his voice with a hunger I couldn't suppress, scribbling notes and wishing the time would slow.

At one point, he paused, glancing meaningfully in my direction. "Can anyone tell me how a microwave works?"

I hesitated, unsure whether to answer.

Someone in the front row rattled off a textbook response. "It converts electric energy into microwaves, which make the water molecules vibrate and heat up."

"That's a good start," Cal said, nodding toward him. "Now—can anyone tell me why it's a bad idea to heat water in the microwave?" Another glance my way. "Say, in an attempt to make tea."

I sank down in my seat, burning and breathless, and hated how much I loved him for it.

So...calling me out in front of the entire class? Bold move, Dr. Hawthorne.

I did no such thing. But at least you won't be microwaving water again, Miss Clark.

I smiled, grateful that I was alone and no longer had to school my expressions. My phone buzzed again.

How was calculus?

My pulse skipped.

Numbing, but I made it through. Now I'm studying. Or pretending to.

Psych at 1?

Good memory.

I'm known for that, love. Where are you?

I glanced around at the chaotic array of tables, chairs, crates, and furniture covered in tarps. Beneath the Page College chapel lay the remnants of a Cold War-era fallout shelter. Now used mostly for storage and accessible only to those who knew how to find it, it was my study spot of choice.

Secluded study spot. Hardly anyone knows it's here. I'm all alone...

A secret lair... Should I be concerned or intrigued?

I hovered over the screen, thumb ghosting the keyboard. It was reckless. A terrible idea. But I typed it anyway.

If you're free...you could join me...

I swallowed hard and hit send.
His reply came faster than I expected.

You're dangerously persuasive when you shouldn't be. Send me a pin. I'm already walking.

I left my things and made my way upstairs to meet him. The cramped storage room behind the chapel was overrun and chaotic—an echo of the shelter below. I wondered if this was too reckless. If he'd turn back once he saw my pin drop.

But a moment later, the door creaked open, and there he was.

Longing spiked through me. He shut the door quietly, his gaze sweeping the room—then locking with mine, burning through every restraint I'd tried to build.

"Covert enough for you?" I asked, voice low as I stepped toward him. Close enough to catch the glint of amusement in his eyes at my audacity. Close enough for my breath to catch at his nearness.

"The chapel? I'd say sacrilegious, not covert," Cal mused, still watching me in that way that made everything else go dim.

We both glanced at the door, as if expecting someone to burst through. But there were no footsteps. No voices nearby. Just dust motes drifting through shafts of light from high windows.

"No, not the chapel. I'm not insane." I reached for his hand and felt him hesitate, tugged by propriety. "Under the chapel. The old fallout shelter."

His posture eased, and he let me lead him down into the stairwell, into the hush and shadows where nothing else mattered but this. The door clanged shut above us. With each step, we left the world behind—one that demanded restraint and reason.

"I thought this place was a myth," he whispered.

"Nope. It was built during the Cold War in case of a nuclear strike. I've heard there are three more around campus, maybe even tunnels, but they might be sealed off."

He tightened his hand around mine—warm and solid, everything I needed it to be. The space opened around us, vast and abandoned. My heart kept a wild rhythm as we reached the bottom landing.

Cal stopped short, looking around the space as if grounding himself in its secrecy. "You weren't joking," he said softly.

I squeezed his hand and pulled him closer. The quiet down here was different—expectant, suspended in time like the rest of the world had vanished aboveground. I slipped my hands around his waist.

His breath was a low exhale against my hair, relief and want tangled together.

"You really shouldn't have called me out like that in class," I murmured into his shirt.

He drew back just enough to look at me, his gaze tracing the curve of my jaw. "That was nothing." His smile was slow, a promise. "You should see what I'll do next time."

Heat rose in my cheeks as he tilted my chin, his mouth soft on mine. It was tentative at first—an almost-question—but I answered before it could form, closing the distance. He kissed me harder, restraint giving way to something deeper and more dangerous. Every hesitation—every careful line we'd drawn—dissolved in the dark. No rules here. No roles. Just us and the quiet madness of wanting what we shouldn't.

Cal gathered me to him like he never meant to let go and pressed me back against a stack of crates. He slipped his jacket from his shoulders, tossing it somewhere behind him.

"You're impossible," I whispered.

He smiled against my skin, his hands at the hem of my sweater, then warm beneath it.

"And you're meant to be studying."

I worked quickly to loosen his tie and undo his top few buttons. He watched me as if every movement burned. I tugged his shirt free from his waistband and slid my hands beneath—finally—pressing against smooth, warm skin and the taut muscles of his abdomen. He shuddered at my touch, each breath a quiet burn against my neck. I splayed my fingers across his chest, felt his heartbeat—wild, a perfect match for mine. He caught my wrist as if to steady himself, then released it just as quickly, like his own restraint had surprised him.

"Gabrielle," he said, voice rough-edged and urgent.

I silenced him with another kiss, tugging him close until there was no space left between us. We were frantic now, heat climbing with every touch. He tangled his hands in my hair, then slid them down my back to grip me tighter. The world spun, free-falling around us.

We stumbled sideways into a battered armchair and toppled over its edge. I landed half on the floor, half tangled in Cal's arms—laughing breathlessly at the absurdity. At how careful we weren't being. His weight pinned me to the cool concrete beneath a threadbare rug, and it was all I could do not to come undone.

He traced his fingers along my ribcage as he kissed me again. "I want you," he said between kisses, "so badly." He pulled back slightly. "I'm genuinely considering ravishing you right here in the chapel. I really am going to hell."

I shook my head as I undid his belt. "No, you're *under* the chapel. There's a difference."

His belt gave way under my fingers, and something shifted in him—restraint melting into something darker, needier. He kissed me like he was memorizing the shape of my mouth. Like he hadn't stopped thinking about it since the last time. Maybe he hadn't.

My sweater was gone before I even realized I'd raised my arms. He sat back just enough to take me in. His hands skated over the curve of my waist, the rise of my ribs—slow and reverent, as if he had all the time in the world.

"God, you're beautiful," he whispered, his thumb brushing the underside of my breast.

Then he moved again—lips at my collarbone, my throat, a trail of heat down my chest. His hands followed—confident, unhurried. He wasn't rushing. He was savoring.

He smiled against my skin—smug, warm, and completely focused. "Is this what you want?" he asked low and gravelly as he slid his hand under the waistband of my jeans.

"Yes," I breathed. "God, yes."

"Good," he said, leaning in. "Because I've been imagining this all day."

He kissed his way down my stomach, fingers following steadily, every motion tuned to me as if I were the only thing that existed. When he slid his hand lower and found me—really found me—my hips arched helplessly, and he groaned into the fabric of my jeans.

"You're soaked," he said, voice thick.

"Your fault," I managed, barely holding on.

His laugh was pure sin, low and close to my ear—and then he was kneeling between my legs, dragging my jeans and underwear down with aching slowness, as if every inch of bare skin was something he needed to see, to memorize.

He dipped his head and kissed the inside of my thigh. Then another. And another, higher each time. I shivered beneath him, the air cool on my skin, my nerves electric.

When he touched me—featherlight at first—I jolted. Pleasure flared, sharp and immediate. He dragged his fingers more firmly through the slick heat between my legs with maddening control, learning the rhythm of my breath, the arch of my hips.

"You're trembling," he murmured.

"Because you're not *doing* anything."

He smiled against my skin. "I'm doing plenty."

He slid a finger inside me, slow and deliberate, and I moaned—tipping my head back, my spine lifting off the floor. He added a second, pumping gently, curling just right, just enough.

Still working his fingers inside me, he sealed his mouth over my clit, tongue stroking in perfect sync—unrelenting, terrifyingly precise. He pinned me with one arm braced across my thigh, holding me steady as I writhed against him, unable to stay still.

"Cal," I cried, broken and breathless.

He hummed against me, the sound vibrating through

every nerve. My hands scrambled for purchase—his hair, a crate, the rug beneath us—anything to hold on to.

Every flick of his tongue, every press of his fingers, every low sound in his throat wound me tighter.

When I came, it was all at once—blinding and helpless, a full-body shudder that tore through me like a live wire. I cried out, legs trembling, breath ragged, but he didn't stop. Not until I gasped his name again and pulled at his shoulders, needing him with me.

He kissed the inside of my thigh, then my hipbone, then dragged himself up my body, blanketing me in his warmth again.

"You're so beautiful when you come," he whispered, brushing his lips over mine. "I could die right here and not regret a thing."

His breath turned to a low groan against my mouth as I kissed him harder, hands everywhere.

I fumbled with his fly. He froze—just long enough for me to look up and meet his eyes.

"This is insane," he murmured.

I brushed a kiss to the corner of his mouth. "Then stop me."

He didn't. Of course he didn't.

The zipper gave, and I pushed his trousers open, slipping my hand just beneath the waistband. His face was flushed, breath ragged—but he was still holding back. Barely.

I paused. We hadn't exactly…planned this.

"You didn't, by any chance, bring anything…did you?"

I expected a no. Prayed for a maybe.

He paused. Just for a second. "Wallet. Back pocket."

I blinked. "Seriously?"

He let out a breath. "It's not what you think."

I raised an eyebrow.

"I don't sleep around, Gabrielle." His voice was low,

rough. "It's just a precaution. I always keep protection on me —a habit ingrained from boyhood."

I searched his face. He looked half-guilty, half-desperate—not for forgiveness, but for me to believe him.

I kissed him—slow, certain. "Well," I said, reaching around to fish his wallet from his back pocket, "thank God for outdated male conditioning."

He laughed—breathless, wrecked. "I swear it's not expired."

"Better not be," I said, tearing open the foil. "I'm not going to hell *and* the health clinic in one afternoon."

I guided him down to the floor and straddled him, hands sure and steady as I rolled the condom on. He sucked in a breath through his teeth, hands fisting at his sides, like if he touched me now, he might break.

I didn't give him the chance.

I sank onto him slowly, inch by inch, until he was fully inside me. The stretch burned—delicious and deep. He gasped as if it broke him.

"God," he breathed. "You feel like sin."

"I was going to say heaven." I rolled my hips, and his hands flew to my waist, fingers digging in like he was holding on for dear life.

We moved together—slow at first, testing the rhythm—then faster as heat built and the world slipped away. His hands roamed, reverent and greedy. I leaned in to kiss him, and he met me with everything—teeth, tongue, breath—as if I was the only air he had left.

The rug burned my knees. The air was thick with sweat and want and the soft, rhythmic thud of bodies meeting in secret.

He tangled his fingers in my hair. "Let me see you," he said, voice wrecked. "Please."

I sat up just enough for him to watch me ride him—eyes

locked, hands everywhere. Desperate worship, nothing to do with religion, everything to do with us. With now.

He brushed his thumb over my nipple, and I gasped. With his other hand, he gripped my hip, guiding the rhythm—anchoring me as he moved, deeper, slower, then harder again.

"Come for me again," he whispered. "I want to feel it."

The words struck somewhere deep. I closed my eyes and gave in—to the friction, the steady drag of him inside me, the way my thighs trembled from the strain, from the pleasure, from the wave cresting higher with every breath. I clutched at his shoulders, then slid one hand between us, circling my clit, desperate for just a little more.

Then everything went hot and sharp and brilliant.

I shattered with a cry I didn't mean to make—body clenching, every muscle locking down as the orgasm tore through me. I pulsed around him—greedy, relentless—and he groaned.

"Fuck, Gabrielle—" He thrust once, twice—then he was gone too, undone beneath me.

We had no words for a long moment. Just the echo of what we'd done. And knowing that nothing about this was safe anymore.

I collapsed onto his chest, both of us breathless, hearts pounding in sync. He wrapped his arms around me—like instinct, like shelter—holding me through the aftershocks.

When I finally stirred, my muscles trembling, I eased off him with a soft, spent sound. The rug scratched my shoulders as I rolled onto my back, blinking at the flickering overhead lights. Cool air licked across my sweat-slicked skin, a sharp contrast to the molten ache still humming through me.

Cal stretched out beside me, then he rolled over and crawled over me with slow, deliberate care, as if he couldn't bear the loss of contact. He pressed kisses up my thighs, over my hip, back to my lips.

"Now," he whispered. "Now I'm officially going to hell."

I pulled him down. "As long as you take me with you."

CHAPTER 27

CALLUM

I walked the long corridor back toward my office, the fluorescent lights buzzing softly as if registering my altered state. My tie hung loose around my neck, a small rebellion that felt enormous after years of polished convention.

The university's old boiler clanged in the basement below, heating the building with all the elegance of a steam train on its last legs. The smell of it was evident even on the third floor —a metallic tang beneath the more familiar scent of scorched coffee from the departmental lounge. But nothing could overpower Gabrielle's lingering presence. It clung to me like static—sweet, charged, and impossible to ignore.

I ran a hand through my hair, trying for decorum before anyone noticed how thoroughly unraveled I was.

"Cal!" a voice called down the hall, cheerful and persistent. "I was about to text you."

I turned to find Bill Watkins lumbering toward me, his gait no match for his exuberance.

"There's a student camped outside your office," he managed between breaths. "He's been there long enough to make himself at home."

I stopped short, blinking as if he'd pulled me from a dream. "A student?" My mind spun through possibilities—Gabrielle first among them, despite all logic. Unlikely. Bill had clearly said *he*.

"Jackson, I think," he added. "One of your research students."

Jackson. Of course. I checked my watch—12:57 p.m. *Damn it*. I'd completely forgotten the meeting about his revised project proposal.

"I'm heading there now," I said, brushing back a stray lock of hair that had fallen across my forehead. "His appointment is scheduled for one, but Jackson is…eager."

"That's one word for it." Bill chuckled and then looked me over, his round face lit with curiosity. "Everything okay, Cal? You look a little less put-together than usual."

Heat flushed beneath my collar as images of Gabrielle in the underground bunker played fast and reckless—breathless laughter, rumpled clothes, her taste on my lips. I shoved them back.

"Brisk walk over lunch," I said, straightening my tie like that could undo what I'd just done.

Bill gave me a look of amused disbelief but didn't press. "There's something different about you lately. I can't quite put my finger on it." He squinted at me like a scientist peering through a microscope. "You seem less…brooding. More pep in your step."

I barked a laugh, slightly ragged. "That won't do. I have a reputation to uphold."

He shook his head, all friendly exasperation. "Whatever it is, it suits you. It's nice to see you happy." Bill clapped me on the shoulder, then gestured down the hall toward Jackson, who sat cross-legged on the floor, consumed by his phone. "Don't keep him waiting."

"Thanks for the message." I straightened, the scholar's armor sliding back into place as I turned toward my office.

That was close.

I made it through the meeting with my composure mostly intact. Jackson left a little after three—freshly annotated proposal in hand, an ambitious glint in his eye, and no idea my attention had been…divided the entire time.

I sank back in my chair and let out a long breath. My shirt clung to the small of my back. The air felt too warm, too tight.

I didn't know how long I stared at the same corner of my desk before pulling out my phone.

> Did you make it to your afternoon class on time?

Her reply came a minute later.

> Barely, but yes. Physically present anyway.
> Mentally, I was still with you.

Heat flushed under my collar again, but it was different this time—lower, deeper—slow and consuming. I hesitated only briefly before typing:

> Can I pop by tonight? I've got something for you.

A beat. Then another. Then—

> More than you already gave me today?
> Because I'm not sure I'll be able to walk
> tomorrow…

I laughed, silent and helpless, dropping my forehead to the edge of my desk. God help me…

Another message followed:

> Yes, of course you can come over. I was going
> to order Chinese. But fair warning—I won't
> share my egg rolls unless you bring dessert.

I stared at the screen, grinning like a fool, the day's weight slipping off my shoulders one scandalous message at a time. I typed and deleted a dozen responses before landing on something that wouldn't get me arrested. Or fired. Or both.

> I'll be there at seven. And I never arrive empty-handed.

~

I knocked once on Gabrielle's door, briefcase slung over one shoulder and a brown paper bag in my hand.

"It's open," she called.

I stepped inside and shut the door. Gabrielle stood barefoot in leggings and an oversized tee, her hair piled up in a way that was somehow more dangerous than formalwear. She looked at me and smiled like I was the only thing she'd been waiting for all day.

"You made it," she said, padding over to kiss my cheek. "And with dessert. You're officially welcome."

"I was promised egg rolls," I said, shrugging off my coat and setting my briefcase by the sofa. "And as I said, I don't arrive empty-handed."

"So, what'd you bring me?"

I pulled a pint of Bluebell from the bag and held it up like an offering. "I was told Bluebell is the only acceptable ice cream to bring to a Texan's home."

Gabrielle laughed, the sound wrapping around me like silk. "You've done your homework."

I opened the carton, noting the clean split down the middle. "I wasn't sure if you preferred chocolate or vanilla," I said as she took it, "so I was pleased to find The Great Divide offers both."

"I should have known you'd find a diplomatic solution," she said, grinning. She replaced the lid, carried the carton to the kitchen, and popped it in the freezer. She pulled down two plates and dished up Chinese takeaway. The scent of soy and ginger filled the small kitchen, mouthwatering and warm. "Beef and broccoli," she said as she opened a carton, voice tinged with apology. "I hope that's okay."

"It's perfect," I said, watching the way she moved as she spooned the food onto my plate. She handed it to me with an egg roll perched atop a bed of pork fried rice. "Smells heavenly."

"Good." Her meal was vegetable-based, a neat pile of tofu and broccoli next to a mess of lo mein. She glanced over her shoulder. "Fork or chopsticks?"

"Chopsticks," I said, mock solemn. "Of course."

We settled at her small dining table, close enough for our knees to touch. I let mine rest against hers, a slow burn seeping through the thin fabric of my trousers.

We ate in an easy silence at first, the only sound the soft clink of ceramic and wood as we briefly fumbled with our chopsticks. Then we talked about everything and nothing, the conversation airy and light. She told me the salacious back-row gossip from my morning lecture; I told her Bill thought I'd lost my brooding edge. We laughed and stayed mostly on safe ground.

By the end of the meal, she grazed her fingertips across my knee and trailed them like a whisper down my calf.

"I'll get these," she said, collecting the empty plates and retreating to the kitchen under the guise of tidiness. Silence sidled in behind her, less comfortable now. Her restlessness was like a current. She rinsed one plate, then another, then paused. "So…what did you bring me?" Her voice was easy, but her eyes weren't. "Besides ice cream and your company, of course."

I smiled, crossed the room, and fished a large envelope from my soft-sided briefcase. "I have something for you."

"So you said." She peered closely, eyes narrow, as I returned to the kitchen.

"I know it's early," I said, handing it over, "and it's presumptuous as hell, but…"

She took the envelope and opened it slowly—first perplexed, then amused. "You brought me a passport renewal application?"

"Last week at the museum," I said, my heart pounding. "I mentioned taking you to England. You said you'd need to renew your passport."

"I can't believe you remembered that."

I stepped closer and brushed my fingers lightly against her wrist. "I haven't forgotten a single thing about you since we met."

A blush bloomed across her cheeks as she searched my face for more than just an administrative courtesy.

I took a breath. Held it longer than I meant to. "It's…a family event," I said finally, the words catching on the way out. "My sister's wedding. At the end of May. After spring term is over."

Her eyes widened, bright and cautious.

"I'd like you to come with me."

"Oh," she breathed, barely audible. Her fingers tightened around the envelope as if grounding herself in its paper certainty. "To your sister's wedding?"

Shit. Shit. Shit. I had crossed a line.

"Yes." My voice was unsteady but irrevocable.

"As your…" She trailed off, but her expression was expectant.

"Yes."

A beat. "This is major, Cal."

I swallowed. "Yes." *Did I know any other words?* "We'd stay two weeks. I don't go home often, but Isabel—my sister, that is —is important to me. Probably the only halfway sane member of the lot."

Gabrielle laid a hand flat on my chest.

I stilled.

"This isn't just a trip," she said. Her voice was steady, but her fingers curled against my shirt. "It's…stepping into your world. One I don't know the first thing about."

"You'll be with me the whole time," I said quietly.

She nodded once. "I know. But let's be honest—your family isn't going to see me as…" Her eyes flicked to the envelope, then back to me. She ticked off each point on her fingers. "I'm thirteen years younger than you. I'm your student. I grew up reasonably well-off, but my 'status' doesn't come close to yours. That's three strikes, and I don't even know their names."

I started to speak, but she lifted a hand.

"I'm not asking you to defend them," she said. "And I'm not saying no. I just…want to be clear about what we're doing."

"I understand." I stepped closer, voice low. "And for what it's worth, they don't deserve you."

That made her laugh, soft and unexpected.

"I'm not worried about *me*," she said. "I'm worried about walking into a room full of people who've already decided I'm not good enough for *you*."

I reached for her hand again. "You don't have to prove anything—to them or to me. You already belong with me. That's the whole point."

She looked at me, eyes searching—then handed the envelope back.

My heart thudded. "Gabrielle—"

"Relax," she said with a smirk, her dry wit threading back in. "You really think I don't know how to renew a passport online?"

Relief hit me like a wave. But before I could speak, she added, "I'll come with you. But you'd better not let me fall on my face."

"I'll carry you if I have to."

"I know," she said. "That's the part that scares me." A smile graced her lips. "But in the best way."

The envelope fluttered to the kitchen floor as I took her face in my hands and kissed her—tender, earnest, pouring every unsaid word into her.

"Thank you," I said.

"Don't thank me yet. I'm not getting on that plane without a full cultural crash course."

"I'll start drafting a syllabus."

I held her to my chest, grazing my thumb over her cheek.

After a few satisfying moments, I pulled back and clapped once. "Right. Time for pudding."

She blinked. "Pudding?"

I hesitated. "Sorry—dessert."

She smiled. "God, you really are British."

"You say that like it's a character flaw."

"Jury's still out."

I made for the freezer, trying not to grin. "I usually remember to code-switch," I said over my shoulder. "But you make it too easy to feel at home."

Behind me, the room went still.

Then her beautiful, soft voice cut through the air. "That's how I want you to feel."

CHAPTER 28

GABRIELLE

The hallway outside Cal's office felt like a pressure cooker: too warm, too bright, too many students pretending not to panic. I'd been spoiled by having his Thursday afternoon office hours almost entirely to myself. But I suppose the day before his midterm exam was reason enough to draw everyone out of the woodwork.

Two students sat ahead of me, slumped in institutional chairs like prisoners awaiting sentencing. I sat with my notebook open on my lap, pen poised, though I hadn't written anything in ten minutes.

I didn't need help with the midterm. Not really. I just needed five minutes with him. His voice. His air. Plus one more rundown of Faraday's Law before the exam couldn't hurt.

The door clicked open, and a girl stepped out, muttering a halfhearted thanks as she brushed past. That made me next—after Sloane.

"Miss Cartwright?" Cal's voice floated into the hall, calm and clipped.

Sloane stood—perfectly composed, glossy lips set in a smile just shy of sincere. She adjusted the strap of her designer tote and smoothed down her sorority sweatshirt like she was heading into a casting call, not office hours.

"Dr. Hawthorne," she cooed as she stepped inside, "thanks so much for squeezing me in."

I didn't mean to eavesdrop. But the door didn't quite latch.

"I've sent a few emails," Sloane said, her tone rising at the end of each phrase, all faux-question marks. "But I figured it might be easier to talk in person. I was hoping to reschedule tomorrow's exam. I'm flying out first thing, and I really can't rebook."

A pause. No response. But I could picture him—cool, collected, intimidating without trying.

"I'd hate to tank my GPA over an unavoidable six a.m. flight. Surely you can help me out."

A longer pause.

Cal's voice came crisp and even. "While I fully understand the appeal of an early start to spring break—which, I presume, is the only possible reason for the request—the exam schedule stands."

"Would it help if my dad called and vouched for me? He's on the Board of Trustees, after all." She dropped that little nugget like a stone in water. Clever.

"That won't be necessary," Cal replied softly.

"Oh, good, because I'd hate for there to be any… unpleasantness." Entitlement dripped from every word.

"That won't be necessary because that strategy won't work on me, Miss Cartwright." She huffed, but before she could retort, Cal continued, "Your physics midterm exam is at eight o'clock tomorrow morning. Without exception. If you choose not to appear, you'll receive a zero. And in this course, that would be difficult—if not impossible—to recover from."

Another pause. Neither spoke, but the tension spilled into the hallway.

Then, a single line from Cal—*Dr. Hawthorne*. Calm. Unmovable. "Choose wisely."

Sloane emerged with a flounce, cheeks tinted and expression soured. She shot me a scathing look, rolling her eyes so hard I thought they might stay that way.

"Asshole," she muttered as her steps quickened. "Think he'd show a little human decency. Fucking jerk." Her words trailed after her, a scandalized wake rippling down the hall.

I tried not to smile.

"Miss Clark?" Cal's voice was different—warmer, like a favorite song.

I sprang up, notebook tucked to my chest, and stepped into his office.

He looked at me with sweetness, though he tried for the usual façade. "Always a pleasure to see you," he said, gesturing to the chair across from his desk. "How can I help?"

I closed the door behind me, a click as soft as the smile I couldn't quite keep in check. "That sounded…fun," I said, sliding into the chair.

He rolled his eyes, a rare crack in the armor. "Oh, you have no idea."

I bit my lip to hide a grin. "You handled it well."

He leaned in slightly, voice low—just for me. "You're the only one who could ever get away with something like that."

I blinked, unsure if I'd heard him right. "I'd never ask," I said, almost whispering.

"I know." His gaze softened, gray eyes smoldering. "That's one of the many reasons I love you."

The world stuttered to a halt.

Neither of us moved. Neither of us breathed.

He glanced down at the desk—a beat too long.

Then, so gently it almost hurt, he reached for my notebook like nothing had happened. "Now," he said, voice a shade unsteady, "show me where you're stuck."

～

My phone buzzed and clattered on the kitchen table.

Aunt Suzy…

I sighed. I couldn't dodge her forever, so I might as well get this over with.

"Gabrielle! Sweetheart!" Aunt Suzy's voice burst from the phone like a flood of glitter and frosting. I braced myself with a deep breath.

"Hi, Suzy," I said.

"Oh? I'm *just* Suzy now, am I?"

I ran a hand through my hair and sank back in my chair. "Sorry. Hi, Aunt Suzy."

"Well, don't keep me in suspense. How did midterms go?"

"They were fine," I said, trying to sound more relieved than exhausted. "I'm just glad they're over."

"Well, tell me everything," she chirped. "How do you think you did? I'm sure you aced them."

A knock on the door made me jump. I bit my lip, torn between relief and panic, and crossed the room.

"One sec," I said, opening the door.

Cal stood there, backlit by the soft afternoon light. His jeans were worn just right, black turtleneck stretched comfortably across his chest. A leather jacket hung open over it, his motorcycle helmet tucked under one arm.

I swooned internally, glancing over my shoulder. "You're early," I mouthed, signaling him to stay quiet.

He grinned, a silent question in his eyes. I motioned him in, finger to my lips. He nodded, catching on, and slipped in quietly.

"Are you still there?" Aunt Suzy asked.

"Yeah, sorry," I said, watching Cal slip off his jacket. "What were you saying?"

"How do you think you did on your midterms?"

"Calculus and French were As," I said, trying to focus on the call and not the way he looked so completely at home in my apartment. He draped his jacket over the back of a chair.

My pulse quickened, and I risked a glance at Cal. "But the other grades haven't posted yet."

He raised an eyebrow, more amused than surprised. Heat crept into my cheeks, and I knew he noticed. He leaned against the wall, arms crossed, watching me with a look that was equal parts interest and mischief.

"I'm sure you did just fine." I could hear the smile in Aunt Suzy's voice. "Especially since you have that 'special friend' to study with. How's that going, by the way?"

Her question landed with the subtlety of a grenade.

"It's going," I said, aiming for nonchalance. I turned slightly, hoping to hide the way my face had gone embarrassingly hot.

"And when do I get to meet him?"

I shifted the phone to my other ear, avoiding Cal's eyes. "I'm not sure yet. We'll see."

"I don't see what the big deal is. You could bring him to Houston over spring break."

"Yeah, but you'll be teaching. Shame our breaks didn't line up this year," I said, pressing my lips together as Cal stepped closer and wrapped his arms around my waist.

Her voice softened, coaxing. "Then when are you coming down? I haven't seen you since Christmas."

"I don't know," I said, distracted as Cal slipped his fingers beneath the hem of my shirt. "I'll figure something out."

"What are your plans for the week?"

I tried to focus as he traced his hands along my waist. "Nothing exciting. Reading. Spring cleaning. Hopefully some time at the airfield."

"And some time with your 'friend?'" Her tone sliced through the line.

I hesitated, and Cal's breath warmed my neck as he nuzzled closer. "Yes," I said finally.

"Are you spending the whole week with him?"

I bit my lip. "Probably most of it..."

"Gabrielle, this is getting serious."

"Maybe…"

"I'd like to meet him before you rush off and get married," she said, half-exasperated, half-amused.

I choked on my words, coughing so hard I nearly dropped the phone. Cal pulled back, brows furrowed. I waved him off. "Let's not get ahead of ourselves," I managed. Silence buzzed on the line. "Well, if that's everything," I said quickly, "I'll let you—"

"Wait!" Aunt Suzy cut in. "Before you go, I have news!"

"News?"

She lowered her voice. "Remember my colleague who was put on administrative leave for 'allegedly' sleeping with a student? They didn't say it, of course, but we all knew."

I froze. "The one you took over a class for," I said, hoping my voice didn't crack.

"Well," Suzy said, voice rising, "he was found guilty and fired. Good riddance."

The air punched out of my lungs.

"Gabrielle?"

"Yeah. That's…good news, I guess."

"Of course it's good news," she replied, oblivious to the tension in my voice. "But it means I'm teaching a second course this summer."

"You can handle it," I said, forcing brightness into my voice. "Hey, I've got to go. Talk later?"

"Sure thing! Have fun this week, but be safe. Protection and all that—"

"Goodbye, Aunt Suzy," I cut her off, heat prickling at the back of my neck.

"Love you, bye!" she chirped.

I hung up and flopped back on the couch with an exasperated sigh.

But the sigh caught in my chest. Cal was still here. The

week was still ours. I wasn't going to let someone else's scandal steal it from us.

Cal crouched in front of the sofa, bracing his forearms lightly on my knees so I couldn't look anywhere but at him.

"What was that last bit about?" he asked, voice low and even. "You went stiff."

I forced a smile, but it cracked. "It's nothing."

He brushed his thumb along the outside of my knee—barely there, like a touch meant more to soothe than to persuade. "Gabrielle," he said quietly. "Talk to me."

I swallowed, my throat dry. "It just caught me off guard. She was talking about her colleague—a professor who…crossed a line with a student. And got caught." For a split second, I saw Cal in that story—career in ashes because of me. The fear hit sharp, and I shoved it down hard before it could take root.

His expression didn't change, but I saw the ripple beneath it—something fierce and protective rising fast.

"She doesn't know," I said quickly, like the words could unspool the tension coiling between us. "She has no idea about us. She was venting about work. It just…hit close to home."

I blinked hard, surprised by the sudden sting behind my eyes. Cal exhaled, curling his fingers a little tighter around my knee before relaxing again. He didn't try to kiss me. Didn't crowd me. Just stayed there, steady and warm and waiting for me to come back to him on my own.

"I hate this," he said quietly. "I hate putting you in a position where you have to hide. Where you have to lie for me." His voice wasn't angry—just low and raw, like it cost him something to admit it out loud.

"You're not forcing me to do anything," I said, meeting his eyes. "I know what I'm doing. And I know what we have to do to keep us both out of hot water. You're worth every bit of it and more."

For a moment, neither of us moved. The room breathed around us, heavy and light all at once.

Then, mercifully, Cal eased the tension with a small, lopsided smile. "All right," he said, sitting back on his heels. "Tell me about your midterms. Before I take you away and corrupt you for the rest of the week."

I huffed a laugh, the tightness in my chest starting to ease. "Yours was brutal," I said, pointing an accusatory finger.

He looked wholly unrepentant. "Good. Would've been a disappointment otherwise."

I narrowed my eyes. "You're lucky it's spring break and campus is closed. Otherwise, I might have to report you for academic cruelty."

"Why do you think I schedule my midterm the Friday before spring break?"

I shook my head, but a smile tugged at my lips, smoothing the jagged edges of the previous conversation. I clicked my tongue at him. "Driving your students to the brink and skipping town before they can riot? You're positively evil, Professor Hawthorne."

"Now you're catching on." A smile played on his lips as he stood and reached for my hands. "Speaking of skipping town…"

I let him pull me off the couch and into his arms. "Yes?"

"I booked us a week at The Waverly on Lake Rayburn starting Sunday, if that's not too presumptuous."

I pulled back. "The Waverly? Seriously? How much did that set you back?"

He shook his head. "Doesn't matter. I told you early on I wanted to wine and dine you in splendor. There's not much opportunity up here, so please allow me this."

"Wow. Okay. That sounds amazing."

"Truth be told, I chose it for the seclusion and exclusivity. I want a whole week where we don't have to hide or pretend, constantly glancing over our shoulders. I want a week where it's just us. And I don't care where it is, as long as we get that."

I had no words. But he didn't seem to mind.

"I do need to finish grading tomorrow. But the weather should be lovely if you'd like some flight time whilst I drown in exam papers."

"A week at a luxury resort *and* a few hours in the sky? You spoil me."

"That's the idea." He pressed a tender kiss to my lips. "In the meantime…"

"Yes?"

"Go slip into that stunning brown leather jacket, darling," he murmured in my ear. "And let's take the bike out before we lose the light."

CHAPTER 29

CALLUM

The sky burned low over Lake Rayburn, streaked in rippled gold and bruised purple. I tightened my grip on Gabrielle's hand as we wandered the winding path back to the main resort.

The days here had melted into something feverish and unreal—an endless rush of bare skin, tangled sheets, and empty wine bottles scattered across the floor. We devoured each other in the dark, in the sunlight, in every stolen moment we could wrest from the clock. There were nights I didn't know where I ended and she began—nights I would've sworn I could taste her name on my tongue like it was stitched into my blood.

We laughed until our bodies ached. We kissed until the rest of the world slipped off the edge of the map.

I couldn't remember the last time I'd felt so recklessly alive.

Or so terrifyingly at peace.

Gabrielle swung our joined hands between us, humming softly, carefree and sweet. Her golden hair tumbled wild in the lake breeze, her cheeks pink from the chill. She looked so devastatingly free, it punched the breath out of my lungs.

I wanted to stay here forever.

God help me, I never wanted to let this reverie go.

"Penny for your thoughts." Her honeyed voice brought me back.

"I'm afraid they're not worth that much."

"There you go putting yourself down again." She nudged me with her hip.

I smiled, but the weight of what I wanted—everything I hadn't said yet—coiled in my chest, pulling tighter with every step.

The wind kicked up, tossing her hair across her face. She laughed, tucking it behind her ear, and for a moment, I just stood there—admiring this brilliant, maddening, beautiful woman who had somehow become my gravity.

I squeezed her hand. "When's your lease up?"

She shot me a sideways look, sharp and knowing. "End of July. Why?"

I shrugged, aiming for nonchalance, but my voice gave me away—too steady, too deliberate. "Just thinking ahead."

She slowed, pulling us both to a stop beneath a stretch of trees heavy with budding spring leaves. "Thinking about what exactly?" she asked, the teasing edge in her voice soft, careful.

I turned to face her fully. The dying light framed her like something I wasn't meant to touch but had somehow been allowed to hold anyway. "Thinking I'm tired of dropping you off at night," I said quietly. "Of texting you goodnight rather than kissing you. Of waking up and realizing you're not there. Of pretending I'm content with fragments when what I really want is…all of you. Every day."

Her lips parted as if she might speak, but no sound followed. The air between us thickened, charged with everything we hadn't dared say yet. Not properly anyway.

I brushed my thumb along the back of her hand. "I want you to come home to me, Gabrielle. Not just sometimes. Always."

Her eyes shone in the fading light, and for one breathless second, I wondered if I'd pushed too far. Moved too fast.

Then she stepped closer to me, her free hand resting flat against my chest. "You have me," she said simply. "You already do."

The silence was charged. "I sense a 'but' coming."

She sank onto a bench beside the path. "But…how would that work? We already have to be so careful to keep this under wraps. Living together? That's asking for trouble. There's no way we could keep it secret. And then you'll lose your job."

I sat beside her, our knees brushing. Close enough to feel the tremble in her body, the war between wanting and fearing.

"I know," I said quietly. "I've thought about that too."

She looked at me, searching my face, waiting for the rest.

I let out a long, steady breath. "I've been looking for jobs." I turned my hand, offering it if she wanted to take it. "At other universities. So you and I can live however the hell we like without worrying about scandal or fallout."

Her fingers curled into mine like a tether.

"I wasn't going to tell you yet," I admitted. "Not until I found something concrete. But after this week here, with you —I can't pretend the status quo is good enough."

Her gaze was steady, but I felt uncertainty fraying its edges. "Where would you go?" she asked. "You've worked so hard at Page. You're up for tenure soon."

I shook my head. "It's not such a big deal."

She bit her lip, unconvinced.

"There are a few promising positions," I continued. "One in Dallas. One in Fort Worth. Either would keep me fairly close." She tightened her grip, and I knew she understood what I meant. "I came to Page to disappear for a while. And I do like it, but if I'm serious about advancing in my field, I should be at a larger institution."

Gabrielle stared down at our hands, a furrow creasing her

brow. "I've been looking into transferring too," she said, her voice nearly lost in the wind.

I tipped her chin up to meet her eyes. "You came to Page as a legacy student. I thought being there mattered to you."

"The *idea* of it mattered." She exhaled a breath that carried more than just air. "And I like it too. But I think I was trying to live up to my dad." Her words were quiet but firm. "But Dad would want me to do what makes me happy, not walk his path out of duty." Her voice steadied, like she'd finally started believing herself. "Besides, it's really hard being at a place where I'm so much older than everyone else. It's brutal trying to make friends with people who can't even drink yet—legally anyway—and think Greek life is the end-all be-all of everything that's important." She looked at me, a wry smile tugging at her lips. "I'm not sure how many more Sloane Cartwrights I can handle."

I laughed, and the sound felt like relief. "Hate to break it to you, but Sloane Cartwrights are everywhere. On both sides of the Atlantic."

"Great," she muttered, rolling her eyes. "I'll make sure we keep the wine stocked."

Dusk had fully fallen. The air was crisp against my skin, but beneath it, something certain simmered in my bones. The way her eyes locked on mine. The way she leaned into me, like she was ready to fall and only needed to know I'd catch her. I would. A thousand times over.

She laughed softly, out of nowhere.

"What is it?"

She dipped her head, smiling before looking back up at me. "Last week during office hours, you went over the high points of Faraday's Law with me. Do you remember?"

"Of course." *Why the hell was she thinking about exam material now?*

"This"—she squeezed my hand—"is Faraday's Law."

I blinked. "You'll have to explain that one to me."

She tilted her head, that slow, devastating smile pulling at her lips. "You said movement creates change," she murmured. "That if nothing moves, nothing changes. But if you move a wire through a magnetic field—or move the field itself—you generate something new. Electricity. Power."

I stared at her, her words slamming into me before my mind could catch up.

She drew closer, our joined hands locked between us. "That's what this is, Cal. Us. I was fine just sitting still. Safe. Predictable. But then you walked into my world—" Her voice cracked, fierce and beautiful. "And everything shifted. You moved me. And there's no going back."

I couldn't breathe.

Gabrielle smiled—all nerves, defiance, and heart. "You changed the field. You changed me. And I wouldn't want it any other way."

I didn't even realize I was moving until I had her pulled into my arms and crushed against me, her heartbeat pounding frantically against mine. I buried my face in her hair, inhaling the salt and sun and sweetness of her.

"God, Gabrielle," I whispered, my voice wrecked. "You have no idea what you've just done to me."

She tipped her head back, smiling up at me, unguarded and radiant. "Oh, I think I do."

I kissed her then—slow, deep, reverent—the way you kiss the only person who's ever tilted your world and made it stay that way.

When we finally broke apart, she rested her forehead against mine, soft and steady, like she was anchoring me to the earth.

"I love you," I rasped. I knew it for certain—had known it for ages. And at last, I gave the words to her. Deliberately. Too big to cage, too true to ever hold back.

She shuddered slightly in my arms—a quiet, gorgeous tremor that shattered what was left of my composure. "I love you too," she whispered, fierce and sure, like it had been waiting just beneath her skin, waiting for the right moment to break free.

I held her like a drowning man clutching air—only to realize she wasn't just the air.

She was the whole reason I was breathing at all.

And I would never, ever let her go.

CHAPTER 30

GABRIELLE

Finals week was brutal, but it had its perks—chief among them, Cal taking over the cooking and dishes so I could study. He stood at my sink, sleeves pushed to his elbows, water sluicing over the dinner plates. His black collared shirt clung to the lean lines of his body. His coffee-colored hair was slightly mussed, that one rebellious lock falling across his forehead as he worked. A kitchen towel hung loosely over his shoulder, and he looked so utterly at home that my heart ached.

I sat cross-legged on my living room floor, calculus book open and notes strewn around me like leaves. The numbers and symbols blurred together, tangled and stubborn, refusing to resolve into anything meaningful. My gaze kept drifting back to him—caught in the tempo of his movements, in the way he belonged so completely in this space. With me.

He glanced up, catching me in the act. "Back to work, love," he called, a teasing lilt in his voice. "That calculus exam won't pass itself."

I groaned theatrically and let my head fall onto the coffee table with a soft thud. "It should," I mumbled into the wood, though I couldn't help the smile tugging at my lips.

He laughed, low and warm, and the sound wrapped around me, softening the edges of my frustration. "You'll do brilliantly," he said, rinsing the last plate and setting it in the rack with a satisfied clink.

I lifted my head, propping my chin in my hands. "How's your workload?" I asked, watching as he wiped his hands on the towel and slung it over the faucet.

"Rather light, actually." He moved to the couch, his presence filling the room with a quiet, electric ease. "Other than marking exams, I'm essentially done for the term."

I tracked his movements as he settled beside me, the cushions dipping under his weight. He pulled a thick folder from his soft-sided briefcase and tapped it with a red pen. "You study," he instructed, a mischievous glint in his eyes. "I'll grade quantum physics finals."

We worked in companionable silence, the room filled with the rustle of paper, the scratch of his pen, the soft brush of pencil against my notes. Every so often, I'd sneak a glance at him—the way his brow furrowed in concentration, the deft movements of his hands as he marked each exam.

Time slipped by, measured only by the soft ticking of the clock and the growing stack of graded papers beside him. There was a strange comfort in knowing he was there, just an arm's length away, sharing this small piece of life with me.

At last, I got tired of the numbers refusing to arrange themselves into anything comprehensible. I snapped the calculus book shut and leaned back against the cushions with a sigh.

He looked up, a playful arch to his brow. "Finished?"

"If it's not in my brain by now," I said, stretching my arms overhead, "it never will be."

His eyes lingered on me, a tender warmth there that made my chest tighten.

I popped to my feet and rummaged through my purse.

"Before I forget…" I pulled out my wallet. "I need to give you your credit card back."

He shook his head as he stood, a sly smile tugging at the corner of his mouth. "Absolutely not. Hang on to it, in case anything else comes up."

I hesitated, heat rising in my cheeks. "Are you sure? I… might have gotten a bit carried away."

"Positive." He slipped the card back into my wallet with easy authority, his fingers brushing mine. "Did you get everything you needed for the trip?"

I wrinkled my nose. "Come see."

I led him into the bedroom, where two half-packed suitcases spilled onto the floor with the aftermath of a shopping spree. New clothes hung in my closet, tags still dangling from their sleeves.

His eyes widened slightly as he surveyed the scene. "Did Isabel help you figure out what to buy?" he asked, his tone apologetic. "I know I'm useless when it comes to that sort of thing."

"She was great," I said, though guilt prickled beneath my words. "I hate bombarding her with questions while she's knee-deep in wedding chaos."

Cal plucked a deep violet cocktail dress from the closet, its satin shimmering under the light. "I really like this one." He turned to me, a wicked gleam in his eye. "I can't wait to see you in it," he said, his voice low and teasing. "Then take it off of you."

I swatted him lightly on the arm, but a shiver of anticipation curled through me. He caught my wrist, pulling me into him with a swift, playful motion.

"Do we really have to dress up for dinner every night?" I asked, dread creeping into my voice. "I thought Isabel was joking."

He laughed, a rich, unguarded sound. "It's not bloody

Downton Abbey, but yes. The family is…" He paused, searching for the right word. "Traditional."

I groaned, burying my face in his chest. "I don't know how I'm going to get all this into two suitcases."

"Then take a third." He rested his chin on the top of my head, the motion tender and reassuring. "Pack what you can, and don't stress. I suspect Isabel will have a few things waiting for you there."

I pulled back slightly, looking up at him. "You're joking."

"She likes you." He kissed my forehead. "And she's thrilled I'm finally bringing someone home. Between you and me, she doesn't much care for my brother's wife, Caroline. But if you repeat that, I'll deny it."

I ducked away with a half-smile and returned the dress to the closet—anything to keep my hands busy. "I just don't want to epically screw up in front of your family. I already feel like an impostor."

"You won't, and you're not," he said, gentler now. "You're exactly who I want them to meet. Who I want them to know."

I turned toward him, heart soft and sore and full. But before I could speak, he wandered a few steps across the room, attention drifting. His gaze landed on my desk, where my laptop sat closed and two letters lay stacked beside it—cream stationery, embossed university seals at the top. One from Southern Methodist University, the other from the University of Texas at Dallas. I hadn't realized I'd left them there.

He picked them up and scanned the text. "When were you planning to tell me?"

I blinked. "Tell you what?"

He held up the letters like they spoke for themselves. "Accepted to the engineering programs at both SMU and UTD? Gabrielle!" He looked at me, eyes bright and disbelieving. "This is incredible. Why didn't you say anything?"

A flush crept up my neck. "I figured I'd tell you when I decided what to do. I have until July first to commit."

He shook his head, caught between pride and exasperation. "And you weren't even going to mention it?"

"I didn't want to make a big deal." The words tumbled out too fast. "They're both excellent, but I'm not sure which to choose."

"What's holding you back?"

I hesitated. "UTD is great, and I could swing it without taking on debt. But SMU..." I shifted. "It's so expensive. I qualified for a scholarship, but it's still going to be a lot."

He set the letters down on the desk. "Don't worry about that."

I pulled a face. "You can't just say that like it's nothing."

"It's not." He stepped toward me, slow and deliberate. "Where do you want to go?" His voice was calm and steady, like the answer was all that mattered.

The quiet thickened. He held my gaze, waiting, and I felt the truth rise in me, unshakable. "I want to go to SMU," I said at last. "I do. But I can't let you—"

"You can," he interrupted, already knowing. "And you should. I want to do this for you."

I shook my head, letting out a small, incredulous laugh. "Fixing my car or beefing up my wardrobe is one thing," I said, knotting my fingers. "Subsidizing college is another."

"It's an investment," he said, reaching for my hands. "And one I'm more than willing to make."

I felt the familiar pull of him—like gravity—the way he made everything seem possible and within reach. Still, I held my ground, my stubborn streak refusing to let him carry this too. "We'll talk about it later." I kissed his cheek. "Because it won't make a lick of difference if I don't make it through my last two finals."

"Calculus and..."

I nudged him, a playful challenge in my smile. "Don't ask questions you already know the answer to."

"Ah, physics…" He trailed his fingers up my spine, slow and deliberate. "Then let me help you…"

"You mean distract me?"

He slid a hand between my legs, claiming my breath in one swift motion. "I prefer to think of it as…relaxing you."

His touch pressed warm and insistent through the soft fabric of my leggings. I tipped my head back, a faint shiver running through me as he brushed his lips along my neck, lingering and tender.

"Cal," I breathed, a halfhearted protest that melted into a sigh.

He shifted his weight, coaxing us both toward the bed. "Yes?" he asked, the word a drawn-out rumble against my skin. He slipped warm fingers beneath my waistband, his touch electric. I drew in a sharp breath, dizzy with want but still clinging to some thread of responsibility.

"I really do need to study," I murmured, the protest faint and feeble.

He let out a low, wicked laugh that sent a jolt of heat straight through me. In one breath-stealing motion, he tossed me onto the bed, his body quick and sure above mine.

"Ask me anything," he whispered, peeling my leggings and panties away in a slow, deliberate tangle.

His touch was teasing and relentless, until I could barely remember why I was supposed to resist. "I don't want to take advantage," I said, the words tumbling out, uneven.

He stilled, a sly grin curving his mouth. "You've never asked for help in my course outside of class or office hours," he said, fingers grazing across my skin, unraveling my defenses. "Not once."

I bit back a gasp as he thumbed my clit. My body yielded to his touch, aching. "I'm trying to keep…separation of church and state," I managed, my voice catching.

He teased me with his fingertips, deliberate and devastating. "We fucked in a chapel, Gabrielle." His breath scorched my neck, his touch dizzying. "That act alone obliterated the line."

I shuddered—a sharp, exquisite wave—as his fingers finally slipped inside me. "Underneath the chapel," I corrected, the words almost lost in a rush.

"Still sinful." He pumped his fingers, drawing a ragged sound from deep within me. "You're only my student for two more days." He nudged my thighs apart, settling between my knees, his breath hot and demanding against my skin. "And you've followed all the rules." His tongue flicked against me, quick and devastating. "Be a bad girl now and break those rules for me."

I moaned low, drawn out.

He looked up, gray eyes molten and urgent. "Consider this office hours," he said, his voice dark and coaxing. "House call edition." He paused, teasing. "What do you still need help with, Miss Clark?"

I shivered, head spinning, fingers clutching the sheets. "Waves," I gasped, the word catching on a breath. "I get how frequency and amplitude work. Technically. But…"

"But?" he prompted, that smirk tugging at the corners of his mouth.

"But why does higher frequency feel…stronger?" I breathed. "If the amplitude's the same, shouldn't it all feel the same?"

He stilled, a wicked smile playing at his lips—hot and unholy. "Funny you should ask." He slid off the bed. "Where do you keep your vibrator?"

I blinked at him, dazed. "My…what?"

"Every woman has one," he said, amused. "Or so I'm told. Where's yours?"

Heat flushed through me. "Second drawer of my nightstand." The words were a reckless, breathless confession.

He moved to the drawer, retrieved the vibrator, and held it loosely in his hand—off, but somehow humming with promise. He returned to the edge of the bed, his gaze sharp, scientific, and entirely indecent.

"Frequency is measured in…?" he asked, dragging the smooth curve of the toy along my inner thigh. Not enough pressure to satisfy. Just enough to make my skin chase it.

"Hertz," I whispered, my voice barely there.

"Good girl." His mouth curled. "And another way of saying Hertz?" He teased the vibrator against my clit.

My breath hitched. "Pulses…per second."

He nodded, pleased. "Exactly."

He clicked it on at the lowest setting. The vibration hummed through me. I gasped and arched beneath him.

"This lovely little device is delivering energy to your nervous system at…" He paused, voice dark and wicked. "Let's call it fifty pulses per second. Fifty Hertz."

He moved the vibrator in slow, tantalizing circles. I whimpered, my body tightening with the effort of staying still.

"Now," he said, coaxing me, "assuming amplitude stays the same…but I increase the frequency to…" He turned the dial. "One hundred pulses per second. Are the pulses any stronger?"

The new intensity crashed through me, and I struggled to find my voice. "No," I gasped, the word nearly lost on a breath.

The vibrations were relentless and consuming as he asked, "Then what have I done to the amount of energy delivered to your…stimulated nervous system over time?"

I shuddered, my whole body taut and trembling. "Doubled it," I moaned.

His laugh was unrestrained, full of delight and mischief, and it sent another wave of heat through me.

"Precisely." He turned the dial as high as it would go. The vibrator whined, and the surge of sensation lit up every nerve ending I had. Too much. Almost unbearable. But I couldn't pull away.

He pinned my hips down with his forearm, the force of it exquisite, and the vibration seared through me, fast as lightning. He watched as I writhed, as my body strained against his hold, desperate for more but too overwhelmed to take it.

"With all this energy I'm sending through you," he said, teasing and sure, "there's only so much these sensitive nerves can take until they…overload."

The words barely registered before the world shattered white. My muscles clenched around the sensation, my voice breaking into a cry.

I came back to myself slowly, breathless and undone. The duvet was bunched beneath me, and my skin pulsed with aftershocks. Cal shut off the vibrator and eased it away, his eyes never leaving mine.

"In biosexual terms," he said, his mouth curving into that wicked grin, "that 'overload' is called an orgasm."

I let out a shaky, incredulous laugh, the sound raw and unconfined.

"That was your best lecture yet," I managed, my breath still catching.

He pulled me up, wrapping me in his arms, the motion tender and possessive. "I know," he said, cocky, unrepentant.

I tipped my chin up, lips grazing his ear. "Five stars, Professor," I whispered, letting the title drip like sin between us.

He went still for half a heartbeat—just long enough for me to feel the shift—then let out a low, dark groan and gripped my hips.

"Say that again," he growled, voice thick with hunger, "and I won't stop until you forget your own name."

I leaned in, lips brushing his jaw. "Thank you for the lesson, Dr. Hawthorne."

He let out a low, guttural sound and buried his face in my neck, tension rolling through him like thunder. "Christ, just get me through the next two days," he breathed. "Freedom is so close I can taste it."

I didn't answer. I just kissed him like I could bend time.

Chapter 31

Callum

S pring term was done, but the ghosts of it still lingered —scattered papers, red pens, the sterile scent of the physics lab clinging to my skin. I sat in my office where the overhead fluorescents buzzed faintly. Absently, I reached for the coffee cup on my desk as I reviewed the next row of grades. The first sip caught me off guard—bitter, thin, and tepid. I grimaced but swallowed it anyway. It was the standard office blend: weak, industrial, and barely drinkable. A far cry from what I brewed at home. But I needed something—anything—to push through the end-of-term tedium. A stimulant and a distraction. Both were in short supply as I entered the last of my grades.

Two screens flanked me like sentries—one with my online grade book, the other with the university's portal. I worked methodically, the names blurring into numbers, into decimals, into letters. A few more entries, and I'd be free. Free of this place. Free to take Gabrielle to England, where there would be no secrets and no pretense, only the truth of us, laid bare in the long shadow of my family's approval.

I reached her name.

    Clark, Gabrielle Suzanne

My fingers hovered over the keyboard, a slight tremor in them as I paused, savoring this last act. She had scored a 94 on the final exam, well above the class average of 85. Her overall grade was a 95.7. I let the numbers settle in, let the pride unfurl in me like a slow bloom. She'd done an exemplary job, and in one decisive motion, I entered an A for her final mark.

Sitting back, I allowed myself a moment to bask in the quiet triumph of it, a smile tugging at the edges of my mouth. "Well done, love," I said softly to the empty room. She had earned every bit of it on her own—no favors, boosts, or advantages. Merely her determination. Her brilliance.

A sharp chime from my laptop fractured the quiet, and the name flashing on the incoming video call sent an icy spike through me: Father. Unscheduled, though hardly a surprise.

I stood—briskly enough to send my office chair skidding with a muted scrape against the linoleum—and crossed to shut the door. The old handle stuck slightly before clicking into place. I turned the lock. Then I slipped on my headphones—a preemptive shield against the hallway beyond —and perhaps against what I was about to hear. I drew a full breath and accepted the call.

His face filled the screen—those familiar lines and angles sharpened by distance and disapproval. Crisp shirt. Immaculate tie. Silver hair. Eyes like twin blades.

"Father," I said, clipped and cool.

"Callum."

The use of my full name grated like a dull saw. "To what do I owe the pleasure?"

His eyes flicked over me, thoughts no doubt forming, crisp and predictable as a ledger. "You look...comfortable," he said, dry as a bone.

I glanced down, noting the loosened tie, the rolled-up sleeves, the too-casual state of everything. "Yes, well," I said evenly, meeting his gaze. "I find it rather liberating."

He sniffed, displeasure crackling across the Atlantic. "You're still arriving Monday?"

"We are," I said, tight and measured.

He pressed his lips into a line. "And you're still bringing your…guest?"

The pause stung like a nettle, but I schooled my features, refusing him the satisfaction of a reaction. "I am."

The leather of his chair creaked like an old joint as he shifted. "And she…knows what to expect?"

"What should she expect, Father? Other than the *warm* reception of my family?"

"Come now, Callum."

I raised an eyebrow. "We're being candid, then?"

His expression barely shifted, eyes sharp and narrow. "Only as much as the situation requires." He folded his hands, cuffs perfectly aligned. "You'll be bringing…Miss Clark, correct?"

"That's right."

"There's not much we know about her."

I paused, just long enough to let the implication settle. "Don't insult us both by pretending you haven't already looked up everything there is to know."

A flicker passed over his face—disapproval, perhaps, or irritation. Likely both. Hard to tell with him.

"She's considerably younger."

"So was Mother, if I recall."

He ignored that. "Is she aware of what's expected?"

"She knows she's meeting my family. That's all she needs to know."

Father gave a slow, precise nod. "Well. I hope she knows how to conduct herself."

"She does," I said. "And she doesn't rattle easily."

We stared at each other for a long, unblinking beat—his face impassive, mine immovable—until he gave a single nod. "Monday, then."

"Monday."

The screen went black.

I exhaled, slow and controlled, and let the silence close in around me like armor. Then I reached for the stone-cold coffee again—and drank it down like penance.

CHAPTER 32

GABRIELLE

The stone steps were warm beneath me, baked smooth by the May sun filtering through the ancient oak overhead. From here, I had a clear view of the green, where rows of guests sat in white folding chairs. The ceremony moved steadily, graduate by graduate. They were in the S-names now—only a handful of students left to cross the stage.

I wasn't technically supposed to be here. I wasn't graduating. I wasn't family. And I wasn't seated in the guest section. But no one had stopped me when I'd wandered over here alone, tucked into the shadow of the stone steps leading to the old science building. And if they had, I'd have found a reason. Because Cal was out there, seated on the aisle in full academic regalia. Hood, gown, tam. Regal, unreadable, breathtaking.

And entirely out of reach.

My heart pinched as another graduate paused for a handshake and a photo. I twisted my fingers in my lap. All I wanted—really wanted—was to be beside him. Not hiding. Not stealing glances from behind a tree or scraping excuses to exist on the edges of his world.

But we were leaving for England tomorrow. And there, for the first time, he wouldn't be keeping me a secret. The thought was equal parts exhilarating and terrifying—like jumping off the high dive without knowing how deep the water was.

My phone buzzed in my lap.

Aunt Suzy.

I grimaced. Worst possible timing. Still, I swiped to answer and lifted the phone. "Hey," I said, soft and cautious. Before I could get another word out—

"What do you mean you're going to England?" Aunt Suzy shrilled.

"Hang on," I said, grabbing my purse and popping to my feet. I hurried down the length of Melvin Hall. "Let me get somewhere I can talk."

"Where are you now? You haven't already left, have you?" Her voice was screechy and strained.

I slipped around the side of the building, out of sight of the ceremony—and any watchful eyes. A gust of wind tugged at the hem of my dress as I tucked behind the limestone corner and braced for impact.

"I'm at commencement," I answered. "But I stepped away."

"Why are you at commencement?"

"A friend is walking," I answered. Not technically a lie… "But I can talk for a minute."

She huffed. "Okay. What's this business about England?"

I took a deep breath. "I thought my email was pretty clear. My…boyfriend…"—another deep breath—"asked me to go with him."

For once in her life, she was silent.

"Are you still there?"

"I'm here. I just don't like it."

I plopped down on a bench outside the library. Sunlight filtered through the trees, casting dappled patterns on the sidewalk that shifted with the breeze. "I'm still going." My tone was quiet but resolute.

"If your father were still alive, he wouldn't stand for you gallivanting around the globe with someone you barely know."

"If my father were still alive," I countered through gritted teeth, "he'd trust my judgment. Trust me to make my own decisions."

"Gabrielle!" she hissed.

I said nothing.

"How are you even affording this?"

"Great deal on airfare," I lied. Well, not technically. Actually, I'd never asked Cal about the airfare. But even if I had, it wouldn't have mattered. He'd have told me not to worry, that it was already taken care of. "And we're staying with his relatives, so no lodging cost."

"Gabrielle, I've never even met this boy."

"He's a man, not a boy. And I'm not a child either."

"I know, I know. But it's still my job to look after you. I promised my brother—your dad—that I'd make sure you were taken care of."

"And I appreciate you, Aunt Suzy. I do. But I'm fine." A beat. "And I'm going to England with him."

"Can I at least know his full name?"

"Cal—" I hesitated, blood thudding in my ears. My gaze darted around until it landed on the carved name above the library entrance. "Calvin Green." The lie hit the air, and my stomach clenched. To her, that name was real now—anchored, permanent. I'd have to remember to ask what Cal was *actually* short for…if I ever planned to tell her the truth.

"Calvin Green," she repeated, testing the name on her tongue. "Okay." She went quiet for a beat. When she spoke again, her tone was subdued. "And you leave tomorrow?"

"Yes. We'll be gone two weeks."

Her controlled exhale whispered through the line. "All

right," she said at last, resigned. "Have a great time, and be safe."

"I will." Cheers erupted in the distance. The ceremony must have been drawing to a close. "Hey, I've got to get back. I'll talk to you later."

"Message me when you land. I don't care what time it is. I love you."

"I love you too."

I ended the call and made my way back to my sentry post on the stone steps of Melvin Hall. I loved these steps. I used to play on them as a kid, back when my dad brought me along to alumni events.

Final cheers erupted, echoing off the buildings around the green as the ceremony ended. Caps flew like startled birds against the blue sky as music swelled from the loudspeakers. I strained for a glimpse of Cal among the robed faculty, but from my vantage point on the outskirts, the once-orderly procession had already dissolved into a jubilant chaos. Families surged forward, hugging and snapping photos while graduates shed their gowns, the air alive with laughter and celebration. The weather couldn't have been more perfect— sunny and warm. A soft breeze tugged at the leaves above me, the scent of freshly cut grass sweet and sharp on the wind.

I scanned the crowd and finally spotted Cal walking alongside Dr. Watkins, chatting amiably as they headed toward the science building. Cal's scarlet Oxford robe billowed behind him like a banner, the deep blue hood vivid against it. His velvet tam sat slightly askew atop his dark hair—careless, rakish, unfairly elegant.

My stomach flipped when he cast me a sideways glance. Even from a distance, he seemed to fill the entire landscape. I'd seen that robe hanging on the back of his office door before, but never like this—never on him. Pride swelled inside me, fierce and uncontainable.

God, he looked good.

I ducked my head, scrolling aimlessly through my phone as I stole another glance at him. He was drawing closer, robes flowing with each long stride, his pinstriped slacks peeking out from underneath.

As they neared the steps, Dr. Watkins spotted me, his face lighting with recognition. "Gabrielle!" he said, pausing with a wide grin. "I thought that was you. Congrats on finishing the year. How'd you do?"

I slipped my phone into my purse and stood, smoothing my dress. "Thanks, Dr. Watkins. It was a tough semester, but I pulled all As by some miracle."

"So I hear," he said, eyes twinkling as he glanced at Cal. "Dr. Hawthorne says you were one of his best. This man doesn't hand out praise easily, you know."

Cal kept his expression carefully neutral, though I caught the faintest tug at the corner of his mouth. "I do when it's earned," he said, holding my gaze for a second too long. The way he said it—quiet, deliberate—sent a shiver low in my spine. "And she certainly earned it."

Dr. Watkins chuckled, but his eyes flicked between us. One eyebrow ticked—barely perceptible. If he noticed the undercurrent, he didn't say so. Still, I had the distinct feeling he'd logged something away for later. He turned back to me, sincere again. "Well done, Gabrielle. We're all very proud."

"Thanks," I said, heat creeping up my neck. The breeze played with the hem of my dress.

"Will I see you in my Modern Physics class next fall?" he asked, smiling over his sunglasses. "Fair warning, we hit Einstein by week two."

Before I could come up with an answer that wasn't a lie— but didn't reveal that I was planning to transfer—Cal nudged him with an elbow. "Don't frighten her off. Let her enjoy the break before you start unloading the syllabus."

"Fair enough," Dr. Watkins said with a laugh. "But if you're around this summer, stop by. We just got a brand-spanking new piece of equipment for a project Dr. Hawthorne and I are working on."

I glanced at Cal, then back at Dr. Watkins. "What sort of equipment?"

His eyes lit up. "A femtosecond laser system for ultrafast spectroscopy."

I blinked. "Sounds intense, but all I got out of that was 'laser.'"

"It can basically 'freeze time' at the quantum level," he explained, his voice animated. "Perfect for studying how particles respond to electromagnetic fields or testing quantum field theory predictions."

Cal's mouth tipped into a sly grin. "You spend a million dollars to watch the universe blink."

Dr. Watkins laughed. "Theoretical physicists," he said with a wink. "No appreciation for the experimental wonders of the world."

I laughed, bright and unrestrained. "And they say science is boring."

He chuckled, his face flushed with enthusiasm. "You're always welcome in the lab, Gabrielle. Anytime."

I smiled, grateful and guilty all at once. If he'd known I was considering a transfer—no, planning on one—I doubted he'd be quite so eager.

Cal must have sensed my hesitation. "The equipment will still be there in the fall." He clapped Dr. Watkins on the shoulder. "Come on, let's get these blasted robes hung up. I'm boiling."

Cal started up the steps, then paused. He glanced back, eyes cutting through the shade like a flash of silver. A half-smile pulled at his mouth—just enough to register, gone just as fast.

"Enjoy your summer break, Miss Clark." Even and polished. Nothing out of place.

I dipped my chin. "You too, Dr. Hawthorne."

A flicker lit in his eyes. Nothing overt—just a spark caught and banked. He nodded once, turned, and disappeared inside, scarlet robes whispering behind him.

CHAPTER 33

CALLUM

The first-class cabin was calm by design—soft lighting, carpeted silence, and the curated hush of affluence. No announcements. No scramble for overhead compartments. Just the low murmur of conversation, a glass clink here and there, and the slow parade of the rest of the aircraft hidden behind the curtain.

A flight attendant with a sleek blonde chignon appeared at my side, her smile polished and professional. "May I take your jacket?" she asked, her English accent crisply enunciated. One step closer to home.

"Yes, thank you." I slipped off my blazer, handed it over, and stowed my carry-on in the overhead locker.

I slid down the central divider between our pods, and there she was—curled into the cocoon of her seat, wide-eyed and luminous. Gabrielle was quietly cataloging the amenities, her expression a mix of disbelief and delight as she gestured to the toiletry kit, pajamas, slippers, comforter, and memory-foam pillow.

"You said we were flying first class," she said, trying for nonchalance and falling short. "You didn't say it'd be like this."

I chuckled as I settled into the soft, indulgent leather. "If we have to fly, darling, we may as well be comfortable."

Gabrielle shook her head with a soft laugh. "You really don't like planes, do you?"

"No, not particularly."

She leaned toward me. "Then why on earth did you let me take you flying when we first met?"

I sighed. "Because you asked." I reached across the divider, took her hand, and pressed a kiss to the inside of her wrist. "I may not have admitted it to myself at the time, but I was desperately trying to impress you."

She blinked, caught off guard, but her hand softened in mine.

Another flight attendant, an impeccably polished brunette, leaned in to offer warm towels and flutes of sparkling white wine. Gabrielle accepted both with a giddy grin she couldn't suppress.

She swirled the wine, watching the bubbles rise. "Bubbles before takeoff…like bubbles before dinner. See? I pay attention."

I lifted an eyebrow. "To what?"

She raised her glass to me. "To you. That first dinner date in Dallas." She took a sip. "And Isabel. And Google. I took copious notes on everything—what to wear, when to wear it, which fork means what…" She trailed off with a quiet sigh. "I just want to do everything right."

I shook my head. "You're worrying too much."

"I don't think I'm worrying enough," she countered. "I don't even know what to call your parents. Mr. and Mrs. Hawthorne?"

I hesitated, then took a drink.

She looked at me, eyebrows raised. "Not that?"

I cleared my throat, eyes on my glass. "Actually…my father is titled."

"I don't know what that means."

"It means that while Hawthorne is our surname, my father is the Baron Branleigh. So, my parents are Lord and Lady Branleigh."

"Baron?" Her voice lifted in disbelief. "Like, actually noble?" She blinked. "Not just posh and judgy?"

I nodded.

"Were you planning to tell me, or did you just forget to mention it?"

"I didn't forget," I said. "I just…didn't think it mattered. Or rather—I didn't want it to."

"So…are you in line for something?"

"Oh, heavens no. That dubious honor falls to my dear brother, James. Better him than me."

"I'm sensing some tension…"

"Just a bit. But that's a story for another day."

She studied me for a moment, lips pressed together. "So what does that make you, exactly? Do I have to call you anything special?"

I leaned across the divider and nipped her ear. "You can call me anything you like."

She swatted me. "I'm serious. I don't want to mess anything up."

"Just Cal."

"What's that short for? I've been meaning to ask…"

I blew out a quick breath. "Callum." I rolled my eyes. "My great-grandfather's name. Ghastly, I know."

"No… Just not what I expected."

"What did you think it was?"

"No idea. I panicked and told my aunt it was Calvin."

I laughed. "*Calvin?*"

She shrugged. "What? I panicked."

The flight attendant returned to collect the towels and glasses before takeoff.

"So…just Cal. Not 'Lord' or 'Sir' or—"

"Just Cal. I technically have a courtesy title, but that only shows up on formal correspondence and place cards."

"And that would be…"

"Technically?" I sighed. "The Honourable Callum Hawthorne."

Gabrielle snorted.

"Yes, go on, get it out of your system."

"Sorry," she said, still grinning. "It's just…"

I rolled my eyes again. "It's absurd, I know."

The overhead chime sounded, followed by the familiar cadence of a flight attendant's voice. "The boarding door is now closed. Please ensure all carry-on items are stowed, and your devices are in airplane mode…"

Soft thuds echoed down the aisle as the overhead compartments clicked shut. The engine hummed beneath us, and my pulse jumped. I tightened my seatbelt—like it would help—then turned back to Gabrielle.

"The only titles I've ever cared about," I said, "I earned myself."

She reached across the divider and brushed her fingers against mine. "Massive respect." Leaning in close with a wicked gleam, she added, "And I do love that look you get when I call you 'Professor.'"

The car hummed beneath us, the soft thrum of tires on damp country roads muffled by layers of luxury insulation. The countryside blurred past in a wash of green hedgerows, moss-covered stone walls, and distant oaks dappled with muted mid-morning sun. The sun had actually come out for my homecoming—miracles did happen. Or perhaps the universe just had a twisted sense of humor.

Gabrielle slept against my shoulder, her breath slow and even. One hand curled in her lap and the other rested against my chest, a featherlight warmth through my jacket. I cradled her, fingertips grazing the ends of her hair where they spilled over her shoulder.

She trusted me. Entirely. Without hesitation.

God help us both.

I let my thumb drift over the crown of her head, slow and careful, as if I could hold on to this quiet moment a little longer. She'd fallen asleep less than half an hour into the drive, lulled by jet lag, the softness of the seat, and the way I'd pulled her close when she leaned into me. She hadn't even fought it. Just exhaled and let go.

I envied her that.

The driver—someone new and unfamiliar—had offered a clipped "Welcome home, sir" at the airport and then had fallen into blessed silence. I hadn't asked his name. He hadn't offered it. Small mercies.

We were a mile out, maybe less. I knew this road—the gentle bend through the woodland, the slow rise before the estate walls came into view. I'd walked it. Driven it. Sprinted down it as a boy, trying to outrun the weight of everything that lurked behind those gates.

Now I was bringing her into it. The legacy. The expectations. The precision-polished façade of a family that had never once accepted anything they couldn't control.

I'd spent years carving out a different life—measured, ordinary, my name just ink on a syllabus in a town where my father's name didn't reach. No titles. No press. No obligations dressed up as tradition. And now I was undoing all of it, one mile at a time.

I'd told myself this was necessary. That she deserved to see it, to know what she was stepping into. But part of me knew better. Part of me had known, the moment she pressed her palm to my chest and said she wasn't afraid, that it was already too late to protect her.

They would be civil, of course. That was the danger.

Civility could cut sharper than cruelty—and in that house, it always did.

And somewhere in the marrow of it all—still—was Claire. Not her presence, exactly. Just the echo of her absence. The way her name was never spoken, the ending of her story rewritten before her body was cold. Not to protect me. To protect themselves.

I could never unsee that. And I could never unring the silence.

And still—here was Gabrielle. My love. Tucked against me like I was safe.

I let my eyes close. Just for a breath.

Then I turned my head, speaking low beside her ear. "Gabrielle." I gently brushed her arm. "We're nearly there."

Chapter 34

Gabrielle

Cal's voice was soft, a gentle breath against my ear. "Gabrielle, we're nearly there."

I blinked awake slowly, disoriented. The car's interior was softly lit, the windows bright with a kind of sunlight I didn't recognize—gentle and diffused, like it had passed through lace before touching the earth. Nothing like Texas. No glare. No weight. Just warmth without burden.

Cal's arm was still around me, warm and steady—but the rest of him had gone rigid. I shifted to look at him. His expression was unreadable, carved from something colder than usual, his gaze locked on the road ahead. The calm he wore so convincingly had gone brittle around the edges.

I straightened, rubbing at my eyes. "How long was I out?"

"About an hour," he said. "You didn't miss much. Fields. Trees. Cows."

His words were light, but not his tone.

I turned to the window, and the world outside took my breath away. It was green—but not the green I knew. Not the bright, sunbaked green of home. This was softer. Deeper. Alive in a way that felt untouched. Hedgerows lined the road like living fences, tight and neat, their edges blurred with dew.

Trees stretched wide and high, their branches dense with leaves and shadow. Fields sloped gently into one another like a patchwork stitched by hand.

It felt older here. Quieter. Like the land had secrets and was in no hurry to tell them.

Then, just beyond the bend, where the narrow road brushed past a thicket of trees, the gates came into view—tall black wrought iron, latticed with delicate scrollwork, their hinges sunk into thick pillars of weathered stone. Ivy climbed up the sides, dark and glossy. A modest crest was carved into the stone—unpainted, easy to miss unless you were looking.

The car slowed, and the driver rolled down his window to tap a code into the stone-faced keypad tucked beside the gate. No fanfare, no delay—just the smooth swing of iron as the gates opened and we passed through.

The air changed. Cooler, cleaner. Even the light shifted—crisper somehow, like the trees had stepped politely back to let the estate come into view.

The drive curved gently. Trees gave way to a manicured lawn—sweeping and precise, edged by formal hedges and cone-shaped topiary. Flower beds bordered the path with disciplined bursts of color. Beneath it all, the crunch of gravel marked our arrival, steady and sharp.

And then—just beyond the final bend—stood the house.

I actually laughed. Quietly. To myself.

It looked like Wayne Manor.

Not the cartoon one—the cinematic version Dad and I used to watch on old *Batman* DVDs. Broad-shouldered and regal, with symmetry that stared you down. The kind of house that didn't just sit on land. It ruled it.

Solid brick, three stories tall, with chimneys rising like sentinels into the sky. Tall windows framed in pale stone lined the façade in perfect rows. Nothing out of place.

This wasn't a house. It was a legacy. A statement.

Cal hadn't said a word.

I glanced over, but his expression hadn't shifted. Eyes locked straight ahead, jaw tight. Whatever this place meant to him, it had already started to close in.

The car crested the final rise and slowed to a stop in front of the house. Or manor. Or whatever this kind of building was technically called. The front door stood beneath a carved stone portico, two columns rising to support an arch weathered by centuries of wind and rain. The wood was dark, the brass hardware gleaming. No welcome mat, no wreath. Just the kind of entrance that made you check your posture without thinking.

The engine stopped. And for a moment, the world outside held still.

The chauffeur stepped out and moved briskly to open Cal's door. He unfolded from the car with that long-limbed ease he always had, adjusted his jacket sleeves, and glanced back inside.

"Come on," he said, offering his hand.

I slid my fingers into his, and he helped me out, steadying me on the gravel. It crunched underfoot—pale and fine, like it had been raked smooth just for us.

"Welcome to Branleigh Park," he said, giving our interlaced fingers a gentle squeeze.

Behind us, movement caught my eye—two men emerging from a side door to collect our luggage. Efficient. Silent. Not a word exchanged.

The front door eased open, and a man in a sharply tailored black waistcoat stepped forward. He wore a crisp white shirt beneath it, the collar set neatly under a slim black jacket with satin-trimmed lapels. A silver watch chain curved between the pockets. His trousers were pressed to a knife's edge, his shoes gleaming. He stood with one hand lightly folded behind his back, the other resting at his side.

He was older—sixty, maybe more—but moved with precision, like every step and breath had been rehearsed until the man and the role were one. His expression was unreadable, save for a faint crease at the corners of his mouth that might have once been a smile.

"Welcome home, Mr. Hawthorne. Miss Clark."

Cal gave a faint nod. "Thank you, Avery."

The butler—I assumed—inclined his head. Not a bow. Just enough to say, *I see you.* He didn't look at Cal for long, shifting to me instead.

Measured. Not cold. Not quite warm. Just…observant.

I had the distinct feeling he missed nothing. Not the way I still clung to Cal's hand. Not the way my travel-worn flats stood out against the gravel like punctuation. Not the way I was trying very hard not to gape at the house towering over us.

I wore jeans and my green sweater. Clean, presentable, comfortable. But not what one wore to be received.

Whatever judgment passed through his mind, he didn't show it. He simply stepped aside to let us through. "Her ladyship is in the drawing room." There was something in the tilt of his voice—gentle, practiced, but pitched just slightly toward kindness.

Inside, the hall was cool and vast. Painted portraits stared down from their gilded frames. The red-and-blue mosaic floor gleamed underfoot, and my footsteps sounded too loud.

As we passed under an archway, I leaned close to Cal. "Why 'Mister' Hawthorne?" I whispered. "Not 'Doctor'?"

He didn't glance at me as he answered quietly, "Because a doctorate is a professional title, not a social one. It doesn't mean anything here. Not in this house."

Avery led us down a wide corridor lined with pale wainscoting. The drawing room waited at the end, its double doors open but still.

Cal didn't slow. He didn't knock. He simply walked in.

A woman sat near a tall window in a high-backed chair, a

glossy magazine open across one knee. Beside her, a silver tea tray gleamed, not a cup out of place.

She looked up as we entered and rose with effortless grace.

Her movements were smooth, practiced. She wore tailored cream slacks and a soft blue blouse with a silken sheen—no jewelry except a strand of pearls and a watch that probably cost more than my car. Her silver-and-ash-blonde hair was perfectly swept back. She didn't smile, exactly. But something faint shifted at the corners of her mouth.

"Callum, dear," she said, stepping forward.

She kissed his cheek—twice, one side then the other. Light. Deliberate. The sort of continental greeting that suggested affection without surrendering to it.

Cal inclined his head. "Hello, Mother."

Then he turned to me.

"May I present Miss Gabrielle Clark? Gabrielle, my mother—Lady Branleigh."

Her eyes met mine at once—clear, pale, and appraising. "Miss Clark," she said with a cool sort of grace. "How lovely to finally meet you. Do sit."

I looked to Cal. He nodded, so I crossed to the nearest tufted red velvet sofa and sat—carefully. The stiff cushion barely gave. Cal remained standing a moment longer, then lowered himself beside me. The room was flooded with soft light from tall sash windows draped in heavy gold curtains. Pale yellow walls were trimmed in white, and delicate filigree traced the corners where ceiling met cornice. Everything gleamed with restrained opulence—meant to impress without appearing to try.

Lady Branleigh gestured toward the tea tray, though she made no move to serve. "Avery, two more settings, please."

He nodded and withdrew without a word.

She turned back to me. "You do take tea, don't you? I ought to have asked."

"I do," I said. "Thank you."

She took her seat again with a slight incline of her head, as though that confirmed something she'd already suspected. "How was your flight? It must be rather long from Texas."

"It was, but comfortable," I said. "Thank you for having me."

She gave a soft murmur of approval. "I'm so pleased you've come. You must be exhausted."

I offered a polite smile. "A bit. But I'm glad to be here."

"Good," she said. "Isabel will be joining us for luncheon."

I glanced at Cal, who gave nothing away.

"And Father?" he asked.

Lady Branleigh's mouth tightened by a fraction. "He had to go into London on business. But he'll return by teatime." She smoothed an invisible crease from her sleeve. "James and Caroline will join us for dinner this evening."

Avery returned, carrying a tray with two patterned porcelain cups and a matching teapot, which he placed on the table beside the existing service.

"Shall I pour, ma'am?"

"No thank you," she said, leaning forward to lift the pot. "I'll be mother."

She poured the tea, and its strong, earthy scent rose with the steam—sharp and clean, no hint of fruit or flowers. Proper tea. I kept my hands still in my lap.

She turned her attention back to me. "You'll be in Lady Amelia, Miss Clark. Avery will show you up shortly."

Lady Amelia? Was that...a room? A person? A ghost? Cal didn't even blink. Apparently, the rooms had names. Of course they did.

"Luncheon is at one," she continued. "That should give you time to freshen up and change after your journey. Milk and sugar?"

"Um...yes, both please."

She prepared the cup with unhurried composure, then passed it to me on a delicate saucer.

"Still milk only, Callum?"

"Yes, Mother."

She handed him his cup and returned the pot to its place —a soft clink of porcelain, then silence.

"And you'll be in your old room, of course," she added, eyes fixed on her tea. "Everything is just as you left it."

Cal nodded once. "You got my note about Gabrielle's dietary preferences?"

A flicker—too brief to be warmth, but close—passed over her features. "Yes, of course," she said. "I've spoken with Chef. Everything's taken care of."

She returned to her tea, as if remembering hadn't cost her a thing. But beside me, Cal's posture eased, just slightly, like the smallest weight had lifted.

Lady Branleigh set her cup down with a faint click. "Well," she said, rising in one graceful motion. "We'll get properly acquainted over luncheon."

Cal stood at once.

I started to rise too, but Cal brushed my hand, just enough to keep me seated. A private signal in a house full of rules I didn't know.

Lady Branleigh didn't appear to notice. Or perhaps she did and chose silence. She merely inclined her head. "I'm sure you'll want a moment to settle in. I'll see you at one."

She moved toward the door, crisp and unhurried.

Avery reappeared at the threshold as if summoned by scent. "Miss Clark?"

"I'll take it from here, Avery," Cal said, offering me his hand. "I do remember my way around."

The butler's eyebrow lifted—just enough to suggest *that's not how we do things here*, but not enough to challenge it. "Very good, sir."

Cal led me up the main staircase, his hand resting lightly at the small of my back. The banister was dark wood, polished to a satin sheen, and the runner beneath our feet was so thick it muffled every step. Brass stair rods held the runner in place, and the intricate iron balustrade—painted white and gold—curled like filigree along the curve of the stairs. More portraits adorned the walls—landscapes, stiff-backed ancestors, the occasional hound—each one perfectly lit by the soft glow of antique sconces. It was beautiful, yes—but curated. Composed. Like walking through a museum someone still lived in.

"I've never seen a house like this," I said softly.

"You get used to it."

"But you haven't."

That earned me a faint smile. "Not quite."

He stopped in front of a tall oak door and turned the engraved brass handle. The room beyond was large, light, and crisply elegant—muted blue wallpaper, ivory trim, a tall window framed by floor-length drapes. The bed was massive —carved mahogany with a pale quilted coverlet—its wood gleaming in the morning light.

I stepped inside slowly—absorbing.

"Separate rooms?" I asked, glancing back at him.

Cal leaned against the doorframe—casual, but eyes sharp. "From what you've told me of your Aunt Suzy, she's fairly traditional. Would she put us in the same bedroom?"

I gave a quiet laugh. "You're probably right."

A flicker of shared ground. Cal stepped inside, and I turned, scanning the room again. "Where are my bags?"

He crossed to the wardrobe, opened one of the tall doors, and stepped aside. My things were already inside, hung and folded with military precision. No suitcases in sight.

I blinked. "You've got to be kidding me."

He smiled. "Welcome to Branleigh."

CHAPTER 35

CALLUM

I poured just enough sherry to coat the bottom of the glass. The pale gold caught the light as I swirled it once, then took it in a single pull—a small fortification against the hours and days ahead. I let the warmth linger, then set the empty glass on the silver tray, the sound ringing soft and clear through the vacant room.

The drawing room was, as ever, regal and immaculate. The chairs and settees were upholstered to repel comfort—as stiff and unyielding as the legacy they represented. It hadn't changed much since I was a boy, and probably never would.

The sherry clung warm and smooth to the back of my throat. I considered pouring another—slightly more generous —but thought better of it. The day would be long. The fortnight longer. I needed to pace myself if I had any hope of remaining upright, let alone sober, in a house where the temptation to fortify—or anesthetize—was as plentiful as the family's expectations.

A sharp staccato of heels echoed down the hallway, moving with precision and purpose. I abandoned the decanter, loose and half-wild with relief, and turned toward the open doorway.

Isabel swept in like a gust of air too vivid for these walls. Her auburn hair caught the light, and her eyes—blue, bright, incisive—locked on mine. She wore a crisp blouse and dark trousers tailored to perfection. Effortless elegance, as always.

"Cal, darling! You made it!" She crossed the room in two long strides and folded me into an embrace that somehow maintained equestrian posture. She smelled of florals and leather. "I thought you might've lost your nerve and gone into hiding."

"Not yet," I said, stepping back to take her in. "But I haven't ruled it out."

She swatted my arm lightly. "I've missed you, you dreadful man."

"You have no idea how glad I am you're here."

She smiled, bright and knowing, then glanced around the room. "And where's this mysterious young woman you've imported? Have you frightened her off already?"

"Upstairs, freshening up," I said, settling into one of the red velvet sofas. "We've only just arrived."

"Good. That gives us a moment to conspire before she realizes how mad we all are."

I laughed, the sound echoing off the high ceiling. "I think she's already worked that out."

Isabel sat in a chair across from me, her movements smooth and precise. She crossed her legs. "And how's she handling it?"

"Brilliant, actually. Far more composed than I am. And she survived meeting Mother."

She raised a brow. "Impressive."

"Yes. Granted, it was only five minutes, but hopefully it's a good sign that she'll actually last the trip. And not run away screaming and never speak to me again."

Isabel leaned back, studying me. "You care for her."

"I do."

Her gaze didn't shift, but her voice softened. "Then let the rest of them be damned."

I let out an unsteady breath, some tightness easing in my chest.

"Father included," she added, rising to pour herself a sherry.

"How livid was he when I insisted on bringing her? You know he'd never admit it to me."

"Livid?" She shook her head. "Not really. Caught off guard, maybe. But…"

"But what?"

She retook her seat and took a measured sip. "Talk to him, Cal."

I narrowed my eyes. "Since when are you so cryptic, Isabel?"

Whatever retort she had planned vanished when Gabrielle appeared in the doorway, tentative and wide-eyed. Her gaze swept the room, as if unsure she'd stepped into the right place. But when her eyes found me, they softened with relief.

I sprang up, crossing to her in a few quick strides. She shifted instinctively into my side, and I slipped a protective arm around her waist, pressing a kiss to her cheek.

"There you are," I said softly, guiding her in, letting the warmth of her presence melt away my tension. I turned to Isabel, whose eyes shone with interest. "Isabel, meet my Gabrielle."

Gabrielle extended a hand, her smile careful but genuine. "It's so nice to meet you in person."

Isabel took Gabrielle's hand in both of hers, warm and gracious. "Likewise. Cal talks of little else."

Gabrielle's cheeks colored, her eyes flicking to mine. I squeezed her waist gently and felt the faint tremor of nerves beneath the fabric of her blouse.

"Please, sit," Isabel said, gesturing to the sofas with a graceful sweep. "Cal, get the poor girl a drink."

I crossed over to the drinks tray. "Sherry before lunch, darling?"

Gabrielle shrugged as she perched on the edge of the sofa. "If that's the protocol."

I smiled as I poured a modest measure and brought it to her.

She lifted the glass and took a careful, controlled sip. The liquid glowed amber in the early afternoon light, catching the faint tremble in her hand before she politely set it down on a side table, trying with valiant effort to mask a grimace.

"Not to your liking?" I asked.

"Not really, no. I hope that's not wrong."

I reached over, took the glass, and finished it in one swallow. "More for me, then."

She flashed me a smile, then turned her attention back to my sister. "How are the last-minute wedding details coming along? I hope the chaos hasn't consumed you."

"Not yet, but it's doing its best. The florist is a menace—keeps trying to sneak in lilies, which I detest. And the caterer—" She let out a theatrical sigh. "Don't get me started."

Gabrielle's laugh was soft, an attempt at finding her ease. "Sounds like a nightmare."

"It's a bloody circus," Isabel said, though more amused than frazzled. Her eyes flicked to me. "And don't you dare smirk. Your turn will come soon enough."

The last of the scones sat half-eaten on my plate, its sugared crust crumbling slightly where I'd broken it open. Not too sweet. Still warm. Proper. I'd spent years insisting you could get a decent one in the States, but sitting here now, I knew better. You could replicate the recipe, perhaps. But not the taste. Not the texture. Not the memory baked into it.

Late-afternoon light slanted through the tall windows,

gilding the edge of the china and casting long shadows across the library rug. Teatime. A pause in the day that served no urgent purpose—except perhaps to remind us that life needn't always be rushed. The Americans, for all their strengths, had never quite grasped the value of a ritual built around slowing down. For all I'd cast off…this, I had missed.

I eased back into the cushions and wrapped an arm around Gabrielle's shoulder. She leaned into me, easy and unselfconscious. Mother pressed her lips into the faintest line but offered no comment. The library air was steeped in the scent of tea and the low, smoky trace of my father's tobacco still lingering in the wood. He hadn't smoked in here for years, not since Mother had drawn the line. But the room hadn't forgotten.

I brushed my thumb along Gabrielle's arm, tracing the soft wool of her jumper and the grounding weight of her closeness. Across from us, Isabel and Mother exchanged a glance—a wordless flicker—then both turned toward us with a well-practiced sort of interest. I shifted, the old upholstery creaking beneath me, and set my empty cup down on the table.

"Do you have everything you need?" Mother asked Gabrielle.

"Oh yes, thank you," Gabrielle replied.

"Dinner is served at eight. We usually gather in the drawing room at half seven."

Gabrielle glanced at me, confusion on her face, though she desperately tried to hide it.

"Seven-thirty," I explained, low next to her ear.

She gave a small nod, then turned back toward my mother with a composed smile. "Everything's been wonderful so far. The house is…breathtaking, really. And the tea," she added, gesturing gently toward her cup, "perfect. Thank you for making me feel so welcome."

A pause—only a beat—but I felt it. Mother inclined her

head. "How kind." Her tone was neither cold nor rude. Just... final. Like closing a magazine without bothering to read the rest.

Gabrielle didn't falter, but beside me, I felt the faintest hitch of breath.

Avery appeared in the doorway, unobtrusive as ever—waistcoat immaculate, expression unreadable. "Mr. Hawthorne," he said, his voice smooth as the polished floorboards. "Lord Branleigh has asked to see you in his study."

Mother looked up sharply. "I didn't realize he was back from London."

"He returned just over an hour ago, ma'am."

"And he didn't want tea?"

"He said not."

She shook her head. "London must not have gone well."

I looked at Isabel, and she caught my hesitation. Before I could speak, she stood, smoothing the lines of her trousers with a brisk motion. "Gabrielle," she said, her tone conspiratorial, "shall we take a turn in the garden before dinner?"

Gabrielle looked at me with the faintest trace of worry, but the warmth of Isabel's invitation was hard to refuse. "I'd like that," she said, voice bright, if not quite steady. She stood with care—poised but tentative. She was trying so hard, and I tried not to imagine the weight of it—of all of this. "Thank you for tea, Lady Branleigh," she said, her voice polite but edged with the slightest uncertainty.

Isabel looped her arm through Gabrielle's, drawing her out with ease. Avery remained, waiting with precise patience, the timeless clockwork of the house ticking smoothly around him.

"I'll show you to his—" he began, then stopped as I shook my head.

"I know the way," I said as I rose to my feet, the words

firmer than I felt. I leaned down and kissed Mother on the cheek.

Avery stepped aside, and I passed him, my footsteps measured down the long corridor. The walk to my father's study felt longer than I remembered, as if the house had grown in my absence.

The door stood ajar, a thin strip of light slicing into the shadowed hall. I hesitated, my pulse quickening, then pushed it open with a steady hand and stepped inside.

Father sat behind a broad mahogany desk, glasses perched low on his nose as he studied a fan of papers. The curtains were half-drawn, muting the afternoon light, and the air was thick with the residue of tobacco woven into the old leather bindings that lined the walls, the scent heavier still in the crevices of the ancient carved bookcases with their worn crests and scrolled emblems.

An ashtray sat on the sideboard—polished and unused. A half-empty teacup rested near his hand. The only sound was the quiet, relentless tick of an antique clock.

He looked older than I remembered. It had only been two years since I'd last seen him in person, but it might as well have been ten. His face had thinned, the skin drawn tight across sharp cheekbones. Still immaculately dressed, of course, but the fingers that rested beside the cup looked leaner, the joints more pronounced. Knots beneath a polished surface. He didn't look diminished, exactly. Just…smaller. Still iron, but iron left exposed to the weather.

He looked up. "Callum."

"Father."

Formality hung between us like dust motes in the still air. I waited until he gestured, then took the seat across from him.

His gaze flickered over me, assessing. "I suppose I should ask how you've been. But I expect you'd tell me very little."

"Come now. We've never been ones for small talk."

He folded his glasses and laid them on the desk. "I do

care, you know. Contrary to whatever poison you've fed yourself."

I let the words sit, unsorted.

Poison? No. Just memory.

But there was no use in saying so. Not here.

Instead, I leaned back, arms loosely crossed. "Funny, I always thought silence was the family tonic."

He didn't flinch, but his jaw ticked. "This woman you've brought."

"Gabrielle? What of her?"

"Is it serious, or just a passing dalliance?"

"I wouldn't have brought her if it weren't serious."

He fingered the handle of his teacup but didn't lift it. "She's American."

"You've noticed."

"So does that mean you've cast off for good now? No chance of ever returning home?"

I let out a breath—not quite a sigh. "I cast off a long time ago. Long before Gabrielle. You know that."

He didn't argue. Just watched me with those razor-edged eyes, still calculating the damage.

"Why the sudden concern?" I asked, quieter this time. "It's not like I have a place here—not truly. James is the heir and your company man through and through. He was born and built for it. And I'm more than happy in academia. He's where he belongs. I'm where I belong. End of story."

"Yes, I gave up on getting you interested in business years ago. But why not come home? You've made your point. I could get you a post at Cambridge."

"Then clearly I *haven't* made my point. I don't need you to get me anything. I'm perfectly capable of building a career on my own."

"By sleeping with one of your students?"

I didn't blink. "That's beneath you."

"Other way around, I should think."

I stood. "I'm not here to ask permission, Father. Gabrielle is my choice. And if you're expecting an apology for how or where we met, you'll be waiting a long time."

"Oh, do sit down, Callum," he said, biting and dry.

I paused, the tension between us stretched taut.

He coughed—a hack that rattled like a loose shutter in the wind.

I sat hesitantly, studying his face. "Are you all right?"

"Don't fuss. It's the spring air." He waved a hand, dismissive. "Gets me every year."

I waited, but he didn't elaborate. Just pinched the bridge of his nose and drummed his bony fingers on the desk.

"What's this really about, Father?"

He looked up, eyes narrowing into sharp lines. "Your intentions for the girl. What are they?"

The question landed like a blade. I held his gaze, unwilling to let him see how deep it cut.

"Will you marry her?"

I let the silence draw out. "If she'll have me," I said at last, my voice steady. "Then yes."

He picked up his cup, studied the contents, and set it down again. The soft clink of porcelain rang louder than his voice when it finally came. "In that case, I insist on a prenuptial agreement." He slid a business card across the desk. "That's my solicitor. He can sort everything for you."

I tapped the card once, then eased it back toward him. "What exactly do you think she's after?" I asked, voice sharp as cut glass. "My vast fortune as a physics professor?"

"You know that's not what I mean."

"Then what do you mean?" I leaned back, arms crossed. "The trust you set up when I turned eighteen? The one I haven't touched? The company shares I let sit idle? She doesn't even know those exist."

"All the more reason to protect them."

"From what, exactly?"

"Callum," he said with a sigh, as if I were the one being unreasonable. "It's the proper thing to do. You know that."

Proper. That word. Always that word.

"I know she doesn't care about the money. Or the name."

His expression didn't change. "And you're sure of that?"

The air suddenly turned thin, brittle. "Yes," I said slowly. "I am."

"Then it shouldn't matter to her."

He held my gaze, the old challenge still there. But something behind it shifted. He didn't argue. Didn't repeat himself. Instead, he reached for his cup and took a long, measured sip of tea that had surely gone cold.

Chapter 36

Gabrielle

Avery approached with a plate distinctly different from the others. I caught the scent first—earthy and rich, with a hint of wine-steeped shallots. When he set it down, I saw the difference: a golden galette, delicately folded and ringed with a reduction that looked brushed on by hand. Unlike the others, there was no filet, no jus—just a beautifully composed vegetarian dish, as intentional and elegant as the rest.

"Thank you," I said.

Avery gave a tight nod and moved on. No one else acknowledged him. I couldn't tell if that was the norm here, or if I'd already broken yet another invisible rule.

The table gleamed beneath polished silver and cut crystal, everything symmetrical, like it had been arranged by an architect with OCD. Candles burned low in silver holders, their light dancing across porcelain plates and the deep ruby of the wine. The room itself was grand in a way no photograph could capture—wood-paneled walls, oil portraits with steady eyes, and windows framed in heavy damask. It was warm, but not cozy. Elegant without feeling lived in.

I'd sat at my Aunt Suzy's dining table plenty of times—

formal meals with cloth napkins, matching china, and a centerpiece that changed with the seasons. But this wasn't just formal. This was curated. Historic. Like every piece had a story and a pedigree.

The people matched the setting. Women in shimmering beaded silks, men in tuxedos—though they called them "dinner jackets," which sounded woefully inadequate for what they actually were.

And then there was Cal. Cal in a tuxedo was so sinful it should be illegal. Clean and crisp. Polished and devastating. I'd seen him dressed sharply before—shirt, tie, and jacket for class. But this—this version of him was something else entirely. All control and filigreed elegance. He looked like he belonged here.

And somehow, impossibly, he was holding my hand under the table.

I smoothed my napkin and adjusted my dress. Deep violet silk, sleeveless, with a neckline that had derailed Cal's train of thought more than once. I had worn it for him, not his family, but now, under their collective gaze, I wasn't sure if it read confident or naïve.

Seated on Cal's other side, Caroline—James's wife—leaned in just enough to make it look casual. "Remind me how you two met. I don't think I've heard the full story." Her tone was honeyed, her expression poised, but her eyes held a flicker of mischief. Or maybe it was warning. Either way, it was a performance. They all knew.

The moment settled over the table like a second tablecloth.

Cal, mercifully, didn't miss a beat. "At the university," he said smoothly. "Gabrielle is an exceptionally gifted engineering student—brilliant and annoyingly self-sufficient. At least until her car battery died at the start of term."

A few brows rose. Caroline's smile tightened slightly.

"It was late, cold, and pouring rain," he went on, his tone

just conversational enough to mask the significance. "I couldn't very well leave her stranded in the car park, so I offered her a ride home. Seemed practical at the time, though in hindsight—"

"It was a bit cinematic," I finished, managing a smile.

Lord Branleigh gave a low hum of amusement, finally glancing my way. "Letting a battery go flat? I wouldn't have pegged that for an aspiring engineer."

The corner of Cal's mouth ticked upward. "She had an emergency kit. Just no one to call."

"I'm resourceful," I said, keeping my tone light. "Not a magician."

Lord Branleigh's voice came again, crisp and composed. "Engineering, you say?" His gaze shifted to me—not unkind, but cool. Like he was cataloging the information, not engaging with it.

"Yes, sir," I said. "Aerospace engineering."

"Ambitious," he said, lifting a brow. "And your prospects? What is it you hope to…engineer?"

Cal's hand brushed mine under the table—just enough to ground me.

"Aircraft design, with any luck. I've always loved aviation. Anything with wings."

Across the table, Isabel smiled with unmistakable approval.

Cal's gaze fell on me, sweet and proud. "Gabrielle is quite an accomplished pilot," he said, smirking faintly. "And she's been accepted into two top-tier engineering programs."

"So…" Caroline probed, tilting her head, "you'll no longer be at the same university?"

"Correct," Cal answered mildly.

"I daresay that's for the best," Lady Branleigh said, lifting her glass without so much as a glance in my direction.

I drew a breath and aimed for levity. "Cal didn't tell you how I completely botched his tea the night he drove me home."

His eyes met mine, a hint of amusement there. "I hadn't planned to embarrass you on your first night at Branleigh Park."

Isabel lit up with mischief. "You can't just leave the story there. Tell it."

Cal chuckled, low and unguarded. "Well, as I said, it was pouring, so I stayed to wait out the weather. Gabrielle offered me a cup of tea—already a point in her favor—but hadn't the faintest idea how to make one." He turned to me with mock reproach. "You're not English, so I could forgive that."

Polite laughter rippled around the table.

"But you taught me the correct way," I said, smiling at the memory.

"And now she makes an excellent cup of tea." He patted my hand.

"So you haven't been a total corrupting influence then?" Isabel ribbed.

A brief, companionable silence settled. I sipped my wine, the dry red warming my throat. Candlelight flickered, shadows leaping like dancers across the paneled walls. Somewhere between the chandelier and the shadow-dappled walls, disbelief crept in. Me. Here. Draped in silk, sipping something older than I was, beside a man who looked like he'd stepped out of a Bond film and held my hand under the table like it was nothing at all. I wasn't intimidated, exactly. But the reality shimmered at the edge of my thoughts like heat rising off asphalt.

Finally, James spoke for the first time. "Seems she's had some influence on you as well." He looked at Cal, his expression cool. "You've picked up quite the American accent."

The words hung in the air, threaded with challenge. Cal's fingers stilled. His lips thinned, but he held James's gaze with practiced indifference.

I turned to Cal, eyebrows raised. "Have you?" I asked. "I hadn't noticed."

"It has gone a bit muddled, darling," Isabel chimed in, her tone mock-dramatic. "But it's hardly surprising, is it, since you've been away for…what now? Ten years?"

"Nearly," Cal said evenly. The tension in his jaw eased, but it was still coiled just beneath the surface.

"Give him a few days," Isabel went on, mouth quirking into a half-smile, "and he'll drop the twang and revert to form."

Lady Branleigh shifted her attention to me with the grace of a swan turning on water. "Do tell us about your family, Miss Clark," she said, her tone impeccably polite. She cast a glare at James. "I imagine they're far less prone to… dramatics."

I smoothed the napkin on my lap. "My family is considerably smaller," I said. "But I suppose we have our own drama. Growing up, it was just my dad and me." I took a sip of wine, letting the words land softly.

Lady Branleigh's expression turned politely curious. "And your mother?"

Cal stiffened beside me, but I met Lady Branleigh's gaze with a steady smile. "She left when I was very young," I said, careful to keep my voice light. "We haven't had contact in years." I set my glass down with deliberate calm. "It was better that way, really. Just me and Dad. He worked a lot, but he was always there when it counted. We were very close."

Lady Branleigh tilted her head, precise and curious. "Were?"

"Mother…" Cal warned.

The air thinned, but I kept my composure. "No, it's okay," I said, forcing warmth into my voice. "He died about a year and a half ago."

Silence fell over the table, dense and awkward. Isabel's

gaze flicked from Cal to me. Lord Branleigh cleared his throat.

"How very difficult for you," Lady Branleigh said with practiced gravity.

"Thank you," I returned, finishing the wine in my glass. No sooner had I set my glass down than Avery appeared to refill it. The second pour seemed richer, darker. Or maybe that was just the room. I took a slow sip, kept my smile intact, and reminded myself to breathe.

The drawing room looked different at night—curtains drawn, fire banked low, lamps casting amber light that pooled like melted gold on polished wood. It should have been cozy and inviting, but the quiet—too careful, too composed—put me on edge. I sat close beside Cal, my hand brushing his knee, the warmth of him a quiet tether. Around us, conversation drifted like smoke, refined and inconsequential. But when Lady Branleigh looked my way, the room shifted. Voices faltered, trailing off mid-sentence.

"Do you ride, Miss Clark?" Her voice was cool, inquisitive, and I nearly choked on my coffee.

"You mean horses?"

"What else should I mean?" she asked, tilting her head with the faintest amusement. "I assumed, being from Texas…"

I laughed—a little too brightly. "I do," I said. "Or I did. I haven't been on a horse since I was twelve."

"Then Callum must take you while you're here," she said, the suggestion clearly meant for him, not me.

Cal's mouth tipped into a reluctant smile. "I suppose I could manage that. If you're up for it."

Lord Branleigh pushed heavily on the armrests and rose

from his chair. "If you'll excuse me," he said, weariness edging into his voice. "The day has caught up with me."

"You look tired, dear," Lady Branleigh noted, a crease between her brows. "I told you that trip into London would be too much."

"I'll be fine. Just need to turn in." He turned to Cal, and for a moment, something faltered in his gaze—a flicker of vulnerability, quickly hidden. "Callum, son—welcome home." Then he shifted to me, and his expression softened. "Miss Clark, we're pleased to have you."

Cal's surprise was a barely perceptible shift, but he recovered swiftly. "Thank you, Father. Good night."

As Lord Branleigh shuffled toward the door, Lady Branleigh rose before anyone could prompt her. "I'll come too."

"Don't fuss, Eleanor," Lord Branleigh muttered, more habit than protest. "I'm perfectly capable."

She ignored him with polished indifference. James stood as she passed and dipped his head to kiss her cheek. Cal followed suit, straightening as she turned to me.

"Breakfast is in the dining room between half seven and nine," she said, her smile precise. "You're unfamiliar with the household routine, but I'm sure you'll catch on."

"Thank you," I answered, unsure of how else to respond.

"Good night, Miss Clark," she said, her tone smooth as porcelain.

"Good night, Lady Branleigh." I didn't know whether to rise, nod, or curtsy—so I simply smiled.

And then she was gone, the door closing softly behind her, leaving the five of us in a room that suddenly felt more fragile than grand.

Caroline set down her empty coffee cup and broke the silence. "What else do you have planned for your visit?"

"Nothing specific," Cal answered, saving me from the awkward pause. As far as I knew, we hadn't planned anything beyond Isabel's wedding on Saturday. "Just introducing Gabrielle to the joys and slower pace of country life," Cal added, slipping his arm around me and drawing me closer.

James gave a low, sardonic laugh. "Shouldn't we all be so lucky—to shirk our duties for a few glorious weeks?"

Cal met his brother's gaze, sharp enough to cut glass. "Like you've never taken a holiday?"

"Play nice, boys," Isabel said, a warning and a plea. It held for a moment, the air thick with history.

James held his tongue, but only for a breath. He reached for his whiskey, took a slow sip, then looked straight at Cal. "Do us all a favor, little brother," he said, voice low and precise. He glanced at me, then back to Cal. "Don't take this one to Switzerland like you did the last. It took us years to clean up your scandal."

His words cracked through the room like a slap, and Cal's arm tensed around me. I didn't know what Switzerland had to do with anything, but I knew a calculated strike when I heard one—and so did Cal.

He drew a sharp breath. The air shifted like he might stand and storm out. Instead, he took my hand—firm, not desperate—his eyes fixed on James with cold, measured fury. The room felt smaller, stifling. I tried to pull away, to give him space, but he held me close.

The tension crackled—hot, sharp, brittle—before Cal finally stood. His silence held a beat longer than the air could bear. "As much as we'd love to stay and reminisce, I'm afraid we're far too travel-worn to be pleasant company," he said, his voice so polite, it dripped with venom. His accent was the strongest I'd ever heard it. "If you'll excuse us."

The room went still, the air thick with the echo of what hadn't been said. Cal extended his hand, his grip sure and steady as I rose.

James stayed sprawled in his chair, his smile thin and

knowing. He tipped his glass in our direction—a salute or a dismissal, it was hard to tell.

Isabel rose, apology soft in her eyes. "Good night, darling," she said, kissing my cheek with a warmth that only deepened the fracture in the room.

I managed a faint smile. "Good night."

Cal's grip tightened as we left the drawing room. We walked in silence, my pulse loud in my ears, the weight of his stillness pressing in from all sides. He moved with tense precision, like the slightest misstep might shatter him.

The corridor felt endless. Our footsteps swallowed the space, and I wondered how much longer he could carry the strain.

At the bottom of the stairs, he stopped and turned to me. The mask slipped—just for a second—and I saw the anguish underneath.

He didn't say a word—not aloud, anyway.

He walked me to my room in silence.

Lingering in the doorway, he finally spoke. "Would you mind if I stayed a while?"

I turned to him and cocked my head. "I'd be offended if you didn't."

He gave a thin smile that didn't reach his eyes, then closed the door, shrugged off his jacket, and loosened his bowtie.

"You don't have to wear the mask with me, you know."

"And for that"—he unfastened the first few buttons of his shirt—"I'm more grateful than I can say." He sank into the blue-and-white patterned armchair in the corner. "Not even twenty-four hours, and you're already seeing us for what we really are. I'm so sorry for dragging you into this madness, Gabrielle."

A thousand questions crowded my mind, but now wasn't the time. I sat on the ottoman in front of him and laid a hand on his knee. "I'm tougher than I look."

He shifted under my hand, eyes weary. "I know you are," he said, voice low with something close to awe. "But you shouldn't have to be." He laced his fingers with mine, curling slowly, like he was afraid to let go. "I want you to see *me*—not this." He gestured vaguely at the room, the house, the legacy hanging over it all.

I shifted onto the arm of the chair, leaning into him until the tension began to bleed away. "I do see you, Cal. I always have. Not my professor, not the son of a duke—"

"Baron," he corrected.

"Whatever he is. It doesn't matter. I see you—who you are, not what you are. And I love you, no matter what wrapping you come in."

His breath caught, and for a moment, I thought he might say something. But instead, he pulled me closer, pressing his forehead to my shoulder—a small act of surrender that said more than words ever could.

We stayed like that for a while, the silence thick, calm, until I felt the tightness in him begin to soften. His breath steadied, his body relaxing against mine, the strain of the evening slowly unwinding its grip. Finally, he shifted, his eyes meeting mine with raw, unguarded honesty that sent a shiver of tenderness through me.

"Thank you," he said, his voice rough around the edges.

I awkwardly raked my fingers through his hair—thick with dried gel—and kissed his forehead. "Anytime." I fingered the silk of his bowtie. "And by the way, you look absolutely devastating in a tux. Hot doesn't begin to cover it."

For the first time, he smiled—truly smiled.

He pulled me onto his lap, and I let out a soft, surprised sound as his lips found mine. "I'm bloody glad you wore that dress," he murmured against my mouth, fingers brushing my bare shoulder—a slow, deliberate tease. "The one I liked so much."

His smile ghosted across my skin, his breath warm and insistent against my neck. Then he nipped at my ear, setting off a shiver I couldn't hope to contain. "I've been imagining taking it off you all night."

I swatted him playfully, my hand grazing the curve of his jaw. "Cal…"

He paused, pulling back just enough to search my face. "Are you tired?" he asked softly.

I sighed and let my head fall against his shoulder. "Physically, I'm absolutely exhausted. But mentally, I'm wide awake. It's weird."

He chuckled, the sound vibrating through his chest. "That's the time change," he said, holding me tighter.

We stayed like that for a long, sweet moment—his arms a refuge, the world beyond his heartbeat falling away. The room was hushed, the heavy drapes cutting out the moonlight and leaving us in a soft, woolen dark.

"I know we're supposed to be in separate rooms," I whispered against his neck, then pulled back to see his reaction.

He rolled his eyes.

"Are you going to stay?" I asked.

"Try and stop me."

Chapter 37

Callum

The morning air tasted like memory—clean and sharp—laced with wet grass, turned soil, and distant woodsmoke. Beneath it, the musky sweetness of horse sweat mingled with the earthy tang of leather and hay. Birds rustled in the hedgerow, unseen but singing—thrush, blackbird, maybe a pheasant startled into flight. Hoofbeats, softened by the damp turf, echoed around us, steady and grounding.

I hadn't realized how much I'd missed it. Not Branleigh. Not the house or the bloodlines or the silent judgments served with breakfast. But this—open land uncoiling to the horizon. The steadiness of a good horse beneath me. And the sun, breaking through a veil of cloud, just long enough to gild the fields in gold.

Gabrielle pulled up beside me, cheeks flushed from the ride, eyes alight beneath the brim of her borrowed helmet. Her seat wasn't perfect, but it was better than I expected. She looked…right. Natural. Like she belonged here in a way that twisted something behind my ribs.

"You're catching on," I said, unable to hide the grin tugging at my mouth.

She laughed, winded and triumphant. "My dad put me in lessons as a kid. Western, mostly. But I guess I didn't forget everything."

My gaze followed the sway of her hips in the saddle, drifting down the line of her leg and over the borrowed riding boots, polished and dusted with trail grit. "Western, hmm?" I said mildly. "I'd love to see you in cowboy boots."

She shot me a look—half-amused, half-scandalized. "Would you now?"

I leaned in enough to draw a spark without fanning it. "And nothing else."

She rolled her eyes and nudged her horse ahead. "That'd make for an uncomfortable ride."

I followed, smile lingering. "Depends what you're riding."

She slowed, letting the horse fall into a gentle walk. "Sorry I missed breakfast. Was it a big deal?"

I came alongside her. "Not at all. You were jet-lagged. I didn't want to wake you."

She bit her lip, still uncertain. "I hope your family doesn't think I'm rude."

"I handled it. And my father begged off as well, so…"

She glanced at me, worry still lingering. "I just don't want to make a bad impression."

I reached for her hand, steadying her reins. "You haven't. And besides, I don't care what they think."

A lull settled. Only the soft snort of horses and the rustle of wind through the trees remained. I waited a beat, then spoke. "You never asked me what James meant last night. Switzerland and scandal."

She tightened her grip on the reins but didn't flinch. "I wasn't going to pry," she said carefully. "I figured you'd tell me if you felt you needed to."

The clouds shifted like breath from a snuffed-out flame. I felt Gabrielle's eyes on me but kept mine fixed ahead.

"Do you remember the first time we drove to Dallas together, and you asked about the last time I was in love?"

"Yes," she answered simply.

"I told you I was engaged once, and that she died. Which is true."

"I'm guessing there's more to the story."

"I took Claire to one of my father's ski resorts in Switzerland. It was an engagement gift from the family. After a long day on the slopes, we ended up in the hot tub and, shameful to admit, high out of our bleeding heads."

Gabrielle frowned. "You mean…*high* high?" she asked, bringing her thumb and index finger to her lips, miming a puff of smoke.

I let out a dark laugh and dragged a finger beneath my nose. "Think powder, not pot."

Her expression sobered. "Oh."

"I don't know how I even remember everything. I probably don't. She got out of the hot tub to fetch more drinks—like we needed anything else. But we were young and stupid. She slipped on the deck, fell back, and smashed her head on a stone bench."

Gabrielle put her hand to her mouth.

I stared straight ahead but saw nothing of the landscape. "She was dead before I got to her. The family wanted to keep it quiet, so they rewrote the story. Made it something else entirely."

"What did they say?" Her voice was soft, the question hesitant.

"Father couldn't risk bad press—heaven forbid the resort should suffer. The official story was that she hit a tree skiing and died in my arms. He cast me as the innocent, grieving fiancé." I blew out a shaky breath. "And I let him."

"What happened after that?" she asked, her voice gentle.

"There were questions," I said. "Her injuries didn't match the story, for one. The resort staff and witnesses had to be bought off. And Claire's family…" I swallowed hard. "Money solves a lot of problems. Everyone has a price when it comes to it."

The horses plodded on. Gabrielle said nothing, her gaze distant.

"Please say something," I pleaded. "Even if it's that you can't stay with me."

Gabrielle blinked, eyes snapping back into focus. "Why on earth would I say that?"

I looked down, tightening my grip on the reins. "I can imagine what you must think of me now."

"I'm thinking it's odd you talk like you're guilty of something." She brushed my arm. "It was an accident. You didn't kill her."

"Perhaps not," I said, my voice low. "But I brought her there. And I got her high."

"No. You were 'young and stupid,' like you said. It just as easily could've been you. Though selfish as it may be, I'm glad it wasn't."

"But I helped cover it up."

A pause, as sharp and clean as the morning air. "Is that how you ended up in the US?"

I nodded. "There was too much talk, too many rumors. I was a young lecturer at Oxford, but it was clear that my career was…tainted." I met her gaze, clear and unwavering. "England is a small country. And the upper class? Smaller still. There was nothing left for me. So my father pulled some strings and got me a post-doc at Princeton. After that, I got my position at Page on my own—no strings, no favors." I let out a breath. "And you know the rest."

The weight of it all—the years, the silence, the shame— fell away with the words. Gabrielle's hand covered mine, warm and steady.

"I'm sorry," she said, her voice a soft tether. "That sounds…brutal."

"It was," I admitted. "But I'm not sure I'd have found you otherwise."

She looked at me, her expression unreadable for a moment, then softened—something tender blooming behind her eyes. I couldn't look away.

"I know now," I said, steady and certain, "you're it for me. The one I want beside me for the rest of my life. I can't live without you—and don't intend to try."

She blinked. "Is that a proposal?"

I tilted my head. "If you like."

She laughed, loud and unbridled. "That's how you ask me to marry you?"

I arched a brow. "Would you rather I throw myself from the saddle and kneel in the mud?"

"Honestly? I'm not sure what I expected, but…a little more ceremony wouldn't hurt."

I made a show of patting my jacket. "Afraid I didn't bring a ring."

"Pity. I didn't bring a pen," she said, grinning. "You do seem to have a thing for asking big questions with government paperwork."

I narrowed my eyes. "I beg your pardon?"

"You invited me to England with a passport application, remember?"

"It was a very efficient method."

"It was a form, Cal."

"A very official form."

She shook her head, laughing as her horse sidestepped a low branch. Her laugh, bright and genuine, loosened something in my chest I hadn't realized was still coiled.

"You're not saying no," I said, watching her from the corner of my eye.

"You haven't asked me anything."

I drew a slow breath, reining in until we were perfectly side by side. My pulse ticked hard at my throat.

"Marry me, Gabrielle."

She stilled. Her reins slackened. For a moment, all I heard was saddles creaking and hooves on damp turf. Then she reached across and caught my sleeve, fingers curling into the fabric.

"God, I love you."

I leaned in just enough for our foreheads to touch, the reins gathered loose in one hand, hers tangled in the other.

"Shall I take that as a yes? Or would you prefer it in triplicate?"

Her voice was warm against my cheek. "It's a yes."

CHAPTER 38

GABRIELLE

Gravel crunched beneath our boots as we walked back up to the house. Cal looped an arm around my shoulders and pulled me close. I basked in his warmth, anchoring me to this moment.

He'd asked me. He'd really asked me.

"Shall I shout the news from the rooftops?" he murmured against my ear as we climbed the steps to Branleigh's towering double oak doors. "Or shall it be our secret for now?"

"Just us for now," I answered, nuzzling into him. "At least until after Isabel's wedding. I don't want to steal her thunder."

"See? You're already keeping me in line."

The entry hall was cool and still. As we stepped inside, Cal slid his arm around my waist, his touch easy and sure. James cut across the foyer, a leather satchel slung over one shoulder.

He paused, eyes flicking to where Cal's hand rested on my hip.

"Look at you," he said with a sneer. "Rather public, aren't we?"

Cal tightened his hold around me, his smile sharp. "Don't you have an empire to run?"

"I do, in fact," James replied, his tone so casual it stung. "Not that you'd know anything about it." His eyes glinted with veiled contempt. "We can't all run off and be mad scientists, now can we?"

Cal stiffened, then kissed my cheek—a soft brush of lips that lingered like a promise. "See you at lunch?" he asked, his voice warmer than I expected.

I nodded, and Cal let go, his hand trailing down my arm before he turned and left me at the foot of the stairs. James joined him, and together they disappeared behind the heavy oak door leading to the library. I couldn't hear what they said once the door shut—but I could guess.

I went back to my room, which had been serviced while we'd been out. After a quick rinse to wash off the morning's ride, I slipped into a blouse and skirt—simple but polished for lunch. My body moved on autopilot while my mind ricocheted like a pinball machine.

My phone buzzed, dull and insistent against the polished nightstand. I almost ignored it, cocooned in that blissful haze where nothing else seems to matter, but a second buzz followed. I grabbed it. Two new texts, both from Aunt Suzy.

12:04 p.m. here. That meant it was just after six in the morning in Texas. I could see her now: bare feet on the kitchen tile, coffee maker whirring, glasses perched low on her nose, and a crime podcast humming from the Bluetooth speaker. She'd wake the whole house just to check on me.

The first message:

> Good morning, sweet girl! Just checking in.
> How's England? Is he treating you right? Send
> pics!

The second:

NEED PROOF OF LIFE! If you get murdered by a serial killer, I better be quoted in the documentary, LOL.

I smiled despite myself, thumb hovering over the keyboard. The house was still—no voices from the corridor, no footsteps from Avery or the other staff—just the distant rattle and whine of a lawnmower somewhere on the estate.

I opened the curtains wide, flooding the room with wet, milky light, and snapped a shot of the view—a sweep of emerald lawn, tidy hedges, the pewter blanket of cloud cover. I took a mirror selfie to show off my outfit and sent them both.

Alive and well and having an amazing time!

Umm. Where's the mystery man? I demand photographic evidence.

I laughed—of course she zeroed in on the omission. I set the phone on the dressing table and watched the cursor blink. I'd never sent a photo of Cal. Not one. Every time she'd asked, I made an excuse—he hates pictures, it's not that serious, he's shy. And there was always a next time. Always. Now, even an ocean away, she saw right through me.

I scrolled to the blurry, off-kilter shot I'd taken of Cal outside the stables—his hair ruffled by the wind, the sharp line of his jaw softer in profile, a hint of a smile shading his lips. For a second, I considered it. The urge clawed at me—weird and primal—to show him off like a trophy. Proof that this was real.

Then I came back to reality and typed out a safe reply.

I told you he's super camera shy. I promise he exists, and he's treating me like a queen.

A read receipt popped up, and for a moment, nothing. Then:

> I'm on to you, Gabrielle. If you show up married and he's an 87-year-old lecher, I WILL call the police.

I snorted, then caught my reflection in the mirror—eyes bright, skin flushed, smiling like a girl with her first crush. I didn't look like myself. Or maybe I looked *exactly* like myself— for the first time in forever.

The phone buzzed again—this time a call. I let it ring out, watching the screen pulse with Aunt Suzy's name and a photo of her grinning with sunglasses and a Houston Astros ball cap. The urge to answer flared sharp and bright, but I couldn't do it. Not with my voice liable to give everything away. Not with my heart crowding the air from my lungs.

Instead, I typed a brisk reply:

> Can't talk, bad reception. Heading to lunch. More pics soon. Love you!

It was half true, which was better than nothing.

I set the phone face down and stared out the window. The lawn rippled in the wind, shadows skimming the grass like ghosts.

I was engaged.

I pressed my forehead to the glass, trying to focus on sensation—the faint chill, the distant echo of my breath. I was engaged.

To Cal.

To my professor.

No. Not my professor. Not anymore. That was the line I kept repeating, the excuse I wore like a shield.

If we got married—and it was no longer an if, not really— the truth would have to come out. I'd have to tell Aunt Suzy, tell everyone, that I hadn't just fallen for some charming Brit with an aristocratic surname. I'd fallen for my professor. I'd crossed the one line everyone agreed was uncrossable. Even if I transferred and started fresh with a new school and a new story, the damage was already done. The rules were clear, and I'd broken them. No revisionist history would change that.

And it would be a scandal. No matter how many times Cal said it would be fine, that my life wouldn't be ruined. I could see the ripples already: Sloane Cartwright savoring the gossip, the story spreading from one group chat to the next, strangers acting like they knew me—like they were owed the details. I could already hear the whispers trailing me down hallways I'd never walk again—at least, not as a student.

The thought swept cold through my chest, harder than the wind rattling the windowpanes. I thought of the headlines that had chased Cal out of Oxford and across an ocean. I thought of my own shaky alibi—the half-lies I'd fed Aunt Suzy, the bland, forgettable name I gave her so she wouldn't look too closely. A day would come—and soon—when the truth would crash through it all, shattering the neat compartments I'd built to keep my worlds apart.

In that moment, I didn't know which was heavier—the secret or the love. I wondered if Cal's family had reached the same conclusion. On the surface, they seemed to have accepted everything—the age gap, my Americanness, the certainty that I would never, no matter how hard I scrubbed, fit within the outline of their world. My family was considered well-off back home, but nothing compared to the Hawthornes.

There had been no awkward questions about how long we'd known each other, or when exactly the shift from student and professor to something more had occurred. Instead, they had welcomed me—politely, if not warmly. But who knew what they said behind closed doors?

I glanced at the clock.

Shoot!

I'd let forty minutes slip past, lost somewhere between the blue damask wallpaper and my own reverie. I slipped on a pair of ballet flats and checked my outfit in the mirror. Not my best work, but it would have to do.

I hated the sherry—this family's preferred pre-luncheon ritual. But today, I might need it more than I'd ever admit.

CHAPTER 39

CALLUM

The library door sighed shut behind us, and the hush inside pressed close. Late morning light slanted through the east windows, striping the Persian rug in ochre and indigo.

James crossed to the drinks trolley, uncorked the decanter, and poured two fingers of whiskey—none for me. He made a show of the omission, as if it might sting. I leaned against the marble-topped sideboard, hands braced on its edge, and waited for the opening volley.

He offered none—simply swirled his drink.

"A bit early to be drowning your sorrows, isn't it?" I said, finally breaking the silence.

James's gaze sharpened behind the rim of his glass. "What would you know about sorrows?" His tone was a slow scalpel slide. "Or responsibility?" He set the glass down. "And you're hardly in a position to lecture me on appropriate behavior."

Heat prickled at my collarbone, but I kept my shoulders set, arms folded. "Well, go on then," I said. "Let's have it. A homecoming wouldn't be complete without a sermon from my perfect older brother."

He didn't rise to my tone, only shifted his weight, slow and deliberate. "You know what I hate about the prodigal son story?" He let the question hang, daring me to mock it. "It was forced on us every Sunday, if you recall."

"I do," I said, wary. "I didn't realize you were so fond of Sunday school parables."

James ignored me. "The younger brother's a wastrel. He fucks off, squanders their father's money, ignores every expectation, and then—when he's wrecked, when he's bled the world dry—he stumbles home, and his father throws him a bloody feast."

He tossed back the last of his whiskey, voice leveling out. James stared at the cut crystal glass, as if clarity might emerge from the play of refracted light.

"They drilled that story into us for years. But the punchline was always the same, wasn't it?" He looked up, a tight smile curving at the edges of his mouth. "The elder son stays behind. Sacrifices. Holds the line for the family. And where does that get him?" He traced a finger along the rim of the glass, eyes fixed on its slow revolution. "No feast. No celebration. No gratitude. Just more bloody work."

I braced myself against the sideboard, the cold bite of marble grounding me. "If you're saying you've never had anything handed to you, forgive me if I don't quite buy it."

James's laugh came out low and bone-dry. "Oh, I've been handed plenty, little brother. The business. The expectations. The duty. The slow, choking certainty that I'll die of boredom at a board meeting or one of Father's interminable charity events." He set the glass down, face hardening. "You, though —" He pointed, the gesture sharp as a chess move. "You get to fuck up. Publicly. You get to crash and burn—kill your fiancée, shag your student, whatever you bloody well like."

That was the point where most men would've thrown a punch. I just locked my jaw and let the fury settle into ice. "Anything else?"

James's smile sharpened, mean and precise. He leaned

close, voice dropping. "Do you know what's most galling? No matter what you do, someone's always there to clean up after you. Wipe the slate. Sweep away the mess. What mess is it this time, hmm?" His gaze flicked up, cold and bright. "The American girl upstairs? Did you at least give her top marks for fucking you?"

A pulse hammered in my throat, slow and savage. The library blurred—sideboard, dust motes spinning in the slant of sun, bone-white knuckles around a clenched fist. I forced air through my nose, measured and deliberate. "You're out of line." Each word balanced on the thin edge of my control.

"*I'm* out of line?" He stepped closer. I caught the bite of aftershave, the sour drift of whiskey. "You can't even see the line. You never could." He took a step back and gave me a once-over, all clinical disdain. "Or could it be that you've knocked her up?"

The words hit like a whipcrack, every old wound rising at once. I lunged—fast, thoughtless. The decanter rattled as my fist stopped just shy of his jaw. I could picture it—his bones cracking, blood blooming, my raw, fleeting satisfaction. None of the rules we'd grown up with—not age, etiquette, discipline —held a candle to the heat flaring in me.

"No," I spat, my hand trembling an inch from his face. "She's not pregnant, you absolute bastard." My breath tore in and out, wild and raw. I swallowed hard, the taste of blood sharp in my throat. "Say one more word about her—about us —and I'll put you through that fucking window."

James didn't flinch. Not even a tick in his jaw. "Go on," he said, almost gently. "One more mess for me to clean up."

My fist hovered, suspended between impulse and consequence. The past unspooled—the somber pageantry at Claire's funeral, the stinging shame of my first Oxford faculty meeting after the tabloids bled our story down every corridor. Humiliation, helplessness, rage—seething in my temples, cracking down my wrists like cold fire. I wanted to hit him. For the world to fracture beneath my knuckles.

But I didn't. Not for him. Not for the ancestral ghosts in the walls. For myself. For Gabrielle. Because striking him would mean he'd won. It would make me the beast he always said I was.

I let my hand fall, slow and controlled, and stepped back. My chest shook with the effort to leash the rest of me.

"When are you leaving?" James asked, like it had just occurred to him, voice flat with boredom.

"Not soon enough."

He nodded, lips twisting into a sneer masquerading as a smile. "Good. And when you do, feel free to make it permanent. I'm sure no one will mind." A pause, just long enough for the venom to seep in. "And when I finally have my way, every door here will be shut in your face. So, go on—shoo."

"Counting your inheritance a bit prematurely, aren't we?"

"I wouldn't say that. But I doubt you've noticed."

"Noticed what?"

"Typical," he scoffed. "You've been too busy fucking students to see a thing."

"Noticed what?" I asked again, stepping in.

James studied me, head cocked, and gave a short, humorless laugh. "Father is upstairs in his room. You should go see him." He paused. "If you can tear yourself away."

He didn't wait for a response. Just turned and walked out, leaving the door ajar.

I stayed rooted for a breath, pulse still pounding, then pushed off the sideboard.

Upstairs, the corridor was hushed, the air different—warmer, stuffy. I knocked once on Father's door, then let myself in.

The room was dim, curtains half-drawn against the midday light, the air heavy with the faint metallic drift of oxygen and disinfectant. My father lay propped against a bank of pillows in the great four-poster bed, its carved mahogany posts dwarfing his frame. His pajamas were crisp, the dressing gown belted neatly, but the fabric hung loose, no longer fitted to the man who'd once filled them out with authority. A thin cannula looped over his ears and into his nostrils, the clear tubing snaking down to a portable oxygen concentrator. A youngish nurse in a blue uniform—unfamiliar, likely agency—hovered near the bedside, checking the IV flow and making quiet notations on a digital tablet.

I stood there for a moment, unable to summon the right greeting. I hadn't seen him in bed since he'd shattered his ankle on a fox hunt two decades ago. Even then, he'd looked ferocious. Now he looked…small. Gray. His eyes were still sharp, but the skin around them had folded and thinned, like parchment baked too long in the sun.

I hovered in the doorway, caught between embarrassment and something colder. No one had warned me.

"What's all this?" I managed, the words brittle as chalk.

"You're the academic, Callum," Father rasped. "Surely you don't need it explained to you."

I pulled a chair to the bedside. "A little wouldn't hurt."

Father took a deep breath, followed by a series of hacking coughs. "Lung cancer." He said it without drama, like he was reporting the price of copper or an overnight devaluation of the pound. The nurse glanced up, then returned to her work, the tablet's blue glow casting her face in spectral relief against the half-light.

"Stage?" I heard myself ask, clinical and dry. I hated everything about my voice just then.

"Four." He held up four skeletal fingers, as if the number itself were distasteful. "It's been a busy quarter."

I pressed my palms to my knees. "When were you planning to tell me?"

He tilted his head, almost surprised. "When there was a

point to it. What would you have done with the information, Callum? Booked an earlier flight?"

The words should have stung—once, they would have opened a vein—but now they just hung there, as inert as the oxygen hissing at his nose.

"How long?"

He shrugged. "Six months, if the next round of treatment works. Less if it doesn't." He shrugged again, softer this time, the bones of his shoulders shifting under the fabric like driftwood.

"Mother knows?"

"Of course I know. Everyone knows." Mother's voice pierced from behind me.

I hadn't heard her enter. I stood, but she moved past me to the side of the bed, elegant even in her quiet. She rested her hand, featherlight, on the blanket at Father's knee. She didn't look at me. Her gaze flicked to his face and lingered there, searching for a sign that he needed her, or perhaps permission, some unspoken signal. They operated like an old ballet, every gesture second nature after decades of choreography—gracefully intertwined, even, or especially, at the end.

"Callum, you mustn't exhaust him," she said, her voice measured and velvet.

Father gave a sardonic grunt. "Let the boy talk, Eleanor. It's not as if conversation will kill me. We're well past that stage."

I nodded at the IV pole, its plastic tubing curled toward the crook of his arm. "Is that chemotherapy?" My voice was steadier than I expected.

Father's eyes flicked to the rig and back. "No. The poison comes next Thursday." He turned toward the nurse. "Remind me which cocktail we're on now?"

"Just some vitamins and fluid to keep you hydrated, Lord Branleigh," she answered without missing a beat, her tone gentle yet businesslike. "Should help keep your strength up for the festivities."

I watched her check the drip, her hands quick and competent, skin freckled and papery, her wedding band spinning loose on one finger. The line ran clear, tinged pale yellow—the color of weak tea. For a moment, I caught the edge of his forearm beneath the sleeve—like flaky parchment.

"How much longer?" he asked.

"Half an hour, give or take."

"I'd like a few moments alone with my son."

"Of course, sir. Ring if you need me, and I'll come straight in." She smiled at me. "He's a bit of a troublemaker, this one. Don't let him overdo it."

Father barely acknowledged her, but I did. "Thank you."

Mother watched the nurse's departure, then checked her watch—a slim Cartier, so thin it was more an idea than a timepiece. The gesture was subtle, but it landed like a gavel brought softly to the bench. "It's nearly one. I must go down for luncheon," she said, her words brisk for efficiency. "Miss Clark will think we've all abandoned her." She smoothed a crease from the blanket, then turned to me. "Will you come, Callum?" The question hung like an ornament, bright and fraught with the knowledge of what I would choose.

I tried to wipe the hesitation from my face. "If it's all the same, I'll stay here a bit longer." The old instinct—deference, or something that mimicked its lines—kicked in, but she only nodded, lips pressed into a thoughtful seam. "But please save me a place."

"Of course," she said. "The time alone will allow me a chance to get to know your young lady a little better," she added with the softest edge. Her tone, while light, allowed no counterpoint. She smoothed her skirt and swept from the room, heels thudding softly on the carpet.

The door softly snicked shut behind her.

Father let his head sink a notch deeper into the wedge of

pillows. One hand lay slack on the blanket, the other gestured to the chair at his bedside. "Sit."

I obeyed, and we considered one another across the expanse of white linen, the air between us thick with the muffled hiss of the oxygen concentrator. I waited out the silence, let it build until it threatened to smother us, years of practice finally serving some small purpose. He broke first.

"Well," he said at last, "have you found what you were looking for?"

I realized, too late, that I hadn't the faintest idea how to answer.

His tone was equal parts indulgence and acid. "All those years chasing your own blueprint. Carving out a life nobody had crafted for you. Cutting ties with everyone who ever supported you, just to prove you could build something entirely your own. So, answer me, Callum, was it worth all the trouble?"

He watched me with a hunger that startled me—a rabid need to balance the ledger before the world closed out his accounts. I looked for the familiar tics of manipulation, the old tells, but there was nothing left in him but directness—raw and crumbling, stripped of power.

I should have lied, told him something comforting. I should have said yes, I have everything I could ever want.

"I don't know," I said, surprised by the truth of it. "I thought so, once. But now…" The words stuck. What did I want now? For Gabrielle to be safe and whole and somehow delivered from the shadows I'd cast over her. Maybe even for my father to look at me and see a man, not a disappointment in a tailored suit.

I stared at the faint trace of his features reflected in the window glass. Not so long ago, I'd have met his parries flourish for flourish, carving clever wounds to savor in private. Now, all I could manage was honesty, leached of venom.

I turned to face him. "I'm happy," I said, and let it hang, plain. A confession, not a defense.

He tilted his head, studying me like an unfamiliar equation. The cannula pulled the line of his cheek taut, blue veins just visible beneath the skin. "Good." The word limped out. "That's all I wanted to know." He tapped the blanket, a rhythm too slow to be impatience. It struck me: he was nervous. "About the girl," he said, his eyes fixed somewhere just past my shoulder. "I've seen enough to know you're serious."

I waited, not trusting myself to speak.

"I won't lie," he continued, his voice gone low, "it's not what I'd have picked for you. Certainly not the… circumstances. But even I can see that she settles you, which you so desperately need." His gaze finally met mine. "So, if this is the path you've chosen, then you have my blessing. If it's worth anything."

Something caved in my chest, soft and hollow. "Thank you," I said, and to my horror, the words cracked.

He gestured vaguely toward the window, at the hazed green of the parkland stretching beyond the glass. "There's no mending you and James." His voice was distant but not dismissive—more like he'd finally accepted it wasn't worth the cost of hope. "I used to think it would come with time. That you'd settle your differences and find a way to coexist. But I see now you've both gone too far down your own lines for that." He shifted his hand, veins stark against his skin. "Which will make things complicated…after."

He didn't say after what. He didn't need to.

I waited, letting the silence thicken until he drew a deeper breath, shallow as it was.

He coughed—dry, serrated—and motioned toward the nightstand, where a glass of water waited on a silver tray. I handed it to him. He drank, then set it aside, the act costing more than it should.

"When I'm gone," he said, and the words caught in his chest. "There will be no one left to referee. James will inherit the title. He'll run the estate, the business, the family. It'll be his. All of it."

I nodded. My pulse drummed in my throat. The truth wasn't surprising, but hearing it put so plainly—without prelude, grandeur, or the upright posturing he'd always insisted on—cut deeper than it should have.

"I don't need a referee," I said. "We're not children anymore."

He smiled, though the effort left a fresh seam in his cheek. "You actually are. Isabel has more sense than the two of you put together." He looked all the way through me, a flicker of his old cunning beneath the haze of painkillers and disease. "I've changed my will," he said quietly.

"Finally cut me out?" I meant it in jest. At least halfway.

"Yes."

I snapped my head up. I shouldn't have cared, but the brutality of it still stung.

"But it's not what you think." Father took a moment, as if weighing not just the words but their velocity and impact. "That's why I was in London yesterday. I've signed over several assets to you. Directly. Not through the will, not funneled through the family trust."

"Father, I—"

"It's a sum of money and a few properties. I know James. He'll be the next baron, and he'll stop your allowance before my body is cold. And I know what he'll be like as executor. He won't honor anything in my will that doesn't suit him. I want what's yours to actually reach you."

I flinched, not at the act but at the expectation. "You don't need to do that," I said, the words out before I could retract them. "I'm the spare. I know my place. I'm not going to fight James for—"

"It's not up to him," Father interrupted. Then, careful and

precise, he continued, "And it's not for you, strictly. I know you'll give most of it away or let it sit untouched. It's for whoever comes after you." His gaze drifted back to the window, the fields beyond glazed over with haze. "I know you never wanted any of this, Callum, but you're the only one of my children to see the world as it truly is. Not as you'd have it, not as you'd like it to look in the press release. You *see* it." A short laugh broke up his breathing. "And maybe…maybe you've drawn the short straw too many times. So, please, son, let me do this for you."

I wanted to say, *You could have shown this softness before now.* I wanted to ask why he'd never bothered to try. But I wasn't a child, and petulance missed the mark when one was this close the end. Instead, I opted for a simple, quiet, "Thank you, Father."

He closed his eyes, his skin translucent over the sockets, and after a moment, he reached out and set his hand over mine where it rested on the duvet. The gesture was so unfamiliar I almost pulled away on instinct, but I made myself stay, feeling the dry, papery palm and brittle fingers.

"My solicitor will handle the deed of gift. This is strictly between us."

I nodded, and for once in my life, I didn't argue.

CHAPTER 40

GABRIELLE

Brooding.

There was no other word to describe Cal. He'd been this way since lunch. And I had no idea why.

Well, I had an idea. I just didn't want to think about it. Which meant, of course, that I couldn't think about anything else.

He sat slouched in the armchair of my bedroom, navy-and-burgundy dressing gown belted loosely around his waist, staring at the carpet. Or through it.

"Are you going to tell me what's wrong?"

"Why should anything be wrong?" he said flatly, never lifting his eyes.

I shook my head. "This is what you warned me about, isn't it?"

He looked up, gray eyes dull, but said nothing.

"You've been here for two days. Two. And they're already rubbing off on you. This doesn't work if you shut me out."

He dropped his gaze back to the carpet. "It's not what you think."

"Then fill me in. Because I just went from walking on clouds this morning to the most awkward day of my life. One minute, you're asking me to marry you. The next, you go off with your family, and now you won't look at me. I'm not an idiot, Cal."

"It's not you."

"'It's not you, it's me?' Wow…" I flung myself back on my pillows and stared at the ceiling. "I've heard that line before, but I never thought I'd hear it from you."

He stood and moved toward the bed. Bracing his hands on the footboard, he looked at me. The brooding was gone, replaced by pain rolling off him in waves.

I sat up and hugged my knees to my chest. "You told them, didn't you? You told them you wanted to marry me, and they shot you down."

"No," he said softly.

"If you're trying to spare my feelings, it's not working." I dropped my chin to my knee. "I was stupid to think I was good enough."

"*Damn it*, Gabrielle! This isn't about you." His words hit like a slap. And they stung just as much.

I rolled onto my side, curling toward the window. Tears welled, hot and stinging. I blinked hard to hold them back, but it didn't work. They spilled anyway.

I sucked in a shaky breath, trying to keep the tremors from my voice. "You should sleep in your own room tonight." Another breath. "I'm tired."

He didn't argue. I heard him shuffle toward the door. The knob creaked. His voice—smooth but frigid—coasted across the room.

"Funny thing about Branleigh Park—it changes people. Seems neither of us is immune." A beat. Then, clipped and formal, "Good night."

The door clicked shut.

And the waterworks began. Sobs ripped through my chest. I smothered my face in the cool pillow—partly to muffle the sound, partly to press it all back down. Like that ever worked.

I'd told myself this was different. That *we* were different.

Maybe I had been a fool to believe that a man like him—thirteen years older, Oxford-educated, so sharp and sure and finished—could really want someone like me. A girl still trying to make sense of her life, her grief, her future.

He was an accomplished physicist, and if the universe was just, a breath away from tenure. I didn't even have a bachelor's degree yet. He had old money, old manners, and a name people recognized. I had student loans, a flimsy résumé, and a heart too easily handed over.

What had I actually thought would happen? That we'd somehow outrun the odds? That his family would raise their crystal glasses and toast the scandal? That I'd be enough?

It was stupid. *I* was stupid.

What was I even doing here? I didn't belong in this house, in this family, in his world. Maybe I never had.

There was no version of this story where we belonged together. Not really.

And the worst part—the part that ached deepest—was that I still wanted him to come back. To walk through that door, lie down beside me, and say he didn't mean it. That he was scared too. That he'd shut me out because that's what he does when he's hurting, not because he didn't love me.

But the hallway was silent.

And I was curled in a strange bed, crying over a man who'd asked me to marry him that very morning…and walked out that night like I'd never mattered.

I don't know how long I lay there—long enough that the sobs quieted to hiccups, and the hiccups faded to silence. My head throbbed, my throat burned, and my body ached from exhaustion.

I hated crying like this. Hated the mess of it. Hated that it always ended the same way—leaving me hollow, humiliated, alone.

A soft knock sounded at the door.

I stiffened, every nerve suddenly wide awake.

The door opened with the softest click. I didn't move. I couldn't.

"Gabrielle?"

A fresh wave of tears slid down my face and onto the pillow.

Cal's voice came low and ragged, almost raw. "I'm shit at this." He let the words sit, wrecked and breathless. "Not just relationships—all of it. I know I've made a mess of today. I made a mess of everything after lunch. I made a mess just now, and I don't know how to…" The bed shuddered a little as he sat down—not too close, but not far.

He let the silence spool out, the pause trembling with whatever it cost him to speak.

"James and I had a row. It shouldn't matter, but it does. It dredged up…so much old rot. All the things I thought I'd finally left behind." He let out a sound halfway between a laugh and a sigh. "And then there's Father. He's dying, Gabrielle. Lung cancer. Maybe six months left, but that's optimistic. Apparently, everyone knew except me, and today he just…" Cal trailed off, voice thin and stunned.

I rolled to face him. He was sitting on the edge of the bed with his back to me. "I'm sorry."

"You have nothing to be sorry for."

I sat up. "No, I'm sorry your father is ill." I folded my legs under me and dashed away the tears with the back of my hand. "I know better than most what that's like."

He hesitated, hands knotted tight in his lap. His voice, when it came, was smaller than I'd ever heard it, shorn of every armor. "I know you do." He turned to me, and when his eyes met mine, his face fell. I'm sure I looked a wreck—eyes bloodshot, face blotchy.

Cal recoiled as if he'd been struck, his mouth folding into something raw and wordless. The next instant, he gathered me, careful but urgent, as though I were a glass cracked at the base but not yet fully shattered. My cheek found the warmth between his chest and shoulder, and he cradled me there, his palm cupping the crown of my head, thumb combing gentle paths in my hair.

"Don't," he murmured, the word a plea and a command and an apology all wound together. "Oh, love, don't ever let me do this to you."

I shook my head, but more tears leaked out, hotter for the embarrassment of them. He caught each one, stroking them away as if he could erase the evidence along with the wound.

"I never want to be the reason you cry," he said, voice low but hard-edged with self-loathing. He traced the curve of my jaw, the lines beneath my eyes. "Please, Gabrielle—don't let the rot of my family touch you. Not like this." His movements were desperate, almost frantic, as though he could paste me back together with sheer proximity.

"It's the jet lag," I blurted, forcing a laugh that faltered on the catch in my throat. "And the stress. And the end of the semester. It's a miracle I made it through customs without ugly-crying at some poor border agent." I sniffed, trying to find levity in the mess, but my voice sounded soft and pathetic, even to me.

Cal didn't take the out. He kept stroking my hair, sweeping slow arcs from my temple to the nape of my neck. He tightened his hold and pulled me fully onto his lap, the dressing gown soft against my skin. Dark stubble dotted his jaw, and fine lines gathered at the corners of his eyes.

"I'm sorry," I repeated, and this time he winced, shutting his eyes as if the words themselves hurt. "I thought your family convinced you I wasn't good enough," I said. I heard the acid in it, the raw scrape of pride. "That I was a phase, or an embarrassment, or something you'd regret later. I thought you'd finally seen how stupid our relationship looks from the outside." I forced the words, because if I didn't, I would shatter again. "If you want out, I won't stop you."

Cal drew a long, stuttering breath, his chest pushing into mine. His voice, when it surfaced, was crisp as a starched shirt but shaded with disbelief. "You are a prodigiously brilliant woman, and yet somehow you've arrived at the most daft conclusion imaginable. Truly staggering work." He said it like he'd stepped straight out of the House of Lords—vowels pure cut glass, diction so precise it could have been ironed. But beneath the theatrical scorn was something else entirely—devotion, worn thin by fear.

The laugh that burst out of me started as a hiccup, then a tumble I was too spent to restrain. It felt new and fragile, trembling there in the hush. "Wow," I managed, letting my head fall back. "You went full *Downton Abbey* on me."

He rested his forehead against mine, eyes closed, a rueful smile curving at the edge of his mouth. "You really think my family could change my mind about you?" He scoffed, and the warmth of him, the utter shock of his confession, was enough to start the tears again—except this time they tasted like relief. "And, if you must know, they've never tried to dissuade me. Even if they had, it wouldn't have made a lick of difference." Cal tightened his arm around my ribs, as if he needed the resistance to anchor the words. "Because, truthfully, it's the other way around. I'm not good enough for you. I still don't know why you bother with me."

I angled back, just enough to see his face—pale in the dim bedroom light. He was smiling, but it was a smile folded in on itself, paper-thin and crushed at the edges. I touched my fingertips to his jaw, let them follow the subtle graze of stubble to the hollow beneath his ear. "Now who's being daft?"

He huffed a laugh, but the sound was more a shudder than anything, equal parts relief and defeat.

I nestled my cheek against his shoulder, letting the silence yawn between us until my pulse evened out and my breathing fell back into a slow, measured rhythm. "Thank you," I said, so quiet it might have been a thought. "For coming back."

"I never should have left," he murmured, his voice vibrating beneath my ear.

I pressed my palm to the warmth of his chest, his muscles shifting restlessly, breath uneven beneath my hand, and I steadied myself against the uncertainty of what came next. "If you want to talk about your dad, I'm listening."

"I wouldn't know what to say." He drew in a breath and continued before I could reply. "It's odd—I'm perfectly happy delving into string theory, complex quantum entanglement, or working out the mathematics of a universe with twenty dimensions. But dying? A universally natural part of the human condition? It doesn't feel real yet. Or maybe it does, but the wrong parts do."

Cal's words hovered there, thoughts unfinished. He held me as if I were the axis of his world and he wasn't sure whether to spin or simply hang suspended.

I let the silence fill up with the sounds of his slow breaths and the muted tick of the ancient clock on the dresser. The last time I'd felt this particular brand of ache, I was perched on the foot of my dad's hospice bed, watching the shadows lengthen on the wall, waiting for a future to start that I couldn't for the life of me imagine. The awkwardness of impending loss was so specific—so metallic and cold—that it seemed to filter into the very air in the room. I could almost taste it here now, in England, nestled against Cal's ribcage.

"When my dad was nearing the end," I finally said, "I didn't think or act or feel like I thought I was supposed to. Cold as it is to say, I was ready for it all to be over so that I could finally move on. I mentioned that to the hospice chaplain, and his response has stayed with me to this day."

"What was it?"

"He said, 'In an abnormal situation, any response is normal.'" A beat. "That's the only useful thing anybody ever told me."

Cal didn't answer. At least, not with words. Instead, he

kissed my forehead—gentle, reverent. With a quiet exhale, he eased me off his lap and onto the bed, just long enough to shrug out of his dressing gown. He slipped beneath the covers and drew me in, curling his body around mine with a tenderness that undid me all over again.

He reached across me and flipped off the lamp. Darkness swept in, soft and complete. The strength of his arms around my waist anchored me more than words ever could.

And in that silence, held tight against his chest, I finally let myself believe we were still us.

Chapter 41

Callum

"So, is this what you want?" I asked, one hand anchored at Gabrielle's waist as I spun her across the makeshift dance floor. She felt right in my arms. Around us, guests mingled beneath fluttering bunting and tall hedges, late-afternoon light gilding everything in gold.

"You mean for a wedding?"

"Mm-hmm."

I drew her into another turn, her dress flashing a shimmering pale blue in the sun, and let her answer unfold at its own pace. She was exquisite in motion—shoulders bare, hair pinned up in that whimsical mess stylists spend hours perfecting.

Isabel's reception whirled around us in full gloss: linen-draped tables on the east lawn, waitstaff weaving through clipped boxwood and peony borders, silver trays held high. Champagne flutes sparkled in the light. Silk lanterns swayed from the marquee ceiling like moons caught mid-rise. Even the air was curated—gin and sweet vernal grass, strawberries steeping in Pimm's, and beneath it all, that deep green note of loam that only an English summer could summon.

"I could give you all this, if you wanted," I said. "The

pageantry, the spectacle, the perfect venue—though perhaps not Branleigh Park." I glanced toward James, deep in conversation with some pinstriped relic. Caroline, perched on his arm, nodded at all the right moments. Born to ingratiate. I turned back to Gabrielle. "Once James takes the helm, I doubt I'll be welcome. Maybe for my funeral, though probably not even then."

"Is it really that bad between you?"

"It is," I said, drawing her closer. "But James is the last person I want to think about right now."

She smiled—small, private, wry—as if she'd already drafted a hundred versions of this conversation and tucked them away in her back pocket.

"Is this what *you* want, though?" she asked.

Sunlight caught the blue of her dress, flashing it nearly silver.

"You're stalling," I said. "Try again. Do you want a wedding like this?"

She angled her head, scanning the crowd—old men in tailcoats and women in hats you could land a pigeon on. Peacocks, the lot of them.

"It's…beautiful," she said at last. "Gorgeous, really. Every detail—it's like something out of a movie. But for us? I don't think I could ever be the center of all this."

I sighed and leaned in, murmuring in her ear, "Thank God."

"I figured something like this would be expected of you."

I kissed her forehead. "Come now. You know me better than that."

"So what were *you* thinking?" she asked. "For a wedding?"

"Well…I don't much care to be the center of attention either. But a little excess can be fun. So…Vegas?"

"Vegas?" she repeated, lifting an eyebrow. "Seriously?"

"I've never been. But I've heard it's quite something."

"I've never been either," she admitted. Then, with a smile

that bloomed like a secret, "But yeah. That sounds perfect. If you're sure it's what you want."

"I want *you*," I said. "With as little interference from the rest of the world as possible." I tightened my grip on her waist, greedy in claiming her. "I want to wake up and drink coffee with you. I want to watch you make a complete mockery of British tea. And I want a life where the only approval that matters is yours."

Gabrielle didn't speak. She just looked at me with a softness that unspooled the tightness in my chest.

My gaze drifted past her shoulder, across the green swell of the lawn, to Isabel. She was dancing—bright and effervescent—with her new husband, her laughter trailing through the air like perfume. From a distance, no one would have guessed at the nerves she'd carried this morning—the panic over missing boutonnieres, the way she'd frozen in the kitchen and nearly called the whole thing off. You'd only see the hostess in her element, radiant and composed, a woman born to outlast every cliché the world had ever thrown at her.

She caught my eye. And just like that, she was weaving through the crowd toward us.

Isabel descended in a flare of silk and champagne, eyes bright as she looped Gabrielle into an embrace. "You two look far too conspiratorial for your own good," she said, voice pitched for our ears alone. Still the picture of grace, I caught the slight slurring of her words and alcohol-induced haze in her eyes. She let Gabrielle go but kept her hand, pressing it in both of hers. "What are we plotting?"

Gabrielle's smile was tentative but real. "Congratulations, Isabel. It's all...breathtaking, honestly. I've never seen anything like it."

Isabel's mouth curled around satisfaction. "Aren't you a darling?" She lifted her glass, eyeing Gabrielle over the rim. "With a little luck, it'll be you next. Save yourself the headache and elope."

Gabrielle blushed—not faint or bashful, but a surge of color that climbed her throat and set her ears aflame.

Isabel was too tipsy to notice. "So, what are your plans for the rest of your visit?"

I fielded the question for both of us. "We'll take a few days in London next week—show Gabrielle the city, play tourist. She's never seen it, apart from Heathrow."

Isabel lit up. "Good, you'll love it. London's lovely this time of year." She gave Gabrielle's hand one last squeeze, then turned to me. "Cal, you must take her to Dennis Severs' House—the old Georgian one in Spitalfields. It's deliciously strange. Just the right kind of theatrical. She'll adore it."

She tipped back the rest of her champagne. "Today's it for me. We're leaving on honeymoon first thing tomorrow, and we'll be gone for weeks." Her gaze flicked to Gabrielle, then, a beat slower, to me. "You two will have vanished across the Atlantic before I'm back." She jabbed a finger at my lapel. "You at least owe me a dance if you're going to abandon me again."

I cast a sidelong glance at Gabrielle. She nodded, wordlessly surrendering me to my sister's grasp. Isabel seized my hand and, with a fluidity that belied the champagne, swept us into the slipstream of the other dancers. We settled into step, her palm light on my shoulder. The band—a local orchestra plus a jazz pianist of some renown—played something old and clever, slipping over the crowd like a well-tailored coat.

In heels, Isabel nearly matched my height. She led, or thought she did anyway. For once, I didn't mind letting her.

"You've done well, Cal."

"Thank you for that."

"I'm serious. She's clever, charming, and somehow manages to put up with your bullshit." Isabel laughed—not her society laugh, but the unguarded one I remembered from childhood. "If I weren't so fond of you, I'd say she's far too good for you. But you deserve the best, darling."

She balanced her words on that knife-edge between fondness and fragility. For all her polish, Isabel was not invulnerable. A shadow flickered in her as we passed the white marquee, the custard tarts, and the lawn's serried ranks of children—sticky and wild, playing rounders in their formalwear. Today was her triumph. And her reward? A brother still half in exile, a mother who'd never mastered the maternal, a father unlikely to see another Christmas, and another brother already taking measurements for the drapes. Perhaps Father was right—Isabel had more sense than the rest of us put together.

"She's happy, Cal." Isabel pressed my hand, her gaze landing briefly on Gabrielle, who stood beside a rose trellis, fingers curled nervously around a fresh glass of Pimm's. "I can always tell. Don't you dare ruin it."

I matched the pressure in her palm. "I wasn't planning to."

"See that you don't." Isabel exhaled the softest sigh. Around us, the music swelled to a close. Couples peeled away in laughter or retreated to the drinks tent. "Take care of her. And yourself. And don't be a stranger. I don't care what James says. You're always welcome *chez-moi*."

I opened my mouth to reply—something sardonic, something easy, the old script we'd perfected—but the words fell short. "Thank you," I managed, drawing her into an embrace. I kissed her cheek.

She swatted my sleeve. "Off with you now."

Chapter 42

Gabrielle

"*S hit.*"

I looked up from my book, still jet-lagged and foggy. Cal was staring at his phone, brows cinched. "What is it?"

He didn't answer—just set the phone on the coffee table and stalked off toward his office.

I blinked, then leaned over to check the screen. A text from Bill Watkins was still open:

> Hey, sorry to bug you while you're off the grid, but heads-up: Dr. Lemke and Dr. Singh are asking pointed questions, and the rumor mill is flying. You should check your university email. Stat.

I waited a minute. Then another. Curiosity finally corroded my resolve. I trailed after Cal, my pulse thrumming in my ears, the hardwood cool beneath my bare feet. His office door was ajar, just enough to see him hunched at the desk, laptop open, the screen's blue-white glow carving exhausted shadows into his face.

I hovered just outside the doorway—close enough to see

him, far enough to give him space. I folded my arms, knuckles digging into the soft cotton of my sweatshirt, and waited. If Dr. Lemke and Dr. Singh—deans, VPs, or whatever high-level thing they were—were sniffing around, the digital gossip at Page College would have already gone nuclear. I slid my phone from my pocket and opened the only social media app that mattered. I searched for Cal's name—first, last, full academic honorific—and the results flooded in, each thread more unhinged than the last.

It was Sloane Cartwright's post, naturally, that set the tone:

—prof hawthorne caught in "close relationship" with a student. paging the ethics committee lmao!

She'd paired it with a GIF of a flaming dumpster rolling downhill. The replies were a demolition derby of snark, thirst, conspiracy, and unholy Photoshop crimes.

—"Close relationship" is doing a LOT of heavy lifting. Girl, blink twice if you're trapped in a thesis defense with benefits.
—Professor Hawthorne gets extra credit in bed!!
—ikr he's hot as hell.
—Welp. My tuition's funding somebody's sex life, I guess.
—Who's the lucky bitch!?!?!
—Not me emailing him my quantum physics homework and a nude.
—Someone said "academic rigor," and Dr. Hawthorne said "bet."
—I'd risk the honor code for that D.
—Did she call him "sir" before or after the final? Asking for science...

There was a poll—an actual, five-choice poll—on who the

"mystery student" could be, with the top vote going to "some grad-student honeytrap." Nobody had my name. Not yet.

I scrolled with a weird detachment, like it was happening to someone else. The posts spread from the college subforum to the wider university feed, then spilled out to the usual sewage conduits. Someone had screen grabbed Cal's faculty photo and slapped it beside a screeching tabloid headline. I'd always known the internet was a bonfire. I just never thought I'd be the kindling.

I closed the app, shoved the phone in my pocket, and leaned against the doorjamb. Cal sat rigid at his desk, one hand buried in his hair, the other clicking through screens at lightspeed.

"Is it what I think it is?" I finally asked.

"I won't insult your intelligence by pretending otherwise." He spun the laptop to face me, open to an email.

I stepped forward and read.

Subject: Formal Notice of Allegation
From: Dr. Amrita Singh, Vice President of
Academic Affairs
To: Dr. Callum Hawthorne
CC: Dr. Michael Lemke, Dean of Students; Ms.
Maryann Jennings, Human Resources
Date: May 29

Dr. Hawthorne,

This email serves as formal notice that the
Office of Academic Affairs has received an
allegation regarding a potential violation of
the Faculty Code of Conduct, specifically
Section 4.1.3: Improper Relationships with
Students.

You are required to attend a preliminary
meeting regarding this matter on Monday at
8:30 a.m. in my office, located in Suite 300,
Administration Building. The meeting will
include myself, the dean of students, and a
representative from human resources.

Please note that this is not a formal
disciplinary hearing; however, your full
cooperation is expected. Until the matter is
resolved, you are hereby instructed not to
discuss it with students or faculty.

A copy of the relevant policy is attached for
your reference.

Sincerely,
Dr. Amrita Singh
Vice President of Academic Affairs
Page College

I pulled away from the screen. "Monday? That's tomorrow.
We literally got back in the country yesterday."

Cal nodded. "No rest for the wicked."

I came around the desk and rested a hand on his shoulder.
"What do you need me to do?"

He blinked, as if the question surprised him. "Nothing,
love," he said quietly, not looking up. "I'll go in, sit through
their little performance, and wait to see if the axe falls before
or after lunch."

"Shouldn't there be a formal inquiry or something? It
can't just be a one-and-done meeting."

"Depends how much they know. And I don't know that

yet." He leaned back slightly, eyes fixed on the wall. "It's all optics. If they've got the upper hand, they'll use it. Pressure me to sign something, disappear quietly, spare the college the scandal. Nothing worse than bad press."

He took my hand and kissed my knuckles, slow and distracted.

"I'm more concerned for you than for me."

"Why? It's your career on the line, not mine."

He didn't answer. He closed the laptop and stared at it. "How bad is the social media fallout?"

I feigned ignorance. "The what?"

He looked up. "I presume that's what you were checking just now. So, how bad is it?"

I hesitated, replaying the worst of it in my head. "What you'd expect." It felt glib, but I said it anyway. "Just gossip. No real meat."

"Are you named?"

"Not that I can tell." I bit my lip. "Not yet, anyway."

"That's a small mercy, at least." He snapped his chin up, as if remembering something vital. "Have you formally withdrawn from Page yet?"

"Not yet. I was going to submit that this week."

"Best hold off. At least until we know what they've got."

CHAPTER 43

CALLUM

Monday, 8:25 a.m. The administration building reeked of fresh paint and filtered air—an industrial sort of sweetness. The glass on the third floor was so clear it felt more like an absence than a window, a silent threat of falling straight through to the campus quad below.

Suite 300 was a frosted-glass affair with an incongruously cheerful secretary—her hair dyed copper and nails lacquered in what could only be called "litigation red."

"They'll be ready for you in a few minutes."

"Lovely," I said and sat, hands folded, as careful as a bomb technician.

The clock ticked forward in increments too small to trust.

At 8:30 precisely, the interior door sighed open, and Dr. Amrita Singh appeared. She wore a navy linen pantsuit and a smile so geometrically thin it could have been etched with a diamond stylus.

"We're ready for you, Dr. Hawthorne."

The worst they can do is fire you, I told myself. With a controlled exhale, I rose to my feet, adjusted my cuff links, and followed her in.

Dr. Michael Lemke, Dean of Students, and Maryanne Jennings from Human Resources were seated on one side of a large circular conference table. A third chair—Dr. Singh's, presumably—sat between them. Opposite them, a lone chair awaited—clearly mine. So much for the egalitarian promise of the round table.

"Please have a seat," said Dr. Singh, closing the door behind her and taking her place between Dr. Lemke and Ms. Jennings.

In no particular hurry, I crossed to my assigned chair and eased into it.

"Thank you for coming, Dr. Hawthorne," she began, clipped and formal, like reading from a script. "I've asked Ms. Jennings to be present as this matter may affect your employment status at Page College. Dr. Lemke is here because the issue involves a member of the student body."

"Alleged," I corrected.

"Pardon?"

"Alleged issue." I matched her tone, syllable for syllable. My time at Branleigh Park had served its purpose after all— my armor was intact. "I don't even know what I've been accused of."

"Very well," she said, amending herself with faint distaste. "*Alleged* issue."

Beside her, Dr. Lemke loomed—broad shoulders filling out a royal blue button-down, his bright orange tie geometrically knotted, his face arranged in professionally moderated concern.

Dr. Singh steepled her fingers, the motion as elegant and precise as the rest of her. "Dr. Hawthorne, I've called you here today to address a serious allegation that has recently come to my attention." She glanced at the HR rep, then back to me, offering a brief, icy smile. "This is not a formal disciplinary hearing. Consider it an opportunity to clarify the situation before such measures prove necessary."

Ms. Jennings nodded with bureaucratic solemnity, pen already poised above her notepad.

"We know you're just back from vacation," Dr. Lemke said, voice smooth as worn leather, shaded with the easy cadence of a Texas drawl. "So we really appreciate your coming in first thing on a Monday."

Ah. So he was to be the good cop.

Dr. Singh opened a slim folder and slid a printout across the table. "We received an email last week. The sender alleges that you, while employed as a member of the faculty, engaged in an unduly personal and physically intimate relationship with a student currently enrolled at Page College. The relationship is described as 'ongoing.' The message cites several specific incidents and claims the involvement began during the spring semester."

She waited for me to pick up the paper, but I let it sit. It was clearly an email, but the sender's name, address, and every line that didn't directly reference me had been reduced to a series of thick black bars. Even the subject line was redacted, as if the very premise of my existence had been deemed classified.

I scanned the visible lines.

```
"…a student under the direct
instructional supervision of Dr.
Hawthorne…"
"…unduly familiar relationship with
multiple encounters outside the
classroom…"
"…overnight travel during spring break."
```

The final lines, most damning, read:

```
"…traveled with Dr. Hawthorne to England
after the end of the spring semester,
```

```
where they stayed for an extended period
at an estate owned by Dr. Hawthorne's
family."
```

The sender's name was blacked out entirely, along with any detail that might point to the original observer. I recognized the cadence—fastidious and self-important—almost certainly written by an elite or an academic. Not a student.

My thoughts landed, however briefly, on James. This knife-in-the-back maneuver was certainly his style. But I doubted he cared enough to bother.

"Is there a name attached to the complaint?" I asked, not looking up.

Dr. Singh shook her head. "The sender requested complete anonymity."

"And the identity of the alleged student?"

"I can't disclose that either. I have a responsibility to protect their confidentiality."

"How very convenient for them," I said. "And for you."

She blinked, unruffled. "We take all allegations seriously, especially those which could bring harm to the institution or its students."

"Dr. Hawthorne," said Dr. Lemke, shifting forward, "this isn't personal in any way. You and I have always gotten along great. But you have to understand, we're in a tough position here. Priority number one—we have to look out for our students."

"Of course."

"So, help us out. Is there any truth to these claims?"

"What claims, exactly?" I asked, keeping my voice even. Dr. Lemke's eyes darted to Dr. Singh, waiting for her to take the lead.

She gestured to the printout. "The ones enumerated in the email. The ones you just read."

"A heavily redacted, nameless complaint absent credibility or context?" I tapped the table, the sound louder than I expected. "How am I supposed to respond when I don't even know what I've been accused of—by whom, with whom, or when?"

"You understand the need to protect student confidentiality," Dr. Singh said, her tone almost chiding.

I matched her tone. "Of course. But surely you see that asking me to respond to a redacted, anonymous tip is not only improper—it's legally dubious." I folded my hands in my lap. "You haven't even told me which student I'm meant to have… ensnared."

Dr. Lemke leaned in, speaking like a coach addressing a promising but difficult player. "Cal—may I call you Cal? We're not trying to trip you up. But this is serious. We want to give you a chance to clear the air before it escalates."

"Michael—may I call you Michael?"

He bristled a bit but didn't back down.

"Do you have corroborating evidence, or is this strictly an exercise in creative reading?"

He looked to his colleague and then back at me, but didn't answer.

"No? Then I'd say the air is clear. As is my conscience."

Dr. Singh turned the full weight of her scorn on me. "Dr. Hawthorne, this is not a negotiation. We're asking you plainly: have you, at any time, engaged in an inappropriate relationship with a Page College student?"

Silence thickened. The HVAC grumbled as it kicked on, blasting frosty air across the room. The printed email—more thick black ink than white space—fluttered to the floor in the artificial gust. I met her gaze, then Dr. Lemke's.

"No," I finally answered. "I have not engaged in an inappropriate relationship with a student." I chose my words carefully, echoing her exact phrasing. I should have left it there. But pride or ego or sheer stupidity got the better of me.

"If this is about optics, then what I've done—or haven't done—is already irrelevant. But I will say this. At no point have I exploited my position, nor have I coerced, endangered, or manipulated anyone. Are we finished?"

Dr. Singh pressed her lips into a pale seam of distaste. "Dr. Hawthorne, it is the determination of this office that there is sufficient cause to refer this matter to a formal disciplinary review. You will be notified of the date, and your full cooperation is expected." She glanced at Ms. Jennings, who rustled a folder open without looking up. "Ms. Jennings will brief you on specifics."

"You are hereby placed on paid administrative leave, effective immediately," she began, her voice as flat as a spreadsheet cell. "You are not permitted on campus except when specifically requested by the review board. You are not to have any contact with students, and you are prohibited from engaging with any faculty or staff regarding this matter, except through approved channels."

She opened a second folder—copies, no doubt, of the same bureaucratic terms she'd just recited.

"Further," she continued, "until this inquiry is resolved, you are not to represent the college in any public or professional capacity. Any public statement, including those made to media or on social platforms, will be considered a violation of the terms of your leave."

She handed me the top sheet—a crisp printout on university letterhead, its paragraphs already numb on the page. "Do you understand?"

I nodded, resisting the urge to laugh. Even the language was a performance.

"Then please sign at the bottom. You're only acknowledging receipt and understanding. This is not an admission of guilt."

I signed, the gesture crisp, and slid it back with a flourish I hoped read as final rather than fatalistic.

Dr. Lemke folded his hands like a vicar leading a funeral prayer. "No one wants this to turn ugly, Cal. Least of all me."

I said nothing.

Dr. Singh stood. "That will be all, Dr. Hawthorne."

I rose without a word, walked to the door, and didn't look back. If I had, I might not have kept my mouth shut.

Chapter 44

Gabrielle

al was gone. Physically, at least. His coffee mug sat half-full on the kitchen counter. I rinsed it out and put it in the dishwasher—not out of obligation, just to give my hands something to do.

I'd been drifting all morning—from couch to table to floor to couch again—touching random objects like they could tether me to the present. Like he'd walk back in if I just kept moving. The nerves in my stomach had gone full-time and were billing by the minute.

I checked my phone again—8:45. Still nothing. I hoped for a call, a text, an email—anything. At this point, even a text from Aunt Suzy would have helped. Anything to break the silence.

Speaking of Aunt Suzy… She'd gone quiet ever since I got back from England. Her last message, sent the day I'd landed, was still sitting there:

> Good luck with the jet lag, kiddo. Glad you're home.

That was two days ago.

I hovered, then thumbed out:

Are you free?

Yes

Call?

Sure...

The ellipsis tripped me up. Was it passive-aggressive punctuation? Or just the casual dot-dot-dot favored by anyone over fifty?

I called. Three rings.

"Hello?"

I put on my sweetest voice. "Hi, Aunt Suzy!"

"Hey, hon." Her voice was pitched oddly stiff. Cable news murmured in the background.

"You busy?" I asked, immediately regretting it.

A rustle. A clatter. "Always." A door clicked shut. "But I can talk. What's up?"

I curled up on the couch, phone pressed tight to my ear. "Just…checking in. Haven't heard from you."

"Can't say I've heard much from you either, sweet girl." The endearment hit like a sugar cube with a razor in it. "Did you have a nice time in England?"

I laughed—light, maybe too light. "Honestly? It was incredible. The countryside looked like something out of a fairy tale. The house was unreal. His sister's wedding was *Vogue* meets *Downton Abbey*. And we rode horses! I didn't break my neck, which—" I caught myself babbling.

"That's nice," Aunt Suzy said. Flat as a pancake. "Sounds like a once-in-a-lifetime experience."

"I know you're mad I went, but it really was—"

"I'm not mad you went, Gabrielle."

"Then what?"

The silence stretched, taut and unforgiving.

Then, finally, she said, "I'm mad you lied to me about it."

My stomach dropped. "What do you mean, I lied?" I asked, careful to keep my voice even. "I told you I went to England with my boyfriend, stayed with his family, and got back Saturday."

"Your boyfriend." It wasn't a question. "Remind me, who is that again?"

I scanned the room for a lifeline and found only the sun pooling on the carpet and the dull hum of the air conditioner. "You…don't know him."

Her spoon clinked, followed by the slow drag of her inhale. "Calvin Green, you told me. Another student from your physics class?"

"I—" The pause was my only defense. "I know him from physics, yes."

A rustle—papers, maybe. When her voice returned, it held the brittle sweetness of a pie crust about to crack. "So, here's the funny thing. You know me—I'm nothing if not a diligent aunt," she said. "I tried to look him up, but I couldn't find any Calvin Green associated with Page College."

"No…?"

"But you know who I found instead?"

My mouth went dry. "Who?"

She let it hang, relishing the power. "A dashing physics *professor* by the name of Cal Hawthorne."

For once in my life, I had no words.

"I did a little more digging, reached out to a few friends, called in a few favors. Turns out, he's not just any professor. He was *your* professor this spring. He's quite British, and, according to one of his colleagues in the physics department, just spent two weeks visiting family in England."

I swallowed hard, then found my voice. "How many privacy laws did you have to break to get all that?"

A brittle laugh. "Honey, there's no such thing as privacy once you're on the internet. Or in a faculty directory."

I pressed the heel of my hand to my eye. "I didn't want you to think—"

"To think what?" Her voice wasn't loud, but it cut with a serrated edge. "That you were dating your professor? That you got on a plane with a man twice your age and flew halfway around the globe?"

"He's not twice my age."

"*That's* the part you defend?"

I answered with silence.

Her inhale was shaky, hard. "You should have told me the truth, Gabrielle."

"You wouldn't have been okay with it."

"No," she admitted. "I wouldn't have. I don't know what I would've done—maybe thrown a fit, maybe tried to talk you out of it. But at least I wouldn't have had to find out like some dumb suburban mom on a *Dateline* rerun."

"You're not my mom." It came out hotter than I'd intended. Acid laced with exhaustion. But I didn't take it back.

She paused. "No. I'm not. But I'm the closest thing you've ever had." Her voice dropped. "So I'm going to ignore that."

The silence after that was so absolute I could hear the blood move through my ears.

"Are you going to tell me the whole truth now?" Aunt Suzy asked. Her voice was gentler than I expected, more stunned than angry. "No more redactions. No more 'Calvin Green' bullshit. I want the whole story. Start to finish."

I took a breath and tasted metal. "Okay." My voice came out thready.

She waited, not filling the space, and let me do the heavy lifting.

I told her everything—the dead battery in the rain, the tea fiasco, the motorcycle ride to Oklahoma, the pull we couldn't fight, the week on Lake Rayburn, my decision to transfer so we could be together legitimately, and finally, the trip to England to meet his family. I left out the engagement detail, but only because Cal and I had agreed to keep that to ourselves for now.

"Wow."

"Yeah…"

"So this is the real deal, then? He's not exploiting you, coercing you, or abusing his position?"

"Not even a little. This is real, Aunt Suzy." A beat. "I love him. I really do."

She blew out a long breath. "You really should have told me sooner."

"I know. But I'm telling you now. I've been accepted—with scholarship—to the engineering programs at both SMU and UTD. I'm choosing SMU, and I'll file my withdrawal from Page this week. So everything will be…legal."

Suzy was quiet. Too quiet.

"You're not saying anything."

"I'm thinking," she said finally. "Trying to decide whether to be relieved…or scared out of my mind."

"I'm not in danger," I said, keeping my voice as steady as I could. "We've been careful. No one at school knows. Well…" I caught myself. "At least not officially."

"What does that mean?"

"Someone knows something—I just don't know what or how much. Cal got called to campus first thing this morning."

A breath crackled through the line. "Gabrielle…I need to tell you something."

My stomach turned. "Okay…"

Her voice dropped. "I didn't mean for this to spiral. I just…I didn't know what else to do. So I sent an email with what I knew and asked the administration to look into it."

The room went still. "You *what?*"

"I just…gave them enough to ask questions. To make sure this wasn't—" She exhaled shakily. "God, Gabrielle, I was scared. Yes, you're twenty-five, but this is the first time you've really been out on your own. He's your professor. What if it wasn't what you thought? What if you got hurt and I sat back and did nothing?"

I stared at the blank TV screen, my heart thudding. I didn't know what to say. All the words dissolved on my tongue, sour and useless.

"I'm sorry, Gabrielle," Aunt Suzy said, voice quivering around an unfamiliar burr. "I was just trying to protect you. I hope you can see that."

I pulled the phone away and stared at it, like it might offer some guidance from the digital ether. Then I pressed it back to my cheek. The garage door rumbled open—low and steady, like a warning bell. Cal was back.

"I can't talk to you right now."

Disconnect.

I stood, walked into the kitchen, checked the water level on the kettle, and switched it on. Tea made everything better, right?

CHAPTER 45

CALLUM

"Thank you, love," I said as I accepted a cup of tea from Gabrielle. The warmth seeped into my fingers. I held it like it might keep me afloat.

She didn't say anything. Just gave me space.

I took a sip. *Perfection.* She'd come a long way. At least I'd been good for something.

"Formal inquiry is going forward," I said at last, when it was clear she wouldn't ask. "They've put me on administrative leave. Full pay, health insurance, the works. I can't set foot on campus, talk to students or staff, or so much as send an email. I am, for all practical purposes, persona non grata at Page College."

She nodded, her gaze steady. "How long?"

"Until they reach a verdict." I took another scalding sip. "They'll convene a review board. Gather evidence. Interview anyone named in the complaint."

Gabrielle stirred her tea, though every sugar crystal had long since dissolved. "What was the complaint?" she asked, not looking up.

"A heavily redacted email. But it was enough."

"What did it say?"

"From the bits I could actually read, it alleged we've had an ongoing relationship since spring term. That we're sexually involved. That we spent spring break together. And more recently, two weeks in England. All of which is true. Not that I confirmed any of it."

She was silent.

"They wouldn't say who sent it, and they didn't name you. But whoever it was had an alarming amount of insight into our lives." I took another drink of tea. "The email was eloquent and polished. I suspect my family. James, most likely. He has both the motive and the cruelty. And enough detail to wound with precision."

"It wasn't James." She looked away, burying her face in a long sip of tea.

I set my cup down. "If not James…then who?"

She hesitated, then placed her mug on the table. Her fingers lingered at the rim. She wouldn't meet my eyes. "Please don't get mad."

My gut clenched. I swallowed, throat dry. "I won't," I said. Then added, because I had to, "Unless you tell me it came from you."

Her mouth twitched into a pained smile. "Not me."

A beat.

"It was Aunt Suzy." Her voice was hollow. Then she looked up, eyes red-rimmed but dry. There was no apology in them. Just the bleak certainty of delivering a wound she couldn't take back. "She's the one who reported us."

I blinked. Then reached for my cup—not to drink, just to anchor my hands.

"Your aunt?" I said slowly. A faint, incredulous laugh slipped out before I could stop it. "I thought she didn't know."

"She didn't. But I guess…all the little lies I told, the half-truths—they didn't hold up. She didn't buy the classmate boyfriend story, so she started digging. She's got tons of university connections. And she found you."

I closed my eyes. Let the weight of it settle.

Of course.

"That explains why Dr. Singh took it seriously," I said quietly. "Your aunt's faculty at the University of Houston, isn't she?"

Gabrielle nodded. "Education professor."

"And you've known since…?"

"Ten minutes ago. I was literally on the phone with her when you pulled into the drive." She looked up, pleading. "I'm so sorry, Cal. I know it doesn't count for much, but I am."

I don't know how long I stood there—frozen somewhere between heartbreak and logic, between the urge to lash out and the certainty she wasn't the one holding the knife.

She stepped—slowly, deliberately—toward me.

"What can I do to make this right?" Her voice barely carried the short distance to me. "I'll go to campus, make a statement, talk to the review board—whatever you need. Just let me fix this. Please."

I exhaled and looked toward the window. "You can't fix this, Gabrielle."

She flinched like I'd slapped her. But I kept going.

"Because it was never your mess to fix." I turned back to her. "I knew the risk. Knew it when I let myself want you." I traced my fingertips along her jaw. "Knew it when I kissed you. Knew it every bloody day after. I just…" My throat tightened. "I thought if we were careful enough, smart enough, we'd make it through. We were so close."

She opened her mouth, but I shook my head.

"No one's dragging you into this. I won't allow it. They'll come for me, and I'll take it. But you—" I laced my fingers through hers. "Your hands stay clean. Got it?"

Her tears brimmed on the ledge but refused to fall. "You think I'd let you take the whole hit for this? That's not—"

"It's exactly what's going to happen."

She steadied herself, voice trembling but stubborn. "You

don't get to decide what I can live with. I choose you, Cal. Even if it means choosing the fallout too."

Silence. The kind that seeps into drywall cracks, baseboard seams, the marrow of old houses built on shifting earth.

I tried to memorize the angle of her jaw in profile, the wary intelligence in her eyes, the pale ring of baby-fine hair at her forehead. Assuming, of course, that one day I'd be asked to reconstruct this moment in painful detail—for a committee, a tribunal, or some future version of myself. Or for the version of her that survived whatever was coming.

She deserved more than memories. More than careful erasures, closed doors, and whispered I-love-yous in the dark.

I kissed the inside of her wrist. Let my lips linger a breath longer than necessary.

Then I looked up. "Take me flying, Gabrielle."

She blinked. "Flying?"

"You heard me."

"Now?"

"I'm on leave. It's not like I've got pressing plans."

She pulled back an inch, like she was checking to see if I was joking. "You mean in a—what did you call it—'tin can with wings'?"

"Flying tin can," I corrected softly. "But yeah."

"Cal…" Her voice dropped. "You hate flying."

"I do."

She stared at me, trying to make sense of it. "Then why?"

I gave her the only truth that mattered. "Because fear doesn't get to decide anymore."

CHAPTER 46

GABRIELLE

"You know you don't have to impress me anymore." My voice echoed in the headset, metallic and oddly detached—a sound I still hadn't gotten used to. I leveled the plane out of a gentle turn. Above and around us, the cornflower sky stretched like a glass dome, seamless and vast. The heat rising off the earth wrapped around us, thick and close—a sunbaked June embrace.

Cal's voice crackled through the intercom. "I'll never stop trying to impress you. Not ever."

He gripped his harness so tightly his knuckles were white, but he still managed a show of bravado. His hair was mussed from the headset and wind, and I loved him more for the faint sheen of terror on his brow.

I angled the Cessna into a slow climb, the world outside resolving into that private geometry known only to pilots and gods. Heat and light shimmered over Lake Texoma. The air above us was clean—ancient, unjudging.

"You know, for a physicist, you're showing a tragic lack of faith in Bernoulli's Principle," I teased.

"I trust Bernoulli completely. What I don't trust is how his principle was applied in building this aircraft. That's why I'm a theoretical physicist. The maths never lie." He released his grip on the harness long enough to fumble for his pocket. "But…"

"But what?"

"I have complete faith in *you*."

I shot him a sideways glance. "I'll remind you of that when I'm ready for wingovers and negative G maneuvers."

"Before you do that…" He inhaled sharply. "Keep in mind that I'm putting my life completely in your hands."

I laughed, but his eyes were fixed on me. I went to answer him—to fire back some clever retort, but he got there first.

"But that's rather the point, isn't it?"

"What is?"

"That I trust you completely with my life in your hands. Which is as it should be if"—he snapped open a black box— "I'm going to ask you to trust yours in mine."

The diamond glinted in the intense summer sun. My throat went dry as sandpaper. I had no words.

"I know we've talked about this, but the last time I proposed, it was all a bit spur of the moment. So, I'd like a chance to do it properly." The headset crackled behind his beat of silence. "Gabrielle Suzanne Clark—will you marry me?"

I choked, my voice wavering between a laugh and a sob. I looked down at my trembling hands on the yoke. I tried to center myself on the horizon line—how the world was always straight and true if you knew how to read it—but my vision blurred. "I already said yes."

Cal pulled out the ring—a princess cut with channel-set diamonds on a gold band—and held it out. "Humor me. Say it again."

I grinned until my cheeks ached. "Yes."

Cal took my left hand from the yoke—always with that impossible gentleness—and slid the ring onto my finger. His hands were cooler than mine. My pulse moved like a slow tidal current under my skin. The diamond caught a sunbeam, scattering rainbows across the instrument panel.

I stared at it—at the certainty of it—as the horizon leveled. Below us, the world blurred into a patchwork of green, brown, and blue—boundless, impersonal—but in the cockpit, it was just us and this impossible, shining future.

"How long have you been sitting on this?" I managed to ask, as I flexed my fingers, watching the stone catch the light.

He smiled, faintly embarrassed. "Picked it up in London, actually. Just before we left. I wanted it to be…proper."

I swatted his shoulder, letting my fingers linger on the soft blue of his shirt. "You liar. You said you had to meet your father's solicitor."

He gave a theatrical sigh, but the corners of his eyes crinkled. "I did. But the appointment was conveniently next to a charming jewelry shop."

I nudged his thigh with my knee, the control stick trembling with the motion. "You didn't have to risk death by turbulence to propose. You could have just…I don't know, knelt at dinner like a normal person. Dropped the ring in the champagne."

He arched an eyebrow. "And then I'd be every other man. Is that what you want?"

I considered it, then shook my head. "No. I couldn't stand it."

"Precisely." He glanced at my hand, now heavy with promise, and the tension in his jaw eased. "Besides, it's more poetic this way. Permanently affianced at three thousand feet, entirely at the mercy of your piloting."

I rolled my eyes and angled toward the cloud bank, letting the sky swallow us in blue. After a minute, the adrenaline ebbed, and with it the mad, shimmering disbelief. In its place came a weightless kind of happiness—the kind I'd never trusted before. I flexed my left hand—the ring foreign, yet oddly reassuring—and just for a moment, I let myself forget about what waited for us on the ground.

"How did you know my middle name?"

He gave me a faux-wounded look. "Darling, I spent an entire term staring at your name on my roster. I memorized every detail."

CHAPTER 47

CALLUM

I pushed a thumb drive across my desk. Bill stared at it, scratching his beard before picking it up.

"That's all my course content: syllabi, slide decks, lecture notes, exams. Everything."

"You're really leaving, Cal?" He tucked the thumb drive into his shirt pocket.

"It's for the best." I stacked another three volumes—Griffiths, Feynman, and a battered copy of *The Road to Reality*—into a white banker's box. They thudded against the corrugated cardboard like bricks mortared into a wall.

"But the board cleared you."

"Technically, yes. But you and I both know that the damage is done." I dropped a stack of research notebooks into the box. "If I stayed, I'd be looking over my shoulder, second-guessing every interaction. I can't live like that."

"I thought for sure you'd stay, even if only out of spite."

I chuckled darkly as I slid the lid over the banker's box with a tight, satisfying seal.

"Where will you go?"

"I've got a few feelers out. A visiting professorship in Switzerland. A private research post in Austin. Possibly consulting for an aerospace startup. Or I might take a sabbatical. Get some real writing done for once. I haven't decided."

He nodded, eyes drifting over the stripped shelves. "You'll hate Switzerland."

I busied my hands with a tangle of power cords, winding them into neat, choking loops. "Probably."

Bill hovered in silence, hands shoved deep in his pockets, knuckles straining the fabric. The question gathered like a storm front over a flat horizon.

He shut the door.

"Cal, since you're leaving anyway, I have to ask." He squinted, as if bracing for the answer. "Was there any truth to the rumors?"

My tongue stuck to the roof of my mouth. I looked up, surprised less by the question than the timing. Bill stared at the far wall, where sunlight leaked through a narrow slit in the blinds.

"I'm flattered you think my life is that interesting." I shifted the box lid, buying a second before I went on. "But do you really believe I'd risk my career—never mind my dignity —just to coax a student into bed? I assure you, I'm perfectly capable of finding someone of age and above board." I punctuated my words with a tight smile. "Should I ever be so inclined."

The smile held, but a muscle ticked in my jaw.

Bill dropped his gaze, letting the silence grow roots. He picked at the frayed hem of his shirt. Then, as offhandedly as he could manage, he said, "So, I heard Gabrielle Clark has withdrawn from Page."

The statement caught me off guard, a sharp flick to the solar plexus. I let the shock settle, leaning on old habits of detachment. "Did she?" I kept my voice as casual as possible. "That's unfortunate. She was one of the best I've taught."

"Same here. I was hoping we could lure her out of

engineering and into a physics major." He grunted, belly straining his shirt buttons. "I haven't heard where she's going —only that she's not coming back." He paused, fingering the hem again. "Any idea why?"

I shook my head. "Not a clue. But she's brilliant and quite capable. She'll do well—wherever she lands."

He nodded, but the twinkle was gone.

My phone skittered across the desk. Gabrielle.

> SOS. All hell just broke loose online. Can you talk?

I glanced up at Bill, careful not to betray urgency. "Would you mind giving me a minute? I need to make a call."

He nodded, stood, and made for the door. "Sure, no problem. I'll be in my office." The latch caught with a soft click.

I waited for the echo of Bill's heavy tread to fade, then thumbed Gabrielle's name and hit Call.

She picked up on the first ring. "Hey." Her voice was brisk, all business.

"Hey," I echoed, voice softening instinctively. "What's going on?" I kept my tone and words neutral, conscious that the walls were paper thin.

"Yeah, so—social media just exploded. About you. I don't even know where to start. It's a bloodbath."

"Same old, or something new?"

"Sloane Cartwright has been on a posting spree since eight a.m. She's got, like, three different threads saying the school 'let you off' because you're a 'fancy British physicist with connections.' Somehow, she got the board's official finding—probably from her dad—and posted it online."

"So much for confidentiality."

"Now she's telling everyone to come forward if they've got stories about you. Doesn't matter if they're true—the more scandalous, the better. It's her personal mission to take you down. This is going to blow up."

My skin prickled. I pinched the bridge of my nose, the headache already settling behind my eyes. "I fucking knew she'd be trouble." The expletive slipped out before I could stop it. "Sorry."

"No need. I think you've earned an arsenal of F-bombs."

"Are you named?"

"No," she said. "Which is honestly a perk of not making too many friends this year."

The line beeped with an incoming call. Dr. Amrita Singh. *Shit.*

"Darling, my boss is calling. I have to take it. Can you screenshot those posts? Just in case they vanish. I've got a feeling I'll need every scrap of evidence I can get."

"Yeah, no problem. Good luck. I love you."

"Love you too."

I clicked over.

"Hello?"

"Dr. Hawthorne, are you on campus?"

Despite our current adversarial situation, I appreciated that Dr. Singh always skipped the small talk. "I am—just packing up my office."

"Please come see me."

I switched the phone to my other ear. "May I ask what this is about?" Though, of course, Gabrielle had already given me a good idea.

"I'd prefer to discuss it in person."

"Right. I'll walk over."

"Thank you." She hung up.

The walk across the quad was a trek through an oven. Late June sun bounced white off the concrete, searing my eyes. I kept my head down, unwilling to risk eye contact with students or colleagues. Campus was mostly empty during the summer, but I preferred to avoid recognition just the same.

Outside Administration Suite 300, the secretary's desk sat vacant. I tapped lightly on the glass door.

"Come in," Dr. Singh called from the other side.

I opened the door and stepped into her office. Dr. Lemke sat on the couch, leaning back, one leg crossed in a relaxed figure-four.

No HR rep this time.

"Dr. Hawthorne," she said, gesturing to the seat across from her. "Thank you for coming so quickly."

I sat, sweat slicking my shirt to my back.

Dr. Singh wasted no time. "We've received additional complaints," she said, hands folded in that careful lattice I'd come to recognize as her prelude to unpleasantness. "Fourteen, to be precise. All in the last twenty-four hours."

I stared at her, stunned by the number. "That's—" I caught myself. "What are the allegations?"

She slid a folder across the desk with two fingers. "You're welcome to review the sanitized reports. The themes are consistent: abuse of authority, inappropriate conduct, sexual harassment, and, in three instances, explicit claims of quid pro quo." Her voice was perfectly measured—neither accusatory nor sympathetic. "Some are new. Others reference incidents from previous semesters."

Dr. Lemke chimed in, his tone serious but good-natured. "Cal, I won't lie—the timing is…suspicious. But the volume— well, you understand how it looks."

I thumbed open the folder. Page after page of neatly typed accusations—scrubbed of identifiers but detailing, in jagged terms, an escalating set of improprieties: lewd comments, inappropriate contact, mandatory 'remediation' after hours, and—most egregious—demanding sexual favors for passing grades.

I pushed the folder back across the desk. "A complete joke —that's how it looks."

Dr. Singh didn't blink. "We don't decide how it looks.

We're obligated to review complaints brought forward in good faith. The policy is clear."

Dr. Lemke put on an expression of empathy, but his words rang hollow. "Fourteen students don't come forward out of thin air, Cal."

"They do if they're prompted by someone with an agenda." I drummed my fingers on the table, a tic I couldn't suppress. "Look closely. Half of these are carbon copies. You know why? Because someone is disgruntled and orchestrating this circus." I swallowed, heat rising in my ears. "And you both know it."

Dr. Singh set her jaw. "Do you have proof?"

"Not yet. But a search through social media should give you all the proof you need."

She folded her arms—her tell that the conversation was closed. "Given the volume and nature of the claims, we have no choice but to reopen disciplinary proceedings."

"This nonsense again, really? I've already resigned. What more do you want from me?"

Dr. Lemke cleared his throat. "I'm afraid it's not that simple. Your resignation doesn't take effect until the end of summer."

"Then accelerate it," I said. "I'm already packed. I'll be out by the end of the day. If it makes anyone's life easier, I'll walk out now and never look back."

Dr. Singh's gaze held steady, but her voice edged defensive. "We're under significant pressure from the Board of Trustees," she said. "They've taken a direct interest in this case."

I let the words hang, a sour bloom of disbelief rising behind my ribs. "What the hell do they have to do with this?"

She bristled—just a flicker, a tightening around her eyes.

Dr. Lemke leaned in, palms up in a placating gesture. "Easy, Cal. We're all just trying to do what's right."

I exhaled, slow and controlled, and steepled my fingers.

"Forgive me. But what, precisely, does the Board of Trustees have to do with a faculty conduct matter?"

Dr. Lemke shifted, glancing at Dr. Singh like he hoped she'd take it. She obliged.

"The Board sets institutional priorities. In the wake of recent cases—nationally—they're hyperaware of anything that could damage Page's reputation. They want this handled by the book. More than that, they want the appearance of being above reproach."

I folded my arms and leveled a stare at Dr. Singh. "This wouldn't have anything to do with Trustee Cartwright, would it?"

She exchanged a brief glance with her colleague—a flick, but enough to confirm my suspicion.

"What makes you say that?" she asked.

"His daughter was in my Physics 112 course this spring. We didn't see eye to eye." I let the implication hang. "Her attendance was laughable. She demanded to be allowed to make up missed quizzes and to reschedule her midterm so she could leave early for spring break. Naturally, I refused. At the end of the term, she asked me to inflate her grade. I told her she got exactly what she earned. She threatened to 'take it all the way to the top.'" I looked at Lemke, then Singh. "I assume this is what she meant."

Neither replied. Dr. Singh looked down at her folded hands. Lemke opened his mouth—perhaps for a platitude— but closed again, as if he knew it wasn't worth the trouble.

"It doesn't take a PhD to connect the dots," I added.

My phone buzzed in my pocket. I pulled it out, hoping for Gabrielle's name and the screenshots I'd asked for. But it was Isabel.

Call me.

I ignored it.

Dr. Singh's expression was impossible to parse. On a better day, I might have admired her poker face. "We have to treat every complaint as credible," she said, voice honed to a bureaucratic sheen. "Regardless of the source."

"Of course," I said. "So when does the circus start again?"

"I'll convene a new review board—all new members to avoid any bias."

I scoffed, but she didn't react. My phone buzzed again. Another message from Isabel.

It's urgent, Cal. Call me.

Dr. Singh narrowed her eyes. "Are we keeping you from something?"

I flashed the lock screen. "My sister is asking me to call. She says it's urgent. Do you mind?"

"Not at all. We're done here. You have until the end of the day to collect anything from campus. Then your administrative leave will resume. You'll be contacted when you are needed."

I nodded, stood, and walked out. In the waiting area, I called Isabel. She answered, voice strained.

"What took you so bloody long?"

"I was in a meeting. What's going on? I thought you were on honeymoon."

"I was, but we're heading home."

My stomach tightened. "Tired of each other already?"

She ignored that. "It's Father."

"Go on."

"He passed away overnight."

I raked a hand through my hair. My headache flared. I stepped to the window and looked out over the sunbaked campus. "What do you mean, he passed away? I thought he had months."

"So did we. But Mother said he went to bed knackered last night and never woke up."

I pressed my lips together. "Right," I said, voice flat. "Thank you for telling me."

"I know you were just here last month, but you should probably come back. I don't know details yet, but you know how these things are."

I nodded even though she couldn't see me. "I'll book my flight and send you the details."

We ended the call without pleasantries. None were needed.

With a deep breath, I knocked on Dr. Singh's door.

"Yes?"

I opened it and stepped inside.

"Was there something else?" she asked.

I held up my phone. "I just got off the phone with my sister. My father died this morning."

Dr. Lemke sprang to his feet—more agile than his broad frame would suggest—his face washed in genuine concern. "Oh God, Cal. I'm so sorry."

I nodded. "So you understand—I need to return to England for a bit. I trust that won't be a problem."

"Of course not," Dr. Singh obliged. "Please take whatever time you need. I'll email you with any developments." She paused for a beat. "Safe travels."

Gabrielle glanced up from her book as I walked into the living room. She took one look at me, and concern spread across her face. Whatever mask I'd managed in the car, on the walk to the door—it was gone now. I must have looked absolutely wrecked.

"What's wrong?" she asked, already on her feet, her book discarded on the sofa.

"Page. My career. My father." I met her eyes. "Everything."

She wrapped her arms around me.

I froze. Not because I didn't want to hold her. But because I knew if I let even one crack form, the whole dam would break. She pulled back.

"What can I do?"

"I'm fine."

"No, you're not."

I exhaled. "No, I'm not. But falling to pieces won't help."

She moved toward the kitchen. "Can I make you some tea?"

I laughed—more bark than mirth. "I've trained you well, haven't I?" I blew out a shaky breath and followed. "But no. This calls for something stronger." I reached into a cupboard for a glass, but it slipped through my fingers—shattering on the granite like ice on concrete.

"*Goddamn it!*" My scream hit the cabinets and hung there.

Gabrielle didn't flinch. She didn't even blink. She just reached for the dish towel, wet it under the tap, and began gathering the glass with deliberate swipes. The shards caught the light, each one a splintered refraction of the disaster I'd made of everything. She moved with such methodical calm that it became, for a moment, the only thing to watch—the world shrinking to the woman I loved, a damp cloth, and fractured glass.

I moved in to help, but she blocked me with a single gentle palm.

"I've got it," she said—flat, not cruel.

I stood back and gripped the counter's edge until my knuckles went white. I didn't know what else to do with my hands.

"Father's dead," I said at last. The words fell into the silence without echo or ceremony.

She didn't stop wiping. Didn't look at me, even. Just kept

gathering the shards into a tidy pile. "I'm sorry," she said, soft as cotton, before setting the towel aside and reaching into the cabinet for another glass. "Do you want ice?"

I shook my head, but she was already filling it. The ice cubes hissed and popped as she drowned them in whiskey.

"What else?" she asked as she handed me the glass.

"There are no fewer than fourteen student complaints against me." The whiskey burned down my throat, but I welcomed the pain. "All utter rubbish, but no one cares."

"But you've already put in your resignation."

I shook my head. "Doesn't matter. It's a witch hunt now. Sloane Cartwright and her father have seen to that." I drained the whiskey, then set the glass down before I had the chance to hurl it at the wall. "I could have handled one accusation. Maybe two. But *fourteen*? There's a momentum to it. Once people start believing, it becomes real—true or not. That's the world now. Truth doesn't matter—only who can shout the loudest."

She pressed her fingertips to the island, the gesture somehow both delicate and furious. "I wish I could fix it."

"Not your problem to fix," I said, sharper than I'd intended. "If anyone's to blame, it's me. I should have left when the first round started. No courtesy notice—just out the bloody door. And I should have seen this whole farce for what it is—a slow-motion guillotine."

Gabrielle flinched—only a little—but let it pass through her. "What will you do?"

I pushed away from the counter. "First, I have to go back to England for the funeral. I don't particularly care to…"

"But it's expected," she finished.

I nodded.

"Do you want me to come with you?"

"No." I glanced up quickly. "Don't misunderstand. In a perfect world, I don't want you out of my sight, much less in a separate country. But this trip will be as nasty as it gets. And I can't bear to drag you through that. Not when I've already asked more of you than anyone should."

Surprisingly, she didn't argue with me.

"What about Page?"

"They've already decided what story they want to tell." I dumped the ice in the sink and refilled the glass—to the brim this time. "It's not about truth. It's about optics." I took a long drink. "Page wants a villain, and I just happen to be available."

Gabrielle stepped closer, but not into my arms. She hovered at the edge of the kitchen tile, hands knotted at her sides, assessing the damage—glass, whiskey, me.

"Go sit."

A command. I obeyed it.

In the living room, the afternoon sun slanted across the floor, drawing a gold line nearly to my feet. I sank into the sofa and let my gaze drift over the furniture, the dust motes, the impossible ordinariness of the room.

She sat beside me, knees tucked to her chest, and watched me. The light caught her hair and set it aglow.

"When do you fly out?" she asked, her voice softened to a near whisper.

I looked at the glass. Then at my hands. Then her. "I haven't booked it yet," I admitted, pulling my phone from my pocket. The screen wavered under my thumb. I was too far gone—too scattered—to make sense of the airline apps. All those boxes and drop-down menus, the infinite loop of payment screens and confirmation codes...it was all too much.

She watched me fumble for a minute, then slid her hand over mine and eased the phone from my grip. She set it face down on the coffee table, close enough to reclaim but far enough to make a point. "Talk to me, Cal. Don't let it eat you alive. Let's work through it. What's the worst that could happen right now?"

I slouched back, the cushions swallowing my shoulders. The ceiling above was wide and blank—like a clean whiteboard to diagram all the ways I'd failed myself, my father, her.

"Even if I fight this circus at Page, I'm done. No university will touch me now." I forced the laugh. "Another scandal of my own making. Maybe James was right about me after all."

"Don't," she said, slicing through my self-pity with a clarity that startled me. She swung her legs off the sofa, planted both feet on the floor, and turned her whole body to face me. Her voice was low and steady—no trembling, no tremor, just iron wrapped in silk. "You're not what they say. Not even close. And I won't let you talk about yourself like you're guilty of something."

I opened my mouth to protest, but she cut me off again, sharper this time.

"I mean it, Cal. I don't care how many idiots post stories or how many times Sloane Cartwright tags the college on her socials. You're not a monster. You're not even a villain. You're someone with principles and morals who actually gives a damn. More than anyone I've ever met."

The words should have comforted me. Instead, I felt the gouge of guilt, sharp as a splinter under a fingernail. I looked away, out the window, over the low roofs and parched lawns of the town I'd never truly learned to call home. I swallowed hard. "You asked what the worst thing that could happen was."

She waited, watching me with the kind of patience that made it harder, not easier, to speak.

"It's not losing my job," I said finally. "It's not the public shaming, the institutional fallout, or the fact that my father died thinking I'd torched my career again."

I looked at her—really looked—and the words slid out before I could temper them.

"It's you looking at me…and wondering if any of it might be true."

Her breath caught, just faintly, and I saw the flicker in her eyes. Not doubt. Not fear. Just heartbreak—mine reflected back at me.

"That's what I can't stomach," I went on, voice low. "That somewhere in the back of your mind, even for a second, you might start seeing me the way they do. That you'd question what we are—what we've been."

She didn't speak right away. Just reached out, slow and steady, and placed her hand on my chest. "I know who you are," she whispered. "And nothing they can say could make me forget the man who made me feel whole."

I closed my eyes. Just for a second. Let that truth wrap around me. Let it hold me up when my own spine wouldn't. "I don't deserve you," I whispered.

"Too late," she said, quiet and firm. "You've got me anyway."

She held her hand steady over the hammering ruins of my heart. But instead of drawing back, she leaned in and pulled me into her arms.

For a moment, I didn't move. I didn't know how. My body was still caught in the reflex of holding everything in— shoulders locked, jaw set, spine stiff with pride and panic.

But then she tucked her chin over my shoulder, and I breathed her in—her warm skin, the faint aroma of her shampoo—steady and real. And that was it. The dam broke. Not into sobs exactly, but something more visceral.

I clawed at her back like a man pulled from a wreck, unsure where the pain ended and the relief began. My body shook once, then again—sharp, silent, involuntary jolts I couldn't suppress. I buried my face in her shoulder and held on like the air had gone thin.

She said nothing. Just held me—arms wrapped firm, breath slow and sure. Like she knew the ground was splitting beneath me…

And she was determined to hold me through the fall.

CHAPTER 48

GABRIELLE

"I miss you, Cal. I need you here like yesterday." I wanted to reach through the phone and yank him home by the sleeve.

"Twenty-four hours, love," he replied. "I fly out in the morning, and, trust me, it's not soon enough."

"How are you holding up?"

"As you'd expect. Just glad it's all over." Silence crackled on the line before he continued, "James wasted no time in shutting me out. The funeral had barely ended before he said, in no uncertain terms, that I'm never to darken his door again." Cal scoffed. "He literally kicked me out, so I'm staying in a London hotel tonight. But I suppose I should thank him. Better room service and less chance of me missing my flight in the morning."

"Was he mad about the money and properties your father left you?"

"Livid. But Father sorted all that before he died, so there's nothing James can do." He drew a sharp breath. "I don't particularly care about the assets. It wasn't even that much. James still got the lion's share. But watching him boil over made it all worth it."

I surveyed Cal's once-pristine living room, now lined with boxes of my belongings. A Houston Astros tumbler full of sweet tea sweated onto a coaster on the coffee table. My favorite hoodie slouched over the arm of the black leather sofa. I'd tried to make myself at home, but it felt more like a child's fort in a stranger's parlor.

"This place feels weird without you," I admitted.

Cal's smile was audible through the transatlantic static. "You're my fiancée. It's your house too, love."

Fiancée. The word had its own gravity—bending the whole room around it. I had never been anybody's anything in such a permanent way.

I let the words settle. "Yeah, I know. It just…doesn't feel real yet." My phone beeped with another call. "Hang on, let me see who this is." I checked the screen. Aunt Suzy. "Ugh, she's relentless." I sent the call to voicemail.

"Your aunt again?"

"Yeah. She's been blowing up my phone the past couple of days. I can't—" I pinched the bridge of my nose, trying to unknot the pressure in my chest. "I still can't talk to her. I know she means well, but if it weren't for her—"

"It's all right, Gabrielle. You don't have to explain." His voice was a balm to my frazzled nerves, a pressure bandage over the bruise. "Talk to her when you're ready. Not before."

I propped my feet on a box labeled "WINTER CLOTHES" and picked at a loose thread on my leggings. "Maybe I won't ever talk to her again," I said, though we both knew it was a lie.

He didn't call me on it.

The doorbell reverberated through the house. I nearly dropped my phone.

"Who's there?" Cal asked.

"Not sure," I answered, peering down the hall toward the front door. A vague figure loomed behind the frosted glass. "Probably a delivery."

"What have you ordered now?"

"A few more books."

He groaned. "More? And where do you plan to put them?"

I nudged a knee-high box with my heel—brimming with paperbacks, a few crammed spine-down into the gaps I'd packed too fast and carelessly. "I have a system."

"You have a problem."

"I'm curating a collection," I said, feigning haughtiness. "Besides, you'll appreciate my spicy new titles when you're jet-lagged and desperate for…entertainment."

He sighed, low and theatrical. "If I return home to find you in bed with a paperback…"

"Yes…"

"Let's just say I'll be forced to remind you of the superiority of hands-on research." His voice, even disembodied, was enough to send a sweet shiver down my back.

"That's bold talk coming from a theoretical physicist."

"Who can rock your world in fourteen different dimensions."

A hot flush crept from my neck to my ears. "Okay, you win."

"Damn right."

The doorbell rang again. I stood and walked down the hall. "Maybe I have to sign for it."

A figure shifted behind the rippled glass—solid, broad-shouldered, familiar in a way that knotted my stomach. I'd expected a delivery person, maybe a clipboard and a bored smile. Instead, when I opened the door, the world exhaled a damp waft of cut grass and gasoline and Bill Watkins, standing awkwardly on the step holding a foil-covered Pyrex dish.

"Crap," I said before I could help myself.

"Gabrielle?" Dr. Watkins's voice was cautious and oddly

formal for a man in a sweat-stained polo and white dad sneakers.

Cal's voice crackled through the phone. "What is it?"

"I'll call you back." I hung up before he could argue. "Hello, Dr. Watkins." My voice cracked in a register I didn't know I had.

He blinked. "Didn't expect to catch you here. Sorry. I just…" His eyes dropped to the casserole, like it might prompt his next line. "My wife made this. I thought Cal was back today."

"He gets back tomorrow." I was hyperaware of my bare feet, disheveled hair, and oversized T-shirt.

He paused, eyebrows narrowed. "What are you doing here?"

"Housesitting," I managed feebly.

His gaze darted over my shoulder into the house. "I didn't realize housesitting involved so many boxes."

I tried on a smile that didn't quite fit. "I'll be happy to put that in the fridge and let Dr. Hawthorne know you stopped by."

He handed over the casserole but didn't budge from the stoop. "I'm not here to judge, Gabrielle. What you two do is your business. But let's not insult each other, okay?" He wiped his palms on the sides of his khaki cargo shorts. "May I come in?"

It was phrased as a question, but it was clearly anything but. I stepped aside. "Please excuse the mess."

Dr. Watkins walked into the living room, his gaze snagging on the half-unpacked boxes and the nest of blankets on the couch.

I ferried the Pyrex to the kitchen, cheese and garlic wafting in its wake, and slid it onto the second shelf of the refrigerator. "Would you like something to drink? I made sweet tea," I offered, trying to remember how normal people behaved.

He shook his head as he settled into the armchair. "Nothing for me, thanks." He rubbed at the thinning spot on his scalp, as if starting a fire.

I perched on the edge of the sofa. My phone buzzed with a message from Cal.

> Who was at the door?

I looked up at Dr. Watkins, who met my gaze with an unshakable, almost clinical, patience. "It's Dr. Hawthorne," I said, holding up the phone. "He wants to know who was at the door. Should I tell him?"

He mustered a smile. "Of course. Tell him it's Bill. And that I come in peace." The words were mild but carried a strange finality, as if they were the preface to a much longer, heavier soliloquy.

I typed out a reply, letting him know I had it under control, then set the phone face down on the coffee table. Dr. Watkins waited until the silence had outgrown its natural lifespan before clearing his throat.

"I won't waste your time—or mine. You know as well as I do that Cal is in a heap of trouble." He leaned forward, elbows on knees, and pinned me with a steady, unblinking gaze. "Look, I'm not here to play gotcha. I'm here because I care about Cal, and, to be honest, I care about you too. So I'll ask straight: what the hell happened last spring?"

I folded my hands into the hem of my shirt, hoping it read as poised rather than panicked. "Is this off the record?" I asked before I could stop myself.

"Gabrielle, I'm not a cop. I'm not even your advisor anymore." He glanced at the nearest box—my name scrawled in block marker—and softened. "If I were, I'd have brought a notepad." He looked at me, then added, "But if you want to lawyer up, I'll wait."

I shook my head. "No. It's just..." Was it the urge to

confide, or the terror of what confession did to a secret? "I don't want to get anyone in trouble."

"He's already there. I thought everything would blow over, but it's only gotten worse. New complaints—some downright inventive. And now the Board of Trustees is involved." He leaned in, pain etched across his face. "They're going to make an example of him."

I swallowed, my throat as dry and rough as sandpaper. "It's all bullshit," I said, then regretted the word, but he didn't flinch.

"I know that. Or I thought I did. But apparently"—he nodded toward me—"there's some truth to the talk."

I said nothing.

"I promise I'm on your side. But I need the full picture." He took a breath, let it out slowly, and looked up at me with pleading eyes. "Help me help my friend. Please."

I traced a seam in the couch—rough stitching against smooth leather. "You want the truth?" My voice rasped, older than I expected. "All right. I was in Dr. Hawthorne's class last spring—you know that. We both knew the rules, and we tried not to…" I glanced up. "We were careful. And it wasn't the usual story. There was no power play, no coercion, no favoritism. I wasn't some infatuated kid, and he wasn't…some creep with boundary issues. We were two people who connected at the worst possible time and tried—really tried—not to act on it. But…"

I let the silence settle, heavy as humidity.

Bill's frown softened, like he was looking at an old photograph and suddenly recognized the face. "I've known Cal since he was fresh off his post-doc—back when I had less gray and a higher tolerance for academic bullshit. Cal's never been reckless," he said, voice measured. "He's not manipulative. He's got integrity in spades, even if he can be a smug bastard about it."

I snickered at that.

"I can't say I know you all that well. But I don't think you're the type to twist a situation for personal gain." He glanced down, and his gaze stalled on my left hand. The ring caught a filament of sunlight and threw it across the room in a sharp, dancing glint. Bill's mouth folded into a line that said he'd expected this, dreaded it, and maybe—on some level—approved. "So it's the real thing, then," he said, almost to himself. "I thought as much." His face—creased by sun and worry—settled into a look of deep, almost paternal, resignation. "I've been married twenty-two years. The first time I saw my wife, I knew it was game over. So I get it. And may you both be happy. But you need to understand—this happy ending won't come easy."

I swallowed. For a second, the room tilted under me. "I know," I said. "But I'm not going anywhere."

He shook his head. "You misunderstand. Page is going to hang Cal out to dry. It's his word against a mountain of student complaints. And the only person who can offer any truth in this situation is you."

"But if I say anything, they'll find him guilty."

"They'll find him guilty regardless. But by telling them what's *actually* true, you can help the board separate fact from horseshit. And he might have a chance at redeeming his career. Not at Page, of course. But somewhere else."

"You want me to speak to the review board? Cal wouldn't allow that."

"No, he'd never ask it of you. I know him well enough to know that. But *I'm* asking you. If there's a chance for you to help him clear his name, this is it."

Chapter 49

Callum

The curbside pickup at DFW was a hydraulic ballet of roaring engines, tumbling suitcases, and unbridled American hope. No matter how many times I returned, the air always hit the same: scorched concrete, sunburned tar, barbecue smoke, and the dry shimmer of a grassy plain. I scanned the jumble of oversized pickups and gleaming sedans, and my breath caught when I spotted my car in the queue.

Gabrielle leaned against the rear spoiler, a to-go cup from some local caffeine cartel in one hand and sunglasses perched on her head like a crown. Her blonde hair was down—loose, wild, and unrestrained. She wore deliciously short denim shorts and a soft blue top that fit her like sin. She was breathtaking, and I felt a surge of homesickness for her before I'd even reached the curb.

I rolled my suitcase along the pavement and approached, watching her toy with her phone—oblivious to the crowd and out of step with the frantic choreography around her. She didn't see me at first. Or perhaps she did and wanted to see how long it would take me to break.

I closed the distance and, without preamble, wrapped my

arms around her and swept her off the ground. She yelped against my shirt—equal parts delight and disbelief—and I spun her so fast she nearly caught her heels on the bumper. The suitcase toppled. I didn't care.

When I finally set her down, she punched my arm—hard enough to sting, soft enough to count as affection. "Jesus, Cal," she said, breathless. "You can't just manhandle people at arrivals. I almost dumped my coffee all over you."

"Apologies," I said and kissed her—daylight, diesel, and parched Texas heat crowding around us. The world blurred, but her lips were solid and sure. A car behind us blared its horn, long and insistent, but it made no dent in the moment.

She drew back, cheeks flushed, pupils blown. "That was very public of you."

I kissed her again, slower. "I don't bloody care."

I popped the boot, slid my suitcase and carry-on inside, and took a perverse satisfaction in the way the lid slammed shut—a clean, final closure on the hell of the past several days. Gabrielle moved for the driver's side, but I caught her wrist.

"I'm happy to drive, you know," I said, mostly to assert some token masculinity.

She snorted. "Not on your life. You look half-dead." She kissed the back of my hand. "Still hot. But half-dead. No offense."

I rolled my eyes and slid into the passenger seat. The perspective felt wrong—my car, but not my vantage point.

"Besides," she said, easing from the curb, "I like driving your car. It's smoother than mine. Less…deathtrap-y."

"You are rather due for an upgrade. I replaced your battery in January, but it's only a matter of time."

The sun beat through the glass as Gabrielle navigated the airport maze and eventually merged onto the motorway. The air conditioner whined at full blast, failing to keep pace with the inferno outside. But she looked cool and untouched, the way some people are born immune to climate.

We carved through toll plazas and exurban sprawl beneath an impossibly blue sky streaked with candy-floss clouds. Gabrielle grabbed a bottle of mineral water from the cupholder and handed it to me. I twisted the cap, the plastic crackling over the soft hum of the engine, and drank greedily. My mouth was parched from ten hours of recycled transatlantic air.

"How was your flight?" she asked, her tone light, but her eyes cautious. She always saw past my camouflage, even when she pretended not to.

"Long," I admitted, "but not awful. Shockingly edible food. A few hours of chemically induced sleep."

She smiled, but it didn't quite land. Not hesitation, exactly—more like the moment before a plane touches down, wheels suspended, waiting for gravity to decide.

She waited me out.

I drew a sharp breath. "Boyle's Law."

She glanced over, caught off guard. "What?"

"Pressure's rising, but the volume of this car is fixed. So either we talk…or something explodes."

"Are you seriously making physics puns right now?"

"Technically, it's a metaphor. But yes." I tapped my temple. "It never shuts off."

Her hands worked the wheel with a restless energy, left thumb flicking the rim in nervous taps.

"All right. I'll just come out with it. What did Bill Watkins want yesterday?"

"To bring you a casserole," she said dryly. "It's a Southern thing when someone dies."

"I'm familiar with the custom." When she didn't offer anything further, I prompted, "Can I assume he knows about us?"

She looked over, eyes pleading. "Yeah. I'm so sorry, but

there was no way around it." The words tumbled out fast. "He figured it out the second he saw me in your house. The boxes, the ring…"

"It's all right," I soothed. "It was bound to happen at some point." I rested a hand on her bare thigh. "And it's *our* house, darling."

She fixed her eyes on the road, her face flushed from the sun or the conversation or both. "He's worried about you. Worried about the Board of Trustees. Says they're sharpening the guillotine."

"Not inaccurate."

She placed a hand on mine—solid, grounding. "He thinks I should speak to the review board. Tell them my side."

I pulled my hand. "Out of the question."

"You don't get to decide that."

"I do when it puts *you* in the line of fire."

A horn brayed as a jacked-up pickup cut too close. Gabrielle swerved with an eerie calm. She never missed a beat.

"If you give them a statement, it'll make things worse."

"How?" Her voice was steady, but I could feel nerves sparking off her. "It's already as bad as it can be, and it's ninety-five percent false. If I go in and set the record straight—say our relationship was consensual and that I'm nobody's victim, then what?"

"They won't hear that." I pinched the bridge of my nose, eyes squeezed shut. "They'll hear: student, professor, impropriety. I'll be no less guilty in their eyes, but you'll be slung through the mud along with me." My fingers were trembling. I flattened them against my thigh, hoping she didn't notice. "I can take their contempt. Hell, I deserve it. But you—"

"You *don't* deserve it. That's the whole point." She merged onto the interstate, finally heading north. "Dr. Watkins—"

"Do call him Bill. I think you've earned that much."

"Fine. Bill made a good point—I'm the only one who can set the record straight. Sloane won't back down or admit her role in all this, but if I go in and tell them what's actually true, I can speak to your character. How you'd never behave the way you're being accused of. Bill can too, sure, but I have a front-row seat. And nothing to lose."

I laughed, the sound a dry rasp in my throat. "You have everything to lose, darling. You're about to start at SMU. Don't fool yourself into thinking Dallas is far enough away or that a bigger school is big enough to hide in. Don't you see? If you go on record—if your name gets attached to any of this, the fallout will follow you. It never goes away. And I'm speaking from experience here."

She absorbed it the way she did everything—without flinching, without showing where it struck. "About that..."

"Which part?"

"SMU." She inhaled, her jaw set. I nearly reached for her hand again, but I held back. "Tomorrow's July first," she continued. "That's the notification deadline. I haven't confirmed enrollment yet."

I stared, uncomprehending for a beat, as the bottom dropped out of my chest. "You haven't notified?"

She shook her head, hair swishing softly over her shoulders.

"Gabrielle, no. Absolutely not. You are not giving up your future for any of this—least of all for me." My voice had gone sharp, louder than intended, but I didn't care. "I've already stolen so much from you. I won't take this as well."

She gave me a faint smile—the kind that said she'd rehearsed this and knew every line I was about to speak. "Will you shut up and let me explain?"

"It had better be the argument of your life," I muttered, arms crossed.

She shifted in her seat, subtle as a gymnast's pivot on a balance beam. "Yes, SMU's engineering program is amazing.

And yes, it's the obvious choice. But the only reason I applied there was so I wouldn't be too far from you. I wanted a life with you. And, at the time, that meant you'd still be at Page." She flicked a glance at me—cocky, almost, if not for the sheen of fear behind it. "But that's not a factor anymore. I'd rather we take a beat and figure out what comes next. Together."

"Gabrielle, it's too late to apply anywhere else. You know that, right?"

"For the fall, sure." She shrugged—a sun-warmed roll of her shoulders, like she'd never been burdened by a thing. "But I can take core classes online for a semester or two. Comp sci, calculus, whatever. I won't fall behind, I promise." She changed lanes to pass a slow-moving horse trailer.

"You can still accept the offer," I said. "The deadline hasn't passed. You could be in Dallas in six weeks. I'll come with you, if that's what you want. You know I'd go anywhere."

She smiled at the road. "And do what? You think the Cartwrights—or their sycophants—will just let us start over an hour down the interstate? It'll follow us, Cal. All of it. Sloane's dad is on every board in the Metroplex. I guarantee he's already making calls." She pointed to a gleaming blue glass spear jutting up from the Dallas skyline. "Isn't that their building? Cartwright Tower?"

I watched the spire flicker in the sun, the daylight fracturing along its surface. She was right—the scandal would trail us if we stayed. That was the beauty and the poison of America: reinvention was possible, but only if you were willing to cut loose every anchor.

She swerved around a gravel-streaked semi and exhaled, slow and steady. "I don't regret any of it," she said. "I'd do it all again."

"Gabrielle—"

"Let's just regroup, Cal." Her voice softened, the edge giving way to resolve. She signaled, slipped into the HOV lane, and let the world blur past us at eighty miles an hour.

"We can go anywhere. Anywhere we want. No constraints. Unmoored."

I considered what it actually meant to be unmoored. I'd never been that, not really. Not when I'd first slipped the velvet leash of my family. Not even now, after my father's death and the second implosion of my career. I looked at Gabrielle—gilded in profile, emerald eyes fixed ahead—and knew she was my tether point now. My lifeline. Nothing else mattered. I would go anywhere, do anything, be anyone—for her.

She caught me staring. Color crept into her cheeks. "What?"

"Where do you want to go?"

She licked her lips, eyes on the bright ribbon of freeway. "Somewhere I choose for myself this time. Not because it's close, or safe, or what anyone else expects—because it's right." She glanced at me, a faint smile curling at the corner of her mouth. "And not just for me. For us." She drummed the wheel, thinking. "But since you're asking…let's aim for someplace with amazing food and temperatures that don't make me want to peel off my skin. Mountains might be nice. Maybe somewhere with actual seasons—not just 'hot' and 'surface of the sun.'" She let the idea hang—sounding shy at first, then more sure-footed—before turning it back on me. "Where do you want to go?"

I didn't answer right away. Just watched the landscape rush past, mile by mile, the city giving way to rolling farmland. "Wherever you are," I said finally. "That's home."

She rolled her eyes, but the smile that followed was real. I reached over, threaded my fingers through hers, and held tight.

"But if you're after specifics…" I tilted my head, pretending to consider. "Crisp air. Snow in winter. Trees that actually change color. Somewhere I can research and write. Maybe even teach again." I brushed my lips over her knuckles.

"And build us a life where no one gives a damn what we were —only who we are."

"Sounds perfect. If we weren't in a moving vehicle, I'd climb over there and kiss you."

I grinned. "We've got twenty miles until we're home. Let me have a shower first, and you can do anything you want."

I loved how I made her blush.

Gabrielle braked gently for a construction zone, orange cones flashing past in neat formation.

"Gabrielle, love."

"Yes?"

I kissed the back of her hand and drew in a breath. "I know you're determined to help clear my name. But I would ask—beg, really—that you reconsider speaking to the review board."

CHAPTER 50

GABRIELLE

"Dr. Lemke?" I voiced as I tapped on his door. The dean of students was hunched over his keyboard, staring at the computer screen like he could force its contents to change by sheer willpower.

He looked up, startled, then pushed away from his desk as recognition set in. "Come on in," he invited warmly, motioning to a cozy conversational set in the corner. "Have a seat. Gabrielle Clark, right?"

I nodded as I sat in a minimalist, burgundy leather armchair. "I'm flattered you remember."

He took the chair across from me. "Of course I do. Engineering major. Legacy student. Commuter. You're hard to forget."

"Thanks…?" I fidgeted with the hem of my blouse.

"So, what brings you to campus in the middle of summer?"

I looked down. Maybe this was a mistake.

Dr. Lemke dropped his voice to a hush. "Would this have anything to do with Dr. Hawthorne?"

His candor startled me. I bit my bottom lip until it stung. "Why would you think that?"

He gave a small, not unkind smile and crossed one leg over the other. The creases down his khakis were crisp and even. "Dr. Hawthorne has been a popular topic around here lately."

Heat flared at the base of my neck. My words jammed somewhere between my heart and my teeth. I popped to my feet. "I shouldn't have come—"

He held up both palms. "I only want to help you, Gabrielle." He looked up at me, his expression open and earnest. "I know you're not currently enrolled," he continued, "which is a loss for us, by the way. But I'm Dean of Students for *all* students, even those in transition. My job is to make sure you're safe, heard, and have options." He motioned to my vacated chair. "So…how can I help?"

Reluctantly, I sat back down.

He leaned forward, elbows braced on his knees, equal parts confidential and fatherly. "Clearly, you came to my office for a reason today. You're not in any trouble here—let's lead with that."

I picked at a hangnail until the skin burned. "I know Dr. Hawthorne is under disciplinary review."

He nodded, a small gesture, but his posture sharpened. "I can't go into the details, but yes."

I swallowed hard, the motion thick and uncooperative. "I have information for the college, but I don't know who to talk to."

"Normally, these matters are handled strictly between faculty and the review board. But if you've got information relevant to the case, you could submit a written statement. That's the usual channel."

"That's not good enough." I heard the edge in my voice and tried to soften it. "I don't want to submit a statement. I want to talk to someone. In person. So nothing gets… misinterpreted. I'll answer questions. I just want to make sure the truth actually gets heard. That nothing gets lost in translation."

He studied me, letting the silence bloom, then drummed his fingers on his knee. "Dr. Monroe is the review board chair. She's the one you want."

"I know her. I took her psych class in the spring."

Dr. Lemke stood and crossed to his desk. "She's great—and very fair." He reached for his desk phone. "I'm pretty sure she's on campus today. Want me to see if she'll drop by?"

I chewed my lip while he flipped through a laminated directory. I sucked in a quick breath and answered before I could back out. "Yes."

The next ten minutes crawled by in awkward small talk—weather, summer travel, reading recommendations. Anything but the elephant in the room.

Dr. Monroe clicked her nails on the metal doorframe as she entered the office. She wore dark denim capris paired with a breezy white blouse, and her chocolate-brown hair was pulled into a ponytail that was the right mix of styled and messy.

"Gabrielle, it's good to see you." She said my name with a softness that I hadn't expected, and for a split second, I glimpsed the woman beneath the formidable shell. She nudged the door shut with her wedge sandal and claimed the last seat in the conversational nook.

"I understand you'd like to talk about Dr. Hawthorne," she started, setting a notebook on her lap and folding her hands atop it. Her gaze was direct but patient—a psychologist's gaze, practiced at waiting out discomfort.

I nodded, heat crawling up my neck again. "I want to make a statement. On the record. In person."

She nodded as she uncapped a slim black pen and opened her notebook. "Do you mind if I take notes while we talk?"

"No, go ahead."

She nodded once, pen poised. "Whenever you're ready."

I stared at the striped rug between us, its bright, uneven

weave suddenly fascinating. "I don't even know where to start."

"That's all right," she said gently. "Start wherever feels right."

I hesitated. "It's not just one thing. And I'm not here to—" I paused, struggling for the right phrase. "I'm not here to make excuses. I just want the board to have the full picture. The honest picture."

She nodded. "That's fair. Why don't we go one piece at a time? What do you think the board might not understand?"

I reached into my back pocket and pulled out my phone, scrolling with shaky fingers until I found the screenshots. "There's been a lot of talk online—about Dr. Hawthorne. Angry posts about the original board findings. Students encouraged to file false reports to get him fired and 'do the board's job for them.' Their words, not mine." I handed her my phone. "Most of the posts have been taken down, but I saved screenshots." I pressed my lips together as she swiped through the images. "I hate to be that person and point the finger, but the ringleader is Sloane Cartwright. And..."

Dr. Monroe jotted a few notes, then handed my phone back. "And?"

"I overheard a few exchanges between her and Dr. Hawthorne that—well, let's just say she didn't get her way. And she made it very clear she wasn't happy about it."

She nodded. "Go on."

"Sloane came to Dr. Hawthorne's office hours the day before the midterm and asked him to reschedule her exam so she could leave early for spring break. He said no, and she was furious. She threatened to involve her father on the Board of Trustees, but he didn't budge. She stormed out."

Dr. Monroe said nothing while she wrote.

"And another time, early in the semester, she asked if she could make up a pop quiz she missed because she didn't come to class. He told her no then too. She was extremely vocal about it."

She looked up. "And…how exactly are you privy to this information?"

It felt like a lead, but I sidestepped. "Sloane and I were both in Physics 112 with Dr. Hawthorne last semester. I personally witnessed both interactions. She sat behind me and wasn't exactly discreet about her contempt for him."

Dr. Monroe capped her pen and tucked a strand of hair behind her ear. "Would you mind emailing me those screenshots?" she asked, gesturing to my phone. "I want to be sure they're included in the record."

"Of course," I said, fumbling to slide my phone back into my pocket.

She smiled—measured, but not unfriendly. "Thank you."

A long silence yawned open, too wide for comfort.

Dr. Monroe broke the hush first. "Is there anything else you'd like to share, Gabrielle? Anything at all?"

I almost lied. Almost said no—that this was enough, that I'd already crossed a line just by showing up. But something in her tone—patient, certain, like she'd seen this scene a hundred times—made it impossible to hold the words in. I pressed my lips together, blood surging behind my eyes.

"Yes." My skin tingled. My heart slammed against my ribs. My breakfast threatened to come up.

She let the seconds stretch, like pressure might force something loose. It worked.

"There are a lot of rumors flying around about a relationship between me and Dr. Hawthorne. I'd like to set the record straight."

Dr. Monroe glanced at Dr. Lemke.

He leaned forward. "Would you like me to step out? Give you two some privacy."

I shook my head. "No. I'd rather you hear it from me. That's why I'm here."

I took a breath.
I flashed my engagement ring.
And then I told them everything.

Cal didn't call to me when I came in. The hush was total—no music, no TV, just the faint asthmatic exhale of the air conditioner. I found him in his study, his sleeves rolled to the elbow, dry-erase marker in hand. He was working the whiteboard like it owed him money—dense equations snaked across its surface, all punctuated by angry arrows and half-erased dead ends. He'd written so hard, the marker tip was jammed up the barrel.

I hovered in the doorway, then crossed to the low bookshelf and leaned against it.

"I'm back," I offered, voice soft as a mouse.

"I noticed." The marker squeaked, punctuating the syllables. He didn't turn.

I stared at the board until the symbols blurred into a language I barely remembered. "What are you working on?"

He capped the marker without turning. His shoulders sagged. "Path integrals for a massless scalar field." He recited as if reading from a teleprompter. "I'm attempting to model a scenario where the system's symmetry spontaneously breaks under nontrivial boundary conditions, but the maths keep collapsing."

He'd lost me at "scalar." I sat on the low-slung sofa. "Sounds intense."

"Not really," he said, tossing the marker. It rolled off the desk and hit the floor with a light thud. "It's busywork. Theoretical escapism." He turned, finally, and I saw the stress of the day etched in the circles under his eyes. He looked at me, gaze sharp but unfocused, as if he were searching for the right point of entry.

I supplied it for him. "Aren't you going to ask me how it went?"

He smiled, but it was bitter. "Since you've apparently decided my fate for me, I figured you'd tell me. If you're so inclined, of course."

"Don't do that. Don't act like I wanted to hurt you. I did it to help—to make the board understand the truth. Without me, they'd have filled in the blanks with fiction, and the fallout would be way worse."

"Did you help build the scaffold too?"

"First of all, *ouch*." I folded my arms so he wouldn't see my hands shake.

He looked at me but didn't flinch.

"And I'm the one trying to take the damn thing apart before they hang you from it."

He exhaled—long, barely audible. "I see." A silence opened, and at first, I thought it was anger—some unspoken rebuke. But instead of erupting, he just slouched into his desk chair, spine bowed, hands dangling between his knees. "And did you?" His voice softened a touch.

"I did everything I could. I gave Dr. Monroe the screenshots and told her about every time I saw Sloane Cartwright being...Sloane," I said. "And I told her...what really happened between us last spring."

He narrowed his eyes. "The whole truth?"

I nodded. "Everything."

He squeezed his eyes shut and sucked in a sharp breath. "And?"

"She didn't ask for details—just wanted to know if I felt pressured, or if you'd ever used your position to influence me. I told her 'absolutely not.' That if anything, you'd gone to absurd lengths to keep things appropriate." I tried to laugh, but it stuck in my throat. "I made sure she understood I'm an adult with a backbone and a full set of executive functions—not some naïve eighteen-year-old fresh out of high school.

And that this"—I gestured between us—"is the long-term real deal. Not some silly infatuation or fling."

He looked at me as if seeing a ghost version of himself. "And did it make a difference?"

"I think so." I pictured Dr. Monroe's steady gaze, the way she'd met my eyes after I finished. It was a look I recognized—not judgment, but clinical curiosity. Maybe even empathy. "She said she'd bring it to the full board. But it's out of my hands now."

He raked a hand through his disheveled hair, then dragged both palms down his face. "It won't change anything," he muttered. "They'll protect the institution, not the truth. That's how these things always go."

He leaned forward, elbows on knees, hands slack between them—his whole body curved like he was bracing for impact.

"And you—" His voice caught. "You shouldn't have had to go to them. That should have been me."

"How? You can't talk to them and expect to be believed. It's your word against—how many? It's shitty, but it's the truth."

That almost made him smile, but it collapsed before it could form. "You think you've helped me, Gabrielle, but all I see is that you stepped in front of a firing squad I was meant to face alone."

I crossed the room slowly, the tension between us stretching taut. He didn't move when I perched on his desk, my knee brushing his. "But we're in this together, Cal. Isn't that the whole point? I did it for you." I touched his knee. "And I'd do it again."

He stared down at the rug. "They'll still twist it. You know they will."

"Maybe." I swallowed. "But it won't be because I stayed silent."

When he finally lifted his head, he looked wrecked. His eyes focused on me for a second, then went distant and glassy.

"Protect the family at all costs." He recited it like scripture. "This is Claire all over again."

The lines on his face carved deeper. His jaw ticked as he clenched and unclenched it. He looked older than usual. Not in years, but in history—a man trapped in the sedimentary layers of his past.

I winced at his words. "Cal…that's not fair."

He looked through me. "Isn't it?" His voice went thin and sharp, like wire pulled too tight. "When Claire died, the truth was messy—disgraceful. My father couldn't bear to acknowledge that his reckless, idiotic son was stupid enough to get a girl killed."

"You didn't—"

"So he spun a clean story, wrapped it in silk, and handed it to the press. He wrote it for me, and I had no say. I never got a vote." He let out a soft, brittle bark of a laugh. "You see it now? The pattern?"

I leaned in. "It's not the same. You keep saying it is, but it's not."

"You don't see how you've gone and done exactly what my family did?"

I squeezed my eyes shut and drew in a sharp breath to tamp down the sting beneath my ribs. "I didn't write your story for you, Cal. I refused to let someone else do it while you stayed gagged. That's the difference." I dropped to my knees in front of his chair and pressed my forehead to his. "I didn't lie to protect you. I told the truth because you weren't allowed to."

"You're right. You didn't lie," he said quietly. "But you still went into that room and spoke for me."

"Because no one else would."

He flinched—not because it wasn't true. But because it was.

I took his hands in mine. "Remember when you asked me to marry you?"

"Vividly."

"You said you got into that cockpit with me because you trusted your life in my hands. And you asked me to trust you with mine in yours."

He was quiet for so long, I thought I'd lost him. That he'd receded into the spiral stairwell of his mind and I'd never get him back. But then he tightened his fingers around mine, anchoring me to his plane of reality.

He dragged in a breath. "I also recall promising never to let you fall."

"I haven't." I nudged him with my nose. "Except in love with you."

He laughed. And finally meant it. "That's rather sappy for you, love."

"Maybe I read too much romance while you were gone."

CHAPTER 51

CALLUM

"I was only gone five days. How much did you read?"

"Making up for lost time. I didn't get a lot of reading done during the semester." She grazed her teeth along the shell of my ear. "Tough course load."

A shiver ran down my spine.

I turned, caught her waist, and set her squarely in my lap, her knees bracketing my hips. She squeaked—a sound I would catalog for later, alongside the first time I'd made her laugh, the first time she fell asleep on my chest, the first time she told me she loved me and meant it.

She blinked in mock outrage, then squared her jaw, as if determined not to cede the moment. She succeeded, mostly. I let her.

"Tough course load, you say?" I slid my palms up her back.

She pressed against me. "Brutal."

"Sounds like you've earned a reward…" I traced a slow line up her spine. "For enduring such an exacting, unsympathetic professor." I tangled my fingers in her hair—not to pull. Not yet. Just enough to make her still. "Lucky for you, he offers extra credit." I tipped her chin until her eyes locked on mine.

She held her breath.

"But it's rigorous…and very hands-on."

"Better be. Or I'll be forced to leave a scathing course review." She rocked forward, the motion calculated and criminal.

"You wouldn't dare." I looped an arm around her waist and pulled her in until there was no air, no daylight between us, nothing but the thrum of her pulse under my hands and the soft, devilish curve of her smile against my mouth.

The spell broke with the graceless chime of an incoming email. Gabrielle flinched, and we both looked toward the desk. She climbed off my lap, freeing me to lean forward and tap the trackpad. The preview alone was enough.

```
SUBJECT: Notification of Formal
Disciplinary Hearing
```

I exhaled—a hiss more than a sigh. "Well, they do move quickly."

She hovered beside me, arms folded tight. "When is it?"

I skimmed the message. "Tomorrow at eight. The tribunal's been assembled, and I am summoned to answer for my many and varied sins." The phrase 'expedited process in the public interest' chased itself in a loop behind my eyes. That was code for 'we want this done before the holiday weekend.'

She rested a hand on my shoulder. "What do you want to do today, then? Anything at all."

I looked up at her. The question felt ceremonial—a last meal before the executioner's sword. I wanted to say *crawl under a rug and stay there until the heat death of the universe.* Or *let's drive north until we hit Canada and change our names once we've crossed the border.* Or even *fuck it, let's fly to Vegas and get married tonight. So there's at least one true thing in the record, even if the rest of my life gets redacted.*

"Want to take the motorcycle out?" she offered. "Let me put my life in your hands. Only seems fair."

I glanced out the window. "In this heat? It's a hundred degrees in the shade. We'll absolutely boil."

"Drive fast enough, and the wind will cool us down. Isn't that a thermodynamics thing?"

I snorted. "Cute. Perhaps you *do* need summer remediation."

She feigned offense, emerald eyes wide. "We didn't cover convective heat loss in your class."

"Negligible, in this climate. Besides…" I let my gaze walk up the length of her, basking in the anticipation. "The only ride I want is with you. In bed. Right now."

It was a joke—mostly—but the way her breath caught told me she knew the truth beneath it.

I stood and pulled her flush against me. "I'm a condemned man. Would you deny me this last request?"

She bit her lip and shook her head—cheeks flushed, pupils blown. "Absolutely not. That would be a human rights violation."

I swept her into my arms. "So glad we agree."

She pressed her mouth to mine, hard, and in that moment, every extraneous thought—tomorrow's hearing, every threat and accusation, even the distant echo of my father's voice—evaporated. There was only heat, the flutter blooming in my chest, and the taste of her on my tongue.

We were clawing each other out of our clothes before we even hit the bed. She sprawled beneath me, loose and wild-haired, her body a territory I'd spent the last six months mapping and still hadn't finished.

She looped her arms around my neck, pulled me down, and whispered against my ear, "There's something I want you to teach me, *Professor.*"

She said it with a smile, but the challenge was real.

"At your disposal," I said, propping myself on one elbow.

She trailed her fingers down my chest. "You once told me you could rock my world in fourteen dimensions." She bit her lower lip, her voice sultry. "I don't doubt you, but I'm struggling to picture it."

"Hate to flatten a fantasy, love, but I'm a wounded man. Cut me some slack," I said, slipping my hand between her thighs. She was already wet, her breath catching with my touch. "Besides, you'd need a crash course in string theory to appreciate the full fourteen. And I'm far too impatient." I grazed my thumb over her clit. "Let's start with five."

Her laugh was more gasp than sound. "I know the first three…"

"I'd have never allowed you into my course if you didn't," I said, working her with my fingers, relishing the flutter of her eyelids.

"Length, width, and—"

I plunged a finger inside her. "Depth."

She arched into my hand, desperate and defiant all at once. "And the fourth is…time?"

I kissed the hollow above her collarbone. "Very good." Her pulse bounded under my tongue.

"And the fifth?" she whispered.

"A higher dimension acts on the one below it." I grazed my teeth along her neck. "So let's see if I can stop time." I slid two fingers inside her—and she broke open.

She moaned—long, low, from somewhere marrow-deep, and in that moment, I was certain that whatever awaited me in that hearing, however thoroughly they meant to ruin me— this woman was my salvation. And she was worth it all.

She ground against my palm, greedy for friction, her nails carving crescents into my biceps as I coaxed impossibly sweet sounds from her throat. Her eyelids fluttered, and a terrible, gorgeous ache bloomed at the base of my spine. I pressed my thumb down, slow and relentless, and she clung to my shoulders like she no longer trusted gravity to keep her tethered to the bed. I savored the violence of her need—how the careful, self-possessed woman I knew unraveled under my touch.

I slowed. Withdrew my fingers. She whimpered, a ragged, aching protest. I held her gaze as I drew my wet hand up her belly, pausing at the dip of her ribs, then higher still, savoring the way her chest rose and fell, uneven and desperate. I brought my fingers to my lips. She watched, wide-eyed, as I sucked her taste from them.

But it wasn't enough. I wanted to taste her every tremor.

I slid down, kissing a shaky, reverent path down her ribs, her stomach, the sweet hollow above her hip. She was already trembling when I pulled her thighs apart, and when I licked a slow stripe up the length of her, she gasped, both hands diving into my hair. I didn't tease. Not today. Not when the world might crack open at any moment. I buried my tongue inside her, greedy and worshipful, and she arched into my mouth, her thighs locked around my shoulders. The sounds she made were velvet and thunder—helpless, and entirely mine.

I lost myself in it—in her—in the way she gripped my head, fingers threaded deep in my hair. I could have come right then, undone by the beauty of her helplessness. By the proof that I could remake the woman who had so often remade me.

She was close—she always tried to chase it down early, as if not trusting her body to deliver on the promise. I held her at the edge, tongue and fingers in counterpoint, calibrating every twitch and gasp until she stopped making sense—until logic fled and the raw animal core held court. When she came, it ripped through her whole body, arching her so hard she nearly threw me off her. She pulsed against my mouth, but I didn't let up—not until she went soft and limp with aftershock.

"Holy. Fuck," she rasped. And pride bloomed in my chest.

I kissed the inside of her thigh, then rested my cheek there, unwilling to rush the moment. "Does that mean I successfully stopped time?"

She dragged a hand through her hair, still breathless. "Fifth dimension unlocked."

"And the sixth," I said, pressing a slow kiss to her hip, "is all possible timelines. Every version of reality." I crawled up her body, settling flush against her. "Want to know what happens in all of them?"

She nodded, eyes wide.

"In every timeline," I whispered against her skin, grabbing a condom from the nightstand, "I find you like this." I tore the wrapper and rolled it on. "I make you come undone in my hands, again and again—until the universe runs out of ways to rearrange the stars."

Her breath caught.

"And then I fuck you like the laws of physics never applied at all."

She clung to me, legs locked tight around my hips, hands clawing for leverage on my back. I wanted to savor her—every delectable inch—to kneel at the altar of her pleasure. But my need was too immediate. I was already shaking, already half-mad with it.

I drove into her in one slow, deliberate thrust, feeling the give, the heat, the way she stretched to take me. She gasped— sharp, involuntary, broken open—and clawed my shoulders. I stilled, buried to the hilt, and let her feel me—every inch, every wild heartbeat.

"Fuck," she whispered, voice breaking on the consonant. "Don't stop, Cal, please—"

Not even if the house was burning down around us.

I pulled out nearly all the way, then slammed back in—no gentleness, no pretense of restraint. She met my every thrust, grinding her hips up, greedy and bold, mapping my back, my arms, my ass with her hands, like she meant to memorize every molecule before sunrise.

"You're perfect," I rasped, barely holding back. I kissed her throat, the pulse behind her jaw, the soft shell of her ear. "So fucking perfect." Every thrust was a physics proof—an elegant loop of torque and friction, her body answering mine with equal and opposite need.

She bucked hard, desperate for more, and I gave it. No practiced rhythm now—just brute, hungry pistoning. The sheets twisted beneath us, sweat slicking my back. She was all around me—clutching, clawing—wired directly to me at a thousand nerve endings. The deeper I drove, the more she moaned, a melody of surrender that shorted out all my higher functions.

I couldn't look away, even as my climax built, slow and devastating. Her hair fanned like a corona, mouth open and gasping. Sweat glimmered along her collarbone. She arched her breasts into my chest with each downstroke. She looked like a woman made for sin. And I wanted her to know it.

"Still with me?" I murmured.

She nodded, eyes closed, lashes trembling. "Barely."

"Good. Hold on."

I pulled almost all the way out—then slammed back in. Her breath hitched like I'd knocked the wind out of her. I rocked into her, steady and deep, anchoring myself in the sound of her—those small, helpless gasps she only made for me.

I shifted my weight, angled my hips, and ground down until I found the spot—exactly where she needed it. She bucked, electric, her whole body seizing. She clamped around me, hot and pulsing and wild. Her delicious screams echoed off the walls.

I drove into her, relentless now, every thrust a translation of my undoing. The pressure built, and I let it crest—let it hollow me out, then flood me with a rush that scorched every cell in my body.

I came so hard I could have sworn the air changed, the light flickered, the axis of the planet wobbled. For one wild, ecstatic second, there was only my body and hers, the heat and ferocity of our collision, and then the aftershocks—rippling, unstoppable, rolling through us both.

When my brain rebooted, I was slumped above her, forehead pressed to hers, both of us slick with sweat and trembling in the aftermath. I couldn't have strung a sentence together if someone held a gun to my head. I just breathed, tasted the salt of her skin, and held on to the moment.

Eventually—though I can't say when, since time had well and truly stopped—I pulled out and collapsed beside her.

"I felt that…in my feet," she said between breaths, voice airy and whimsical.

"I felt that in my shoes, and they're across the room."

She laughed—hoarse and loose—and rolled toward me, slinging a leg over mine. My skin buzzed where she touched it. "I bet you can't explain that with physics."

"I absolutely can," I said, curling my fingers around hers. "That's entanglement. Two particles reacting across space, no matter how far apart." I kissed her knuckles. "Rather like us."

CHAPTER 52

GABRIELLE

"Hi, Dad," I whispered, brushing my fingers over the warm bronze.

CLARK, MARTIN GABRIEL — B.A. — 1992

The Honors Court was an open-air colonnade, its walls lined in bronze. Each plaque held dozens of names, grouped by graduation year, stacked from floor to sky in neat columns. Nearly two centuries of students carved into permanence—every graduate of Page College, etched name by name. Not just valedictorians or honor grads. Everyone.

I'd never seen another school with anything like it. Then again, I hadn't seen that many schools. I was a legacy student, so Page had always been the plan.

I used to picture my name in here one day.

I sat on the edge of the fountain and let the silence settle. The morning sun beat against my back.

"Sorry I won't be joining you up there, Dad," I said quietly. "Not on that wall anyway."

I remembered the look on his face the first time I flew a plane solo—pride and terror wrestling for top billing. How he'd gripped my shoulder after I landed, skin pale but voice steady. "Nice job, kid," he said. "You've got this."

"I thought I was supposed to follow in your footsteps. Do everything right, you know?" My voice barely carried. "But I think my path goes somewhere else. I hope that's okay."

A breeze snuck through the corridor, fluttering my hair into my mouth. I yanked it free and tucked it behind my ear. I fought the urge to laugh at myself—talking to someone who'd been gone nearly two years like he was just on the other side of the fountain, waiting with coffee and a crooked smile.

I wanted to believe he'd understand. That he'd forgive me for not seeing this through, for not finishing the arc he started. But I also knew he'd always wanted me to choose my own path.

"You always told me to trust my gut, Dad. Well, it's telling me my path is with Cal." I leaned forward, elbows on knees, and let my chin drop. "I love him. I really do. And this feels right. Even if it means walking away from everything you and I planned together." I blew out a shaky breath, half-laugh, half-sob. "Maybe he and I needed to come to Page to find each other. And now that we have…our roads are entwined, and they lead somewhere else."

My words hovered in the air, unclaimed by echo or witness. The breeze stirred, carrying cut grass and chlorine from the ornamental pool behind me. It was ridiculous, how badly I wanted a sign—one shifting shadow, one bronze plaque rattled loose in the wind. But the dead stayed dead.

"For what it's worth," I said, softer, "I think you'd have liked him. Even if every bone in your body would've wanted to throttle him for how it started. He's stubborn as hell—like you. Way too smart for his own good—also like you. And he makes me feel…whole." I stood and stepped to Dad's plaque. "Wish us luck."

I pressed my finger to his name, just once, then fished my phone from my bag. I snapped a photo of the plaque and sent it to Aunt Suzy with a single line:

Saying hi to Dad

After a few moments, her reply came through.

I needed that, sweet girl. Thank you.

Something eased in my chest. Another message blinked through.

Are you talking to me again?

Apparently so.

For what it's worth, I'm so sorry for what I put you through. Both of you. I promise, I thought I was doing the right thing—protecting you.

I know that. And thank you.

So…how are things?

Cal is in his disciplinary hearing right now. We know how it ends, but my stomach is still doing flips.

What are your plans?

We're still working that out, but…

I snapped a picture of my ring and sent it.

HOLY COW! That thing's HUGE!

She fired off a volley of emojis: "wow," "bling," "heart eyes." I smiled. Truly smiled. The rift was still there and probably would be for a long time. But maybe we'd just put a few stitches in the wound.

Your birthday's in a few weeks. Why don't you come down (both of you) and make a long weekend of it? Kemah, Galveston, whatever you want.

I'll talk to Cal, but…that sounds nice. I'll call you later.

My phone was still in my hand when a low voice made me jump.

"Not surprised to find you up here today."

I turned. Dr. Lemke stood a few steps away, hands in his pockets, his tie a little loose like he'd already had a long morning.

"How'd you know I was here?"

He tilted his head toward the administration building. "Nice view of the Honors Court from my window."

I managed a small smile. "Spying on students, Dr. Lemke?"

He chuckled, then sobered. "Part of the job."

He stood quiet for a second, then came and sat beside me on the fountain's rim. The stone was warm beneath my palms, baked through by the sun.

"I wanted to catch you before you left," he said. "I hope you don't mind."

I shook my head. "Not at all."

He glanced at the colonnade, running his thumb over the edge of his wedding band. "When your name didn't show up on the fall roster, I figured you'd transferred. Don't blame you. A lot of students vanish after a mess like this."

"Are you here to scold me for bailing?" I asked, bracing for it.

"God, no." He looked at me sideways. "I'm here to tell you I admire the hell out of you. I mean that. It takes guts to come forward like you did."

I feigned nonchalance, pawing at my cuticles. "I just told the truth. Not that heroic, really."

He shook his head, smile deepening. "Most people think the truth is like a fire alarm—loud, urgent, impossible to ignore. But more often, it's a smoke detector. Quiet at first, easy to unplug if you don't want to hear it. You could have kept quiet. Stayed out of the line of fire. Let the rumors do their damage. But you didn't." He caught my gaze and held it. "In twenty-plus years at this school, I can count on one hand the number of people who'd have the integrity to do what you did."

I wasn't sure what to say, so I said the only thing that came to mind. "It wasn't for me."

"I know." He let the silence expand, long enough to feel intentional. "So, what's next for you?"

"Honestly, it depends on what options Dr. Hawthorne has after…all this." I paused, then corrected myself. "Cal." I squinted against the sun. "We're still figuring it out. But I've got a long list of engineering programs I'm considering."

He nodded, listening the way a tree listens—patient, unmoving, collecting the words deep in its rings. "I remember your dad—good man," he said, his voice gentle and even, as though we'd been sitting together like this my whole life.

I brushed a thumb across my knee. "From when he was a student here?"

He snorted. "Oh, heck no. I'm not that old." He grinned, then let it settle into something softer. "Your dad was an active alum, though. When I first got started at Page, he was everywhere—alumni council, Greek advisory board, you name it. He was insanely dedicated. Always the first to show up, last to leave. Took a real pride in this place. In legacy." He paused, looking up at the sky. "He used to bring you to campus when you were knee high. I remember you tearing around the quad like your shoes were on fire."

I laughed, but it felt strange.

"And I was real sorry to hear he'd passed."

The words hit somewhere below my sternum. My eyes burned, and I looked away, feigning interest in the warped grid of bricks on the colonnade floor.

He waited, and the silence gave his words a soft landing. "He'd be proud of you, Gabrielle."

I swallowed. My throat had gone tight. "Thank you," I rasped. It was all I could manage.

He turned to me, elbows braced on his knees. "You'll land on your feet. I've seen more than enough to know that." He glanced at the wall of names. "But just because you're leaving Page doesn't mean you're not a part of it. You're in the fabric here, whether you like it or not." He smiled, the lines around his mouth deepening. "You can't get rid of us that easily."

The unexpected comfort of it made my throat burn. I managed a nod, not trusting myself to speak.

He fished a business card from his shirt pocket, the motion oddly ceremonial, and handed it to me. It was thick, textured, with the college crest stamped in crimson and gold at the top. He'd written his personal cell number at the bottom. "If you ever need anything—a recommendation, reference, someone to trash-talk the Ivy Leagues with—let me know." He winked, then smiled, his eyes crinkling at the corners. "I mean it. Don't be a stranger, okay?"

"I won't," I said, blinking back a few stray tears. "And thank you."

CHAPTER 53

CALLUM

The corridor was so silent I could hear my pulse beating in my ears. The parquet floor, an artifact of midcentury public architecture, radiated a sterility that crept through the soles of my shoes and into my bones. On the wall across from me, a framed photograph of this very building from a hundred years ago stared back.

No students wandered these halls in July, save for the odd lost soul searching for an open admin office to sign away their future debt. Even most of the faculty and staff had cleared out on the eve of a holiday weekend.

I glanced at my watch. 9:19. They'd been in there for twenty minutes. I tried to reconstruct the previous hour— every gesture, every inflection that might have registered as uncooperative or, worse, insincere. Not that it mattered. I spun the engraved cufflink on my left wrist.

The conference room door creaked open, just enough for the recording secretary to peek through. "You can come back in now, Dr. Hawthorne."

I stood, straightened my jacket, and made a show of buttoning the cuff that I had undone. The space was mercilessly bright—fluorescents throwing no shadow, glass windows framing the car park's shimmering asphalt. The arrangement was deliberate, almost adversarial—a three-member panel on one side, the secretary at the end, her hands poised above the keyboard. And on my side, a single chair—empty, waiting.

Dr. Monroe sat at the center. Her eyes, soft but unsparing, gave away nothing. The other two—Dr. Huber from the maths department and the new Vice President of Student Affairs, an import from Emory—presented a closed front, their arms folded, pens poised, lips pressed into flat, bureaucratic lines.

I took my seat, carefully smoothing my tie and keeping my hands visible on the table. With the faintest nod from the chair, the secretary began typing.

Dr. Monroe folded her glasses and set them on the table. She cleared her throat and tucked a lock of dark brown hair behind her ear. "We have completed our review and deliberations of your case, Dr. Hawthorne. Before we share our findings, you are invited to make a final statement for the record."

A ceremonial pause. The secretary's keystrokes stuttered.

I considered the script I'd rehearsed, then let it go to rot.

"I won't waste your time with a point-by-point rebuttal. Everything I could say in my defense is already in the record. I would only…" The words caught, unexpectedly raw. "I understand the nature of the rule I've broken—the *only* rule I've broken—and I won't insult your intelligence by hiding behind technicalities. Regarding my relationship with Miss Gabrielle Clark, which I freely admit to…"

I took a sip of water. The plastic bottle crinkled in the silence. "Yes, the relationship began while she was my student. And yes, I knew the policy—knew what I was risking. I've spent most of my life honoring rules and expectations. Family legacy. Academic rigor. Institutional decorum. I have bent myself into a thousand shapes to make others more comfortable. But I will not apologize for falling in love. Gabrielle Clark is brilliant. Fierce. Steady. Utterly extraordinary. She is not a mistake. And I refuse to let her be treated like one. You may say I violated the letter of the law— and perhaps I did. But I upheld its spirit. There was no coercion. No exploitation. No imbalance beyond the kind that exists when one person looks across a room and *knows*—that is the only soul that could undo me. I didn't seduce a student. I fell in love with a woman. And beyond any stretch of my understanding, she's agreed to marry me. If that costs me my place here, then so be it. I'd make the same choice again. Every time."

The panel exchanged glances—a quick, silent relay of consensus.

Dr. Monroe pressed her lips into a thin line and adjusted the documents before her, squaring the corners until they aligned. Finally, she looked up at me.

"Thank you, Dr. Hawthorne. Your candor is noted and appreciated, as is the depth of feeling you've shown throughout these proceedings." Her voice emerged measured —the practiced tone of one who has delivered judgment many times before, and never lightly. She folded her hands atop the stack of documents before her and drew a long breath. "I'll begin with the findings of the board regarding the various complaints submitted by students, both past and present."

She paused for a moment, letting the words coalesce. "We have reviewed the allegations against you in detail. The majority of the complaints were found to be duplicative, contradictory, or lacking in substantive evidence. Several were demonstrably false, propagated by parties with clear bias. It is the board's conclusion that these accusations, in the aggregate, constitute a coordinated attempt to damage your reputation rather than a credible representation of your conduct as a faculty member."

The secretary's keyboard clicked as her fingers flew across it, struggling to keep up with Dr. Monroe.

"Accordingly, the board recommends a deeper investigation into the slanderous nature of the allegations and will refer this matter to Student Affairs."

She tapped her nails on the glass-top table.

"Regarding your relationship with the now-former Page College student, Gabrielle Clark, while enrolled in your Physics 112 course last spring…" She shuffled her papers, then consulted the top sheet. "Both you and Miss Clark have freely admitted that the relationship did, in fact, take place and is ongoing. It is the finding of this board that, regardless of intent, outcome, or personal conviction, the relationship constitutes a clear violation of our professional conduct policy."

She paused to let the weight of the words settle, as if their significance weren't already obvious to everyone in the room.

"Our guidelines exist to protect our students and preserve the integrity of the academic environment. While your long-standing contributions to the college are not in question, the nature and timing of this relationship—especially given the power imbalance and Miss Clark's enrollment in your course—leave the board little room for discretion."

She slid her glasses back on, as though to formalize the findings.

"Therefore, it is the unanimous recommendation of this review board that your previously tendered resignation take immediate effect, rather than at the end of your contract term. We further recommend a one-year interval—a 'cooling-off period,' if you will—in which you refrain from any student-facing instructional or supervisory roles. This is not a lifetime disqualification, Dr. Hawthorne, nor is it meant to be punitive beyond the scope of the infraction. After one calendar year, you are welcome to reenter academia, should you choose."

I nodded. The language was as bloodless as anticipated. But it still stung.

"We're also recommending a mutual non-disparagement agreement to the provost," she continued. "If you're willing to sign such an agreement and comply with the conditions of the one-year professional hiatus, it is our recommendation that all records of this review be kept strictly confidential. The disciplinary file will be sealed and not disclosed to any future employer unless required by law." She let that hang. "Do you have any questions?"

The relief was so sharp it actually hurt—like a cramp at the base of my lungs. "No."

She gathered her papers and tucked them into her folder. "In that case, Dr. Hawthorne, you are dismissed."

The quiet was surgical. I left the room, walking past the secretary at her keyboard, her hands now slack above the home row, as she tracked my exit. The door clicked behind me —a sound that sliced more than closed.

I froze in the corridor. Heat pooled along my spine, my body finally registering the shock. An image drifted up from memory. I was walking the line at Oxford on viva day—the oral defense of my dissertation. The way the walls pulsed with the weight of history, the air thick with judgment. My knees had nearly given out then too. But I'd kept walking. There was no other option.

I made it to the exit, to the baking pavement, before my hands began to shake. I stopped beneath the meager, stunted shade of a crepe myrtle—America's answer to the English yew—and pulled my phone from my jacket. A message from Gabrielle waited, timestamped fifteen minutes ago.

I'm in the Honors Court

It wasn't a far walk. I found her perched on the fountain's edge, her fingers idly combing the water's surface. In the brilliant light of high summer, she looked almost backlit—a projection from a better, less complicated future.

I didn't speak. Just sat beside her—close but not touching—until she curled her hand over mine like we'd never been apart.

"I wasn't sure you'd come find me," she said softly.

"Where else would I go?"

She watched me, pupils pinpricks in the glare, irises flaring seafoam green. Her lavender sundress clung to her in ways I had no business noticing in that moment—yet I did. A faint sunburn bloomed across her exposed shoulders. "Well?"

My shoulders sagged. "It's done."

"And?"

"Gainfully unemployed. Effective immediately." I tried for a smile. "But it's not as bleak as it could have been. I'll work again in my natural lifetime."

She smiled, eyes glimmering with a pride that nearly undid me.

"And..." She hesitated, dropping her voice. "Sloane Cartwright's digital crusade?"

"Thwarted." I kissed her knuckles, one by one. She let me. "Thanks to you. The only crime I answered for was the one I actually committed."

She curled against my side, head on my shoulder. I was baking from the inside out—*why on earth had I insisted on wearing a full suit today?*—but I didn't care. I would have burned alive and never pulled back from her touch.

"I hope you'll still have me," I managed, though my voice came out more thread than steel. "How does it go—'for better or worse'? I believe this qualifies as worse." I meant it as a joke, but the words trembled in their casing.

She nudged me with her knee, all warmth, even in the brittle light. "Yeah, but you're still rich, so it balances out."

Her delivery was so dry I almost missed it. I snapped my head up—reflex, not reason.

She grinned, a bright, unrepentant flash. "Relax, Cal. Let me have my joke." Then she softened, pressing the backs of my fingers to her cheek. "You know I've never cared about any of that."

I exhaled, letting the tension drain from my jaw. The sun sliced like a knife, but the cool of her palm anchored me. "I know."

She kissed me, right there in the open, careless of the optics. Her tongue tasted of mint and the last hint of morning coffee.

I threaded my fingers through her hair and kissed her back with everything I'd ever denied myself: heat, hunger, the absolute abdication of consequence. Sweat traced along my hairline. My heart was a brass band in my chest.

She drew back, breathless, laughing in a way that was all lungs and sunlight. "You've been holding out on me, Dr. Hawthorne."

I nipped at her bottom lip. "What are they going to do? Fire me?"

She laughed again, then met my eyes. "Whatever happens, you've still got me."

And that—God help me—was everything.

GABRIELLE

"What in God's name is that?" Cal stared at the swirling, dark-green-and-black shot on the gnarled wooden table in front of him.

"It's a shot," I answered, sliding into the high-backed leather booth with my matching concoction. I picked up the drink menu of what passed for this small town's local brewpub. "It's called the Reaper. You're welcome."

He squinted at it. "It's eleven in the morning."

I shrugged and spun my glass between my fingers. The rim was sticky from a careless pour, and the licorice burn of cheap absinthe cut through the clamor and yeast of midday bar air.

"If we're toasting the death of my career, that's rather brutal, isn't it?"

"Death, yes. But also the opportunity for rebirth."

"How philosophical." He pushed his sleeves to his elbows —his tie and jacket lay abandoned in the car. A few locks of his dark hair fell haphazardly across his forehead. He lifted his glass. "What's in this?"

I clinked my shot to his. "Doesn't matter. Bottoms up."

We downed them, the liquor searing a path straight to my stomach.

He coughed into his fist and slammed the glass down. "That was revolting. Possibly the worst drink I've ever had. Did you order battery acid?"

"That's extra."

He leaned back in the booth, eyeing me. "You're enjoying this."

"I'm enjoying *you*. Free, unshackled. Slightly singed, but alive." I rolled my glass between my palms, savoring the last bitter warmth of the shot. "You realize this is our first time out in town as…us." The word surprised me with its brazen self-evidence. "No more hiding. No more cover-ups. No more…" I fumbled for the word and came up short. "Pretending."

He tilted his head. "A bar at eleven a.m. isn't exactly the agora of public opinion. But it's a start."

"It's the principle," I said, ignoring the faint sting of absinthe clinging to my tongue. "I like not having to look over my shoulder. I could lean across this table and kiss you right now, and nobody would care."

He glanced around the bar. The only other patron was a grizzled man in a Vietnam veteran ball cap, nursing a beer at the far end of the counter.

"I see your point," Cal conceded. "We're positively blending in."

A waitress with purple streaks in her hair ambled over. "Ready for another round?"

Cal shuddered, pure theatrics.

She laughed. "Yeah, the Reaper packs a punch."

"Understatement of the year," he returned. "Do you serve a proper bitter here?"

She scratched her ear with the back of her pen. "Closest I've got is a decent IPA."

"That's…not even in the same postcode."

"It's on tap and cold."

He shrugged. "That'll do then."

"Two of those," I said, folding my menu. "And a basket of fries."

The waitress drifted off, her purple ponytail swinging behind her.

I nudged Cal's foot under the table. "So, what's next?"

"Next? As in…"

"What do we do next? Where do we go? We can reinvent everything."

He looked around. "You want to plan out our lives in a bar?"

I rolled my eyes. "It's a pub."

He shot me a look from beneath his lashes. "This is *not* a pub."

The waitress returned with our beers and fries, then skittered off again.

He tipped the basket, and the fries tumbled over each other like straws. "I took you to a proper pub back home. This isn't a pub."

I took a long sip of my beer—cool and crisp, exactly what I needed. "Do you want to go back home? We could live in the house your father left you."

The words slipped out before I could think better of them.

Cal's smile faded. He shook his head, more gently than I expected. "No. I don't mind visiting Isabel now and then, but there's nothing left for me there." He said it like a fact, not a wound.

I picked up a fry. "So where do you want to go?"

He studied me for a long moment, as if calibrating an answer. "I've got a year-long cooling-off period. But I'm not particularly sorry about it." He flicked his gaze to the window, where the summer light glanced off the hoods of parked cars. "I could use a sabbatical anyway. I might even finish my book." He paused, laugh lines deepening. "But I'm more concerned with what suits you. Your next steps. Where do you want to go?"

"There's plenty of places I could go. MIT, Georgia Tech, Michigan." I ticked them off on my fingers. "But I was thinking… I'd really love to go abroad."

Cal looked up from his drink, eyebrows raised. "That's rather vague. Did you have a country in mind, or are we throwing darts at the map?"

I sucked in a breath. "Switzerland."

He sputtered into his beer. "Switzerland?"

I shrugged, trying for nonchalance. "Zurich ETH. It's one of the best engineering schools in Europe. Top-tier aerospace program. It'll be intense, but—"

"You're brilliant. You'll keep up."

"Do you mean that?"

His face softened. "I wouldn't say it if I didn't." He took a long drink and gave me a look—not quite sadness, not quite nostalgia.

And then I remembered—too late, of course—Switzerland was Claire.

The beautiful disaster. A continent-sized wound that had taken a decade and an ocean to scar over.

I tried to backpedal, but my tongue tripped on the handoff. "Unless you… I mean, Zurich's not the only option. I don't know what I was thinking. It's stupid expensive, the winters are brutal, and—"

"Switzerland is perfect."

I wanted to stitch up the moment with something witty— my usual arsenal of sarcasm and defense-mechanism humor —but all that came out was an apology. "I'm sorry, Cal. That was thoughtless. I didn't mean—"

He caught my hand, fingers warm around mine, and shook his head before I could spiral. "Darling, if you're worried about my delicate emotional state, don't be. You haven't reopened an old wound. If anything, you're the reason it ever healed."

I stared at him, searching for the wince, the shadow, the ghost. But it wasn't there. The memory was present, and always would be, but it no longer cast him in grayscale.

A strange effervescence bubbled in my chest—pride and gratitude, bright and giddy. I squeezed his hand. "You're really okay with it?"

"Of course I am," he said. And then a sly smile crept in, like he was savoring a private joke. "Switzerland keeps coming up. Third time in as many months, actually. Maybe the universe is telling me something."

"What do you mean?"

"I didn't say anything because I wasn't going to act on it, but back in April, I was approached about a one-year research associate position at CERN. I turned it down, obviously. But I still have the contacts. There might be something for me yet."

My jaw practically hit the table. "CERN? *The* CERN? Home of the supercollider? The physicist's wet dream?"

Cal laughed—genuinely laughed—and his gray eyes sparkled. "I'd have called it the physicist's Olympus. But yes." He leaned back in the booth, lines creasing at the corners of his eyes. "Slight hitch though. CERN is in Geneva. ETH Zurich is, well, Zurich. Bit of a schlep, even by Swiss standards."

"We'll figure it out," I said, waving off the logistics. "I have to get in first."

He looked genuinely affronted. "You'll get in. You're one of the most gifted students I've ever taught. And I've taught at three universities, so that's not hyperbole."

I blushed and drowned in a long pull of my beer. "Too bad I studied French and not German."

"That's right. I'd forgotten."

I nodded. "Four years in high school and two advanced semesters at Page."

He flicked the rim of his glass. "If I end up in Geneva, I suppose I'll finally have to learn the bloody language."

I reached across the table, walked my fingers up his forearm, and gave him my best attempt at coy. "I could teach you…"

A slow, wolfish grin unfurled. "You realize you're tempting me with one of my more persistent boyhood fantasies." He took my hand and grazed his lips across my knuckles. "Not my French instructor at Eton. She was ghastly. But you…" He kissed the inside of my wrist. "I could be persuaded to be a good student for *you*."

I dragged my fingertips along the inside of his collar. "Just so we're clear"—I bunched his shirt in my fist, tugging him closer—"I'm not above giving you homework."

His mouth curved—more sin than smile. "Grammar drills or oral exams?"

I leaned in and kissed him. "Yes."

The look he gave me wasn't a smirk or a smile—it was pure intent, slow and simmering, like he already had me back in our bed.

A low hum lit under my skin—an electric ripple down my spine, blooming behind my ribs and radiating out. God, this man. I'd never get used to the way he could melt me.

I dragged the tip of my tongue across my bottom lip, just enough to make his eyes track. "I'll try not to abuse my power."

He brushed a knuckle down my arm. "I rather wish you would." He raised his glass. "To the future, then. Our personal renaissance."

I grinned and tapped my glass to his. "To us."

Grateful Beyond Words!

Thank you—*truly*—for joining me on this journey.

Boiling Point has been a labor of love (and a fair bit of fire), and I hope you fell for Cal and Gabrielle as deeply as I did. Their story—messy, risky, and incandescent—burned through me from the moment I put pen to paper (or fingertips to keyboard), and I'm honored you chose to spend your time with them.

If you enjoyed the book, I'd be incredibly grateful if you left a review on the site where you purchased it. Reviews help stories like this reach new readers—and they mean the world to authors like me.

A little confession: I once had an indecent crush on a brilliant, stunning instructor—sharp as a blade and kind to the core. Thankfully (and wisely), we never acted on it. But oh, did my imagination have a field day. And that's the beauty of fiction, isn't it? On the page, you get to touch the spark, fan it into flame, and see what happens when desire dares to cross the line. Writing Cal and Gabrielle's story let me live out that "what if" with all the peril and passion it deserves.

Thank you again for reading, for daring, and for burning a little brighter with me.

With love and fire,
Nadine

Acknowledgments

First and foremost—to my husband: You are my rock, my anchor, and my fiercest champion. You cheer me on even when my ideas sound half-mad, offer your perspective when I need to get inside a man's head (especially for the spicier scenes), and give me inspiration in more ways than I'll ever put on paper. You even sanctioned me running off to England for a week in the name of "authenticity." (Research, darling, research.) You make a cameo in most of my books (except the darkest ones), but this time you supplied an epic line I've been dying to use. Thank you, love, for everything—always.

To my village—my family and friends who hold me up through this wild ride: Thank you for listening to my rants, laughing at my triumphs, and reminding me I'm human when the words won't come. For the texts, the coffee, the memes, the late-night DMs, and the "you've got this" nudges—you're the reason I keep going.

To the people who helped make this book the most authentic it could be: The wonderful owners of Rudby Hall in North Yorkshire (the inspiration for Branleigh Park), the amazing faculty and staff at my alma mater who indulged me on my research trip, the tireless volunteer staff of the Perrin Air Force Museum (yes, it really exists—go see it!), my UK friends who patiently fielded my endless "is this phrasing right?" messages. And I'd be remiss if I didn't mention my friend, mentor, and the man who famously coined "potpourri in a cup." (See? I told you I'd use it. Three times, in fact.)

Thank you all for lending me your worlds so I could build mine.

To my brilliant editorial team at HEA Author Services: You rock. Thank you for wrangling my chaos into clarity, catching the echoes of my favorite phrases, tolerating my cherished diacritical marks, and reminding me that deadlines do, in fact, exist. This book is stronger, sharper, and hotter because of you.

To my authenticity readers and subject matter experts: Physics, calculus, aviation, oh my! You double-checked my math, my metaphors, and my Britishisms until Cal actually sounded English. Thank you for catching what I didn't, for challenging me to do better, and for making sure my "forbidden professor" actually read like the real deal.

To the folks at Literally Yours PR and Grey's Promotions: Thank you for helping me get this book into readers' hands and for guiding me through the wilds of book marketing with patience, good humor, and more spreadsheets than I'll ever admit to needing. And to the ARC readers and influencers who shouted about this book from the rooftops—your early love and energy gave it wings.

And finally—to *you*: Whether you've been here since the beginning or this is your first of my books, you are the reason I get to do this. Every review, every message, every word of encouragement matters more than you know. Thank you for taking a chance on Cal and Gabrielle, for daring to follow them into the fire, and for letting their story live in your hearts.

Ohhhh, and one more thing…

To the brilliant instructor who once inspired a rather indecent crush—don't worry, we never acted on it. But fiction is a beautiful thing, isn't it? Consider this book my thank-you note…with interest.

Thirsty for more?

Check out Nadine's other books!

Starcrossed Nocturne

An ancient vampire running from her tortured past.

A human mystic who sees the light within her.

A forbidden love could destroy them both…

A reverse-age gap paranormal romance

~

Letters From Victor

In the city of angels…

She finds her devil.

A midcentury noir forbidden romance, inspired by a true story

~

UNNAMED

(Written as N. Theiss)

I have no name. No freedom. No escape.

A brutally dark survival story

~

About the Author

Nadine Theiss is a U.S. Navy veteran with a sharp pen and a taste for the unexpected. She's been writing since she was twelve—long before she had any idea just how far stories could go. With degrees in Modern Language and Psychology and a passport that's seen some things, she blends rich cultural detail with emotional depth and just the right amount of bite.

Whether she's crafting fierce heroines, bending genre lines, or burning down outdated expectations, Nadine writes with fearless intensity and without apology. She draws inspiration from *The Great Gatsby*, *Memoirs of a Geisha*, and the deep lore of *Star Trek*, *Star Wars*, and *Harry Potter*.

She lives in Charleston, South Carolina, where she's fueled by coffee, chaos, and the occasional trivia night—always chasing the next story that refuses to behave.